D1051762

Also by Kim Green

Is That a Moose in Your Pocket?

PAGING APHRODITE

Kim Green

DELTA TRADE PAPERBACKS

PAGING APHRODITE
A Delta Trade Paperback / November 2004

Published by Bantam Dell
A division of Random House, Inc.
New York, New York

Book design by Laurie Jewell

Library of Congress Cataloging in Publication Data is
on file with the publisher.

ISBN: 0-385-33719-1

Manufactured in the United States of America
Published simultaneously in Canada

BVG 10 9 8 7 6 5 4 3 2 1

FOR GABE

ACKNOWLEDGMENTS

Writing this book was a lot of fun, especially stumbling down memory lane. To my sisters in crime: thank you for being there when it all went down, and don't worry—the names have been changed to protect the guilty.

Gracias to Graciela Villarreal, Elma Tejeda, and Marco Tejeda for speaking both of California's languages so well. Thanks to Rachel Swain, Karen Byrne, Simon Booth, and Heidi Booth for their mastery of all things English, Australian, and chocolate. And to John Jackson, who helped me read like an architect.

Great thanks to all the pros at Bantam Dell, with particular thanks to Jackie Cantor, Kathy Lord, Anna Forgione, and Marietta Anastassatos. I am grateful for the guidance of Victoria Sanders, Imani Wilson, and their colleagues, who represent me with tenaciousness and humor.

The support of family and friends seems unending. Thanks to everyone who asked, listened, read, and commented, and, most of all, wore the sidewalks out walking the baby while I noodled. (Mom, Dad, Grandma, Dana, and B.J.: That means you.)

Gabe and Lucca-bean, this is for you.

PAGING APHRODITE

prologue

SAN FRANCISCO

SYDNEY

LONDON

PARKER

My real name is Rosie, but my life is not. Even though I'm thirty-two and should know better, I can't help but blame my parents for the mess I'm in. If they hadn't named me Rosie Meadow Glass, I might not have spent the past three decades quietly rectifying every little error that wafted under my magnifying glass in a vain attempt to right the original wrong, and missed the Big Mistake that lay, lazy and engorged, right under my nose. Of course, it could have been worse. My sisters are called Cardamom and Tarragon. Carda and Tarra. If Leo and Sue hadn't managed to conceive me during a pink-hued dawn while camping in Yosemite's Valley Meadow, they might have birthed an entire spice rack before someone thought to give Dad a vasectomy. As it is, I was never a Rosie. Not from day one. Like most kids, I spent a great deal of time plotting my rebirth to parents of my own choosing. Parents who let you eat refined sugar and watch TV and name you something normal and anonymous like Jane or Sarah or Chris. And so, one day when I was eight, I had the good fortune to catch a Hardy Boys pilot at a friend's, took one look at

Parker Stevenson's handsome blue eyes and fluffy hair, and became Parker. The fact that he was a boy, and I a girl, didn't concern me in the slightest. He seemed very clean and wore a tie. He was going somewhere in life. I approved.

One thing I really love is my job. Interior decorator. Partner and principal, actually. Glass, Ng & Associates. There are no associates, but only Mol and I know that. My business partner, Molly Ng, says I radiate creative conviction *and* have serious control issues, which is what I believe makes me a good interior designer and project manager. People want their designers to be full of angst and maniacs for detail. It gives you the necessary gravitas. If you aren't tortured, clients question your commitment as well as your talent. They want to believe you would leave your baby on the side of the road in a heartbeat if you spotted a leaf sprouting along the center divider in the precise shade of asparagus that would complement the damask chairs chosen for their living room.

So, really, my work is about keeping fantasies alive. And I'm extremely good at it. So good, in fact, that when my own fantasy life came to an abrupt and classically screeching halt, I was already spinning favorable outcomes in my mind: Neil would get to Uruguay or Ukraine or whatever *U* place Habitat for Humanity sent him, see how unpleasant it was, what a mistake he'd made, come home, and ask me for forgiveness with eyes damp from regret and longing. Our friends and families would give me kudos for sticking by him during his psychotic break, for showing the Glass spunkiness that had skipped a generation, arcing from Grandma Ivy straight to me. "How *arrrre* you?" they'd ask when I ran into them at the SFMOMA or the Slanted Door. "Fantastic," I'd say, spooning lemongrass tofu into my mouth. "We've decided to celebrate our anniversary on the day Neil came back instead of our wedding day. Actual wedding anniversaries are *so* nineties."

But there was a slight delay in the plan.

I'm going to Greece because I had a nervous breakdown while helping Iverson & Bernstein advertising agency select conference-room tables to go with their corporate offices' new atrium look.

It's a shame, because up until that point I was doing really well. Granted, Neil's departure a mere eleven days after our nuptials was a blow, but I don't believe in feeling sorry for yourself, moping about when you could be doing something productive. Also, I believe the bad luck is temporary. The attending psychologist at the hospital where they brought me when I just could not stop screaming told me later that I need to deal with my anger. What he doesn't understand is, I'm not angry. Really. I tried to tell him that it wasn't anger that made me scream but rather nerves, or too much coffee, or—what I really think—that I accidentally took too many Ativan tablets that morning. But he just raised his bushy eyebrows at me doubtfully, a device I feel sure he had witnessed in a movie about a psychologist and decided made the gesturer look Freudian and cerebral. At that point, I decided he was a moron. I checked myself out that night and took an aromatherapy bath in my and Neil's Pacific Heights flat, which we own as part of a tenancy in common, along with a magazine editor/ options trader couple, a retired twenty-six-year-old dot-com millionaire/yoga teacher couple and a gynecologist/dermatologist couple. Neil and I are the intellectual property attorney/interior decorator couple. Naturally, we have the best apartment, though I did some nice work for the doctors, who are now said to be getting a divorce.

Molly is a great gal, and I respect her judgment, which is why I agreed to use the honeymoon tickets—Neil's and mine—and go to Corfu for a few weeks. Mol insisted that I take the whole summer as a sabbatical, but we both know that after a couple of weeks of sun and swimming in the Mediterranean's crystal-clear cerulean waters—this is straight out of the brochure, along with the requisite postcard-perfect photos and pithy marketing copy— I'll be ready to get back to my computer, phone, drafting table, fabric swatches, e-mail, *Real Simple* subscription, and client meetings. Plus, Neil's going to be home soon, and I want to be sure he has someone to depend on when he has to start picking up the pieces of his shattered life.

Sydney

$\sim\sim\sim\sim\sim\sim\sim\sim\sim\sim\sim\sim$

CLAIRE

Apparently, I'm quite mad.

"Claire is quite mad," everybody said when they heard, from my mother to my son Ethan to Deborah from book club, whom I overheard telling the cashier at the milk bar that "Claire Dillon left her husband, Gary, because he was sleeping with that tart who does facials over at Bliss Spa. Now she's off to Greece as if she hasn't a care in the world! She's quite mad, that one."

Maybe I am. Quite mad, that is. If there are rules for this sort of thing, rules governing behavior for wives of philandering husbands with families and mortgages and two-car garages, I'd be keen to know what they are and where I can find them. Perhaps they have books on the subject at the library or the supermarket checkout. Books with splendid self-helpish titles like *100 Things You Can Do to Stop Bloody Crying when Your Bloody 47-year-old Husband Takes Up with a Bloody 29-year-old Masseuse*—excuse me, *Massage Therapist*—or *Yes, with Enough Prescription Drugs, You Can Be Happy Again.*

As it is, when things you never expect to happen do, you tend to float about in a daze for quite a lot longer than you'd wish, and your respect for rules and proper etiquette and the like goes straight into the loo. You cast about for ballast, something to remind you that your life still has form and meaning, that the things you thought were permanent are not *all* going to dissolve like Jell-O packets tossed into a glass of water. Friends, Oprah Winfrey, your mother, are all duly sought out and consulted, and you're still left feeling as though you've been asked to endure something wholly original, some evil psychological experiment created to test the effects of public humiliation on middle-aged, white, Australian mothers who delivered their children by C-section, wash linens on Tuesdays, and make love with their husbands on alternate Saturdays. Some renegade part of your brain keeps piping up, saying you're not the only one, the first one, the worst one, but, ultimately, you don't care. The achy soreness that pesters your head and back and heart with maddening constancy, the ear-ringing mental slap you get every morning when your eyes flutter open and rest on the familiar curve of your husband's sleeping back, your neighbors' eyes sliding away from yours when you go out to collect the post—all conspire to drive you straight out of your bloody mind. Maybe no one ever did feel like me before, you say to yourself. Maybe I *am* the first-ever, real-life, documented Worst-Case Scenario.

"Why are you doing this? Don't you want to fight for your marriage? Gary wants to work things out, Claire!" my sister, Valerie, admonished me earlier today. I was folding a faded sarong abandoned by Ethan's ex-girlfriend, Rachel, the way I'd read about in my Lonely Planet guidebook, rolling it to avoid wrinkles.

"I just want to be alone for a while," I'd answered, which wasn't exactly true.

"But why Greece? Everyone there is going to be about twenty-five and on summer holiday, Claire! For God's sake, you think that's going to help your state of mind?"

"Maybe." If I'm not twenty-five, I may as well act like I am.

Valerie narrowed her startling green eyes at me.

"Claire, you're mad," she said.

Later, my tall, unshakable sister cried when I walked her to her minivan. She tried to give me a few hundred French francs that were moldering in her wallet from last year's European holiday.

"I'm going to Greece, not France," I said.

"Aren't they all on those euro thingies now?"

"Yes, but why would they change French francs in Greece?" I pointed out.

"Oh, God," she said, and stuffed the pretty, fake-looking money back into her purse, backed out of our driveway with the oil spot smack in the center from Gary's motorcycle, and drove off. On the way out, she ran over the lawn sprinkler. I left it as is, broken off at the head. After all, I'm quite mad. What do I care about landscaping and curb appeal?

It's 5:13 P.M.

I'm leaving tomorrow, and the sun's pale orange rays arcing across my bedroom seem to be saying good-bye. Even though I'd been sleeping in the guest room, I still kept my clothes in the chest of drawers we'd had since Brian was born. Skirts, slacks, T-shirts, undies all wobbled in neat rows on the bed. I tried to imagine the sun in Mediterranean Greece. Would it feel softer than Australia's fierce light? Warmer? Familiar or strange? Welcoming or alienating? Would they speak English? Would they understand my accent?

Would the madwoman like ouzo or retsina with her dinner?

San Francisco

ANYA

I was born to be a bride. A beautiful, misty-eyed bride in a tulle confection of a dress. *Vas hacer una novia bella*—you'd make a beautiful bride, everyone always tells me, from the tiny, wrinkled lady at the bakery to the lesbian lady with the man-cut hair at the post office to my six aunties, almost indistinguishable from one another except for the different ages and numbers of children who wrap themselves around their stout legs.

When you're born to fulfill a destiny, and destiny takes its sweet time getting to your case number, people start to blame you for what went wrong. They don't want to believe that sometimes bad things happen for no reason at all. That would mean bad luck is lurking right around the corner, potentially, for all of us.

"Lose some weight, *querida*," Auntie Carlota told me at my cousin Pilar's wedding. "In my day, your figure would be perfect, but today"—she threw her rough, graceful brown hands up in the air—"men want their ladies to be thin."

"You're too independent, with that job of yours. Men don't like a woman who doesn't need them," added Auntie Maria-Theresa, who runs her own travel agency on Mission Street.

Auntie Rita disagreed. "The job is fine. She's just too picky. Always going out with white boys. What's wrong with a nice Mexican boy, *chula*?"

I always smile when they say these things, to show them respect and maintain the illusion that my condition is fleeting and superficial, like a scraped knee or a bit of heat rash. But their words hit me like shrapnel. When my lips stretched back over my teeth, I felt like one of those skeletons in *El Día de los Muertos*, stuck in a perpetual grimace with about a thousand years of history and dead relatives' expectations weighing on my shoulders.

I have a secret. I know why God hasn't sent me a soul mate. What I've never told anyone is that I did something pretty bad once. Something bad enough to turn a lemon tree's youthful leaves dank and heavy with rust in the middle of summer. Something that flipped my life's momentum to the off position and set me to waiting. Something that put my dreams of love on death row.

I know what you're thinking: How primitive is that shit? Even though I'm Catholic as they come, I'm enough of a modern woman to know that God's plans for people aren't that simplistic. I know bad things don't have to equal a lifetime of misery and solitude. Except nothing ever changes. I've tried everything I can think of to jump-start my luck, to shatter the curse. What happens? *Nada*, that's what. My secret truth is permanent, like the *cholos* fighting over those two stinky blocks between 16th and 18th streets. Only one soul on this earth besides a few white people in white coats in a whitewashed building knows what happened, and that person's buried this story so deep you'd need a tractor and a stick of dynamite to get it out.

My friend Carda says the best things in life are worth waiting for. That may be true, but I want to get married when my life is still about beauty and impulse and silly mistakes. Before skeins of white cut through my long, wiry black hair. Before my intended looks at me and sees in my eyes the reflection of his fear of being alone. Before the end of love.

London

~~~~~~~~~~~~~~~~~~~~~~~~~~~

KELAH

Butter or salt? That's what my life's come down to. Back in uni, when I was a budding auteur and got pissed with Fiona and Boz and wittered on about Yeats and Chaucer and Blake, I never imagined for a minute that I'd be dispensing fizzy lemonade and popcorn to zit-faced tossers all day at the ripe old age of twenty-five.

I did the waitressing thing and the receptionist thing, the shopgirl thing and the catering thing and even the leave-me-alone-I'm-applying-for-a-postgrad-degree thing, before I hit rock bottom and resorted to the cinema thing. Honestly, I think it was better when I did nothing at all; my parents could pretend I was on the verge of blinding success, I actually worked on my novel, and I didn't have to dive under the counter when someone from Oxford or my parents' circle of tight-arsed friends popped in to see the latest Kate Winslet or Judy Dench.

But lately I've been stuck in a weird sort of inertia. I think moving back in with my parents was probably a mistake. Hot showers, food, and a clean bed are all well and good, but they come at a price in the Morris household. Ambition, drive, and accomplishment—that's what life's about for people like us. Sometimes I feel like I sold my soul for a warm sofa to watch telly on. I look in the mirror in the morning and the hazel-eyed, kinky-haired, coffee-colored girl in front of me reminds me of someone I used to know quite well but have regrettably lost touch with. She shrugs her narrow shoulders at me as if to say, *I'm sorry I let you down*. I love her, but sometimes I hate her, too, you know? I want to look in the mirror and see someone else, not the best friend who got away.

I think things started getting mucked up for me when Fiona's short story got accepted to the *Ploughshares* literary journal. She rang me first.

"Kay!" she screamed into the phone. She was talking and crying all at once. When she does that, her blue eyes get all red and her nose stuffs up horribly and she's impossible to understand.

"Fee? What happened?"

"I sold a story," she said. " 'The Blue Zebra'!"

My stomach plummeted. I said all the right things about how brilliant she was and inevitability and destiny and American acceptance of the avant-garde.

"Thanks, Kay. I haven't even told Bozzie yet. I wanted to tell you first. I mean, I know it's kind of hard, with all the work you've been putting into your writing, but I knew you'd be happy for me . . ."

"Of course I'm happy for you, Fee, it's fantastic!" I choked out.

". . . it's coming out in the fall issue."

"Don't be an idiot. Send me an advance copy," I said.

When we rang off I reread everything I'd written in the last two years with my finger hovering over the delete key and wept.

That's when I decided I needed to get away.

I haven't told anyone I'm going to Greece this summer. Just me, my laptop, and miles of perfect cornflower-blue sea. No Dr. Charles Morris, world-renowned West Indian endocrinologist. No Candace Grant-Morris, world-renowned English book editor. No Charlie Morris, big brother and investment banker with one relaxed-haired wife and 2.5 bloody perfect offspring. No David Morris, whose only distinction is beating me out for Most Disappointing Morris Scion and being utterly vanquished from Morris dinner conversation. No crap London weather. No friends on their way to publishing success whilst their erstwhile flatmates ring up soft drinks at the till of the Belle Vue Theatre, which has no view and no glory, faded or otherwise, now or ever.

part one

AS THEY ARE
(GREECE)

chapter 1

PARKER

"The bus stop is about twenty-five meters from the bank across the square. It is open from seven A.M. to eleven P.M.," I read.

The guidebook was clear on this point. The village was not. I looked around the plaza, which was not unpretty, with flowers and bits of green poking up out of the cobbled paths. The only thing 25 meters from the bank was a leathery-looking man with a donkey and milky blind eyes selling cheap leather briefcases and backpacks. Anya glanced at me timidly. She was wearing too-tight black synthetic stretch pants and a blouse with sweat stains under the arms. It was at least ninety degrees. Her outfit irritated me.

"I'll just ask someone," Anya said.

"Whatever you want to do." I snapped the guidebook shut.

Anya teetered off on platform sandals toward a knot of women in what looked to be black nuns' habits. I fanned the bench with some newspaper, sat down, and tried not to freak out.

She'd been driving me nuts since we left San Francisco International Airport, what felt like sixty-eight hours ago but was actually closer to fourteen. How the hell did I get into this mess?

What had started out as a little involuntary R & R courtesy of my nonrefundable honeymoon booking, Dr. Moron and meddlesome Molly had morphed into a bona fide Hellenic horror show.

I'd gotten a call from my sister Carda a week before we were set to leave for Corfu. In between crying jags and obsessing about Neil, I filled out my packing spreadsheet in Excel.

"Park? It's Carda."

"Hi," I said. I was debating whether to bring 30 or 45 sunblock.

"I have to talk to you about something."

"Uh-huh."

"I know I'm going with you to Greece to help you get over the Neil thing and all, but I was wondering—"

"First of all, Cardamom, Neil and I aren't a *thing*, and second, there's nothing to *get over*. We're married, and we have an *apartment* and a *life* and I'm sure once he gets this out of his system—" I sounded shrill and stopped myself abruptly. I'm a firm believer in the adage that showing weakness makes you more of a victim. Play your cards close to your vest and no one will know for sure what they're dealing with.

"*Okay.* Sorry. Sheesh. I didn't mean anything. Don't be so over-sensitive, Park."

"Fine, I won't be oversensitive. Look, I'm really busy packing. What do you want to ask me?"

Carda had been appointed my minder for the trip by unanimous family vote for the precise reason that her presence tended to infuriate me ever so slightly less than the other members of clan Glass. There was no point in trying to get out of it—once Leo and Sue took you up as a cause, they would picket, strike, rally, and protest until you came around. I suppose on some level I knew they had my best interests at heart. That, and the slim likelihood of their other children taking care of them in retirement if I went insane.

"Well, I got an e-mail from Jake a couple days ago. You know, the guy I met at Burning Man last year? He was still going out with this batik artist called Sonia then, but I guess they broke up, and he's organizing a trip to the Lost Coast for a bunch of people. It's, um, next week."

"Uh-huh." I fingered my pill case. Does one have to declare Class IV narcotics?

"So, what I wanted to tell you was, I gave my ticket to Anya Soberanes. She had vacation time saved up. Isn't that awesome?"

I dropped the case. "No, Cardamom, it's not awesome. It's kind of crappy, actually. Are you telling me you're not coming with me to Greece?"

"Well, Park, it's like . . . you see . . . Jake and I, we have this amazing bond. Jake says we must have been friends in a former life. I checked with my astrologer, and she said a soul mate would reenter my life this year. I guess I thought you'd be happy for me for a change—"

"I barely know Anya! I'm not going to Greece with her!"

"You don't have to yell at me!" Carda shouted.

"Tell me you didn't promise Anya she could come with me."

"I sort of transferred the ticket to her name already," Carda mumbled.

"What?"

"I said, we already put the ticket in her name."

"Well, transfer it back. Or, better yet, forget you were ever coming. In fact, forget you ever knew me."

"But, um, Anya already asked for the vacation time and got her passport from her safe-deposit box."

"Well, I guess she'll have to go somewhere else. Hey, I heard there's a losers' trip to the Lost Coast," I said meanly.

Carda was silent. I could feel guilt creep up my neck.

"Fine," she said finally, before I could apologize. "Then you tell her."

"*I'm* not telling her. You tell her. You're the one who gave the ticket away."

"Nope."

There's one thing about Carda: She may be flaky, but she's almost as stubborn as I am. I tried to imagine recuperating in the company of earnest, overweight, terminally insecure, Spanish-soap-opera-watching Anya Soberanes and felt my chest muscles constrict.

"Okay, whatever. She can go," I muttered.

"Oh, Park, I'm so glad! I'm sure you'll have a lot to talk about with Anya."

"Tons."

The last time Anya and I had a meaningful exchange was in 1979, when Danny Fischbein dunked her braid in green paint at the Campaign Against Apartheid meeting our parents had dragged us to. She cried so hard she hyperventilated. I had to coax her out from under the table with a slice of my mom's veggie loaf.

"Parker?"

"Hmm?"

"You're the best sister and I love you."

"Hmm."

Thus, this is what my honeymoon had come to. Instead of having good athletic sex with Neil under a canopy of bougainvillea, I was shepherding around a vestal virgin with a faint mustache while my supposed husband raised barns in another hemisphere.

Anya came running back, looking, if possible, even sweatier. "Parker, the grandmothers told me to go to the next block. There's another square there, where the bus stops."

Grandmothers, huh? Funny, I thought they were nuns.

Sleep didn't come that first night. I was prepared for it and had a couple of Halcions lined up along the nightstand, next to a cylinder of Greek bottled water and my favorite essential oil balm of lavender, marjoram, and Roman chamomile, which I'd rubbed on my temples per the instructions. At least the room was clean and nice. Actually, the villa was the best thing that had happened so far: a couple of minutes beyond town, on a twisty road canopied with olive trees that wound its way down to the beach. White and spartan and flanked by pungent flowers in magenta and red, with the requisite bright blue door, it was costing us fifteen dollars a night each. Anya had surprised me by laughing when our landlord,

Mrs. Gianniotis, threw out a number as we stood with our suit-cases in front of the charming house. Anya's teeth had flashed, straight and very white. She'd wrapped her long ponytail around her fingers, laid her hand gently on the stout woman's shoulder, and whispered a counteroffer. Apparently, she was good at it, be-cause after she and Mrs. Gianniotis haggled and came to an agreement, Mrs. G. invited us to sit on the terrace and served us syrupy kumquat juice in shot glasses that said *World Cup 1998*.

I stared at the fissured ceiling, tossed in my narrow bed, and obsessed about Neil. We'd met at Molly's wedding to Scott Ruben. Neil was somebody's date and didn't know anybody. I was Molly's maid of honor and unfortunately knew a couple of the ushers a little too well.

"Excuse me," I whispered to the blond guy in the excellent suit while the smoked-salmon tartlets were being passed. "I think your girlfriend needs some help. She lost part of her dress." The woman in question was entertaining the bartenders with a close-up shot of her pneumatic breasts, which looked like two gigantic bellows poised to blow oxygen-rich air over a thirsty fire.

"She's not my girlfriend," he answered without turning his head.

"Oh, goody." I stood straight and tall and tried to still the stac-cato thrum of my heart while I sipped from the delicate cham-pagne flute and channeled the poise of Carolyn Bessette Kennedy (may the woman rest in eternal peace, ad infinitum).

Finally, he turned around. He had one green eye and one blue, like those freakishly intelligent husky dogs that are always drag-ging their masters to safety from a burning building or nibbling on armed intruders. I immediately wanted to collar him and lash him to the foot of my antique cast-iron bed.

"Are you hitting on me?" he said.

"Yes."

"Good."

"Good?"

"Do you have a problem with good?" His tone was arch.

I certainly didn't later when he took me to his apartment,

peeled off my Reem Acra bridesmaid's dress, and licked me up and down till I was as damp and squirmy as a newborn kitten. I think what did me in was that he actually *hung up* the dress before he went down on me. It was at that moment I knew we were meant to open a joint bank account. We started looking for apartments together three weeks later.

Now, don't get me wrong. We're like every other couple, with our share of problems, our life-negating moments, our tendency to sublimate frustration into guerrilla-type warfare over things like improperly opened milk cartons or the smell of nail-polish remover at six A.M. But we always had a baseline sense of destiny, I think. A sense that we were not just two random atoms knocking about the universe, but rather two random atoms with some special little added neutron or something that drew us inexorably toward each other until we slammed together, complete. It was hard not to be smug; we were happy. We really were. Are. In fact, I don't understand how Neil could have done this to us. I'm so worried about him. What if he's sick? He could have a brain tumor, or a cerebral aneurysm, pressing on the part of his brain that loves me and abhors building barns in developmentally challenged countries. The part that loves our life. The part that rouses him from sleep each dawn and whispers in his ear how much he loves being an IP lawyer and being with me, his sort-of-wife, Parker Rosie Meadow Glass. He could be dying right now in a Uruguayan rain forest or a Ukrainian tundra, from a series of strokes so small, they can only be measured by what isn't there after they've run their course, what essential pieces of his memories of us they'd obliterated as they hurtled through the microscopic tributaries of his brain.

chapter 2

ANYA

If I hadn't heard Parker crying last night, I would have thought what Carda told me was a mistake. Surely, I thought, Carda must be wrong. How could a woman whose husband left her *eleven days* after the wedding not shatter into a million pieces? How could she put on her little white linen pants and boat-necked tank and those Jackie O sunglasses—so damn perfect and defiant and cool—and stare out at this strange and wonderful place as if she were simply downtown exchanging duplicate registry gifts at Williams-Sonoma?

I was sort of glad I heard her, because I was starting to think she was seriously weird. I had thought, when I first blurted out the idea of me coming here to my parents during the Ultimatum Scene, that Parker and I might be friends. But now I see that's impossible. I wouldn't go so far as to say that she hates me, but I can see the way her mind works behind that smoothly pale forehead, and I know I'm just another piece of luggage to her: heavy, ungainly, and not particularly useful.

Take breakfast this morning. I got up first, messed up by jet

lag. The air was still and cool and sweet-smelling. I couldn't believe how quiet it was. Far away, echoing between green hills, the
occasional whine of a moped struggling up Corfu's switchback
mountain roads pierced the silence. Fat bees and butterflies
zoomed around, making lazy circles against the arch of branches.
Between the low khaki-colored peaks, I could see triangles of
still, blue sea. I couldn't wait to slip my feet into the Mediterranean. I don't know how to swim, but I had heard that the sea
was shallow here, rolling in toward the beach on sandy shelves
many hundreds of yards long.

"Good morning."

Parker had on a red halter top and trimmed cutoffs that
showed off her skinny legs. She moved slowly and carefully, as if
she had been in a car accident or had her nose done. Her eyes
were hidden behind her gigantic movie-star glasses, so I couldn't
tell what she was thinking.

"Hi," I said. "Want some water?"

She shook her head and slid into a deck chair. All around us,
birds sang and twittered. I thought the smell was glorious: as
green and olive-y and flowered as San Francisco's summertime
inner city was redolent of garbage and grilled meat. In spite of
myself, I felt something tug at the blanket of disappointment I'd
been wearing like a shroud, and it shifted slightly, leaving a little
gap. I tried to smile.

"Oh, God," Parker muttered, to no one in particular.

"Parker, are you all right?" I said.

The opaque black platters turned toward me. "No, I'm not all
right. In fact, I'd say I'm pretty fucked."

I thought I saw a tear slip out from behind the shades, but
Parker said nothing more, just stared out blindly at the shrub-
filled gully.

I have two sets of standards when it comes to love: one for me,
and one for everybody else. My standard for everybody else is

simple: Everyone deserves love—the real thing—no matter who they are or what they've done. I know it's not fashionable these days, but I truly believe that love redeems people. Makes wrong things right. Changes the world. Bestows second chances.

For me, it's a little more complicated.

I was at work one day a few weeks ago, before I came to Greece. I raise money for a nonprofit that develops technology programs for inner-city youth. My salary, which falls somewhere between feeble and pathetic, depends entirely upon grants that I secure myself. The office is in a run-down part of the Mission that used to house undocumented garment workers. Even our computers sit on stacks of old magazines and newspapers. (We could probably afford the monitor stands, but I think the director secretly likes the shoestring look.)

How's that for a do-gooder résumé? There are six people on staff at the AFT (Alliance for Future Technology), plus the executive director. Six are women—one married, one in a long-term relationship, one single and dating, one single and not dating (by choice), one divorced mother of two, and me. Michael, the only guy, is gay (and in a long-term relationship).

Anyway, one day our office manager, Robin Flores, came in at 8:46 A.M. I knew immediately something was going on, because, one, Robin never comes in early, and, two, it was Thursday, and Robin always has the new *SFWeekly* with her, which she claims to read for the features. In actuality, she spends most of her time in the personals, in case her current relationship doesn't work out. That day, she had nothing in her hands but her car keys and her small turquoise purse.

"Hey," she said to the rest of us, and sat down at her desk. I watched out of the corner of my eye while she took off her sweater and laid it over the back of the chair. Then she adjusted the snow globe with the photo of Sanjay, my ex-boyfriend, in it.

Then I saw it. The rock. Husky as a water bug, crouched on the fourth finger of her left hand, it seemed to be winking at me from the dim recesses of Robin's keyboard.

I felt the blood drain from my face.

Before anyone else could notice it, Robin spun around and exploded. "Omigod, *chicas,* guess what? I'm getting married!"

While everyone gathered around the petite girl and oohed and aahed over her extended left hand, I sank into my broken-armed desk chair and tried to collect myself. After all, it wasn't like Robin started up with Sanjay before he was, well, through with me. It wasn't like she'd *stolen* him.

"Anya." Robin beckoned me toward her with her (ringless) right hand. Her huge sherry-colored eyes were filled with sympathy. I floated toward her like a barge being tugged into harbor. She grasped my hand.

"Anya," she said again. "I just want you to know, both Sanjay and me would be honored if you'd come to the wedding."

"Thank you," I whispered.

That night, poring over my overstuffed hope chest, I had to say it to myself over and over again: Everyone deserves love. Even that dirty dog Sanjay Singh and two-faced Robin Flores. Especially them.

I don't know why I'm so obsessed with romance. I know it's the opposite of what a strong, self-respecting Latina's supposed to believe these days. That she needs a man to save her from the big, bad world. It's just that I can't stop hoping there's someone out there for me. Someone tall and strong, with warm brown eyes and a nice family and a job he actually likes. College-educated, that's a must. He should like taking long walks, like me, and reading. And he has to think I'm beautiful.

Sitting with Parker this morning, watching her cry over that *pendejo* husband of hers, I actually felt the tiniest bit jealous that she was married. Jealous! Okay, I know it only lasted a week and a half, but if her vacation wardrobe's any indication, I'm sure her dress was amazing. That's how crazy I am. The way I see it, if you're divorced, at least someone wanted to marry you. Once.

chapter 3

CLAIRE

The taverna is wonderful, the kind of place one sees in films about middle-aged divorcées who bolt for exotic locales after the house is sold and have torrid sex-based affairs with men twenty years younger than themselves with names like Roberto and Sven. Perched atop a knoll high enough to overlook the checkerboard of village rooftops below, Tony's is often near empty at this ungodly island hour of ten A.M. It's too early for the Scandinavian and Italian kids who drink and disco deep into the night, rising only after the sun has arced past midpoint. They mostly skip breakfast anyway, grabbing a loaf of white, seedless Greek bread and motoring to the beach to deepen their already chocolaty tans. There they roast, cans of Amstel beer stuck in the sand next to their silky heads and beautiful flat stomachs.

In the corner of the taverna, tucked into green plastic chairs against the white veranda, a sunburned British couple argued over the merits of the Greek salad versus the fried cheese. I myself have enjoyed the same perfect breakfast—perfect because it is predictable and fresh and I don't have to prepare it—for six days straight. Today, for the first time, when Tony waved me into what I'd started to think of as my chair on the western edge of the outdoor terrace, he brought my salad and espresso and squeezed juice without asking for my order. And so I dug into the sugary tomatoes and crisp cucumber, with the slab of feta on top glistening from a golden layer of olive oil, and felt delicious gladness course through my veins. I had arrived at last. In Pelekastritsa.

"How you are doing today, Mrs. Dillon?" Tony, the proprietor, is gnomelike and just this side of swarthy, with shaggy, 1970s hair, warm brown eyes, and a slight hunch to his back that has not prevented a succession of young Swedish women from making love with him in his apartment tacked onto the back of the restaurant.

"I'm very good, Tony. Thank you. But call me Claire."

He squinted out at the expanse of blue beyond the scrub-covered hill. "It's good today. You go to the beach?"

"Maybe. Do you have any recommendations?"

"Vilades is good. Or Lifada. Not too many people. White sand. No wind this time of year. Very nice. You are okay with the nude beach?" Tony's eyes gleamed and he grinned raffishly.

"It's nothing this old lady hasn't seen before," I said.

Tony leaned back and studied me, as if in appreciation of van Gogh's *Sunflowers* or, more accurately, a piece of ancient Mayan pottery.

"Claire, you are a beautiful woman. 'Old lady'!" He snorted as if I had suggested Constantinople had it up on Athens, and I fought the urge to kiss him right there in the taverna.

Two young women came in, so Tony left me to go seat them. New arrivals, I guessed from their pallor and hesitancy, though the plump one already had the deep olive skin of a Latin. I grabbed my sunnies and slipped them on so I could study them better without being caught.

I could see Tony flirting with them as he pulled their chairs out. Both had that carefree prettiness that shouted youth. Taking in their doe eyes and girlish shoulders, it was hard to believe they had lived, felt pain, run their feet along the silty scrabble of rock bottom. Watching them, the euphoria I'd felt a moment ago dribbled out of me, water spiraling down an emotional drain. I felt suddenly quite old. What was I doing, thousands of kilometers from home, without Gary, Ethan, and Brian? Among these human sylphs and fauns cheerfully lapping up life. Younger than I felt I'd ever been. Maybe everyone was right. Maybe I was quite mad.

I forced myself to finish my salad, swirling chunks of sour cheese through the oil, waiting for one of Zeus's lightning bolts to deliver a revelation.

If Brian were here, my beautiful, irrepressible, impractical son, he would love this room. The sarcophagus, I'd taken to calling it, because it was truly coffin-shaped. Like many of the rented rooms I'd seen when I'd first staggered off the bus and been accosted by the squat women of Pelekastritsa with offers of accommodation, this one had the hard lines and odd angles of an exercise in entrepreneurial architecture, of something added on at the last minute. Set on top of the main house, it was slender and long, with French doors on one side opening up onto a small veranda and cool tiled floors. It still smelled of fresh white paint. The only furniture in the room was a single-size, chaste-looking bed and a rickety chest of drawers, in which I'd laid out my dresses, trousers, and admittedly ratty underwear. (There's something constructive I can do: improve state of undergarments.) The loo occupied a neat rectangle next to the door, the toilet butting up against the peculiar Greek shower, a curtainless square with a spigot sticking straight out of the wall at waist height, which made for interesting bathing.

It felt strange to be occupying this monkish little room. I associated hotel rooms with family holidays, long weekends in Melbourne or Tasmania, Gary's and my honeymoon on New Zealand's South Island, the biannual trips with Valerie and her family to Europe or America. What struck me was the utter quiet: without the constant stream of *Claire*s and *Mum*s punctuating the silence, my mind was free to produce the most extraordinary thoughts. Mind music, I'd taken to calling it. Sometimes it was real music, long-forgotten melodies from that sliver of time in between uni and marriage that I'd shut the door on, thrown away the key to.

I pulled a brush through my thick auburn hair. It was fading, that's for sure, and I hadn't thought to color it before I left. Once a deep auburn and glossy as a wet Labrador, it was now flecked with gray, rolling in slightly coarser waves to mid-back. Still, my best feature. Gary always said it's what made him first notice me, at that show where I was singing, Adelaide Festival, 1976.

I remember that night as if it were last week: me, Bobby, and Carlo, my accompanists on guitar and piano, arranged deliberately on the small stage at angles like cheeses on a platter. Nervous. Our biggest venue yet. I was as lean as I'd ever been, too in love with singing to feed myself properly, in a flame of a red dress that harkened back to a time before hippies, clutching the microphone and finding the face in the crowd to hang my gaze on, my voice. Gary's face, pegged with stubble, roughened by sun, hazel eyes hooded, and, yes, staring at me with unchecked lust. So I sang to him that night, my hair sliding over my shoulder in a red river, spilling into the white V where the slinky dress cowled around my breasts. I'd always been self-conscious of them, even before children blued their veins and swelled them to a disproportionate weight. But that night I saw something in the young man's eyes I'd been thirsty for all my life, something hungry and deep and thrumming and utterly appreciative, and I sang Roberta Flack and Joan Baez and Carole King covers with everything I had, every ounce of yearning and desire I could summon, while Bobby and Carlo's music lifted me up and seemed to bear me aloft, out over the marijuana-perfumed concourse.

There. That would have to do. Hair smoothed into obedient waves, flowered sundress skimming over full hips, chest no longer the smooth expanse of unblemished flesh of the young, but not crepey, thank goodness. Eyes an interesting rusty amber that used to match my hair, large, maybe still beautiful? Ethan and Brian had inherited my eyes. Looking at them when they were babies, I'd felt they could see inside me, spot the goodness. Long lashes and not-olive skin too bronzed by the sun.

Still, people always said I didn't look forty-six. "Claire, you look great," they'd say. "From twenty meters away you could be thirty," they'd murmur, as if being separated from others by a moat made of distance, forever blurry to the other side, was an enviable condition.

chapter 4

~~~~~~~~~~~~~~~~~~~~

KELAH

Ten pages done. Euphoria. The most I'd written in one sitting since, oh, maybe ever. I deserved a reward. A beer, perhaps. In one of the tavernas that dotted the town's main—only—thoroughfare. Pelekastritsa, where I would finish my novel. My new home. Maybe.

I had seldom left the room since I'd arrived a week ago. It wasn't intentional; it just happened. If I sat there long enough, I reasoned, the insights that lurked inside me, my own personal gold mine, would eventually show themselves, unraveling into something I could weave into the stark pages of my notebook or blank computer screen. If I left, to go swimming, or walk along the gravelly trails that tentacled out from town, or drink with the international community of fun-seekers that gathered down in the village, the vain Italians, the moody Swedes, diligent Germans, drunk English, I might miss it. The critical moment. So I stayed in, slicing tomatoes and cucumbers for dinner at dusk, watching tourists buzz by on mopeds, chattering over the sound of the exhaust.

But tonight I would go out. Experience life. Create something to write about.

I picked up the olive cargo trousers off the floor and slipped them on. Tight white tank. Flip-flops. Leather amulet Boz gave me last summer in Budapest with the single blue bead at the center. The letter from Mum was on the bureau, folded in three and printed on the letterhead of the literary press where she worked, in a computer font made to look cursive. I didn't have to read it again. Thinking about it was like a gong going off in my head.

Dear Kelah, it said. *Your card came in today's post. I'm disappointed that you didn't choose to discuss this holiday with your father and me before you left. Naturally, we are concerned about your state of mind, your career, and your life. Whatever would prompt you to go to Greece when you've just begun the cinema position? Please call me collect or on the phone card. You must know we have your best interests at heart.* The letter ended with her usual closing salutation, *Candace Grant-Morris, Executive Editor,* stamped out in the spirally script. Somebody—her assistant, Nicola?—had pressed a stamp bearing her name into the space between the closing and the *Very truly yours.* It was crooked, so one side had the dark, clotted look of chocolate syrup in the bottom of a mug, and the other the faded paleness of old denim. I thought about Nicola reading the letter, in between form manuscript rejections and royalty checks, and felt my jaw clench. The single time Mum and Nicola and I had lunch, at the Avenue, one of Mum's acquaintances had shaken Nicola's hand gravely and said, *What a pleasure it is to meet you at last, Kelah. A First! Your mother must be so proud.* Mum and Nicola flushed pink, Mum in irritation and Nicola in embarrassment, looking absurdly identical with their straight ash-blond hair and sky-colored eyes all squinched up at the corners. Nobody corrected the poor man. I got up and said I had to use the loo, where I smoked two fags whilst sitting on the toilet until I had stopped trembling.

I checked my billfold—some euros and a wad of ancient drachmas I'd pinched from Charlie's old room, left over from some holiday where he'd pretended to be a professional footballer and claimed to have shagged a dozen women. My hair was crap, so I tied a multicolored scarf around my head to push it back. Even stuck inside, it had lightened in the Greek sun during brief trips to the greengrocer, and the end bits were a startling yellow, which made me look a bit like a demented Mel B.

I locked the door to my room and strolled down to the village. The streets were narrow, labyrinthine, and paved, as if someone had gotten the wise idea to pour concrete down Corfu's bush-studded slopes, in between the nested houses. When I passed Greeks, they usually made that funny backward wave the islanders used to say hello. *"Yasu, yasu!"* they called to me, and I would wave back. On the main street, a half dozen old people sat together on a brick wall. The women wore thin, flowered house-coats and their cottony hair was tied back with scarves, not unlike my own. The men wore black woolens and smoked. One man flicked a switch back and forth, pretending to flog the foreigners, who laughed and ran, their bare brown legs scissoring in the fading light.

There were three pubs in Pelekastritsa: the Dallas, Spiro's, and Coyote Club. The Dallas was an American-style bar favored by the English speakers, the Irish, Aussies, Kiwis, Brits, and Canadians. It was patronized by the serious drinkers, men who slipped away from Melbourne or Christchurch, Liverpool or Limerick, with just a rucksack and a pair of greasy blue jeans. The ones who had hours of stories to tell, who woke up on the beach under the melting sun and practiced the name of the town they'd arrived in before they ventured out: Pelekastritsa, Koh Samui, Sousse.

Decoratively challenged Spiro's was empty until eleven or twelve, at which point scores of men in colored jeans and gold-chain necklaces would sidle in and deliver oft-refused overtures to giggling Italian girls and flaxen-haired Scandinavians. Spiro's had the desperate air of the place that was run by the brother who stayed home, the one who didn't go to Paris and become a fashion designer or attend university in Athens. The Coyote Club felt the most neutral and the least desperate, so I went there first.

Already it spewed music into the night, so loud and throbby, you could feel it in your chest. American songs, two or three years old, and European acid house. I sat down on a barstool.

"Heineken," I said to the bartender, a wren-colored Norwegian with pale eyes and very low pants.

Wordlessly, she placed it in front of me and I sipped. Boz has told me I'm socially retarded, which is probably true. It's not that I don't like people per se, but if I neglect my writing in favor of making friends, how will I ever finish my novel? Writers are observers by nature and thus not as inclined to participate. Besides, I place about as much stock in Boz's assessment of my character as I would my own brothers'—he's simply too close to judge my interpersonal skills fairly.

Also—and I say this with the highest regard for Bozzie as a friend—we come at things from, well, opposite sides of the universe. I'm perfectionistic and highly strung, which anyone who knows me will tell you. Boz is easygoing and calm. Also, I have been told I am ambitious, while Boz is happy just to write his little essays on onomatopoeia and magical realism in Latin American literature that nobody but Fiona and I will ever read. He has that luxury, you see. My family is well-off, true, but my dad's West Indian and won a scholarship from Kingston, whereas Boz's father is a British Petroleum executive *and* the nephew of a viscount, so he grew up with a nanny and Christmas trips to Chamonix and the like. The fact that our first—and only—date produced fewer sparks than a wet match is neither here nor there. I'd trade in every boyfriend I've ever had in a heartbeat for a stand-up friend like Boz. The one thing we *do* have in common is an astounding run of bad luck with boyfriends and girlfriends. I'd like to see Boz settle down with someone of his caliber, you know? Bright, well read, with a sense of humor and the character to look beyond the obvious. Frankly, I always thought he might go for Fee, who's his type anyway, with her blond hair, tits, and bit of arse. It's not like I haven't seen him mooning at her with those big, blue, near-sighted eyes of his. But every time I give him a subtle push in that direction, he acts like he doesn't know what I'm talking about. What do the Americans call it? Denial. That's right. Denial.

chapter 5

PARKER

"Park, what do you say we go out tonight?"

Anya sat in one of our spindly terrace chairs, painting her nails a violent shade of pink that called to mind a Barbary Coast bordello. I'd just finished my run and was panting hard. I passionately hate running, but without Bikram yoga, and with all that feta cheese and fried calamari we'd been eating, I had little choice. There was no way I was going to let myself go. That's all I needed—for Neil to come back from Uzbekistan and find a fat, calamari-padded wife waiting for him. No, thanks.

"I was planning on reading," I said, and watched her face drop.

"Just one drink?"

I sighed, thinking of *The New Yorker* I had saved for the occasion. The one with the profile of Martha Stewart.

"Okay," I said. "But just one. And not at that nasty Dallas place. Or Sergio's. They're disgusting."

"Spiro's," she said.

"That's what I said."

Anya went back to her nails, and I went inside to shower. It is a common device in Hollywood movies to throw two wildly different people together under stressful circumstances. Tempers flare, chaos ensues, and then something temporarily tragic happens so that they realize how deeply fond they really are of each other, how relatable their respective torment. Think Harrison Ford and Anne Heche in *Six Days Seven Nights,* anything with Katharine Hepburn and Spencer Tracy, or the entire cast of *Gilligan's Island* and the many years their shenanigans amused us. Unfortunately, that has not been the case with me and Anya. We've been shipwrecked, all right. Shipwrecked on Corfu. But so far we've stuck to our own sides of the island. We cross the swiftly flowing river between the two camps on occasion to borrow necessities, water or food or Kodak film. Then we go back to the other side.

The truth is, I have never felt so alone. Without Neil, I am just another frustrated interior decorator, searching fruitlessly for the perfect shade of blue.

"Has anyone ever told you you look like the actress Jennifer Connelly?"

"No," I lied. Actually, I hear it a lot.

"Come on. You've got the same long black hair, light eyes. Those eyebrows . . ." he persisted.

I rotated slightly, so that the curly-haired guy's gaze hit my right shoulder.

He tapped it.

"Are you American or Canadian?" he said.

"San Franciscan," I muttered from behind the bottle of Amstel Light.

He laughed. "You're funny. Last time I checked, San Francisco hadn't seceded yet."

"Give us a few more months of that tacky Dubya person and we will."

"A fellow lefty! Be still, my bleeding heart."

I turned to face him. Dark hair. Brown eyes. Broad shoulders. Unexpected freckles on an ethnic nose.

"I'm not a liberal, I'm a decorator," I finally said. And a wife, I wanted to add. Sort of.

"Nice to meet you, Ms. Decorator. I'm Josh. Josh Lido."

I nodded and squeezed into the far corner of my barstool. I could feel the warmth radiating from his thigh. Disturbing. I concentrated on my beer, which was disappointingly watery and tepid.

"Normally when someone introduces himself, a response is called for."

He had one skewed front tooth, which I tried not to stare at. I'm a sucker for the charming flaw. I glanced at Anya, who was deep in conversation with a slim, attractive black girl with an enviable British accent.

"Parker Glass," I said.

"Parker, huh? Like the Hardy Boys."

I quelled the snide response I felt gurgling up and ordered another beer. After all, I could hardly expect to sit drinking in a bar on a Greek island and not be hit on, right?

The beer slid down my throat nicely. Not too foul-tasting this time. Good, in fact. What would Neil think, me sitting in a seedy bar, drinking beer out of the bottle, fending off the advances of strange, shortish men with snaggled front teeth and decorative muscles? I tried to imagine what Neil was doing right now. Sleeping fitfully on a filthy pallet? Hammering nails into planks with soft, IP-attorney hands? Speaking to the indigenous with those little tongue clicks one hears on *National Geographic*? Most likely, he was frolicking with bare-breasted women in a river polluted by international agribusiness.

Sickened, I let my head fall onto my crossed arms.

I had received exactly one piece of correspondence from Neil since I left. A letter Molly forwarded to me via poste restante. By the time I read it, the date at the top was twenty-two days old and the postmark had blurred to a greenish blot.

Parker, he'd written in his spidery, hurried scrawl. *I've been placed on a team with fifteen volunteers from all over the world. It is nothing like I expected, yet everything I had hoped for.—What did that mean?—Each day, when I wake up, I feel a sense of purpose and conviction I never felt before. An overwhelming feeling of gratitude that, today, I'm going to contribute to people's well-being, build something real and tangible that will stand as a testament to people's innate goodness and provide shelter to someone who needs it long after I've come and gone from here. I'm beginning to understand a few things about myself, things I never would have understood if I had stayed in San Francisco. I know I've hurt you, and, believe me, I wish there was some way for me to do this without doing so. But I have every reason to think things will work out for us. For me. Parker, you're my brick. My dear, solid brick. Just picturing you in the apartment, tucking the corners of the duvet in, or watering the hydrangeas, gives me a warm rush. I hope you are having a productive and rewarding summer. I'll write soon. Love, Neil*

And that was it. The idea that my summer could be *rewarding* and *productive* after my husband of eleven days ran off to Uganda made me want to throw my beer bottle through the bar mirror.

Oh, Jesus. I might be a little drunk. It had snuck up on me. Naughty. Like Josh Lido. Rhymes with *burrito. Meat-o. Neat-o!* Where was he? I glanced around. Gone. Good. He'd have better luck with one of the Scandinavians, who seemed to be multiplying like ants, spewing out of tavernas and hostels in blond droves, taking over the island, the European Union, the world.

"I'm not Swedish," I announced suddenly.

A group of Nordic amazons and adonises looked up from their table, their ski-glove-size hands clasped around their beers. One of them said something in a singsongy foreign language and they all laughed. He sounded like the chef from *The Muppet Show.*

"What are you laughing at, asshole? You sound just like a Muppet," I slurred.

I decided it was time to go home. Back to the ranch. Oops, the villa. Anya was nowhere to be seen. Don't blame her for leaving me. I'm such a bitch. That's why Neil left me. It wasn't really his fault. I'm so horrid. What did I expect?

Tears stung my eyes as I fumbled with my purse, which I'd wrapped around the stool.

"Let me help you with that." Josh Lido tried to unwind the long cord from around the seat.

"*She a brick . . . HOUSE!*" I shimmied a little.

His dark, winged brows knitted together. "You're shit-faced."

"That I am, sir. But at least I'm not Canadian. Or Swedish. Oh, sorry, are you Canadian? I bet you are. You look like a Canadian. All muscley and alone." I don't know why I said that.

He grinned. He really did have a nice smile. Such white teeth, with that delightful crooked one. "Actually, I'm from California."

I punched him in the arm. He actually staggered back a little, so it must have been harder than I thought. Decorative muscles. Ha! "You sneak! I said I'm from San Francisco and you didn't say anything!"

"You didn't give me a chance."

I grunted and tried to find the door, which had seemed so big and obvious upon arrival. Finally, it presented itself and I sailed out, stumbling down the path toward the villa. I thought I heard Josh Lido say something behind me but didn't turn around.

"I left my heart in San Francisco," I sang. "High on a bridge, you called to me . . ." I tripped on a rock and stubbed my toe. "Ouch," I called out. No one responded, just the rustling of leaves. Were wild animals indigenous to Corfu?

I skittered along the olive-strewn path under a huge silvery moon. Next to it, a mirror aura of the first. "Two moons tonight!" I yelled, and giggled. "Holy butt cheeks, Batman!"

The two moons guided me onto the soft sand, cool beneath the top layer. I felt it squish up between my toes and sighed. Where were my shoes? Gratefully, I sank onto the pillowy beach, felt sand grains rub my cheek. Ahead of me, the water wriggled like broken mirrors under the moonlight. This was better than the villa, better than home. Better.

chapter 6

CLAIRE

I was on my way home, the Aussie vampire heading back to her sarcophagus, when I heard the woman sobbing.

I could make out a vague outline, a frizzy aureole of hair, shaking shoulders, curved over on a tree stump, a few meters off the road. Should I go on, leave the person to her private misery, or butt in?

"Excuse me, are you all right, there?"

She raised her head. Tears reflected the moonlight off her face. The woman looked to be about my age, thin, familiar. Then I realized: the one from behind the bar at the Dallas, silently wiping beer off the well-oiled counter with a clean cloth, as it was spilled. Over and over.

"Who are you?" she said, hiccuping.

"I'm Claire. Claire Dillon. I'm staying just over the hill. I heard you and, well, was just wondering if I can help."

She sniffled softly. "That's very kind of you, Claire. But I'm afraid I'm just dealing with some hard times. With my husband." Oh, did I ever.

The woman was American, with the flat, nasal tones of the Midwest. A news presenter's voice.

"I'm sorry."

We sat there in silence for a moment. I got the sense she was amenable to my presence, so I stayed still.

"Do you believe in true love, Claire?"

"I guess that depends on how you define true love."

"I suppose that's sort of a dumb question."

"Not dumb, maybe just a bit . . . naive. I mean, we grow up raised to believe in the knight on the white horse and all that, and what we get instead is—"

"—a pile of laundry!"

"—a horrid mother-in-law!"

"—a cheating bastard of a husband!"

In spite of myself, I giggled sharply, a report that echoed off the surrounding hills like a pistol shot. The thin woman's eyes locked on mine. They glinted with unshed tears and spent rage.

"You too?"

"Seems so."

"Is that why you're here?"

"Sort of. My husband went to bed with his masseuse." I hesitated. "I'm hoping to find a male masseuse here who will have me."

We listened to the night birds chirp at each other for a moment.

"Actually, I can't believe I just said that. How embarrassing," I said.

We laughed.

"I know exactly how you feel," she said darkly. An image of me strolling through the Greek isles in a bright silk muumuu, waving at a dark-haired man with a large nose standing on the prow of a ship as the wind whipped my luxurious hair behind me, popped into my mind. Indeed.

The frizzy-haired woman stuck out her hand. "I'm Patricia Halkiopolous."

Then Patricia and I spoke of things harmless and simple,

beaches and beer and where to get the best tomatoes, while the sun flirted with the horizon.

I was pregnant the first time at eighteen. There's a reason I state it that way, "pregnant at eighteen," and not "I had so-and-so at eighteen." After the Adelaide Festival, where I sang to Gary in my carmine-colored dress, we courted almost violently, in that way you can only when you're very young and believe the advent of one single person, one man, is going to turn your world into the thrumming magical place you always dreamed it could be. In 1976, courting meant long summer nights listening to Bobby strum his guitar on the beach, my back sliding up against Gary's chest, bottles of lager pressed into my hand. And kissing. Endless, tireless kissing at the back door of my parents' house, where the neighbor Mrs. Blackburn couldn't see us—though my parents might have, had the low murmurs of pleasure roused them—on the broad seat of Gary's red AMX Javelin, at the beach house he shared with three of his construction blokes, and, once, in the loo at his parents' anniversary party, where Gary succeeded in removing my suede miniskirt before someone hammering on the door startled us into quick propriety.

Back then, that perfect moment in time and in youth, I now see that I had that butterfly quality you see in girls: a fragile, swift beauty that drew its power from freedom. Freedom to sing the sweet, arcing notes of Joni Mitchell's For the Roses. Freedom to choose among the three or four suitors who made their yearnings known that summer, slipping notes to Bobby's wife, Marianne, who was our manager, watching me from the crowd, waiting in line for tickets to a string of packed shows in forgettable venues with spilled beer so deep it rolled up over your shoes.

I sometimes batted my wings against Gary's attentions, ambivalent about him and about our love, feeling him all around me, a human butterfly net. I ran hot and then cold, not to tease him, but because I truly didn't know what I wanted, from him or from life.

By the time the first crisp notes of fall seeped into our days, Gary and I were sleeping together. He was my first lover, and I gave our affair everything I had. Gary never told me about his other girlfriends, didn't need to. I felt them there with us, three or four long-haired, full-breasted, big-bottomed, hourglass-shaped girls, my pseudosisters, though I knew he himself had forgotten them completely.

I think of those nights now when I lecture Ethan and Brian—especially Brian—on protection. "Ma," they say, rolling their matching amber eyes at me and elbowing each other in the ribs. "Nobody else's mother gives them bloody frangers when they go out. Jay-sus!" Then they collapse into each other, brown arms flung around broad shoulders, laughing at my naïveté.

I don't think of that first, lost baby much. At least, not on purpose. Sometimes she'll pop up when I least expect her to, while washing up back at home, my eyes filled with the patch of grass and neat shrubs outside the kitchen window. Or on Saturday night, as I skim fingers across film boxes at the video store. Once I saw her outlined clearly against the backdrop of the scoreboard during Ethan's rugby match. Even though they never actually brought her to me—remember, this was 1977, before they knew the importance of the mother imprinting the still creature with her fierce, landless love—I'll see her, a flash, a grainy black-and-white Polaroid image of a baby or a young girl, flipping away even as I try to grasp it. Then I think, in a sort of wonder, there she is, long-limbed and complete, the only daughter I'll ever have. The instigator of a marriage.

chapter 7

ANYA

There are two primary reasons I hate swimming: bathing suits and water. Each alone would have been enough to keep me out of the sea and firmly rooted on land forever if it wasn't for the Voice.

The Voice has been creeping up on me a lot lately. It started back at home. The first time I heard it was That Day. But I'm getting ahead of myself. I guess that's because I don't really understand what happened. The funny thing is, nothing really bad happened that particular day. Really, it was a day like any other, and better than most. Now, that seems ironic, that I should shower, go to work, put the finishing touches on a grant proposal, stop by the five-and-dime to pick up plastic trash liners, walk the six blocks home, turn on the TV, and then take eleven—or twelve, the doctors aren't sure—sleeping tablets, one by one like Halloween candy, on a day when nothing of consequence was supposed to happen. I was watching *El Privilegio de Amar* at the time, which I consider to be insignificant. I should say that I am alone in that opinion.

So, there I am, propped up against the mustard-colored sofa in the apartment I share with my little sister, Carilu, who had gone for a long weekend in Bodega Bay. The remote had slipped from my fingers, which was frustrating, since I'd muted it for the commercials and now Victor Manuel and Luciana were back on the screen, trying to guess the father of Christina's baby. Things were starting to swim a little. I didn't make the connection between the sleeping pills and the wavering lines in my field of vision, the way my head rocked back on my neck until I was staring up at the cracked ceiling with the water stain in the corner. I even wondered if things were moving around because there'd been an earthquake, not an unusual occurrence in San Francisco, I assure you.

Then I heard someone say, "Anya, go to the telephone." The Voice was so clear, so stark and full of decibel, I thought someone was in the room with me. My eyelids, made of stone, wouldn't rise enough to verify this fact, but it was something I knew, just like I knew I'd wear Vera Wang at my wedding and honeymoon in Venice. Even then I knew the Voice wasn't a by-product of a crazy mind, schizophrenia, a personality disorder, or manic depression or whatever. The Voice was cool-toned and calm, someone worth listening to, I'd thought, like a teacher or a cool young mom who doesn't take *chingadera de nadien*. Maybe it was *La Virgen*, who had come to lay her fine pale hands on me and raise from me the curse that stuck to my life like chewing gum on sneakers.

"Why?" I'd asked, licking at the drool that spilled out of my lips onto my cheek.

"El teléfono," the Voice urged softly.

I was going to get up and call someone. Really. But the next thing I knew I was staring up at a white coat with a white face above it, a terrible bright light boring into my brain, and something horrible was choking me. I leaned over and vomited pink spray all over the tiled floor. Some of it hit the nurse's shoes. For the first time that I could recall, I wanted to die.

Now, shifting from one foot to another on the scorched sand, half a world away, she was speaking to me again: Mi'ijita, *get up off your lazy* culo *and get your toes wet*.

I'd already walked the beach countless times, my ankles and knees feeling the sting of the salt. In the baggy shorts that used to be my boyfriend Rick's and I hadn't managed to get rid of. Yet. (Carda would kill me; I'd promised to box everything up and leave it for her to throw out while I was gone.) But just when the water kissed my knees, I'd stop, backing out of the sea one step at a time until I was back on the beach, stranded and already faint with heat.

Out on the water, a couple of tourists were getting windsurfing lessons, the girls screaming repeatedly as they surged away from shore and the wind ripped the sail out of their hands, flinging them into the sparkly turquoise water. I wanted to be like them. I wanted to lie, slick and gently bruised, on the pointed white board, bobbing up and down on the swells that came to shore each afternoon, nudged forward by the trade winds. I pictured myself, sun-steeped and lean in a white bathing suit—hey, I know, but it's a dream, okay?—leaning back against the pull of the sail and flying, *flying*, across the water. I'd look back at those people on the beach and think, how sad it must be to not be me. Someone who flies on water.

I walked up to the Greek boy who was wrapping sails around big poles at the edge of the sand.

"Excuse me," I said. "Do you speak English?"

He squinted up at me. His eyes were very green against his tan skin, almost as dark as mine. "Of course. You want lessons?"

"Not exactly. I mean, yes, I want lessons. But I need to . . . you see, I can't . . ." I breathed deeply and started over. "I don't know how to swim, but I really want to do *that*"—I pointed to the lovely flock of sailboarders skipping across the waves—"so I wanted to see if you'd teach me to swim first, and then maybe the other stuff." There, I'd said it.

He leaned back on his heels as if pondering such a pathetic pronouncement. Imagine, not knowing how to swim! Up close,

I realized he was barely a teenager, narrow still through the chest and shoulders, with ropy muscles starting to bulge out in the skinny biceps and thighs.

"Maybe this isn't a good idea," I said hurriedly. "I mean, maybe I should go to the pool or something—"

"I teach you."

"—because all I can do is, like, paddle around a little. I've never even been in the ocean all the way, or a river. I mean, I was in a lake once, but that was an accident because my brother pushed me in—"

"I teach you. No worries," he said again, and resumed tying knots in the sail's ropes.

"You'll teach me."

He flashed his pretty eyes at me. "Yes. I taught my sisters to swim, and some cousins. I can teach you. Besides, there's no pool."

"Will I be able to do that?" I gestured out at the glorious wave dancers.

"Are you working hard?" he asked me.

"Very."

"Then probably you can do that by the end of summer. Come tomorrow morning at nine, yes? There's no wind then. No bumps."

For a minute I thought he was talking about me in a bathing suit and I felt heat flame in my cheeks, then I realized he meant waves.

"Oh. Okay. See you," I fumbled.

"Hey, wait!"

I turned around.

"What's your name?"

"Anya. What's yours?"

"Johnny."

He waved, and something tight and unyielding seemed to unfurl in my chest a little. Wow. Me, swimming. Now I just needed to find a bathing suit. That's what I get for listening to the Voice.

chapter 8

PARKER

I had my whole life planned out by the time I was twelve. First, I'd bypass Berkeley High and attend the *Lycée Français*. That way, when I did my requisite year abroad in university, I'd be better prepared to ask for ice in my Coke or politely refuse the advances of the host family's Gauloise-smoking father. Then, college at a small liberal arts school with snow, old brick buildings crumbling under the weight of their own tastefulness, and an emphasis on culturally bracing yet utterly useless courses such as Existentialism in Avant-Garde Film and The Epistemology of Modern Dance. University of California was my backup plan, which, thankfully, I didn't have to use because I got a scholarship to Smith. Later, I'd get my MFA at San Francisco's Academy of Art College, focusing on interior architecture and design. A suitable husband, handsome, with a full head of crisp, wavy hair, WASPy parents, fiscally but not socially conservative, well-traveled and lacrosse-playing and rebellious enough to recognize the storytelling mileage my family baggage brought to the table. Two (terrific) kids. One (fabulous) house. No pets (allergic).

Of course, my parents were terribly worried about me—imagine, the horrors of birthing a tiny, goal-oriented capitalist!—and tried to distract me from my unwavering plotting with summertime incarceration in lefty commune-ish day camps and subscriptions to the *Utne Reader*. But you can't mess with destiny. Inevitably, I'd show up at camp, the only Parker adrift in a sea of Dakotas and Cinnamons and Rainbows and Lambs, five issues of *Architectural Digest* folded neatly into my suitcase, tags I'd sewn myself in my five polo jerseys, and an expertly forged note from my family doctor saying that, regrettably, a rare dual affliction of psoriasis and Ménière's disease prohibited all physical and outdoor activities. By the time I hit adulthood, the only really big thing I got wrong was the color of my 325ci: They were out of champagne, so I went with the indigo.

But lately, it seemed as if a landslide of unplanned events was raining down on me: Neil's bombshell, the meltdown, my leave of absence from work, spending the summer with Anya Soberanes, waking up drunk on a public beach, and, now, this annoying little man, this Josh Lido, following me around everywhere. Oh, and that crazy dog.

But first things first.

The morning after my ill-fated evening at the Coyote Club dawned hot and bright. At least, that's what I gathered when I woke up on the beach with the sun already high overhead, baking me into the consistency of human jerky.

"Aaah," I cried, and tried to sit up. Mistake. Black spots pooled out across my field of vision, as if someone had flung ink in my eyes. I collapsed back in the sand. Gingerly, I brought my hand up over my eyes and shifted to a vertical position.

I was on the beach. The nude beach, it looked like, judging by the lack of tan lines and the teepee at the edge of the rocks, where neohippies smeared themselves with diarrhea-colored mud and burned an unceasing supply of foul incense. I was dressed in last night's clothes—thank God—and there was a deep groove in my right cheek where, presumably, the buckle of my Kate Spade bag had branded me during the night. My left side, exposed to

the morning sun, had assumed the crispy texture of Kentucky
Fried Chicken.

A dirty white dog licked my hand.

"Get off me!" I screeched. The little speckled mutt stopped for
a moment, then resumed his ferocious tongue bath, moving up
over my sun-fried arm, which actually would have felt good if it
wasn't so totally gross.

"Git," I said again weakly.

"He likes you."

I tried to identify the speaker, but the instant explosion of fire-
works inside my skull made it impossible to look upward.

"Purse. Glasses. Get," I mumbled into my chest.

The person handed me my wonderful shades. I slipped them
on and stared into the sun.

Josh. Lido?

Today, he wore a faded Hawaiian shirt, threadbare shorts with
a hole near the crotch, and paper-thin flip-flops where his big,
hairy feet lay in neat slots, like dugout canoes. Under his arm
were the ubiquitous bamboo beach mat, a bottled water, and an
enormous tube of sunblock with a picture of a half-naked girl on
the front.

"Did you sleep out here, Park? You look like you slept out
here," he said, stating the obvious in an extremely annoying way. I
glanced down at my rumpled clothes, dog-saliva-covered arms,
and abraded knees and felt him smiling at me as if his grin were a
splash of warm water.

"Don't call me Park," I croaked.

He handed me his water and silently I grasped it, tipped it
back, and chugged until I dry-heaved and water ran out and down
my neck.

"Hey, take it easy. Here, slow down. Yeah, that's better. No,
don't stop. Go ahead and finish it." He held the bottom of the
bottle so I could gulp better.

"Man, you look like shit," Josh said finally.

"Fuck off," I snarled, which even I could see was startlingly
rude after he'd just let me polish off his water supply. I couldn't

help it, though. Something about the guy rubbed me the wrong way. Maybe it was the cocky rich-kid-pretending-to-be-bohemian charm, the I-don't-give-a-shit quality that reeked of entitlement. Or the springy curls that were beginning to look suspiciously like dreadlocks. Or the patch of hairy ass that begged for attention, hanging out where his shorts pocket should be for the world to see. Guys like Josh Lido were a dime a dozen back in California. I wished he would just crawl back under a rock in whatever nou-veau riche, gated Orange County suburb that had produced him.

"Come on. I'm taking you home. Tell me where your villa is," he said solicitously, as if I hadn't just spewed insults at him.

And that's how I ended up doing a passable imitation of the walk of shame with Josh Lido through the streets of Pelekastritsa, minus one shoe, plus one whitish dog with brown spots on his homely nose.

In a town as small as Pelekastritsa, everyone knows everything in an astoundingly short period of time. Who slept with whom, who struck out at Spiro's, who just got a job touting the ouzo-soaked Athena Palace youth hostel over on the other side of the island. I swear, you can't fart without someone spraying air freshener across the street. I'd been able to operate on the fringes of village society up until now—not going out at night, avoiding the beach by day, and not screwing the townies helped. But in one night of ill-advised overindulgence, I'd managed to obliterate all the bliss-ful anonymity I'd so carefully cultivated for nearly three weeks.

Prior to that, I simply read, ran, dozed, and plotted Neil's and my reconciliation. I might have passed the entire summer with about as much human contact as the Unabomber if Anya hadn't persisted in her daily invitations. I don't know exactly how we ar-rived at an understanding, but by the time Josh Lido escorted me and my single shoe back to Chez Prozac, my and Anya's daily rou-tine typically included at least one meal, outing, or shopping ex-pedition (a.k.a. booze run). In honest moments, I admitted to myself that I was sullen, high, and marginally responsive, whereas

Anya was optimistic, conciliatory, and sweet. Naturally, this irritated me.

The day after my canine tongue bath, Anya and I went to Tony's Taverna, as usual, for dinner. We'd tried all the other places, and nothing else could compare: the view, the squid, the moussaka, the dolmas wrapped delicately in their little blankets of grape leaves—all were the best.

Anya was looking better. She had on some sort of voluminous white shift, which looked like a grandma's nightdress, but did bring out her olive complexion. She'd pulled her hair back into a braid and sprayed it with defrizzing gloss. The skittish-deer look she'd had in her eyes since our arrival was mysteriously absent, replaced with a poised curiosity that made her look regal and Mayan.

Tony showed us to our usual table. The attractive middle-aged woman with auburn hair and large, sad eyes who was there most nights raised her hand as I walked by, and I found myself smiling in return.

After a few minutes, Tony brought us our Greek salads and white wine. "So, I hear you got yourself a dog," he said.

I snorted. "It's more like the dog got me."

"Tony, have you seen it? It's small and white. Maybe someone's missing it," Anya said.

"Oh, no, that's Blakas."

"Blakas?" I parroted. Alcohol and sun: not good for the brain.

"He don't belong to anybody. If we see him, we kick him. Always begging."

"But that's terrible!" Anya looked suspiciously at the plate of calamari a busboy had set there, as if it might be deep-fried dog.

Tony shrugged. "On an island, there's not a lot of food for everyone. It's every man for his self." He grinned wolfishly and left us to go flirt with the auburn-haired woman.

After this lesson in Second World social mores, I was inclined to just shut up and eat while there was still food left, but Anya the Social Crusader was on a Joan of Arc kick and couldn't leave it alone.

"It's the same way in Mexico. I totally understand that people come first, but there's something awfully sad about a poor little dog that doesn't know any better begging for food." A halo was practically glimmering above her head. I decided to change the subject.

"Anya, you never really told me why you wanted to come to Greece," I said as I dug into our calamari, surprising myself. Before, I hadn't much cared. Anya was just another one of Carda's hippie-dippy friends, earnest and hairy-legged and prone to citing Global Exchange poverty statistics of Indians in Chiapas and refugees in Gaza.

Anya turned her head away, toward the sea. In profile, I realized suddenly, she was striking, with a high forehead, strong nose, and eyelashes black and spiky as caterpillar bristles. A tear squeezed out at the corner of her right eye.

"I tried to commit suicide," she said simply.

I paused, a fried squid tentacle dangling between us.

"I think I've been trying to pass it off as something else, but when you take twelve sleeping pills and your aunt finds you drooling down your shirt and takes you to the hospital to get your stomach pumped, well, they usually call it suicide."

"Oh, Anya." I couldn't think of what to say. Out of the corner of my eye, I saw the smart-looking British woman from the bar come in with a busty blonde and a tall, skinny guy with glasses.

Her eyes flashed. "I know. It's pathetic. My parents were going to send me to a loony bin, but I convinced them to let me come here instead. I mean, it wasn't really a loony bin—they called it a relaxation ranch—but I had visions of anorexic men in pajamas with staples in their heads and crazy old ladies with no teeth and, *ay Dios*, Miss Havisham in her wedding dress careening around manicured lawns. . . ."

Her voice dribbled away, and before I knew it, I'd extended my hand across the table and covered hers.

"Anya, you're not crazy."

She nodded. "I know."

"And you're not going to end up like Miss Havisham." Carda had told me about Anya's wedding obsession.

"Sure." Her voice was strangled.

"Besides, you're not the only one who's gone bonkers around here. After Neil left, I had a tiny breakdown myself. Of course, my situation was sort of different. I just took too many Ativans by accident"—even as I said this, the absurdity of it reverberated in my mind. Who cared if it was Ativans or Halcion or vitamin C, it's still some sort of overdose, isn't it?—"and got a little upset in a client meeting and decided to take some time off. So . . . you're not alone."

Anya smiled tentatively. "I'm glad you know. I told my parents that you knew. I lied. It was the only way they'd let me come alone." She said it as if lying was some new and horrible thing she'd discovered and abused, like a stash of drug money, and not a simple survival skill.

"Well, now that we know we're just two loonies, let's celebrate with dessert," I suggested. I'd had my eye on that baklava.

"But you don't eat dessert."

I sighed and stroked Blakas's mangy coat. Sometime during dinner, he'd snuck in and planted himself firmly on my right foot. Like Neil, he had two different-colored eyes. Also like Neil, he had never thought twice about the United Arab Emirates or building barns. Thinking of Neil, my gorgeous, sardonic, weak-ass, rat-bastard husband, I felt something new and red and raw rush into my chest, filling the cavities with heat. Anger? Ambivalence? Animal fat?

"Maybe it's time I started," I said.

chapter 9

~~~~~~~~~~~~~~

KELAH

I backspaced over *proverbial pot of gold*—bloody pedestrian, that—and changed it to *extending tentative feelers into a new life*. There, that should do it. I closed out of my word-processing application and shut down. I love being awake when nobody else is. I glanced at the clock: 4:00 A.M. The witching hour. After staring out the small, square window for two hours, pacing a track in the floor, I'd accepted my writer's block and decided to distract myself by starting a holiday journal. It's just a throwaway, you know? Something to pass time before the next burst of inspiration comes. Something to keep me from going stark raving mad.

I tiptoed to the bathroom, stepping over Boz and Fee, who were wrapped up snug as bangers in sleeping bags. Bozzie's mouth hung open slightly and his glasses sat on the floor next to his hand. He looked like an infant, tender and curled into himself. Sweet Bozzie. Maybe he and Fee would get it together. I for one think that'd be brilliant. I mean, she's dead clever and hyper and chronically lovelorn, and he's dead clever and downbeat and chronically lovelorn. They're perfect for each other and just don't know it. Maybe they're holding back because of the whole friends thing. It's hard, when you've been together as long as we three have, to imagine mucking things up, which love inevitably does. But if I've learned anything in life, it's that you have to take risks or you won't stand a chance at happiness. Plus, I was glad as hell to see them. I think I was starting to get a bit insular, here on the island. I'd had, like, two conversations with real people since I got here: one with Anya from America and one with Claire from Australia, though that one was a bit stunted. If Boz and Fee hadn't arrived, I might have mutated into some sort of dodgy hermit, complete with imaginary friends and extralong toenails and unwashed knickers that could walk away by themselves.

They'd shown up one day bearing silly grins, Marmite, and a peculiar long stick Boz had picked up from a stoned Finn on the bus.

"Kay, you in?" Fee called.

"Special delivery!" said Boz.

I heard the familiar voices and poked my head out of the toilet, where I was trying to get a handle on the whole exfoliation thing.

"Fiona! And Bozzie! What in Christ's name are you doing here?"

Then they poured in and in between hugs and great laughs I gleaned that (a) summer in London was shit, (b) their love lives in London were shit, and (c) London was shit.

"What's that great willy-looking thing?" I asked Boz.

"An Amazonian rain stick," he announced proudly.

Fee rolled her eyes. "This Finnish bloke told him it would increase virility. A load of shite if I ever heard it. Peel back the label and you'll see Made in China."

This cracked us up.

"Hey, I'll take all the help I can get. Besides, it sounds cool." He tipped it over and patters, like an avalanche of raindrops, deluged us.

"So, how long can you stay?" I bounced on my single bed.

"Ten days," Fee said.

"Is it any trouble, our staying here?" said Boz.

"Well, we'll look for a new place tomorrow. Oh, this Aussie I met said there's a suite underneath hers that just came empty. Maybe it's still free." Over at Tony's, Claire had described her room as a sarcophagus. I was intrigued.

"Um, how's the writing going?" Boz said. I could tell he was trying to sound casual.

"Oh, fine. Good." Actually, it was crap, but I couldn't look into Fee's newly minted author eyes and say that. I just couldn't.

"Great!" they chimed maniacally, as if they'd talked of nothing but my famous writer's block for the entire journey.

Then Boz stuck his foot in it again.

"So, when did Davey get released?" he said, and this time I couldn't pretend anything, just stared.

My older brother Davey is an addict. Smack, scag, crank, crack, dope, coke, X, love, comic books, overpriced footwear—you name it, he's done it. Long before we even knew he had a drug problem, you could see glimmers of his weakness. As children, when we went shopping with Mum or our West Indian housekeeper, Miriam, there wasn't a sweet or a toy that didn't migrate as if by magic and find itself nestled in the sticky confines of Davey's dungarees pocket. Davey got kicked out of every school Mum and Dad ever sent him to, a veritable beacon for the truly evil kids who saw in him a good way to stir up trouble and get a laugh out of it at the same time. As he got older, the prizes got larger, the transgressions more blatant, until Mum and Dad couldn't ignore it anymore. I know what you're thinking—cry for help and all that. It's true that for a long time Davey retained his basic sweetness—it's there in the photos, warming his smile and softening the expression in his stout-colored eyes. But eventually the phone call comes. And the voice on the other end of the line tells you things you really don't want to hear, can't accept, won't get over. And you feel your heart leak molten anger that fossilizes into something hard and unyielding. Something that makes your eyes slide away from his when he says, *But we're family, Kay.*

Family.

One night, Davey was walking by a chemist's and decided to help himself to some prescription meds. The chemist was closed. The alarm was silent. He'd just been to the cinema (the Belle Vue, of course), and the fact that he'd been able to describe in not insignificant detail the feature that night—*Planet of the Apes*—weighed heavily in his favor at sentencing. It was not believed to be a premeditated crime, you see. Opportunistic, they called it.

The police found him sweeping shattered glass up with the chemist's broom, heedless of the silent alarm that sent its spitting alert through the heavy night. *Oi,* he'd said, grinning foolishly at the cops when they arrived in full bulletproof regalia, *I just wanted to clean up after meself.* He went with them quietly, politely, reports indicated, as if he felt bad for imposing on them.

On the day Davey was sent to prison, my relationship with Mum hit rock bottom. I was living in a flat with Fee at the time but took the tube to Mum and Dad's in time to drive with them over to the court. Mum answered the door with her briefcase in hand.

"Hi," I said. "Are we leaving already? Are Dad and Charlie ready?"

"You'll be leaving at half eight." Her blue eyes flooded with exhaustion. She set the briefcase down. "Kelah, this is a bit difficult. I've decided it's best if I not go with you."

"What do you mean?"

"I can't . . . I feel that I need some distance. We can't continue as we have. It's taking a terrible toll on everybody. Surely you see that," she said gently.

"But we have to support him. We have to support Davey." Rage and pity for Davey made my voice hoarse, mingled with shame at the feeling Mum's statement inspired: envy.

"Your father and Charlie will be there."

"But it's the mother who counts!" I screamed.

"Kelah."

My father appeared behind her, so tall and ebony, he looked like her opposite twin.

"Kelah! Your mother is terribly upset and you're just making it worse. Now, come in and control yourself. And apologize."

"Sorry," I mumbled. Then we stood there awkwardly, and I wanted to say something more but couldn't seem to find the words. After a moment, Mum left and the door shut and she slipped behind the wheel of her Mercedes and rolled away.

Davey got six months in prison for the break-in and burglary, plus rehab. I got sacked for not showing up at Burger Palace #3 for the afternoon shift. And Candace Grant-Morris acquired a work of literary fiction by first-time author Marjorie Waterford, whose story of a Liverpudlian family that raises Hereford cattle and commits incest won the Booker Prize that year, 2003.

chapter 10

~~~~~~~~~~~~~~~~

CLAIRE

Today, I went on the flying doughnut with three lovely boys from Sweden.

"Omigod," I screamed as the speedboat flung the inflatable tube across an incoming wake. Water churned into our faces and we bounced hard enough to make me wish for an exercise bra—no, two exercise bras.

"You all right there, Claire?" asked Sven. (Yes, Sven!)

"Fine. Um, is this nearly over, then?"

He laughed and I clung a little harder. The flying doughnut is an evil invention designed to make its riders into rag dolls. As far as I can see, the benefits are largely for the beachcombers, who have the pleasure of laughing at us as we pop off one by one and sail into the aquamarine waters.

Finally, we finished. Thoroughly exhausted, I staggered out of the water with my arse hanging out of my maillot, waving good-bye to the boys, who had asked me to be a fourth as I was lounging on the beach having dark fantasies of sending Gary's tart a horse-manure bouquet in the post.

"Have a beer with us, Claire?" the blondish one called.

"No, thanks. Too tired." I mimed sleep and went to find my blanket.

Nineteen days had passed since I'd arrived. I can't say anything much had changed, in spite of me riding flying doughnuts and going for long walks to ancient Greek villages and spending hour upon hour alone with my thoughts. The big revelation, the one that scorches the earth in front of you, illuminating the path you're meant to take, had yet to occur.

I decided to write to Valerie.

Dear Val, I scratched in my notebook with the pretty flowered paper. *Today, I went on the flying doughnut with three lovely boys from Sweden.*

Wait—would she even know what a flying doughnut was? I scratched that out and started a new page.

Dear Val, I began again. *Today, I rode an inflatable water toy with three blond adonises from an unnamed Scandinavian country.*

I read it back a few times and thought it rather pathetic, almost as if I was bragging—ha, ha, you're back in Oz enslaved in marriage and I'm in Greece having a naughty with a boy—three boys—named Sven.

Dear Val, I tried again. *Today, I went swimming in a beautiful turquoise sea. It was filled with Scandinavians with hair the color of corn. They were riding on inflatable rafts shaped like giant dongers.*

Disgusted, I crumpled the sheet of paper and stuffed the notebook back in my tote. God help me.

"Hi, Claire."

The thin American woman I had met on the beach stood next to me. She had on tennis shoes and running shorts and her T-shirt was dark with sweat. I recalled that American women always jogged and did aerobic dance and sometimes shaved their heads and played rugby with the men, something I'd thought wouldn't be a bad development in Australia.

"Nice to see you again, Patricia. Would you like to sit down?" I said.

"Um, okay." Patricia seemed embarrassed. "About the other night . . ."

"No need to explain."

"Well, actually"—she glanced up the sandy strip as if the town lynch mob was about to storm the beach, Normandy-style—"maybe I was a little upset. You know, I may have overreacted a little."

"I understand," I said.

"Do you? I thought you would. Just don't . . . mention our conversation to anyone? My husband and I are going to try to work things out, and I don't want anyone to . . . you know . . ."

"Of course."

She was skittish. "I mean, the thing is, he doesn't know I've told anyone. His family's very old-fashioned, Greek Orthodox. They don't believe in talking about your problems. My sister-in-law, Nick's sister, she owns the travel agency? She's a huge gossip, knows everything. God."

Patricia collapsed in the sand next to me. I wondered what she was getting at. Hadn't she made it sufficiently clear already? The sun was coming down hard. Maybe I'd drop by the dairy, get an ice cream or a drink, read awhile.

The Swedish boys were back from the taverna.

"Hi, Patricia," said Sven. "Would you mind if I came by later to pick up that book I left? We're off to Crete tomorrow and it's got my postcards in it."

Patricia the jogging American had the grace to blush.

Gary had always wanted Dillon & Sons to be the truth.

"Think about it, Claire," he'd say, while I stuffed thick slabs of steak with oysters and wrapped potatoes in aluminum foil in anticipation of dinner. "Me and Ethan and Bri, running the biggest construction outfit in New South Wales. I tell you, it's everything my dad ever dreamed for the business! It's why he came here!" Gary's father had emigrated from Ireland with fifty dollars Australian to his name and had a single son, Gary, to carry on the family name.

But Gary's dream didn't turn out quite that way.

It was summer vacation. Both Ethan and Brian were home with us between terms at uni. Ethan was twenty and helping out his father for the summer, going out with his friends after work, sunburned and muscled from days spent digging pools and laying concrete and working side by side with Gary and his foreman, Tad Conway. Ethan had always been taciturn and solid, the one whose future was forecast in every decisive move he made: graduate with a degree in structural engineering, go into business with Gary, elevate the straightforward but lucrative contracting to more ambitious development projects and architecture, marry his university girlfriend, Rachel, and move into an original Dillon & Sons home a couple kilometers from us in Glebe.

Brian was more mercurial, careening from one tightly held yearning to another, from large-animal veterinarian to aboriginal-rights lawyer and finally to actor. That summer, Brian, just eighteen, spent most of his time holed up in his room with his two childhood friends: Jane, a pudgy, pale girl with dyed pink hair and the sidelong glance of the terminal wallflower, and Biscuit, puny as Brian was strapping, with a garland of tattoos around his skinny neck and a ready smile he'd been giving me since he was eight. They were sharing a flat next year at school.

With three men and assorted friends in the house, I was constantly cooking, cleaning, and shopping in what seemed a never-ending carousel of chores. That day, I was in the kitchen putting together a vinaigrette for the salad when Gary's truck squealed into the drive. I heard car doors slam and then the almost tangible uplift in air pressure as men streamed into the house after a day at work—this time, just Gary and Ethan.

"Dad, easy on," I heard Ethan say, and the reediness of his voice sent a sliver of something dank and fearful into my chest.

"Where is he?" Gary roared. "Where is the little queer?"

I ran into the hallway, a sheen of olive oil still coating my hands. Gary had flung open the door to Brian's room and Brian, peering out from under his thick brows in a way I had often found endearing, stared at him blankly, as if he were studying something terribly strange and insectile.

"Dad?" he said.

Gary slapped him across the face. Brian flinched, brought his hands up, his forearms almost absurdly youthful and strong for such a supplicating gesture. Gary's sunburned face was purple, his pale eyes dark with anger. My husband hit my son again, across the cheek. Brian's head jerked back.

"Stop it!" I screamed. "Gary, what are you doing?" Ethan surged forward to stay his father's hand, but stopped, his own hand frozen in midair, as if unable to consummate the arcing gesture that would result in manhandling his own father. Clumps of dirt from their work boots lay strewn across the carpet, bits of tufty grass sprouting from them like golf divots.

"Shall I tell your mother what I heard today, you little whore? Or do you want to tell her yourself? Didn't give a rat's arse who saw you, did you? *Did you?*"

"Gary, that's enough. There's no reason good enough to talk to him like that, to hit him!" I cried. But even as I spoke, I thought of three or four that would, to Gary at least, justify physical violence.

"Tell me it's not true. *Tell me you're not a fucking shirt-lifter, you little shit!*"

Brian stroked the maroon mark on his cheek almost thoughtfully. For a second, our eyes collided and I realized he'd rehearsed this moment dozens of times, all the minute variations unfolding into stark relief, mind-pictures to be shuffled at will. I saw images of his childhood spool by, extra puzzle pieces finally slipping neatly into slots. How, how, how could I not have seen?

"It's true," he said without inflection.

Gary's fist went through the wall next to a family photo taken last summer in Alice Springs.

chapter 11

PARKER

"Why does everybody stare at me when I call for Blakas?"
I asked Tony. He had nearly succeeded in wooing a pair—yes, a
pair—of busty Dutch girls to bed and was giving his pitch a
chance to ripen while he shared a bottle of tart red wine with me.

"You know what means *Blakas*?"

"No."

He shrugged. "Idiot. Stupid one. How you say . . . fool?"

"So it's like I'm running around calling everyone an idiot?
That's just great. First, I'm a celibate married slut, and now I'm a
celibate, married, abusive slut. That's perfect." As if to apologize
for the inconvenience, Blakas laid his head on my thigh. I tapped
his nose. "Are you my little idiot? Good dog."

I realized Tony was fidgeting in the plastic seat. Over his shoulder, I saw the Australian, whose name was apparently Claire,
slide into her regular spot. We smiled at each other. On impulse,
I beckoned her over.

"I think they're ready for you, Tony. You better go over before
they decide your ruthless good looks are out of their league."

Tony rolled his eyes. "I only put up with you because you are good customer." He turned to Claire. "Nice to see you, beautiful. Free dolmas for my two favorite ladies!" he announced, and lurched off toward the statuesque blondes.

"He's a piece of work, that Tony," Claire said. "I think he's had a different woman in his lair every night I've been in, which is every night."

"I don't know how he does it, but he could bottle it and sell it," I said. We sat silently for a moment, listening to the island's dusk settle around us. During the day, the sun baked the scrubby wild-flowers and shrubs, leaving behind a confectionary tartness in the air.

"I'm Parker Glass. I felt sort of silly not introducing myself, seeing you night after night."

"And I'm Claire," she said in a cheerful Aussie accent. "On holiday with your friend?"

"Yes," I said automatically.

An image popped into my mind of Neil nestled in a foxhole with his face pressed between a buxom aid worker's breasts. The tiny bubble of hope I'd been cultivating swelled and burst in my heart.

"I mean, no, no, I'm not," I said slowly. "Actually, my husband seems to have, um, taken off."

The amber eyes pooled with empathy, which, strangely, did not piss me off.

"We can talk about something else," I said hurriedly.

Claire drank deeply of her wine. "Or we can talk about this," she said, shrugging her shoulders as if either route was okay by her. Something about this woman made the knot of muscle in my neck loosen.

"This trip was supposed to be our honeymoon. Neil—that's my husband—told me our life wasn't right for him anymore and joined Habitat for Humanity, I think so he could assuage his WASP guilt, which kind of fucked up the honeymoon part of honey-moon, you know? I thought things were going okay, but then I had a total meltdown in front of a client. My business partner pretty much gave me the choice of going on vacation to Greece or seeing Dr. Lobotomy every week. Since she's also my best friend and I'm not exactly good at the therapy thing, I chose the former," I said with a hint of pride. Damn, this wine was sour. I squeezed my eyes shut and gulped.

To my surprise, Claire laughed. "Okay, my turn. I'm Claire Dillon. I'm forty-six but I've been told I can pass for thirty. Sadly, all the people who say that are legally blind."

"Here's to the legally blind!" We raised our glasses and clinked them together.

Claire continued. "My husband, Gary, cheated on me. His girlfriend's got three kids by three different fathers and pronounces cabernet 'cabernette' and gives massages for a living. I swear, I'm not usually such a snob, but it's just so . . . I don't know, so perfectly awful. It's not like it would be better if she was an English professor or something, it's just that I have to wonder what it is that she's got that I—" She held her palm upright in the air. "Ugh, I don't even want to go there. It was actually even worse because I used to go to her spa for the occasional shiatsu— Oh, never mind." Claire paused and shuddered as she downed her wine. "Since we're doing the confessional thing, I should add that my younger son is gay and his father hasn't spoken to him for seven years and I don't think I could have stood another year of it anyway. Now I'm just trying to find something other than these awful Sidney Sheldons to read in English and deciding if I should kick Gary out on his arse when I get home."

"Here's to getting out while you can!" I tried to sound as cheery as possible, under the circumstances. We clinked again.

Claire inched her chair closer and lowered her voice. "Just so you know, I was considering having an affair with this gorgeous young bloke called Sven, but then my American friend beat me to it. But I'm not ruling it out. Even if I am forty-six years old."

I stared at the tablecloth until the red checks blurred together.

"God. I don't know whether to laugh, cry, or cheer," I said.

"How about all three?"

I refilled our glasses, spilling just a bit onto the tablecloth. "I would like to say you trumped me, Claire, especially with the whole 'cabernette' thing. But I've got an ace in the hole, you see. I'm afraid I'm a certifiable nut job. Diagnosed!" I cleared my throat and mimicked Dr. Lobotomy. "Control freak, with anal-retentive tendencies, a tad obsessive-compulsive, and possibly a small prescription-drug habit."

Claire nodded sagely. "But I haven't even told you about my singing career, cut short in the bloom of youth by an unplanned pregnancy! It's positively Jackie Collins!"

"Yeah, well, my marriage only lasted eleven days!"

"I cut up all of Gary's boxer shorts!"

"I deleted a message from a law firm I didn't want Neil to work for!"

"I once sang 'You Light Up My Life' to a man in a convalescent home who had died ten minutes before we arrived!"

I paused. "Are you serious?"

"Well, okay, ten minutes after," Claire admitted.

"I'm sure it was no reflection on your singing," I said.

She sighed. "You thirsty?" Claire held up the empty bottle so it swung back and forth. The setting sun cut through it, sending green rays across her pretty, smile-lined face. Her auburn hair flamed red at the edges. I felt something tickle at the edges of my mouth and suddenly realized it was the sort of tingly joy you feel when you've just met someone you really, really like and who seems, miraculously, to like you in return. For a second, I almost forgot that Neil had absconded with our life, that I was a failing interior decorator with an anger-management problem, and that there were three Xanaxes bobbing around in my pocket.

"God, Claire. In this light, you look about eighteen," I said, quite truthfully.

There comes a time in every (jilted) woman's life when she has to recognize that accepting the help that's offered her doesn't mean she's weak. Or a loser. Or that her husband's not coming back. For me, the night following my conversation with Claire was that moment.

In later years, we talked about the concept of fated friendship. And whether things could ever have worked out for any of us without our Tony's symposia. Usually, when you trade stories of shared events, each person plucks something different out of the memory heap, some crucial tidbit that makes you laugh so hard you cry, something that makes you say *I can't believe I forgot that!* while you revel in it all. The thing that struck all of us later on was that we all remembered that first night. Remembered it blow by blow. Recalled it like we'd written it down. It had that kind of resonance.

Anya showed up around nine, somewhat secretive about her whereabouts that afternoon. Even though I wheedled and begged, she wouldn't say what she'd been doing. Whatever it was, it was working; her cheeks were pink with sun and hope, and she hadn't mentioned marriage or her cursed love life in at least twenty minutes.

She brought with her the British woman we'd sat next to at the bar, Kelah Morris. We listened to her tale and deemed her demented enough to gain admittance to the club.

"What do you think?" I asked Claire, who was busy pouring everyone another glass of the ammonia-tasting red wine.

"Absolutely. Kelah's in. No doubt about it. In fact, no offense meant, Kelah, but when we met, before you moved into the downstairs with your friends, I thought, that girl has serious problems."

"No, just a workaholic mother, a distant father, a brother who's trying to pass, and a family jailbird. Plus, I'm a writer," she said cheerfully.

"If we're going to meet like this and talk, I think we should have a name," said Anya.

"Like a lonely hearts club?" Kelah asked.

"Well, sort of. But more inclusive," I said.

"What about Four Angry Women? FAW!" blurted Claire, so uncharacteristically that the rest of us immediately collapsed into hysterics, frightening the Dutch glamazons who were lurking around the bar awaiting Tony the Hunchback's ravishment.

"Too eighties. Too Take Back the Night. What about Elbow Greece? 'Cause we're, you know, working to put our lives back together," I said.

Moans all around.

"Cheesy."

"Atrocious."

"Shoot me first."

Kelah twirled a corkscrew curl around her finger. "Wait. I've got something. I was just reading a book on Greek myths. You know, Zeus and Athena and Aphrodite and all that? Have you heard the story of how Hades spies Demeter's daughter, Persephone, and falls instantly in love with her?"

A chorus of no's.

Kelah continued. "He spirits her down to the underworld to be his wife, and Demeter, the goddess of earthly things, goes into such a decline, such a depression over the loss of her beautiful daughter, that the trees and flowers start dying, the air grows cold, the whole world starts to die . . . bloody awful stuff."

"Winter!" I cried.

"That's right!" Kelah grinned. "This state of things can't be allowed to go on, and Zeus goes down to Hades and says, can't you just let her go? And Hades says he will, but only if Persephone doesn't eat anything. But—and there are different explanations for this part of the myth—apparently Persephone was given seven pomegranate seeds, which she ate. So, as a compromise, Zeus says she has to spend part of the year—winter—with Hades, and can return to the surface the rest of the time." She threw back a slug of red, looking satisfied.

"What do the seeds represent?" I griped. I didn't think my elbow idea was so bad.

"Sacrifice. Compromise. Temptation," Anya offered.

"What don't they represent?" said Claire. "Everything that's led us to lose sight of our gifts, our needs, our . . . oh, bloody hell, there was another, but I'm too pissed to remember. . . ."

"Tony, another bottle please!" I called. "The Seven Seeds of Persephone are dry!"

So we toasted our newfound allegiance, and out of the Seven Seeds of Persephone the SNiPs were born. As acronyms go, it was a little problematic. But, then, so was the state of our lives. Claire, with the deep smile lines bracketing her pretty mouth, her maternal pragmatism, swathed in a blanket of frustration that was fraying more each day. Anya, who had more layers than a redwood tree, full of ricocheting dreams and fears. Kelah, brimming with ambition, skinny and raw with anger, angst, and youth. And me. Parker "My Husband Left Me After Eleven Days" Glass. The sunburned, would-be ho with the heart of mercury and enough illicit narcotics to power a small drug cartel. Oh, and Blakas, honorary canine SNiP.

Clearly, the most well-adjusted of the group.

chapter 12

〰〰〰〰〰〰〰〰〰

ANYA

My ex-boyfriend Rick used to call me his Spanish princess. It was embarrassing, especially since I'm Mexican, and mostly native Indian—mestizo—not European. But, like a dozen other things, I overlooked it because Rick Moody was employed, Catholic, blessed with wide fawn-colored eyes I could gaze at for days, and wanted to get married.

I revised this position when I discovered his marriage plans didn't include, well, me.

We were in Lake Tahoe for the state teachers' conference. Each day, Rick and his fellow high-school teachers and administrators disappeared into one or another of Harrah's meeting rooms for a few hours and talked about reading levels and chronic truancy while they picked at out-of-season chunks of pineapple, honeydew, and watermelon. In the afternoon, they'd head out for the ski slopes, casinos, and all-you-can-eat buffets, trailing spouses, kids, and significant others. Rick taught English and coached junior-varsity soccer. He was one of the new generation of teachers who tried to talk to kids on their own level, with respect. His students were Mexican and El Salvadoran, Chinese and Vietnamese, African-American and Hmong. Rick's team called him *El Burro* because he laughed too loudly. He pretended to be annoyed, but I think he was sort of proud of the street cred his nickname gave him.

The last day, loath to shame Rick completely with my lack of athletic prowess—I'd been hiding out at the indoor pool and taking long walks, pleading injury—I'd dutifully donned my spanking new ski-bunny suit and endured a snowboarding lesson. After three hours of cartwheeling down hills that seemed as hard as concrete, I'd gratefully returned my rental board and snuck back to the lodge for some hot chocolate and the new Susan Isaacs.

"Anyone sitting here?"

Shane McDaniel was one of those guys San Franciscans from the wrong side of the tracks call "Marina" people: With silky hair, preternaturally white teeth, model height, and a sense of entitlement that can only be earned in expensive prep schools, he was everything I hadn't grown up with on the other side of town, in the barrio. He and Rick had gone to college together. Rick was the idealistic one. Shane was an assistant principal in an affluent San Francisco suburb, and his parents still thought he was slumming.

"Sure," I said.

"Sure, as in someone's sitting here, or, sure, I can sit down?"

I could tell he was used to women making things easy for him. "Sure, as in there's no one sitting there," I said simply.

Within a minute, three of the other young teachers we'd sat with at dinner the night before gathered around the fire, one guy and two girls. Unfortunately, the nice art teacher with the slightly crossed eye who spoke fluent Spanish was not among them.

"The snow's so awesome today. I did total black diamonds," said Mandy. Or maybe it was Mindy. Mindy-Mandy taught fifth-grade history and had toned thighs and a cell phone that beeped out an early Madonna song whenever her investment-banker boyfriend called to check up on her, which was often.

"Yeah, it's sweet powder," agreed Kathy. Kathy was taller than the men and had a slight underbite and an enormous engagement ring. Last night she told me she was quitting teaching kindergarten the minute she got pregnant.

"How'd you do, Anya?"

I suddenly felt them all staring at me. Rick always tells me it's all in my mind—the feeling I'm being judged—but that didn't make it any easier. "Well, if it had been gymnastics class instead of snowboarding, I might have been an idiot savant," I said finally.

They were quiet.

"Oh, Rick's honey's funny," said the second guy, Bill, who taught trigonometry at Rick's school and was infamous for having had sex with one of the student teachers in a supply closet after school. For some reason, my mind resisted absorbing additional details about this person.

Mindy-Mandy groaned. "God, Bill, you're an idiot."

"I may be an idiot, but I have a huge—"

She punched him. Rick chose that moment to appear at my elbow. No matter how much I bug him, he never wears sunscreen, insisting his burns will turn into a tan. Beneath his hat line, his face was seared the color of freshly boiled lobster. I was glad to see him.

"Hey, Annie. How was it?" He kissed the top of my head, and I saw something sly pass between Mindy-Mandy and Kathy.

"Fine. Want a sip?" I offered him some hot chocolate.

"Not unless that has schnapps in it! Somebody get me a beer," Rick called. Bill passed him a bottle of Anchor Liberty Ale.

"I'd like to propose a toast," Mindy-Mandy said. "To Kathy and Darren, who I have no doubt will dwarf all of us with their ascent to wealth and fame!"

Everyone clanked glasses. "Just don't get knocked up too soon!" someone called.

"Where's that lazy sonofabitch?" Shane said.

When Kathy smiled, her knife-edged face approached pretty. "Emergency surgery. Some old bag's silicone tit popped out of place and Darren had to put it back."

"Nasty."

"Sick."

"Yum. How do I get that job?" Bill leered.

"So, a little bird told me you two might be making the move too," Mindy-Mandy said to Rick, ignoring Bill's comment. At this, I could feel Rick's shoulders tense from a foot away, as if someone had just suggested he jump off a bridge into piranha-infested waters.

"Where'd you hear that?" Rick said.

"Oh, you know, here and there."

"Well, we're right where we want to be, Annie and I, I can tell you that much." He smiled at me, but it felt vinegary and false. In one of those weird moments of prophetic clarity, I realized he intended to break up with me. I started to sweat underneath my fleece jacket. *Ay, Dios mío.*

"Excuse me," I said, and pushed my way to the bathroom to throw up.

"What's her problem?" Mindy-Mandy sniped as I left. "I only asked if you were getting married."

"Don't let go!" I warned.

"I have to let go sometime, Anya. Come on, just a few meters."

Johnny and I were paddling around a small cove. The water was clear and halfway between blue and green. Beautiful. For days, he'd been dragging me around, first with his hands gently holding my belly, then by the arms while I kicked. While we swam, he told me about his life, his dreams, and his six sisters. He was fourteen and wanted to be a rap star or maybe a windsurfer in Australia or Hawaii or perhaps an architect. I felt safe bobbing in his skinny brown arms.

"Okay, I let you go now," he said.

I steeled myself for the inevitable plunge. I imagined I'd enjoy a split second on the twinkling surface, then sink, submarinelike in my modest black suit, into the depths. There I'd lie, submerged among the silver-backed fish and occasional candy wrapper, for all eternity. From my underwater sanctuary I'd watch the tourists' white legs stir up sediment above me, feel the rumble of motor craft zip by on the surface. *Oh, Anya,* my family would say. *She's lying at the bottom of the Mediterranean. She never got married, you know.*

Splashes sounded behind me and in front. Was something chasing me? Brine trickled into my ears, nose, and mouth. My legs scissored. I can't say my arms churned, but they did flop up and out and down again. I could feel the dryness of air kissing my fingertips as they wheeled out of the water; that's how I knew. Without thinking, I had progressed a few feet. Salty water rode my shallow breaths and I choked a little. It burned. I stopped and treaded water the way Johnny had taught me, moving my arms and legs through the thickness in concentric circles.

"I'm swimming!" I yelled, and promptly inhaled a mouthful of the stuff.

Johnny caught me as I sank.

chapter 13

KELAH

Shipwrecked on Corfu, July 25

*K: Boz told me that Davey got out. I can't believe I had to
hear it from a friend, and not someone in my family. Were
Mum and Dad just going to let me go on thinking he was in
jail? Maybe that's where they want him—locked up and out
of the way, where he can't bring any more shame to the
Morris name. Poor Boz was mortified. I tried to make him feel
better, said it was just the post and surely Mum had written to
tell me already, but those wide blue-gray eyes of his were all
damp with sympathy, and I felt . . . I don't know. Something.*

*But I'm sure what you really want to know is how are C., P.,
and A. doing. . . . I'll tell you a little more about them. C. is
in her mid-40s, putting a brave face to what is obviously a
difficult time. Her husband had a bit on the side. Back at
home in Australia. The vile bastard, she calls him. But fondly,
I think. Sort of like, he's her vile bastard, you know? The
other day I saw C. scribbling madly at the beach, asked her*

what she was doing. Writing a song, she said. Oh, I replied, you're a singer, then? And she got all blushy and shy and said, no, not really. But I think we'll see more on that front. Mark my words. P. Now, there's an interesting one. They say that holiday can change a person, but can it change you from an uptight, retentive cow to a freewheeling party girl in four weeks? When I first noticed her, P. had something long and sharp wedged so far up her arse she looked like the Duchess of Kent at a royal baptism. P.'s also got man problems, it seems. She just got married. In fact, this was to be her honeymoon, but her husband up and did a runner on her. Word is the marriage lasted a whole eleven days before he took off to build barns for the poor in some Third World country, but that's unsubstantiated. Whatever he did in his former life must have been pretty bad to instigate such a guilt trip. P.'s replaced him in her affections with a small spotted dog called Blakas. She claims to be allergic, and the allegiance temporary, but I wouldn't be surprised if they go the distance, P. and Blakas. They have a certain symmetry. A.'s the wild card. She calls what she has man trouble too, but it goes so far back it might be better named Life Trouble. A.'s a bit of a mystery. She's American, but speaks Spanish too, and has a funny homemade tattoo on her shoulder. I want to ask her about it, but it seems a bit forward. I've seen her sneaking out of town to go to the beach very early—8 or 9 a.m. She comes back with wet hair, but claims to not know how to swim. Expect more from that girl—I do.

In between SNiP meetings and touring with Boz and Fee, things have gotten quite lively here on the island. And I've been writing a lot. Not so much the novel—though it's possibly less crap than usual—but my journal at least.

"Kay?"

"Hmm?"

"Put down your pen and get ready. We're going out," said Fee. She had on a crocheted top that made her full breasts look like sacks of onions, and a scary tatter of a mini. For all her physical and intellectual gifts, Fee's sense of style ran toward, well, the sluttish.

"And take off those nasty trousers. Dress like a girl tonight, please."

Boz snorted. "Kay, dress like a girl? The day she wears a skirt, I will too."

"Boz, you great clot. Shove over, and I'll get my clothes," I said.

Fifteen minutes later we were on our way to the nest of bars. It was still early, so we got a table at the Coyote Club. The plastic chairs were placed on an incline, so you had to be careful not to tumble down the hill. Inevitably, some poor sod got pissed and fell over in front of everyone, providing ample laughs. I just didn't want it to be me.

Fee went to the bar to get our beers. I suspect the whole miniskirt ensemble was aimed at winning the attentions of the bartender, a sturdy Nova Scotian with green eyes and thighs the size of U-boats.

"She fancies that bartender," Boz said. He sounded a bit sad, so I figured this was a good time to give him my blessing.

"You know, I wouldn't mind if you and Fee, well, you know . . ."

He was looking at me strangely.

"What I mean to say is, you and Fee are my best friends, and if you want to have it off with each other, don't let me stop you. I mean, don't snog each other rotten in front of me or anything, but I can tell you're into her and—"

"Kay—"

"—it doesn't have to affect our friendship or anything. We'll still be the same, struggling writers and all, well, except for Fee, I guess she's off to fame and fortune—"

"Kelah—"

"—and I have no doubt you'll be fine. You'll get your PhD and be a brilliant prof, Bozzie, I know it. So don't worry about it. I wouldn't mind at—"

"Kelah, belt up!"

Boz's normally placid face was all red. When did that happen?

"Kelah, if you don't mind, I'll decide who I shag, thank you very much. I'm not so desperate I have to start scraping the bottom of the barrel with my own friends." He leaned back in the tippy chair and smoked furiously.

I was stung. Is that how he felt? That Fee and I were bottom-of-the-barrel?

"I was just trying to help," I said meekly.

"Yeah, well, don't."

After a few minutes, Fee came back with the drinks. "I love this place! Hey, Bozzie, pass me a fag, will you? Would you believe Aaron, that gorgeous creature, is going to meet me after shift? Cheers!"

I tried to smile when we cracked our bottles together, but Boz wouldn't meet my eyes.

I was awakened at half four by a solid crash in the doorway.

"Fuckin' hell!" I heard, then a wicked clank as the bucket we use to hold the door open during the day skittered across the tiled floor.

I kept my eyes shut and pretended to be asleep. I'd come home alone at about one A.M. Fee was holding out hope that Aaron the Canucklehead would choose her from among the half dozen international hopefuls who were lurking around the bar. I swear, it was like a fucking Miss Universe pageant. Miss Arse-faced Universe. After our little argument, which I still didn't fully understand, Boz had stormed off to the bar and chatted up a passel of Italians until he found one willing to sacrifice her virtue for a tall, skinny Brit who couldn't see ten paces without his glasses. He must have gotten lucky, because here he was three hours later, knocking about the flat. I prayed he'd already finished with her, whoever the little slag was. I mean, Boz is my friend, and I wanted him to have a real holiday, complete with cheap holiday sex, but the thought of listening to someone who was like my brother shagging an Italian with a gold belly chain and Versace jeans in the room next door was more than I could bear.

"Kay?"

I could smell the alcoholic fumes from here. I tried to breathe deeply, as if I was asleep. He probably wanted to borrow my room or something. Maybe Fee was in his with the Canucklehead?

"Kelah!" he hissed again.

I sat up. "For God's sake, Boz, what?"

"I'm plastered, Kay. I feel like sheer hell," he said pitifully.

I flopped back down and rolled over. "That's nice, Bozzie. Now, why don't you just go to bed, because I'm bloody knackered. Hey, what are you doing? Boz!"

He'd crawled into bed next to me, spoon-fashion, and snuggled up against my backside. Not in the friendly, soberish way I'd expect, joshing around, maybe roughhousing a little, but right up behind me. I prayed he was too pissed to get a stiffie—we'd never live that down.

"This is so nice," he mumbled.

I decided to let him stay for a second. I mean, it was sort of nice. How often to you get a real live man in your bed, you know? Without having to shag him?

"I cocked up, Kay. I'm a fuckin' idiot." He sniffled against the pillow, and I resolved to ask Mrs. Kiriakis for new sheets tomorrow.

"I'm sorry we fought. I shouldn't have taken it out on you. It's not your fault."

What's not my fault?

"I'm so tired of it, that's all," he continued in a slurred voice. "All the lies. I've been in love with you so long it's like a terminal disease, you know? I know you just want to be friends, so that's what we're going to be. Friends. Shiny, happy friends. God, you smell so good. . . ."

He buried his nose in my hair and inhaled noisily. I felt his hands steal around my waist, perilously close to my waistband. Love? Terminal disease? What was he talking about?

Then, with the scent of the voluptuous Italian still clinging to his skin and a hank of my hair wrapped around his finger, my dear old friend Bozzie shuddered against me and fell asleep.

chapter 14

PARKER

In the interest of humoring Molly and my family, I'd left my laptop computer at home. *See, I'm cool,* the gesture seemed to say—*it's a real vacation, complete with bikini, sunblock, beach books, and eight containers of the best antidepressants modern medicine has to offer.* I may go home without a husband, but I'm as safe from the scourges of sunburn and panic disorder as you could possibly get.

This didn't stop me from succumbing to the urge one day when I'd gone into the island's main city, Corfutown. I was dawdling along the shopping thoroughfares, trying to find *something* to put on my credit card—for shame, to go on holiday without supporting the local economy—when I spotted one of those cybercafes hemmed in between a Laundromat and a souvlaki stand. So I slipped into line behind an Israeli with matted dreadlocks and his nose-ringed Japanese girlfriend. I bought thirty minutes and hustled to a terminal.

Ah, relief. Only seventy-five messages. I guess word of my disgrace had filtered out to the masses and people were avoiding contact. I mean, what is there to say, really, when your acquaintance's husband left her on Day 11—*So, Park, what happened on Day 10?*

I skimmed through them, deleting the junk, ignoring messages from Leo and Sue inquiring as to my state of mind and willingness to sign a petition to save something called the Arizona pygmy from extinction, and replied briefly to Carda and Tarra's pleas for news. By the time I'd answered the dozen or so sincere and not-too-invasive queries from my sisters, Molly, and a few other friends, I had my standard answer finalized. It went something like this:

> Dear So-and-So,
>   Good to hear from you. Having a marvelous time here in Greece, given the circumstances. Have spent most of my time exploring the ruins east of Doukades and sunning on the beach [*There were no ruins east of Doukades, but how would they know that?*] and am allowing myself to heal. [*Californians love when you use the word* heal. *It's almost like a palliative drug for them.*] I am sure when I return, Neil and I will have a lot to talk about and will be able to rebuild what we had. Hope you are well.
>
>   Love,
>   Parker/Rosie/Sis

Isn't that what people wanted to hear? That you're sound enough of mind to explore a ruin, eat fried food, have sex—or at least flirt—with a handsome stranger? I didn't feel a bit strange about skirting the truth. I mean, I *did* feel better than when I'd arrived, and our villa was a bit, well, crumbly around the edges, practically a ruin. For all I know, Athena herself slept there, which would certainly qualify it.

I was getting ready to wrap up when a new message appeared in my in-box. If only I had logged off a moment sooner, I could have spared myself for a few more days, weeks, maybe even a month. Would everything have turned out differently? I'll never know.

I scrolled down and saw Neil's name in the handle. The sight released a small, hot river of panic inside my chest. Suddenly, the room seemed to pixilate into squares of color—brown, red, orange, blue. My heart hammered against the walls of my chest. Frantically, I clawed in my bag for respite. I'd removed my little helpers from immediate procurement—stashing them in a variety of hiding places around the villa, but not in my purse—but was sure a few Valiums still floated around along the bottom seam. Hell, I could always turn the bag inside out and lick it—there was a veritable pharmaceutical cornucopia of drug dust down there.

My fingers closed around a couple of brownish-pink tablets in the pocket that houses my favorite MAC lip liner in "Spice" and a few dog-eared tampons. Relieved, I popped them in my mouth dry and swallowed. I, for one, am all for NAFTA: The mud-colored pills from Mexico, which I picked up for cheap while vacationing with Neil in Puerto Vallarta, are every bit as effective as the yellow ones you get stateside.

I waited a few minutes while they worked their magic, sending liquid calm sluicing through my veins, then reluctantly clicked on Neil's message. I don't know why I reacted so strongly—who knows, maybe I possess more prescience than I give myself credit for.

Neil's message read as follows:

Dear Parker,

I don't know how to tell you this, so I'll just say it. You've never been one to beat around the bush, and I have always respected that. Here goes: I've met someone else, and I'm leaving you to be with her. I realize I am a shit, but she is part of my new life, and you are, to my very real despair and regret, part of what is now my old one. I know it won't be any comfort to you, though I hope it might provide some insight, but it's not anything you did—it's all me. I really used to hate who I was, who I had become—Mr. Attorney, Mr. $350,000/yr salary on the partner track. Mr. Pac Heights Flat. Mr. Jerk. I feel like I was living the life everyone had raised me to live, that I had never had an original thought or made an original choice in my life, and it was finally time to grow up and start thinking for myself. Juliette understands all this and has been there for me through this trying time. We met on assignment in a small village in Patagonia—where I was posted after Uruguay. She's with *Médecins Sans Frontières,* a medical organization that helps the poor in war zones and economically depressed areas. She's an MD specializing in poverty medicine in developing countries and is from a town in French-speaking Belgium that is famous for its pancake syrup made by Trappist monks. I think you'd like her, Park. She reminds me a little of your sister Cardamom, except much thinner, of course. Believe me, this decision was incredibly difficult, and I have not made it lightly. But I honestly believe that, in time, you'll realize you are better off without me, that you will find someone more suited to the life you're meant to lead. And I do hope you find happiness, Park. Really, I do. I mean that. I know we'll have to get to the ugly business of the house, divorce, etc., but why don't we take the rest of the summer to let the new reality sink in before we deal with those administrative matters, okay? I've taken the liberty of making all our mortgage payments through September, so that is taken care of. I'm sorry to do this to you by e-mail, but I don't know where to reach you and won't have access to communications for the next few weeks while Juliette and I and the rest of the team are in Tierra del Fuego administering polio vaccine to the Alacaluf Indians. Take care, Park. I hope you can forgive me, as I have started to forgive myself.

Sincerely,
Neil

p.s. You really should be nicer to your parents, Park. I know they've always embarrassed you, but you're really very lucky to have them. If I had had parents like yours, things might not have turned out this way for us. Think about it.

I read the message through twice in a kind of paralytic horror, then the screen blanked out and a message popped up that said, *Your 30 minutes have expired. Thank you, and good-bye.* Crazed with panic, I charged the counter where a harried young Greek sat handing out time cards to backpackers and answering broken-English questions about the nearest ruins. *I'm* the nearest ruin, I wanted to scream. Look at *me*! I didn't have a plan; at that moment, it just seemed incredibly urgent that I hit the reply button and quickly type the words, *FUCK YOU, PRICK BASTARD, I'LL SEE YOU IN DIVORCE COURT. REMEMBER: IN CALIFORNIA, THE WIFE GETS HALF.*

"Excuse me," I said. "Can I get five more minutes on this?"

"I be with you in a minute," the Greek guy said, who just might be the only person in the Ionian isles with an acne condition.

I waited for what felt like ten minutes. The clock said forty-eight seconds had passed.

"I don't think you understand," I said, trying to keep my voice calm, which wasn't that hard considering the Valium gave me the floaty dissociation of a Wes Craven zombie. "I'm dealing with an emergency and I got cut off."

He eyed me suspiciously, as if, being American, I might be packing a gun or a searing-hot Big Mac. "Everyone have an emergency, miss. You are not the only one."

"My husband just left me for a fucking syrup-making Belgian in Patagonia, you asshole! By e-mail! I think that qualifies as a fucking emergency, don't you?" I yelled loud enough to be heard in Santorini. Apparently, Valium doesn't pack the punch it used to.

Quickly, he grabbed my card, slipped it into a little machine, accepted my money, and handed me the newly imprinted one. I sat back down at the terminal, determined to whip off an appropriately stinging reply, but was having trouble seeing, what with the avalanche of tears cascading down my face. Oh, Neil, what have you done? What have you done?

I had to get out of there. Without logging off, I pulled my bag over my shoulder and stumbled out of the place. The street, which had seemed innocuous and even charming an hour ago, now struck me as seething with malevolent indifference, the local traders simmering with hatred of the interloper tourists they were dependent on for their livelihood. I staggered down the street on jellified legs, intent on . . . something. Where was I going? Oh, yeah. The bus. Back to Pelekastritsa. I felt something wet run down over my lips and tasted salty mucus.

But I seemed to have gotten lost somehow. In a two-horse town, how could that have happened? Clearly, even Corfutown had a wrong side of the tracks—a row of dilapidated white buildings fronting the harbor housing bars, pool halls, and a few filthy-looking storefronts with greasy meat roasting on pikes in the window.

A knot of sailors whistled at me as I walked by trying to look like I knew where I was going. I was wearing a skirt, sandals, and scant top, and even in sun-loving Greece I felt horribly exposed. The Valium I'd taken made it seem as if a layer of gauze had been lowered over the world, like the cheesecloth my mom and Lorena Soberanes use to make tofu bars.

I sensed, rather than saw, the men break off from the group and approach me. Summoning all the skills I'd never learned in the urban-survival classes Molly was always trying to get me to accompany her to but I'd invariably skipped, I turned around and faced them. I tried to remember protocol: Challenge them, show them you won't be an easy mark, then drive their noses into their brains with the heel of your hand. See? No problem.

"Get away from me!" I said, trying to deepen my voice in the hopes they would think me a transvestite and search for weaker prey.

They laughed.

A boyish-looking sailor reached out and grabbed my tit for a second. Seriously. I looked down, half expecting to see his handprint there, like a brand. He was staring at me, as if weighing the damage I might inflict if he pounced.

For the first time, real fear cut through the haze of hysteria and drugs. So this was how it ended. Me, Parker Glass, drugged up, soon-to-be divorced, molested by horny seamen, and left for dead in front of a charred lamb shank.

"Get away from me or I'll call the police," I said again, louder this time.

They made no move, so I backed away, planning to make a break for the nearest busy street.

They moved toward me, a pride of lions eyeing a meaty supper.

I tripped over a rock.

Then, a voice.

"Parker? There you are. I've been looking all over for you! Where the hell have you been? Hey, guys. How's it hangin'? Know a good taverna around here? I've got a yen for some souvlaki. No? Well, that's cool. That's cool. Excuse me, we're just gonna get some eats. C'mon, Park. Let's get outta here. Bye, everyone. It's been real. . . ."

With that, Josh Lido put his arm around me possessively and shepherded me with admirable nonchalance back to Callas Square, where the bus waited, along with the knowledge that I was, for the first time in years, single and dangerous—if only to myself.

chapter 15

~~~~~~~~~~~~~

CLAIRE

Something extraordinary happens when you hear the word *Mom* come out of your babies' mouths and realize they mean you. No matter how old they are, how infuriating, how selfish or independent or drunk on lager, that single word will always have an incredible weight to it, a heft that tugs your attention away from whatever you're doing and redirects it, laserlike, on the creature you sheltered in your belly those nine months.

I recalled this power as I lay in the horizontal rays of the lowering sun. My notebook—or, more correctly, *songbook*—was lying across my belly. I'd been playing with something full-bodied and bluesy, about a woman whose lover leaves her to go on a walkabout in the bush.

"Mom," I heard, and for a second thought I was dreaming, as the voice was that of my eldest, Ethan. I rolled over and tried to fall back asleep. It was six P.M. or so, my favorite time at Mirtiotissa Beach, sun-steeped and dreamy.

"Mom," I heard again. This time I sat up. The other voice belonged to Brian.

And there they were, my two strapping boys, so alike they could be twins—both tall, slim, and broad-shouldered, with thick, wavy chestnut-reddish hair and amber eyes that matched mine. Brian had on a tight gray T-shirt and baggy shorts, Ethan, tattered climbing trousers and a tank top with a bandanna around his neck. Both had rucksacks. My chest filled with love.

"Boys! Whatever are you doing here?" I cried, and lunged up to hug them both.

"We were worried about you, Ma—" Brian said.

Ethan cut in. "Yeah, Aunt Valerie said you were thinking of having an affair with some guy named Sven, so we thought we'd come over—"

"—and check him out for you," interrupted Brian, and we all laughed.

"I can't believe you're here!" I said. "What about work and, um, everything. . . ."

"The play I'm in closed. Bad reviews," said Brian cheerfully.

"I told Dad I needed six weeks off." Ethan dropped his gaze to his hands when he said it, as if Gary's mention would stain the day.

"I see." I hesitated. "Didn't think your dear old mum could handle Greece on her own, eh?"

"Ma, that's not it at all! We just wanted to be with you, that's all. We missed you."

When Brian speaks that ingenuously, I'm smitten. Always have been. Turns my resolve to mush.

"Well, I guess that's it, then. You're here. Ah, boys. The truth is, it's been a bit hard going. I'm so glad to see you! I can't believe you came all this way. Just appearing on the beach like that. I thought I was dreaming. I guess first off we'll have to deal with a place to stay. Mine's not big enough. . . ." I paused, considering the options. Maybe a bigger flat outside of town?

"Oh, that's okay, Ma. We've already got one. Tony set us up. His cousin's husband's business partner has a room at a villa up the hill from yours. We're good to go. They're just cleaning it now. Or maybe it was his partner's cousin's husband. It was sort of complicated." Ethan smiled, and I could see a bit of Gary's decisiveness around his eyes. Ethan looked knackered, though. The truth is, he hadn't been the same since he and his college sweetheart, Rachel, broke up, what was it, a year ago? That's the trade-off, you see. The more your life goes the way you want it to, the more control you think you have, the more fate responds to your gentle prodding, the harsher it is when she lets you down.

I twined my fingers through theirs. "Well, that's sorted, then. The bad news, I suppose, is that I never managed to get it off with old Sven. And the good news is, we've got a festival to go to tonight. With some new friends."

By the time we got to the *panigiri,* the music was in full swing. Dozens of people were gathered under the grove of olive trees next to the church, where candles and lanterns were hung, casting arcs of intermittent light as if a hundred fireflies had just risen in formation. My landlady, Mrs. Kiriakis, had explained that *panigiri* honored the patron saint of a particular church. In this case, it was Saint Spiros, guardian of the entire island of Corfu, who was being celebrated. This explained why every other Corfiote was named Spiros, I suppose.

The festival was held in a neighboring village. To my dismay, both boys had rented motorcycles for the duration of their holiday. I'd heard the statistics about tourists getting into smashes on them, but I held my tongue. I'd never wanted to be one of those mothers who pounce on every little bit of fun their children conceive, dead set on obliterating all traces of danger. Of course, it was a constant battle: There've been times my boys came home drunk on beer or bruised from fighting, and it was all I could do not to lock them in their rooms and throw away the key.

At first, I rode behind Ethan clasped to his back like a limpet. Then something tight and withholding inside me unfurled, and I let myself go to the moment. The truth is, it was marvelous; the wind whipped my hair into a froth, the scent of night-blooming flowers seemed magnified by our speed, and the sweet undulations of the hills lent the journey a kind of magical cadence. The idea of me, Claire Dillon, on a motorcycle was so outrageous I'd laughed out loud, causing Ethan to steer us into a joyful—if treacherous—jig.

We parked the bikes on the road and melded into the throng. Laughter tinkled around us, and people waved and honked at friends and neighbors as they drove by, looking for a spot. At the edge of the grove, tables laden with beer, retsina, and soft drinks groaned under the weight of the platters. A whole goat turned on a giant spit, dripping sizzling juices onto the fire. You could wait in line and one of the local taverna owners manning the fire pit would press a succulent, pita-wrapped gyro into your hand.

I spotted Parker, Anya, Kelah, and Kelah's English friends sitting on a blanket. They waved us over.

"Hi!"

"Hey, guys."

"Hiya."

"Everyone, these are my sons, Ethan and Brian, up from Oz to make sure their mum doesn't shame the family"—laughs all around—"and this is Parker from San Francisco, Anya from San Francisco, Kelah from London, and her friends. Sorry, I don't know your names. . . ."

"I'm Boz and she's Fee," said Boz.

"Good on you. I'm going to scrape up some grog. Anyone else?" said Ethan.

A chorus of yeses. He went off to the bar.

I sat down on the blanket next to Brian. About ten meters away, a cluster of black-clothed men played a frenzied jig, traditional Greek music, I guessed. Three of the men were white-haired and craggy. They played with a businesslike dourness, plucking complicated melodies from their funny-shaped instruments. The fourth was youngish, late twenties, I'd say, slim and dark with a Mona Lisa smile and a long, sensual nose. When he stood up with his instrument, some sort of stringed lute with a bulbous body, and danced sinuously along the perimeter of the circle, fingers urging the lute to release a plaintive cry, I thought: *satyr.*

"Isn't it beautiful?" Anya whispered.

I nodded. I couldn't tear my eyes away from the satyr. His hands flew over the strings like white doves released from a box. There was something about him I would have called dangerous, except it felt too familiar to cause fear. My eyes fluttered shut, and I felt that visceral pull toward the music, the sweet longing to weave my voice in and out of the lute's song in an age-old mating dance.

Ethan was back with the beers. "Mum, here's a middy for you. Bri. Parker and Anya, is it? These are for you. . . ."

I sat back and sipped. The satyr played on, beautifully. The night sky draped over us, a starry net perfect for catching dreams.

chapter 16

ANYA

One of the best things about swimming is the way it takes you inside yourself. Thoughts seem louder and more insistent, echoing in your head while the rest of the world floats somewhere beyond the horizon of vision and sound. Now that I can swim across the cove by myself—well, if you can call my thrashing and kicking swimming—I have discovered being alone with my imaginings is not entirely unpleasant. The day I learned to breathe, for instance, I was able to summon a precise memory of the smell of *Mami*'s kitchen, crisp corn tortillas popping in the pan, onions and tomatoes and chilis mingling, six-hour beans wafting their musty goodness across the house. Under the odorless, soundless blue ceiling of water, it's as if you have to try twice as hard to conjure things, and the renderings, when they come, are as deftly defined as those thick black eyebrows on Frida Kahlo.

I pulled my head out of the nothingness and checked my progress. Johnny kept trying to make me breathe out the side, but sometimes I stopped and did the seal thing, gulping great mouthfuls of air. Drove him crazy. Now he was up there on the beach, talking with a tall man, probably selling him windsurfing lessons or arranging a tour of Corfu's "secret" beaches. Juan, my little *amigo*.

I paddled in, feeling the tingly ache of sore muscles. This morning, when I put on my bathing suit, it sagged in the butt. Skinniness must be contagious, 'cause I've been spending a lot of time with Parker Glass. Either that, or it's the exercise. I was almost ready for a bikini. Almost.

Out of the water, it was nearly cool. I dragged my heels through the tightly packed sand, leaving snaky trails. When I got there, I realized Johnny was with Ethan, Claire's son. He was so good-looking, not to mention that great Australian accent. He and Parker had talked a lot at the *panigiri*. I guess with Neil officially out of the picture, she was free to have her fun.

"*Hola*, guys," I said to them.

Johnny smiled. "Anya, tomorrow we go to Glyfada, okay? I take you on the waves."

"Sure." I dug into my backpack and handed Johnny a bunch of euros for the lessons. He crammed them in his shoe.

"Well, see you tomorrow," I said.

"*Yasu.*"

I trudged off through the sand. I wanted to get over to the travel agency before they closed. I had postcards to send home and needed to change more money.

"Anya? Hold on."

Ethan ran up to me. His reddish, wavy hair was dark and glossy and flopped becomingly over his forehead in a curl like Hugh Grant's. Noticeable muscles bulged along his arms and shoulders. I caught myself staring and blushed.

"Are you going back to town?" he asked.

"Um, yeah."

"Need a lift? I've got a motorcycle."

"Oh, that's okay, I like to walk."

"Come on, it's dusk. My mum always says that's the most dangerous time to be on the road."

"Yeah, I'll be considerably safer on a motorcycle."

He laughed. It's such a cliché, but he really did have a nice smile.

"All right, but don't blame me if we crash. I'm terribly accident-prone," I said.

"Really? I wouldn't have thought . . . You looked very athletic out there, swimming around. Intimidated the hell out of us land-lubbers."

Was he making fun of me? I glanced at his face. He was grinning at me as if . . . as if I was someone he desperately wanted to talk to. Well, maybe not desperately. But he wasn't running in the opposite direction, that's for sure. Involuntarily, I reached for my long ponytail. I have a whole repertoire of nervous tics for times like these, guaranteed to radiate self-consciousness and quell male lust: hair twirling, eye blinking, teeth sucking, eyelash smoothing.

We walked in silence for a few minutes. Ethan's motorcycle was black and sleek. I realized I would have to wrap myself around him to stay on and felt heat slide up my cheeks again. It seemed so intimate. I'd never been that comfortable with the easy sexuality of other girls. Growing up, it seemed like every other *chava* had on hip-slung jeans that exposed their tan bellies and a G-string peeking out the back. By the time they were twelve or thirteen, before the babies came, they were streaking their brown or black Latina hair with champagne-colored stripes and outlining their juicy lips in maroon pencil. In spite of being nominally Catholic, the girls in my neighborhood had a damp, overripe sensuality that promised Friday nights spent kissing against graffiti-scrawled alley walls and boyfriends in lowriders blasting hip-hop down 24th Street and giggling trips to Macy's juniors department to try on flared pants, handkerchief blouses, and glittery makeup. Fat, thin, pimpled, angel-featured, it didn't matter—the key word was *ready*, and that's what they were. Not me. It had taken six dates for me to let Rick kiss me; twenty-three before we had sex—not counting the time we took each other's clothes off during a hike on Mt. Tamalpais (no consummation).

I jumped on Ethan's bike before I could have second thoughts and wrapped my arms tightly around his waist, which was hard and enviably flat. His hair tickled my nose and smelled clean and green, like Irish Spring soap. I wondered if he could feel my breasts and belly pillowing against him and concentrated on sucking in my stomach.

"So, what's San Francisco like these days? I was there once, a long time ago. I was just an ankle-biter, though. Don't remember much. My dad didn't realize you had to pay toll on the Golden Gate Bridge and tried to turn around. Mum almost divorced him on the spot," Ethan yelled over his shoulder, against the wind.

"I grew up in the barrio. Do you know what that is? A lot of people think the Mission's sort of downtrodden—that's where I live—but it really isn't. It's a great neighborhood, all Mexican and Central American families and taquerias and cheap markets and the best nightclubs and restaurants too." Whenever white people asked me about my neighborhood, I stuck to chic dive bars and *enchiladas verdes*. It was just simpler that way, you know?

We hit the main road, and Ethan zoomed ahead. Ethan's motorcycle was much more powerful than Parker's scooter; I could feel plump bees bouncing off my cheek and forehead, and the white-washed villages swept by us in a blur. When we took corners, we lay sideways so the ground rushed up to within a foot of our faces. The insides of my thighs were hot from the engine. I closed my eyes for a second and fantasized that Ethan Dillon was my *novio* and we were on vacation together, discovering quaint little places we would tell our kids about someday.

"So, there's supposed to be this little village about thirty-five kilometers away that has a monastery up on a hill. Are you in a hurry to get back, or do you want to go?" he said. My lips were three inches from his stubbly cheek, so close I could feel his jaw working when he talked. If I were bolder, I'd trace my finger along his chin, right to where the rough skin melted into chamois-soft temples.

"Let's go," I said.

Alexiou's Travel was situated at the nexus of Pelekastritsa's two main thoroughfares. Typically for Greek villages in the islands, the travel agency doubled or tripled as bank, post office, and gossip outpost. It reminded me a little of my *tía* Maria-Theresa's store back home on Mission Street, littered with brochure stands and computer terminals, always a couple of friends or relatives filling up the three or four dented office chairs. At four o'clock on a Thursday afternoon, the place was crammed with tourists selecting this or that ferry or booking their flight back to Copenhagen or Miami or Glasgow.

Nia Alexiou was trying to help a group of young Spanish boys and girls in Day-Glo backpacks with the Athens train schedule. Between their poor English and her inattention—a plump baby was wailing on her knee—they weren't making much progress.

"What. Day. Do. You. Want. To. Leave," she said, clearly ready to go home or scream.

The group's representatives, a blond boy in a Shakira T-shirt and a thin-lipped girl with spirally curls, stared at her blankly. I stood partially hidden behind the rack of postcards featuring pictures of fat-free women in yellow thongs frolicking in radioactively turquoise waters. I felt the kids' frustration shimmering off them as they conducted a quick, Castilian-accented conversation. I stepped forward.

"Um, I speak Spanish. Do you want me to translate?" I asked the woman.

She looked instantly relieved. "Wonderful! Thank you very much! Ask them their travel dates and what class seats they want for the trip from Athens to Barcelona. Write them down on this pad, yes?" Assignment thus given, she turned her hennaed head away and began exchanging a wad of euros for Canadian dollars.

I explained the situation to the Spanish teenagers, who looked equally relieved, then wrote down their information, explaining that they should drop by tomorrow and Mrs. Alexiou would have their tickets. They nodded gratefully and left in a clump, calling out *hasta mañana*s.

Before I could slip away, a couple of pretty German lesbians I'd met at the Dallas asked me if I could check the ferry schedule to Kárpathos. I tried to catch Nia's attention, but she was deep in a shouting match with a sunburned couple who wanted their money back for a disappointing fishing trip.

"Um, sure," I told the Germans. I'd learned the Sabre travel-booking system by working weekends at my aunt's. I sat down at the terminal and found the information they wanted after a couple of tries. They thanked me and left, looking like twins in white tank tops and baggy linen pants.

In quick succession, I sold a lovesick-looking Greek boy overseas stamps, three mainland ferry crossings, and wrote down directions to the charming monastery I'd visited with Ethan yesterday. Before I knew it, Nia was handing me the baby, Spiros, and locking the front doors. Spiros had dimpled hands and chubby cheeks that looked as if they had been stuffed with cotton candy. I jiggled him on my knee and hoped being transferred to a stranger wouldn't start him screaming again, but he just stared at me with sleepy-lidded eyes and curled into the crook of my arm.

Nia came back with a smile on her face. "So, I can pay you twelve euros an hour, plus free drinks at my brother's bar. I'll need you most afternoons and some weekends. No freebies for boyfriends, but if you sell four round-trips to Athens in a day, I'll give you a bonus."

"Fifteen an hour and you have a deal."

Nia grinned. "Done. Now, *zahkarenia mou,* what's your name again?"

chapter 17

⌒⌒⌒⌒⌒⌒⌒⌒⌒⌒⌒⌒

PARKER

What's the obvious reaction to finding out your husband's been *shtupping* a European doctor somewhere in South America? (By the by, we had taken to calling Dr. Tramp such childish and belittling epithets as "The Belgian Waffler," "Aunt Twirp," and "The Brussels Sprout." I swear, once I almost laughed. Then I remembered I was in relationship mourning and put my scowl on and ordered another T&T with lime.)

Anyway, the obvious reaction is, of course, getting laid. Porked. Screwed. *Shtupped.* Bonked. Fucked silly. Whatever you want to call it. There's a poetic symmetry about it, a sort of cleansing I imagine will take place when the first post-Neil penis enters the hallowed tunnel, thrusting away all recollection of Neil's conjugal visits, his tendency to pump to the exact beat of Bruce Springsteen's "Born in the U.S.A.," or the way his kosher-pickle-sized cock curved slightly to the left. Not that I want to fuck anyone else up during my rebound. No, thank you. I'm not really the trail-of-destruction type. I'll make sure I'm honest and up-front with my first custodial (i.e., cleanup) fuck. I could post a sign:

Beware All Ye Who Enter Here, Enter At Your Own Risk, or simply, *Danger: No Lifeguard On Duty.* I could leave a stack of condoms on the nightstand so massive and intimidating, a veritable leaning tower of Trojans, that they'd be absolutely clear as to my expectations and their role in the proceedings. I could glue Swarovski crystals to my baby-doll T-shirt spelling out the words, *Actually, I'll call you.* I could cover all my ethical bases, so no one could accuse me of sending out the wrong signals. I didn't want a relationship, after all, just a nice extramarital plundering of the region I'd pledged to that rat bastard Neil Wentworth in front of God, our families, friends, clients, and that Episcopalian priest who always looked as if he smelled something nasty.

Getting plundered, however, had turned out to be more challenging than I'd thought.

After the devastating message from Neil, my unfortunate confrontation with the Greek navy, and my subsequent rescue by bong-toting wonder boy Josh Lido, I'd gone into, well, a slight decline. It was understandable. For almost eight weeks, I'd been operating under the assumption that Neil and I were merely taking a break from each other, that we were at the crest of a blip in the great Glass–Wentworth Love Story, destined to return to each other's embrace with the careening force of a Caribbean typhoon. Now that I knew that wasn't going to happen, I'd found it difficult to maintain my focus, brush my hair, clip my toenails, or even leave the hammock that rocked in the breeze under the villa's laundry line. I think I was really starting to let myself go by the time SNiP staged an intervention.

After I skipped the third gathering in a week at Tony's Taverna, Claire, Anya, and Kelah burst into the villa like a gaggle of clucking hens.

"Parker, you have to get up. All this . . . it's just not healthy," Claire said, gesturing toward the bureau, which, I saw now, was littered with miniature vodka bottles, damp bathing-suit bottoms, crumpled letters that invariably began *Dear Goatfucker,* and drugs. I could tell by the way the others looked at one another that my situation had been discussed and action decided upon.

"Don' wanna," I mumbled.

Obviously, Claire had been appointed Mother Hen, perhaps because she was, well, a mother, and her husband had cheated on her as well. "Parker, I know how you feel, but this isn't going to help you. It's best to get up and put a good face to it and pretend that things are okay. Eventually, you'll feel a little better."

"Your ability to shame me is masterful," I thought snidely. Then I realized I'd said it out loud. Oops. That's one issue I have with Ativan—makes you talk out of school.

"What you need is a good shag," Kelah said firmly. The others stared at her as if she had suggested I nibble on some hemlock. "I'm serious. There's nothing like a quick, easy fuck to ease the pain of rejection."

How'd a twenty-five-year-old get so much wisdom?

"I agree," volunteered Anya. "I mean, of course, I don't agree, but in this case, I make an exception. Anything that will shatter Neil's hold on you is a good thing. *Ay, Dios mío,* it's like the evil eye! And you've got to countercurse him, *chica.*"

Anya's willingness to violate her strict moral code for me touched me deeply. Slowly, I removed my hand from the Polaroid photo of Neil and me someone had taken on our wedding day. I had been clutching the smooth square to my chest for so long under the blanket that the heat from my fingers had melted the surface slightly, turning our faces into blurry mush. With my forehead elongated slightly, I had discovered I looked a little like one of my all-time heroines, Kate Spade. Thank God for small favors, eh?

Feeling faint, I swung my legs over the edge of the bed. They looked like ivory pipe stems in the grim light. "Fine. Just hand me one of those blue tablets over there and I'll be ready in five minutes," I told them.

My designated ravisher was tall, drunk, Nordic, and fond of shouting *"Opa!"* whenever the music paused.

"You're so hot," he said in my ear. He pronounced it as if it was a question, his voice curving upward at the end. His accent had the generic European quality of a Mentos commercial voiceover. I wasn't sure if he actually spoke English or had heard the phrase in an NSync song.

"Um, thanks," I replied, trying to keep out of the way of his swiveling pelvis. For the time being.

"You want to go for a walk?"

"Yes," I said gratefully. I had been on the island for nine weeks. I knew that "go for a walk" was Corfu tourist-speak for "fuck like bunnies."

He grabbed my hand as if we had met in high school and enjoyed a long, innocent courtship. I simpered across the floor, prom-queen-like. Across the room, I could see Josh Lido putting the moves on a willowy redhead. His eyes swept over me and I turned away. Somehow, I felt like he had crossed the line from holiday stranger to actual acquaintance, guardian angel, I don't know what—someone with the power to bear witness to my transgressions. I hate it when my guardian angels see me screwing Swedes built like brick shithouses.

Our evening jaunt through the olive trees lasted about thirty seconds before Nordic Guy's tongue was rammed down my throat, systematically cleaning my tonsils. He was so tall I had to bend my neck ninety degrees to lock lips with him. Under his jeans, his hard-on was intimidating to say the least, its size seeming to rival that of Catherine the Great's equine paramour.

"Aaach," I choked.

He either didn't hear me or was swept away on a sea of ouzo-marinated lust. Before I knew it, we were through the blue-trimmed door of a dormlike dwelling and writhing around on a cot the width of a Hershey bar.

"Um, the lights . . ." I said. It was one thing to have sex with a stranger. It was another to recognize him when you went to the grocery to buy yogurt.

Nordic Guy leaped up and flipped the switch, finding time to strip off his pants, banana-hammock underwear, shirt, and drug-dealer-style pager. He lowered himself over me, cock extended like a handgun. I tried to ready myself for the upcoming waves of bliss. For some reason, the out-of-body, out-of-mind pleasure I'd envisioned had thus far eluded me. While Nordic Guy chewed on my nipples through my favorite Calvin Klein bra and grunted as if enjoying a particularly savory porterhouse steak, I found myself thinking about a living room I'd passed on to Molly when I left. The Bergmans had insisted on sunflower-yellow walls. I'd tried to talk them out of it, thinking it too country for their modern space, but they'd insisted. I wondered how Molly was dealing with it.

Suddenly, I felt something crushing me. Anxiety flooded my chest. *Here goes,* I thought. *I managed to pick the only Scandinavian psycho on the island and he's trying to smother me with a pillow.* I edged up on my elbows and realized there was no pillow, just Nordic Guy. Immobile. From a stiffie to a stiff in two seconds.

"Hey, are you all right?" I said. "Hey, get off me. What's going on?" I pushed at him, finally succeeding in shifting his deadweight mass to the side, nearly shoving him off the bed in the process.

Apparently, my charms aren't what they used to be, because my Nordic sex toy had passed out and was beginning to emit a soft, babyish snore. Disgusted, I pulled my skirt back on, slipped my feet back into my sandals, grabbed my purse, and tiptoed out into the hallway. I hurried toward the door, anxious to escape the scene without being spotted. Outside, it was cooler than I'd expected.

"Watch the stairs," a voice said.

I stifled a scream and turned toward the sound. A small red ember glowed on a deck chair, indicating a cigarette. I let my eyes adjust and was not surprised to see the shape of Josh Lido emerge out of the gloom.

"Oh, it's you."

"Don't be too excited."

"Are you following me?" I said, not furiously, but close.

He inhaled deeply. "Are you asking me to? I'm pretty busy at the moment but can probably work something into my schedule. Those naval regiments can get pretty squirrelly sometimes. Not to mention those Scandinavian types."

"Thanks, but I think Blakas can cover it on protection patrol."

He nodded. "Drink?"

"All right. But just one." I sat down on the steps and popped open the Amstel Light he handed me. It went down cool and crisp.

"Lars pass out?" Josh said.

"How'd you know?"

"You're not the first chick I've seen storm out of there with pantyhose wrapped around her waist."

"Lovely."

He hopped out of the swing chair and sat next to me on the stairs. His deep eyes looked black in the moonlight, his teeth very white. He was short enough that we sat shoulder to shoulder.

"So, how long are you planning on spending here? Most folks move on after a couple of weeks, you know."

"I don't know. My return ticket's open-ended. I can't seem to summon the energy to leave," I said truthfully. "How about you?"

"Oh, I don't know," he said vaguely.

"Don't know or won't tell me?" My mom always said I had a *shmecker* for lying.

For a second, something pinched and weary enough to be pain seeped into his cola-colored eyes. By the time Josh looked back up at me, it was gone. He smiled tightly. "How about don't know and wouldn't tell you if I did?" he said.

We stared at each other for a second. I felt it again, that gentle tugging at my thoughts that made me want to know things about him, Josh Lido, in spite of myself. I ignored it.

"What do you do, Josh, back home in California?" I said instead.

"Oh, a little of this and that. Sales, mostly."

"I'm a decorator," I said.

"I know. You told me that the first night we met."

"Oh, yeah. That night . . . it's kind of a blur," I confessed.

He laughed, a rich, chocolaty rumble that stirred something in me. "Yeah, well, it's okay to make a fool of yourself once in a while, Park."

"You think?" I decided to let the Park go this time.

"I know."

I don't know what possessed me. Still don't know, in fact. Maybe it was the botched encounter with Lars. Or the promise I'd made to myself in the presence of the SNiPs to get me some action. Or a flashback to how I'd felt, reading Neil's Dear Johnette letter in a shoddy cybercafe. But there, on the staircase of what I now saw was the ramshackle "hotel" the tourists called the Putrid Palace, I leaned forward toward Josh Lido, closing the paltry inches between us until I could feel his breath sweet against my face. It felt like the moon, stark and wide over the trees, was pushing against my back, nudging me toward him. Josh's face was bathed in the light, the panes of his cheekbones standing out in stark relief, freckles sprinkled like a dusting of paprika. I noticed that the V of his upper lip was very deep and was stricken with the inexplicable desire to grab it in my teeth.

Then our mouths were mashed together and we were kissing. His kisses were a surprise. Expecting aggressive bossiness, or at least impudence, I was startled to feel his tongue sweeping gently against the underside of my lip, tasting. He found time to rub his shaven cheek against mine, running his lips against the arch of one eyebrow, then the other. One of his hands traced a burning trail along my collarbone, exploring the little hollow at my neck. His gentleness spawned in me a kind of mad passion, and I nearly tore his hair out burying my hands in his wild thatch of curls. Dizzy with lust, I pulled away, expecting to see my desire matched in his eyes.

"Josh," I rasped.

"Um," he said, kissing the side of my neck.

"Josh," I said again, firmer this time.

"Hmm?"

"Josh, I want to go to bed with you." The words bubbled out of me in a stream, like air unleashed from a bottle of Pellegrino.

He leaned back and stared at me, his hand holding my knee with the same confident ease he had holding a beer bottle or a Frisbee. I realized I'd been imagining those long fingers clasped around my waist for weeks now, buried under my post-Neil widow charade. Admitting it to myself felt delicious, comparable to taking a pee after a three-hour movie.

"Parker," he said, unlacing his fingers from mine, his withdrawal sending me spiraling into a dark hole. "I'm sorry, but this is a really bad idea."

chapter 18

KELAH

In terms of neuroses, I, Kelah Morris, am a textbook case. Or, better yet, a textbook.

Neurosis #1: narcissistic self-absorption.

On more than one occasion, I've been accused of prioritizing my writing above my relationships. This has always stymied me. I mean, writing *is* a relationship, isn't it? It lets me down, makes me feel trapped, provides occasional satisfaction, even ecstasy, and boggles the mind with its rules, rituals, and power to make me feel as if I'm choking. If I talk about it a lot, well, it's because I have a persistent worry I'll die—yes, physically expire—if I don't publish. It's not like I don't care about my friends' problems or my lovers' trials. After all, some of them constitute whole chapters in my novel.

My friends jokingly call me the Six Weeker, because most of my relationships last approximately as long as a pesky urinary tract infection. My last real boyfriend, a lovely Indian artist with paint-gummed nails and espresso-bean eyes called Sami, put it best: "Kelah," he'd said, pausing dramatically to light a Lucky

Strike in my chipped doorway, "you are a fucking bitch, but you're a focused fucking bitch. I'll look for you in bookshops. See you around." I have to confess, it was one of my more flattering breakups.

Neurosis #2: commitment phobia/fear of intimacy.

Related to the first, I can only assume this particular syndrome comes from my reluctance to put myself in a position where someone will let me down. Clichéd? Maybe. True? Certainly.

For instance, I think, more than anyone else in the family, I'd placed my bets on Davey last time around. I'd really convinced myself he would toe the line and stay out of trouble. Consequently, when he went and burgled the chemist's and ended up in jail, it felt almost like a personal affront (see neurosis #1: narcissistic self-absorption). *How* could he do this to me, after all the faith I'd shown in him? *How* could he make me look an idiot in front of Mum and Dad? Over time, life's little disappointments have a way of piling up on you and making you cold. Eventually, withdrawal seems the logical choice in the face of the chronic letdowns. I can see how it could end up for me if this continues: Kelah Morris, would-be writer, fifty or thereabouts. Moldering alone in a garret with only a computer and dusty Darjeeling boxes for company. Hair snarled and gray under an old-ladyish babushka. TV turned permanently on so I don't forget the sound of the human voice. Far too many cats to allow for proper hygiene.

It was too horrible to contemplate.

And, last but definitely not least, neurosis #3: Nothing I will ever do will be enough to please my mother.

There must be some clinical name for this, but I don't know it. It's not like I'm without responsibility here. I mean, I'm as hard on Mum as she is on me. Definitely. In our own separate universes, we're each considered close to normal. Put us together, and we produce a chemical compound that causes fire to shoot out of our mouths and burning acid to coat our insides. Simply put, together, we're toxic. I don't think it's either one's fault. It's one of those aberrations of nature, that's all, like albino elephants or cancer cells run amok, reproducing themselves in a mindless frenzy of self-destruction.

Does it have something to do with the fact that Mum's white and I'm not? I honestly don't think so. I mean, I've been round and round on this point for ages. I did the whole identity-politics thing at uni, flirted with black pride and all that, tried to see Mum as the colonizer, you know? And it just didn't fit. I mean, sure, Mum doesn't understand the black experience, but then, she doesn't understand the teen experience or the female experience or the human experience either. That's just Mum. On the numerous occasions when our relationship as mother and daughter is not presumed, Mum doesn't get on the soapbox and vent her maternal indignation. She's no mama bear. The most such misunderstandings have ever provoked in Mum is a sort of mild irritation, akin to just missing the train or running out of postage stamps. If the fact that I resided in her belly for nine months prompts even a shred of sentimentality in her soul, I've never seen it. It is not uncommon to catch Mum shedding a tear or three over a particularly resplendent bit of literary prose, but try to elicit the radiance of proud motherhood with a letter-perfect school report or a fond hug, and you'll be sorely disappointed.

So, why all these ruminations now, you ask? I guess it's because Fee and Boz just left, and I'm reeling just the tiniest bit due to the Confession. More accurately, the Drunken Confession. They're the worst kind, don't you think? Alcohol, if nothing else, wipes out your ability to prevaricate. So I can only assume that Boz was speaking the truth. It sure complicates things, the truth.

Things got sort of messy the day after the Drunken Confession.

When I woke up that day, the only sign that I'd shared my bed with someone was a slight wrinkling in the starchy sheet next to me. A few of Bozzie's dun-colored hairs lay on the pillow, which immediately set off a giant wave of panic. I hopped out of bed as if the hairs were dipped in plutonium and threw on a T-shirt over my pajamas. I could hear rustling outside.

After a quick pee, I snuck into the kitchen. The teakettle was still hot, so I poured myself a cuppa and went reluctantly to the courtyard. The sun had just tipped over the eastern row of rooftops, spilling rose-tinged warmth over the table and chairs. I especially loved our little aerie in the morning, perched as it was on the highest hill, all whitewashed and stark. Boz was there reading something, one of the village's scrawny cats rubbing against his legs. His hair stuck up in tufts and his glasses were slightly askew. He was very pale.

"Jaysus," I said. "You okay?"

"Yeah. I was sick earlier, but now I'm just knackered."

"Get you some tea?"

"Had some."

I sat down and tried to consider Boz with fresh eyes. It's hard when you've known someone as long as we have, when you've seen him at his worst, with other people, careening about his life, shattering things. As it was, I was just this side of panic at the idea that he would want to talk about last night. What could I say that wouldn't hurt him? Sorry, Bozzie. You're a right brilliant friend, but I wouldn't shag you if all the men on earth were suddenly rendered impotent and they confiscated the world's vibrators?

"Eyebrow," Boz said.

"Oh, thanks." I lowered my hand. When I'm nervous, I rub my right eyebrow. Boz's lifetime assignment is to tell me when I'm doing it. Something tells me that if we gave up our platonic status, his willingness to perform such duties would fall by the wayside.

"Kay?"

Oh, God, now he was going to bring up last night. Oh, shit.

"Um," I answered unhelpfully, slugging back scalding tea as if it were Irish whiskey. If I incurred third-degree burns on my throat, I couldn't say anything regrettable, could I?

"I hope you're not mad at me," Boz said, looking me straight in the eye. His were their usual gray-blue pools of calm, which, strangely, made my panic metastasize into sheer dread.

"Why should I be mad?" I heard someone open the door to Claire's apartment. Great, an audience.

"They were just laying there, so I read them. I know you're kind of private about these things."

Huh?

"The thing is, I think they're really good," he continued. "Especially the parts about Claire and those Americans."

Then I realized: He was talking about my journal. I'd printed out some of it in Corfutown and left it in the kitchen.

"You read my journal? Oh, Boz, why? It's just some crap I've been doing for myself."

"No, Kay, it's really good. I think you should submit it to someone. Maybe as a travelogue or to a newspaper or magazine or something."

"Like *Cosmo*? *Marie Claire*? Is it that good?" I had particular contempt for women's glossies. Boz knew that.

He shook his head. "Kelah, come on. I'm just trying to encourage you to, you know, think of doing something besides that novel. This stuff really *is* good. I mean, you've been working on the book for, like, *years*. Are you sure it's what you really want to do, anyway? Maybe what you're calling writer's block is just . . . just someone trying to tell you something."

I gripped my mug so hard I feared it might shatter in my hand. "That's lovely, Boz. Really lovely. What are you saying, that my writing's for shit? I can't believe this, after all I've been through! You're just like all the others—Mum, Dad, Charlie, shit, Davey too! You know how much this means to me!" I cried.

"That's not what I'm saying at all, and you know it! Exactly the opposite, in fact. Fuckin' hell—you can't take criticism and you can't take compliments either! Sometimes I don't know why I bother with you—"

He stood up suddenly, knocking his tea over so it spilled into a small ashen pool on the table. For some reason, I stood up, too, so we were standing there facing each other, mute. Underneath the nimbus of prickliness surrounding us, a strange idea coalesced, pushing aside my worries about the novel: What would it have felt like if Bozzie *had* said he loved me again, like he did last night?

"Boz . . ." My voice trailed off.

"Kelah, if you want us to be friends come tomorrow, you'll shut your hole right now and we'll forget we ever had this conversation," he said coldly.

We were still staring at each other when Fee came around the corner. She was wearing last night's miniskirt, a metric ton of gummed-up mascara, and a huge grin.

"Hey, luvs, I'll have some of that tea. What are you doing standing there like a couple of eejits? Guess what? I think I finally know what they mean when they say fuck yer brains out!"

chapter 19

~~~~~~~~~~~~~~~~

CLAIRE

It had been a long time since I wanted a man that way. You know how it is: You get married, the babies come, and your dream life atrophies, like a limb whose blood supply has steadily dwindled until only the slenderest trickle remains. It's a major feat just to get dinner on the table; who has time for fantasies involving slim dark men and six-stringed lutes? The you who once rode a bicycle in a suede miniskirt and rubbed her thighs against the fig tree after seeing *Last Tango in Paris* is buried under a mountain of decidedly unsexy responsibilities. Even if you found her, her imagination would be flattened by the weight of them. It's almost better to leave the door closed than to suffer the inevitable disappointment of such pedestrian desires—a fleeting caress, fingers raking long hair, the sublime way the world tips when you're being lowered by strong hands onto a soft bed.

Andreas, the satyr with quicksilver hands, was playing again at Tony's. I'd been the last three nights. At first, it was easy to blend in. To sidle up to my usual seat, hide behind a glass of red wine, and disappear into the throng. Now . . . well, hiding was the least of my worries.

On the first night, Tony came out of the kitchen and hit the side of a homemade wine barrel with a wooden spoon to quiet us. I had just finished eating with Parker and Kelah. Anya was somewhere with Ethan, who was so blatantly smitten I wouldn't dare tease him about it. Since he and his girlfriend, Rachel, broke up, he'd been a bit monkish. I'd been worried about him, actually. Working with Gary from morning till night, an occasional lager with his mates, and too much time drawing up plans for that infernal house of his. No social life or a woman's touch to speak of for the past twelve months. It was as if Rachel's departure left a hole in Ethan's heart where his young man's desire for women's company used to be. It was actually easier to understand when he was just bitter—who doesn't remember such a state?—but the blank detachment he showed whenever he was introduced to someone alarmed me. God knows, a little holiday romance is good for people, but I hope neither of them gets hurt. San Francisco and Sydney aren't exactly commuting distance, you know.

Tony's yelling brought me back to the present.

"Hey, everyone! Quiet. Quiet! We have special treat for you tonight. Our own Andreas Leontarakis is going to play traditional Greek music for you! He come all the way from Corfutown, so clap hard for him—especially you, Fabrizio, you drunk Italian *disgraziato*. Welcome Andreas to Tony's Taverna!"

Everyone applauded as a slim, dark man came out. Ah, the satyr from the *panigiri*! He pulled out a stool without looking at the crowd, sat down, and strummed the lute, releasing a haunting melody that could only be about thwarted love and unrequited passion. Within minutes, mesmerized, I had inched forward to the edge of my chair, my thighs sticking damply to the seat. The usually noisy room had quieted, and most of the women and some of the men were staring at Andreas with naked lust. It wasn't that he was conventionally handsome. He didn't have an aquiline nose, or particularly striking features, or the coveted broad-shoulders-to-narrow-waist proportion. He was on the slender side, with heavy-lidded hazel eyes, olive skin, and a crooked, full-lipped mouth. His thick, shiny dark hair skimmed down over his neck and feathered out in desperate need of a cut. Stylewise, his tight, striped T-shirt and faded dungarees were reminiscent of the 1970s. But when Andreas played, you forgot what he looked like. He displayed a coiled grace that transported you from the ramshackle taverna to the shadowy confines of an olive grove or a bedroom. Any bedroom.

I went home and masturbated for the first time in three years.

Now, on night four of what I'd started to think of as The Siege, I was having doubts about my sanity. Here I was, forty-six years of age, still married by a thread and lusting after a man at least fifteen years my junior, whom I'd not heard utter a single word and who had spared me nary a glance. I wondered if Patricia had felt this way before she invited Sven to see her etchings. Or was it her traitorous husband's face she saw when she was trying futilely to even the score?

"Ooh, there he is," squealed Parker. "God, he's gorgeous."

Gorgeous Andreas Leontarakis wasn't, but sexy, well, that was undeniable. Tonight, he had on jeans so thin they cupped his ass like swaddling clothes. His feet were bare, which reinforced his naughty-Greek-god quality, and his stomach under the loose, barely buttoned white shirt was as hard, flat, and brown as a cutting board. In fact, he looked as if he had just finished playing fiddle with Dionysus himself.

"He looks like he just finished playing fiddle with Dionysus," I murmured into my house red.

"Here's to Dionysus!"

We clinked glasses and sat back to listen. For once, I was glad that neither of my boys was here. Brian had taken the ferry to Mykonos, which was apparently a gay paradise of loose, luscious men and all-night discos, and Ethan and Anya were ostensibly off taking photos of an old church, an absurd excuse for riding double on a motor scooter at night if I'd ever heard one.

Andreas played eloquently, as always, and by the end a gaggle of lovestruck girls had gathered on the floor, sitting Indian-style with their long, tan legs folded under them and incipient tears of yearning springing from their eyes.

"Well, I'm off. Early day tomorrow. I'm taking the boat ride to the other side of the island," I told Parker. I leaned down and gave my lamb shank to Blakas, who was in his usual spot between Parker's ankles. He thanked me with a doggish groan of pleasure and went to work on it.

"See you," she said.

Outside, the night was cool and lightly perfumed with the woodsy scent of trees. I decided to take a walk on the beach before returning to the villa.

I felt different from the Claire Dillon who'd boarded that flight in Sydney seven weeks ago. The Claire Dillon who went to Jazzercise class religiously and drove across town to the farmer's market every Tuesday so Gary could have the fresh goat's-milk gouda he liked and who avoided live music venues where she'd be liable to run into someone from her former life. This new someone would take one look at old Claire's billowy housedress and the disappointed lines around her mouth and think, good Lord, what happened to the Claire Hardy with long bright auburn hair who swayed onstage with her eyes closed like a red-petaled flower? I wasn't sure how comfortable I was with the change either. I *wanted* things now, you see. Things I hadn't wanted in years. And wanting was scary. Without need, you can't feel deprived, right? I thought of all the nights Gary, Ethan, and I had sat at our kitchen table after the workday, a square missing its fourth corner with Brian ostracized to our outer orbit, silently eating our way through dinner, and wanted to cry. Our house in the suburbs, fervently maintained into overlandscaped perfection so it would be a showpiece for Gary's business, portrayed a family so concerned with outward appearances, its members failed to notice when their sad little betrayals mutated into something damaging and permanent *inside*.

God, what a sad sally. A hallmark of the new Claire—the ability to go from wanton hopefulness to self-pitying wallowing in a single drink. I kicked off my sandals, stripped off my sweater, and dipped my feet into the stream of froth at the water's edge. Goose pimples broke out on my arms, the sensitive hairs standing at attention. I leaned back and sang to the swollen moon the folksy-country chorus I'd been working on the last few weeks:

"He told me he'd come back . . . And because the lies hadn't reached his eyes, I didn't have the heart to refuuuse him . . . So we made love onnnne more time, and all the false truths were minnnne . . . Words cease to mean a thing when the joy is all behindddd . . . youuuu . . . Take a walkabout, baby, walk away from me, the future's a vision we're not allowed to see . . . Take a walkabout, baby, 'cause dreams are all we got . . . If you can change the moment, you can undo what you've wrought . . . Take a walkabout, baby, you'll thank me in the end . . . Break me if you must, but don't dare ask me to bend . . . oooh, walkabout, oooh. . . ."

I threw my head back and gave it all I had, ending with a stomp and a splash. Whew.

"Your voice is very beautiful."

I turned around and there he was, his face and body glowing silver in the moonlight. The satyr. For some reason, I wasn't the least surprised. After all, I had willed it, hadn't I?

Denials bubbled up in my mouth. That was old Claire Dillon talking. New Claire Dillon swallowed them whole and tossed her mane of hair back, imagining it streaming like molten copper down her back. With a little luck, the moonlight would mix with the silver strands.

"Thank you," I said with the sane part of my brain. The other side wondered: Was it illegal in Greece to rip a man's shirt off without asking first?

"You are a singer? In England?"

I laughed. "Actually, I'm a housewife in Australia."

"But you used to be a singer?" he persisted.

"Well, yes. But that was a long time ago."

He looked satisfied. "That's what I think. Your name is . . . ?"

"Claire."

"Andreas," he said unnecessarily. The name rolled off his tongue like a lozenge. I had the crazy thought that he could magically pass it to me mouth to mouth: sound candy.

Before I knew what was happening, Andreas had slipped his stringy sandals off and was walking next to me, our forward motion producing two sets of tiny wakes. I don't know if it was the glass of wine or simply the darkness cloaking us, but I felt surprisingly comfortable. He was one of those people you sensed didn't really require the small talk the rest of us relied on as cushion.

With the town glowing softly above us and the infinite expanse of warm black water sweeping out around us, dotted with ferry beacons, I felt small and marvelously anonymous, a dandelion borne on alien winds. It was almost as if I were floating. Claire Dillon, one hundred percent gossamer. A figment of somebody's (naughty) imagination.

We walked down the beach, never touching. I watched my knees flash white in the dark as they slipped in and out of my slit skirt.

"You will sing with me sometime?" he asked after a while in fractured English.

I stopped. Up ahead, I could hear the cottony murmurs of lovers occupying a beach lounge chair, her soft giggles camouflaged by his more urgent whispers.

"Oh, I don't think so. I haven't sung in ages, you see. I don't think it would work."

"Please. Sing with me tomorrow night, Claire."

Hearing my name spill from those sensual lips made tremors shoot down my legs. In a flash, I saw myself lying in my narrow white bed, fingers questing between my thighs. Heat crept up my neck, staining my face. Could he tell what was happening to me? What *was* happening to me? Part of me wanted to flee, to run back to the villa, throw my clothes in a bag, and slip onto a ferry in the depth of night, back to Athens and Sydney and home. Back to old Claire Dillon.

The other part wanted to melt into the sand like the couple out there in the darkness, Andreas looming over me, his satyr body and quicksilver hands obliterating all my secrets and my fears.

"Claire?" Andreas looked at me intently, his eyes never leaving my face.

"Yes," I told him.

chapter 20

ANYA

"Ethan likes you. I can tell these things," Parker said. She was painting her toenails the palest blue, to match Blakas's new bandanna. We were hosting a dinner tonight at our villa for the SNiPs. After getting off work at the travel agency, I'd rushed to buy pasta with olive oil, feta cheese, and lovely ripe tomatoes bulging red and yellow. I'd made flan for dessert and Kelah was bringing her tarot cards.

"Maybe." I couldn't bear to hex it. My sister, Carilu, won't even say a boy's name until she's sure they're exclusive. She's that superstitious.

Parker rolled her eyes. "Come on! He calls when he says he's going to, which is even more impressive since none of us has a phone. He's constantly trying to be alone with you. And besides, he has that kicked-puppy look. Like you could do anything to him and he'd still come back for more."

I felt the edges of my mouth turn up in spite of myself. "Oh, do you think?"

"Definitely."

"Well, I think Josh Lido is into you, *chica*. He watches you when he thinks you're not looking and then—boom!—pretends to be, like, cutting his toenails or something when you turn around."

She snorted. "Josh Lido doesn't cut his toenails. Josh Lido's toenails should be preserved in a museum as a testament to the failure of twenty-first-century hygiene."

"Okay, but you have to admit he has nice eyes."

"Well, if you're into that sort of . . . eyes."

"Everybody's into his sort of eyes," I said.

At least she wasn't pretending Neil was coming back anymore. That was scary. Even more scary than the new Parker, who was friends with a dog and wore blue nail polish and ate fried calamari instead of tranquilizers and was even letting her vampirically pale skin acquire a faint but discernible tan.

"I love his arms," I said dreamily.

"Too many tattoos."

"Not Josh, silly. Ethan. Ethan."

"Oh, well, yeah. And that ass. God. That ass is like Michelangelo's David."

"And that chest," I said.

"Exquisite."

"Plus, he's kind. And smart. And artistic. And *muy guapo*."

Parker screwed the cap back on. "What's *guapo*—handsome? I'll take dumb and loyal and good-looking over smart and scamming these days. Not that Ethan's dumb, of course!" She set her feet up to dry on Blakas's speckled side. "Oh yeah, I have gossip! Claire told me he broke up with his girlfriend a year ago, and they'd been together for years, since college. She said he wanted to get married and have kids, and the girlfriend didn't. I mean, I think the marriage part was okay. It was more about the kids. Apparently, he was *very* into the family thing, and the girlfriend didn't want to interrupt her career. She was a lawyer or something like that. One of those driven types," Parker finished blithely, as if a mere nine weeks ago she herself did not fit the description like her favorite pair of size-six Earl jeans.

When she said that, about Ethan wanting kids, I felt a familiar chill seep into my bones. Of course he would want kids. Who wouldn't? Well, some people, but not Ethan. It was in everything he said, everything he did—even the stuff that wasn't about kids directly. I mean, *mierda,* the guy had *marriage and family material* written all over him, down to the patient, nonpatronizing smile he got when he had to explain something to somebody who's pretty darn slow. Or the way he stopped the motorcycle just to show me a single lavender flower poking up from among the scrubby bushes along the roadside. If I wanted to pursue any kind of future with this man, I was going to have to deal—finally *deal*—with the biggest mistake of my life. I was going to have to tell him the truth. Just the thought of disappointing Ethan that way made my chest ache.

"Oh, shit, they're here. Is the pasta done?" said Parker.

I went in to check on dinner and tried to forget about Ethan and children for a while. That's the problem with destiny: You know she'll get you there eventually, but how she does it is generally a big fat mystery.

"Okay, so what I'm seeing here are two paths. The first possible outcome is signified by the Four of Swords. In some schools of thought, it represents a truce or respite. Solitude, replenishment, self-imposed exile, that sort of thing. Another way of looking at it that's a bit more, I don't know, cynical, I suppose, is that it shows exile or abandonment—"

"That would be about right!" Claire interjected.

Kelah raised one perfectly arched brow. "Well, the important thing to remember is, it's temporary, whatever the state. But see, over here, on the right side you've got the Three of Pentacles. That represents the alternate outcome. This card in this position indicates power and dignity, rank, power, mastery. Perfection in artistic ability. Great skill in whatever you've chosen to accomplish—"

Parker nudged Claire. "It could be your singing, Claire!"

She shrugged. "Or it could be my bloody mind-blowing ability to hem Gary's shirts. What else does it say, Kelah?"

"Well, you've got a reversed Devil—"

"That must be Gary!"

"No, Andreas!"

"Sven!"

"Sven's gorgeous twin brother back in Stockholm!"

"Hey, come on. Actually, the Devil in this position means divorce. Not literally divorce, but freedom from bondage, recognition of need, spiritual understanding. Starting fresh."

"Is it good?"

"Bloody right it is. Better than that one Parker got, with the Tower in the Celtic Cross." Kelah giggled behind her hand.

"Yeah, you gotta love catastrophic destruction and epic misery," Parker said.

"Okay, Anya's turn."

"Yes, but first let's put these dishes in the kitchen and light some more candles. It's getting dark out here."

Parker touched the match to each of the tea-light candles, forming a circle of light around us. Against the pitch backdrop of the hills, it felt like we were a coven of witches, or the only people left in the universe. When we quieted, insects added their voices to the rhythmic hum of the night's song. Then Kelah shuffled the deck and closed her eyes for a moment, as she had with the others. She pushed the deck toward me.

"Which spread do you want?" she asked.

"Um, is there one where you just choose one card, like a yes or no?"

"Yes, you just pick one card."

"Ooh," said Claire. "You're a brave one. I was always afraid to get a reading at all, let alone make it that obvious."

Parker laughed. "Me too. I always thought I'd go into one of those places with a neon palm on the front, and some hag with a crystal ball and a Count Chocula accent would take one look at the cards and say, 'Go, go, go!' in this totally creepy way and, like, point to the door—"

"Did she have really long dodgy-looking fingernails?" Kelah asked.

"Well, *yeah!*"

"I saw her too."

We all laughed.

With my hand hovering over the deck of cards, I closed my eyes and thought about my life at home: the job I thought I'd loved that I hadn't thought about for even a half second; the family and friends I missed sorely, Carilu and my brother, Tomás, and my parents and all the crazy aunties; my crumbling but colorful apartment, with its Mexican rugs and painted-shut windows; the numbness, the faded sense of myself that seemed to follow me around, day in and day out. I thought about the things I wanted and how part of me thought I didn't deserve them, while the other part of me was ready to fight fate tooth and nail for them: a good relationship with a man, marriage, work I could love, friends, people in my life who believed you could be anything if you set your mind to it, and babies—yes, that. Even though it was a pipe dream, I still couldn't let it go. Not completely.

I drew a card slowly from the deck.

Kelah turned it over.

It showed a beautiful maiden in a long, flowing white dress, with a sheet of soft brown waves cascading over her shoulder. She was standing in a green meadow with a roulette wheel behind her.

"Wheel of Fortune," Kelah whispered. "The influence of random chance on the affairs at hand. Coincidence. Balance. The sudden intercession of good luck. The key here is that you have an opportunity. But it's incumbent on you to *exploit* it, and it must be done quickly, before the critical moment has passed."

Kelah looked up, laced her slim fingers together like a sage, her thatch of curls springing out from her head in a golden aureole. "Someone's smiling on you from up there, girl, but what happens next is totally up to you."

chapter 21

PARKER

Josh Lido was everywhere.

As was proof of my humiliation.

Unlike earlier in the "vacation," when I was still pretending I had a marriage to go home to and could maintain that aura of indifference and unconquerability that men clearly find irresistible, now I was simply another spurned career woman in her thirties, looking for love—or at least sex—in all the wrong places and sneaking out of holiday hotels with the tag of her slip skirt digging into her belly button.

All my anger—at Neil, Molly, my family, yes, even the world—seemed to have been filtered through some sort of psychological condensing unit, producing a perfect pearl of hatred that nestled firmly on Josh Lido's bristly head. I knew it was not wholly rational, but that didn't stop me from cultivating elaborate revenge fantasies, wherein the little imp fell madly in love with me and I thwarted all his attempts at carnal pleasure with well-timed interruptions or extended one espadrille-shod foot just in time to watch him tumble off the Acropolis.

The first time I saw him after the Rejection, I was at the general store looking for fabric swatches. I didn't think I could stand the rickety, stained chairs at Tony's another minute and had decided to take matters into my own hands and give him some homemade seat covers as a gift.

I was fingering a lovely bolt of cerulean Greek blue when I spotted Josh's familiar head of hair above the flip-flop aisle.

"Hi, Parker. How's it going?" He was infuriatingly normal.

"Good," I said, seething inside. "What do you think of this?"

"It's nice. What for?"

"Tony's chairs at the taverna."

He grinned, showing off that crooked incisor. "Opening a Pelekastritsa office, are we?"

"Maybe," I said, as coldly as I could.

"Let me know if you need someone in sales. I think I could get used to it here." He cracked his knuckles. I quelled the urge to hit him over the head with a sand shovel.

"Sure thing," I replied. Recalling his sensitive hands and talented mouth, I decided I wouldn't hire Josh Lido to clean my toilet.

The next time was much, much worse. One of the bars along the beach was having the Greek version of a Hawaiian luau, complete with frothy drinks, paper lanterns strung up along the hutlike eaves, and nubile girls dancing on surfboard countertops. I was already in a sour mood that day, having been foolish enough to check e-mail.

Dear Park, Molly had written,

Things are going okay at the office. I hired an intern for the summer to help with billing and mail and phone and stuff. On the first day, she changed the outgoing on-hold message to say that Glass, Ng & Associates are currently busy "designing the most beautiful interiors in Northern California and beyond!" I made her change it back and told her she's lucky you're away or her ass would have been canned. I really miss you, Park ;-) . Scott and I are fine, just the usual stuff. I wrapped up the Bergman project. They went with the marigold for the living room after all, but they did take your advice on the rattan, thank God. Their standard poodle, Muff—what were they thinking?—gave birth in the new sideboard the day after we closed. Barbara wanted me to get them another one at no cost! I told her we're not in the dog-breeding business. She's threatening to sue, but she'll have forgotten about it by next week. Woman's got the brain of a flea.

And now, the bad news. There isn't any way to make this easier, so I'll just say it. I hate having to e-mail you something like this, but I don't want to see you get blindsided. Scott was at one of those lawyer continuing-education courses down in LA, and he runs into someone from Neil's firm, Tyler somebody? Big tall frat-boy type? Anyway, he and Scott got to talking, and somehow it came up that they both knew Neil, and this Tyler guy says, Did you hear about the baby? And Scott's like, what baby? And Tyler says he heard through the grapevine that the Belgian tramp is *PREGGERS*, which might explain a lot about why Neil's acting like such an *UTTER ASS*. Please, please don't freak out about this—okay, that's stupid, of course you're going to freak out. I know I would. It's just, I know you can't see it now, but you're better off without that prick, Park. Someday, sooner than you think, you'll see that. Anyway, I just thought you should know what was going around. I know you like you're my sister, and I know you're probably spending a lot of time worrying about what people are thinking. The truth is, people are too self-absorbed to be thinking about anybody but themselves for more than five minutes, okay? So just concentrate on taking care of yourself and coming back so we can *KICK ASS*. I know you're not supposed to say these things, but I don't care: For the record, Scott and I never thought Neil was good enough for you. You're a star, Park, and you deserve someone who treats you like one. Love, Mol

What a star, I thought. Here I am dancing to pop songs by Israeli drag queens I've never heard of, with a four-foot-tall uni-browed Neopolitan I wouldn't sleep with in a million years trying to bury his head in my cleavage, and the suspicious beginnings of a T&T tire materializing around my waist. Meanwhile, my sort-of-ex-husband was gallivanting around South America in full Jesus of Nazareth regalia, knocking up Flemish floozies and sticking vaccines into babies' butts.

God help me.

I motioned to Anya that I was heading back to the bar. She was locked in a junior-high-style embrace with Ethan, her arms clasped around his muscular neck, his hands clamped firmly to her haunches. Apparently, holiday romance was just what Anya had needed, be-cause she had really bloomed since our arrival in June. In spite of my happiness at her good fortune, I felt a frisson of envy trickle into my heart. They looked so sweet together, so *right*. Oh, to be on the verge of a new love instead of on the bitter outskirts of a failed marriage. Of course, it was going to be hard for her when they went their separate ways come September, but I'd be there to help her through it. I felt ashamed of my initial repulsion of her attempts at friendship and resolved to try harder to make amends.

No sooner had I ordered a water—I intended to begin my diet by cutting back to every other drink for alcoholic beverages—than I felt a thump against my back. Then another.

"Excuse me," I muttered to the interloper.

The next thump almost knocked me off my barstool.

"Hello!" I said to the sun-streaked back of a woman's head.

"Oh, sorry." She giggled. "We kind of forgot what was going on for a minute."

The woman was actually a girl, carelessly scrumptious with tangled goldilocks hair, lots of beads, and enough sun-saturated flesh showing to qualify as a walking nudist colony. She wore a man's arm around her neck like a tattooed scarf.

It was attached to Josh Lido.

I issued an involuntary noise that resembled gagging on spoiled meat.

"Oh, hey, Park. This is my friend Parker. Park, this is Jett."

Jett extended her hand for shaking. Hers was small, square, and bejeweled. She had a crust of dirt under her fingernails. I took it reluctantly and glanced about for an escape hatch.

"Josh and I were just talking about what I could do after I graduate," Jett breathed.

"Oh, are you in graduate school?" I said.

"Not even! Just college. I'm a sophomore at Florida State."

"Oh," I said faintly, feeling the crow's-feet around my eyes furrowing, as if the mere presence of such callow youth was like a perverse aging serum.

Jett smiled sweetly. "Parker, right? Maybe we could meet sometime and do, like, an informational interview? Then I could tell my parents I'd really been working while I was in Greece, you know?"

I couldn't help myself. "How old are your parents, Jett?"

"My mom's thirty-six. She had me really young."

I nearly fell off the stool. "Bye!" I called out semihysterically as I staggered out the door, tossing Josh Lido the Child Molester an evil look. There but for the grace of a couple dozen years go I.

I had decided the way to salvation was work.

After my first failed attempts at extramarital sex left me cold, I swore off lurid thoughts and vowed to live out the rest of my holiday with the purity and fervor of a convent novitiate. Good-bye, Parker Glass, pill-popping, high-living, Scandinavian-straddling, abandoned wife of Neil the Goatfucker. Hello, Nun Rosie, dedicated to the eradication of egregious design flaws and unseemly color schemes wherever they might raise their ugly heads. I would glide from needy galley kitchen to lightless living room like an angel of aesthetic mercy, dark hair winging out from my freshly scrubbed face like a wimple.

Unfortunately, I had no job. So I set about creating one. My first foray into redesigning the interiors of Corfu was Tony's Taverna. One breezy afternoon, I marched into Tony's before the dinner rush.

He was hunched in a corner with an accounts notebook and a calculator, his brow knitted.

"Hi."

"Oh, hi, Parker."

"Whatchu doin'?" I was Sister Rosie, communing with the children of the street in their own language.

"Trying to figure out how to avoid the bank to foreclose." He scowled. "We make all the money on drinks, but with this new tax on spirits, I'm afraid we won't even—how you say?—break level this month."

"What about, I don't know, investors?" I suggested.

"Not a good chance at this point. I'm in debt already to my uncle. He lend me the down payment when I renovate this place." He shoved the papers aside in disgust. "But enough of that. What can I do for you, beautiful girl?"

I decided to be frank. "Well, I have a proposition for you." He raised his brow, so I went on. "I've been here for ten weeks. I'm not the type to sit around going to the beach or getting a tan or whatever these people do all day. I'll be here till at least the end of summer, because I can't go home. My husband left me and got a Belgian doctor pregnant in South America. Before that, at home, I had a nervous breakdown and my partner made me come here. I want to make over your place for free," I said simply.

Tony nodded, tugging on his chin in unintentional mockery of the eternal wise-man image.

"You can do something to increase business?" he said.

"Well, there are things we can do to make the space more inviting and get you more foot traffic." I was starting to get excited. "Actually, there are some possibilities—theme parties, or happy hours, maybe a festival of some sort? Things that would make you more of a destination. . . . Look, do you have time to talk about this more?"

He pulled out the chair opposite him. There was a suspicious wet spot with a yellowish tinge in the middle of the seat.

"Start talking," Tony said.

chapter 22

CLAIRE

Valerie called me in the telephone center approximately ten minutes after the appointed time. I occupied myself by scribbling in my songbook and counting old women in babushkas.

"Hello?"

"Claire?"

"Val?"

"The line's all crackly," she said. There was a slight delay on the line, so that my sister's voice sounded like it was bouncing off the ceiling of a church.

"Modern technology hasn't quite made it to the islands," I said.

"Claire, how *are* you?" she cried as my final words seemed to careen around in the telephone.

I've noticed that when people think you're mad, there's a tendency to overemphasize the second syllable, as if you might misunderstand the purpose of the question. Due to your madness, of course.

"Oh, fine. It's been good having Ethan and Bri here. Ethan's fallen for an American, it seems." I didn't say anything about their mother. What was I supposed to say, *Well, you see, Val, there's this man. He plays lute and wears his shirts open to the waist and just might be thirty.*

"Ethan's in America?"

"No, Ethan's involved with an American girl," I repeated into the echoing chamber.

"Well, I'm sure America's as good a place as any to find a girl," she said finally.

I decided to ignore the exchange and move on.

"So, how are things at home?"

"Oh, good. Josie and Chris are back from winter camp. Chris came back with his tooth broken off."

"No!"

"Oh, yes. Apparently, one of his dormmates dared him to bite off the cap of a Coke. We've had to visit Dr. Duffy and get him a crown."

"Not in any pain, I hope?"

"No. Stupid boy's getting a summer job to pay for it, though. Stef insists." Val's husband, a former Australian army lieutenant, tended to view their offspring as insubordinate privates who would benefit from a few hundred push-ups or half marathons through the bush.

"So, Claire," Val continued. "I had a little visit from Gary a few days ago."

"Gary?" I said vaguely, as if I couldn't recall the name of my husband of twenty-eight years.

"And he was quite, well . . . not himself. I think the separation's really getting to him, Claire. He said quite openly he wants a reconciliation. I think he's really suffering without you all. Honestly, he looked like he'd aged twenty years. If he wasn't my own brother-in-law, I might not have recognized him."

I thought of Gary at home on the couch, surrounded by aluminum TV-dinner trays crusted with the remains of Salisbury steak and chicken enchiladas, falling asleep in front of the television while the dog licked his hands, sticky with bathroom caulk and Foster's.

"Is he still seeing . . . her?" I asked cautiously.

"Absolutely not. I wouldn't even have seen him if he was. Hang on a minute. . . ." I heard Val scream something to Josie about putting on a jumper. Then she came back. "Are you still there? Okay, what was I saying? Oh, yeah. So, it's stone cold over, he says. And I believe him. You'd have to have seen his face, Claire. He regrets what he's done. He said he'd do anything to have you back. Claire? Are you listening?"

"Yes."

"So, when are you coming back?" she said. *Baaack, baaack, baaack,* went the echo.

"Well, I've sort of committed to something here. . . ."

"Committed to something? What are you talking about? What's there to commit to, the ultimate tan?" Val laughed her horsey chortle.

"Actually, I'm going to be singing." I winced, saying it.

Silence.

"Just a little gig in the local taverna. I've got an accompanist and everything. Something to do, you know? Things actually get a little boring here on Corfu."

"For God's sake, Claire! You're a wife and mother! Just because Gary chose to have a midlife crisis doesn't mean you have to."

"Val, I think that's really unfair. What's the harm in it? I like singing. I had to stop a promising career *because* I became a wife. Why not pick it up again now that the kids are grown?"

"I don't mean to be harsh, but don't you think that's a little unrealistic?"

"Actually, no. People here happen to think I'm reasonably good," I said.

Val sniffed out my duplicity like a dog after a meaty bone.

"People? What people?"

"Oh, nobody. Just some people who heard me sing."

"Claire, are you having"—Val dropped her voice to a whisper—*"an affair?"*

"No," I whispered back. "I'm not having an affair. Oh, except for that big Swedish babe. Oh, and that hunky Italian rock star. And the Ghanaian writer's not bad either."

"I'm serious, Claire. Don't make your situation worse than it already is. Shagging a bunch of young boys isn't going to solve anything."

Acid laughter burst out of me. "How could it be worse than it already is, Val? My husband cheated on me, ruined our marriage, embarrassed me in front of all our friends! He's also estranged from my son, whom I love very much. I'm having doubts about whether I want to recommit to Gary. I've made friends here, real friends. People who don't laugh when I say I'm a singer. Do you know how long it's been since I had a friend who wasn't married to one of Gary's mates? Except for you and Laurie, who I never see anymore anyway since she got remarried to that professor, I haven't had my own circle in I don't know how long."

"Well, I'm sorry my friendship means so little to you," my sister said tightly.

I sighed. "It's not that, Val. What I'm trying to tell you is, I'm not ready to come back. There are things I have to do here, and Gary and everyone else will just have to accept that. Friends?"

Val sniffled. I could hear the smile in her voice when she answered.

"So tell me, do those flying-doughnut thingies really look like giant dongers?"

"What do you think?" I asked Andreas.

He nodded, contemplating. "Let's do one more time."

We were literally on top of the village. Anxious to get away from the distractions of town, we'd traversed the whitewashed paths upward, higher than I'd ever gone before, until we came to a nest of unfinished villas on top of a small mountain. Concrete had been laid already, flat and pale gray, forming a sort of dais where Andreas and I stood like an offering to the gods. Singing, with Andreas joining me on lute and acoustic guitar, I felt as if we were being lifted toward the sky. We were so high, even the birds' voices had thinned.

I belted out the song we were working on, trying to settle into the right balance of fervency and cool objectivity. We struggled a couple of times, but it sounded good. I could tell. More importantly, it felt right, me gripping the battery-operated toy microphone we'd borrowed from Nia Alexiou at the travel agency, my voice becoming less thready and deepening into juicy ripeness with each passing day, Andreas weaving lovely melodies in and out of the lyrics. Drenched in sweat, breathless from the high pale air, Andreas's proximity, and my own daring, I'd forgotten to be nervous.

I finished with a flourish, and for a second we simply stood there. My heart thumped like a metronome. Heat raced to my toes and back. I felt my eyelashes flutter damply against my cheeks, as if I was awaiting a kiss from a lover. Something dark and wild had risen in Andreas's usually cool eyes. The current between us seemed to snap, like a dormant electrical wire that had suddenly been doused with water.

"Claire . . ." he said hoarsely.

Then, quite suddenly, I panicked. I gripped the mike harder and started chattering. "Thanks for coming tonight, mates. It's been a great show, and we appreciate your overlooking that broken high C. . . . On the lute and guitar tonight, Andreas Leontarakis. Give him a hand, people! Thank you!" I mimed applause, aiming for levity.

Ignoring me, Andreas came closer, until he was near enough to sway my hair with his breath. Gently, he placed his hand on mine and uncurled my fingers from around the microphone. A late-afternoon breeze swirled around us. The tart odor of stubborn mountain flowers wafted over. I felt as if everything was beyond bright, saturated with color, smell, texture. The fear miraculously lifted and scudded off, light as strata clouds. I was ready to jump into the abyss. The smallest caress would tip me over the edge, arms pinwheeling.

But Andreas just put the microphone back in its Day-Glo box.

"How about something to drink?" he said, smiling at me with the patience of a sated tiger who could take or leave tonight's supper.

chapter 23

KELAH

We were in, of all places, America—Florida, actually—when Mum read my work for the first time. I was fifteen, Charlie was at uni, and Davey was hanging on to public school by a thread, Mum and Dad having bribed the place with a modest scholarship fund for attention-deficit-afflicted boys. I hated Florida with a passion usually reserved for math and football wankers. I hadn't wanted to go on the dreaded family holiday, but Dad had a conference in Miami and we were forced to go or forever endure Mum's wrath. It was like Mum needed a mental snapshot of the perfect family to keep her going through the years' endless rounds of launch parties, conferences, and awards ceremonies. As long as she could call to mind the five of us, tanned and gleaming, around a hotel dining table or on a speedboat, she could forget Davey's troubles, my unpopularity, Dad's workaholism, her own teeth-clenching ambition.

Florida was everything I wasn't: cute, sunny, frivolous, happy. That year, I was wearing my hair in fuzzy, poorly tended, shoulder-length dreadlocks. I listened to Primal Scream and My Bloody

Valentine, Walkman glued to my much-pierced ears most waking hours, and parted company with my favorite T-shirt—a yellowing affair with an anvil and a Nike symbol on the front that said STRIKE: JUST DO IT—only with great reluctance. What's worse, instead of having my brothers on my side in angry rebellion, Charlie and Davey thought Miami was brilliant. For once, they got along like proper brothers, taking windsurfing lessons, playing American football at the beach, flirting with Cuban girls who spoke to them in Spanish. Mum was either on the phone with authors and agents or sitting in a lawn chair at the hotel pool, holding a frothy drink with a tiny magenta umbrella in it. Dad was giving and attending lectures. I was alone and miserable.

My daily journal was filled primarily with juicy descriptions of all the familial wrongs perpetrated against me: bathing-suit shopping, hotel buffets larded with hormone-laden beef, sharing a pigsty suite with my brothers, wasting my time among silly, sunburned Americans. Each day, I'd set up a miniature encampment under the most distant umbrella at the pool: pens, notebook, cassette tapes, and attitude. I'd charge a few unexciting beverages to our room and hunker down in my army-surplus trousers and jumper, looking like a freak next to the tanned, naked flesh surrounding me. Then I'd scribble madly, channeling all my loneliness and self-consciousness into essays, short stories, and diatribes against the catastrophic unfairness of life.

Around five or six P.M., mindful of Dad's warnings about scurvy, I'd wolf down a couple of oranges or mangoes—the tropical fruit was Florida's only good point, as far as I could see—and go for a furtive walk along the boardwalk. The characters I'd spun were alive in my head, so real, I'd forget where I was and wander into indignant Rollerbladers and scantily dressed joggers.

I don't know what possessed me to give Mum some short stories. I mean, sure, I'd shown them stuff before, but not since I was in primary school, too young to know better. I guess in spite of my raging teenage unhappiness, I still had a child's fearlessness and incessant optimism. I hadn't had time enough to fail, so I still clung to my future with romanticism and longing.

One night, when Mum and Dad were out, I ripped fifty-three carefully handwritten pages from my binder, slid them into an envelope embossed with the Hilton's gold-leaf letterhead, and wrote Mum's name on it. I slipped through the connecting door to their room and laid it almost reverently on her pillow, as if it was a bomb that might go off if handled too roughly.

The next morning, I waited for her to say something, to tell me her verdict: Was I going to be a respectable mid-list author, or achieve true brilliance? But we went through our holiday motions without a twitch: spearing chunks of pineapple on rainbow-tipped toothpicks at breakfast, a round of lawn bowling after lunch, mindless television in our room before dinner.

Finally, I snapped.

I knocked on their door and let myself in. Mum was reading a manuscript on the terrace, a red pen between her long fingers. Her glasses had slid down her narrow nose and she had sequined flip-flops on her manicured feet.

"Mum, did you read what I left for you?"

"What's that, love? Oh, your stories. Yes, I did. Most of it. I've still got a bit left."

"Well, what did you think of it?" I said doggedly.

"Do you really want to talk about your future this very minute?"

"If that's what you want to call it."

Mum gazed at me with something like sympathy. "Kelah, I think your stories are very creative. They have a certain . . . energy that is not unusual in a young writer."

She seemed about to say something else but stopped.

"What?"

"Nothing important. It's just . . ."

"*What?*"

She put down the manuscript and looked me full in the face. "How badly do you want to write, Kelah?"

"Badly." Was that a trick question?

"Well, then, you need to be able to take constructive criticism. You must possess a level of emotional maturity that lets you be objective about your own work. Talent . . . well, talent is a small part of it. Hard work, discipline, patience, and the ability to resist self-indulgence—these make up the lion's share of the writer's toolbox."

I felt salty tears flood my eyes. "I don't care about any of that, Mum! I just want to know if I'm any good. Obviously, I'm bloody awful, or you wouldn't be giving me a speech about the sterling qualities I clearly don't . . . don't"—I struggled to come up with something powerful and writerly—"have!" I finished lamely. Shit.

Mum was impatient. "Kelah, don't be paranoid. I'm just trying to impress upon you that what you see in films and in journals is not the reality. Writing is a painful and competitive life. People go mad doing it, and nothing's ever enough to keep the wolves of rampant insecurity at bay. Believe me, I've seen it time and time again, even from my most talented authors. It's not a career I would choose for any of my children unless they were very, very committed."

What lies! There was nothing that would please Mum more than her own daughter writing a brilliant novel. If anything, she was more tribal, more clannish, than Dad, who had distanced himself from his Jamaican family with the focus of someone who didn't have time for messes or less-than-stellar familial memories. I'd seen it in her face when Charlie inevitably won some athletic or academic prize, the shining, almost manic glow when the recipient up on the dais was *hers*. Staring at her sharply drawn, aristocratic face, I realized: Mum just didn't think I was good enough. Sobs burst from me with startling ferocity, as if every minute I'd spent not crying prior had been a farce.

"You think it's shit, don't you?" I cried, ignoring the neighboring guests, who wisely picked up their drinks and slid their balcony door shut with a swooshing thunk. "You just don't think I can do it. Answer me, Mum! I want to know!"

"Of course I don't think it's shit, as you so delicately put it. I think you have talent. But raw talent's not enough to ensure success, and I just don't want to see you get hurt. You should know what you're getting into. Besides, I'm only one person, and postmodern, avant-garde literature is hardly my area of expertise. I don't know everything," she said.

"Mum, you're a fucking editor!"

"Kelah Christine." Each word dripped caution.

I flung my notebook across the terrace. It hit the ice bucket with a satisfying crash, sending champagne and ice cubes showering over the tabletop. My hands trembled. In spite of the hot flush scorching my cheeks, chest, and arms, I felt as if the temperature had just dropped twenty degrees. Beads of sweat chilled on my skin, left me pallid.

Mum crossed her silk-clad arms. "Okay, Kelah. You want the truth? This"—she strode across the terrace and grabbed the crumpled notebook—"is what I'd expect from a talented aspiring writer. You have potential, and your characterizations are compelling. Your stories are original and your voice is powerful. Plotting is a bit fractured, which doesn't matter that much in short fiction, I suppose. One aspect of your work you'll have to overcome is an overdone, self-conscious, flowery prose style, but that's something that comes with maturity and experience. Frankly, your biggest challenge is going to be your attitude. When you harangue people the way you do, you can't expect them to lend their assistance freely. When you make every little critique so personal, well, perhaps it becomes so. It certainly makes others uncomfortable." She placed the notebook on the table and smoothed out its tattered corners. "I don't understand what you're so angry about, Kelah. Your characters . . . they're some of the most unhappy people I've ever met."

For a second, her caramel voice faltered, and the pity almost undid me. Then her blue eyes got steely again and she handed me back my notebook.

"You're a smart girl, Kelah. Your father and I have always known that. But writing requires dedication and, more importantly, self-awareness, and only time will tell if you develop either."

———

Got a letter from Fee today.

Kay, Shmay,

It's absolutely horrid here. No hols, no calamari, no ouzo, no gorgeous men. I can't believe you're still there, and we're stuck in this pit. I have interviewed for a job at Maximum magazine as a "researcher," which I'm told means filing, answering the phone, pouring coffee for the editors, and avoiding getting your bum pinched by dodgy contributors like Nigel Webb and Arthur Fitzsimmon. I'll let you know what happens (i.e., send you photos of said black-and-purple bum). Boz is copyediting texts for Marta San Giacomo in the Comp. Lit. department. I went over there to get him out of the dungeon for a pint and he looked the very image of the living dead. He was wearing that tatty jumper that makes his skin look green and has been surviving solely on a diet of Cadbury milks and Irn-Bru. We went to my mum's and she gave him one of her shepherd's pies to take home. However, incipient malnutrition has not prevented him from finally getting laid: Marta apparently took pity on him and set him up with her twin sister, a postdoc doing a dissertation on Kierkegaard's existentialist arsehole, or some such shite. As far as I know, they've gone out three times. Don't know if he's shagged her yet. I find the twin thing a bit creepy—wouldn't it be a bit like having it off with your boss?—but then, our Boz has never been known for his judgment in love. If I didn't know better, I'd say he's acting like someone broke his heart, moping around and listening to "Maggie May" over and over, but there's been nobody, so???? In any case, I look forward to your return, dear Kay. When you get back, I'll get you a job at Maximum Misogyny, so you, too, can feel the precious pinch of literary fingers on your bum. Maybe something will rub off?

Love,
Fee

I rubbed the flimsy airmail sheets between my fingers. I was glad I hadn't told Fee about what happened between Boz and me. At the time, I'd felt it—the urge to dangle the secret like a ripe plum. To say it out loud so it wouldn't loom so large in my mind. But some small warning voice cautioned against it. The delicate balance we had—three friends, three tempers, three egos, currently intact—it seemed heartless and unwise to bugger it. Still, it was weird; it had been a long time since I'd kept a secret from Fiona. But *Marta's twin*! How could he? Marta was young for a professor, but still at least six years older than Boz. She cultivated a sort of bohemian chic—sheer peasant blouses, batik skirts, slouchy ballet-style leg warmers, goat-hide-ish clogs, crocheted caps that hugged her glossy dark wavy hair. Her stained, shaking fingers always held a cigarillo, and her father was an Italian nobleman slash criminal person, which added to her mystique. She was brilliant. Assuming her twin had even half Marta's looks and brains, she'd be a formidable woman.

Suddenly, I hated her.

Was I one of those women who won't have a man but begrudges him everyone else too?

I was so distracted by my self-disgust that I wrote not a word more on my novel during the next ninety minutes. Finally, I gave up and did a journal entry. I was pretty sure Claire was shagging that Greek ukulele player, but she hadn't said anything to us, so I merely speculated.

chapter 24

ANYA

He traced a finger along my shoulder. The touch was feather-light; the hairs on my arm sprang up. I knew if I looked at him I'd go crazy, so I stared ahead like a damn zombie. My eyes focused on the third shelf of canned goods in the pantry: pinto beans, hominy, canned guavas, yucky *nopalitos*, serrano chili peppers, a cord of shriveled garlic, and Juanita's menudo, which *Mami* used to stretch her own leftovers when there wasn't enough. (I knew that was a secret we couldn't tell nonfamily, even though *Mami* never said anything.)

I could hear people talking in the other room, soft murmurs mixed with tinkling china. Everyone loved my *abuelo*, Grandpa Arturo. Everyone said it was good he wasn't in pain anymore. I'd learned that sometimes people say nice things to make themselves feel better, not just you. When they say them, you have to smile as if the pain is a little less. That's the way it works.

He leaned in closer. Something in his breath, the hard rhythm of it, gave me a queer feeling in my stomach, as if I had just walked too close to the edge of the freeway overpass. His lips kissed the air next to my ear. I was wearing new earrings. Cubic zirconia studs on a 14-karat gold post. *Tiá* Maria-Theresa gave them to me on Tuesday, when Grandpa died.

The hem of my skirt brushed against his legs. I could feel heat coming off them under the black pants. I had a vague memory of a scar on one of those brown knees, but it had been so long since I'd seen them, I couldn't be sure. It might have been his brother Manuel. Without thinking, I shifted my weight from left to right. Then we were together.

"Anyita," he whispered.

In front of me, the neat rows of red, white, and green cans blurred, a desert mirage instigated by a terrible thirst.

"Anya! Anya, wake up."

I sat up. My heart beat against my chest with birdlike velocity. I felt damp all over. Ethan traced his finger along my shoulder. I shuddered.

"You were having a nightmare," he said.

"I know."

It had been years since I'd had this one. Already, it was slipping away, leaving the still-familiar residue of guilt and damp lust. Why now? Like destiny, memory is a trickster. She likes to mess with you when you're living large, remind you that you're still the small, weak schoolgirl you always were.

"I'm sorry," I said.

"Why?"

His Australian accent was strong and naked this morning. Ethan thinks my Mexican-accented English, which I can turn on and off at will, is sexy. Sometimes I turn it on for him, do the Latina thing. With some ex-boyfriends, I had been so vigilant about passing, you could have cut glass on my *R*s. With Ethan, who says it reminds him of Elizabeth Peña in *La Bamba,* I find my conversation sprinkled with Spanish, from love words to the best barrio curses.

"For scaring you?" I finally said.

"I wasn't scared. Just for you, I guess. What were you dreaming about?" His amber eyes were sleepy.

"Something that may or may not have happened a long time ago," I said. It was inside me, burning a hole in my belly. Well, it would have to burn a little longer. "I mean, I knew this guy once, and he made me uncomfortable, that's all. I was actually dreaming about my grandfather's wake," I said, not untruthfully.

"That guy who made you uncomfortable"—Ethan turned on his side to look at me—"did he hurt you?"

"No, nothing like that. Look, can we not talk about this right now? I'm kind of tired," I evaded.

He rolled on top of me, smiling. I let his weight quell memories of the girl I used to be.

"Anyita, that's what you called out in your sleep," he said.

"Anya, can you mind the shop for a few hours? I have to bring Spiros to the doctor."

"No problem."

Nia thanked me and gathered up her purse and gigantic baby bag.

"If those English come back and want to change their departure date, do you know how to do that?"

I glanced at the notes I'd taken. "I think so."

"Good enough. *Yasu.*"

"*Adiós.*"

I always liked late mornings at the agency, before the tourists rose and after the locals had come in to buy stamps or post letters. I could read, write letters, use the Internet. Sometimes Ethan would stop by and bring me coffee, before he and Brian headed off somewhere on their motorcycles.

Nia kept a small newsstand in the front, filled with Greek newspapers, day-old *International Herald Tribune*s, and moldering European gossip magazines in a dozen languages with Juliette Binoche and Prince William on the front. I picked out a British magazine called *Flounce* and started paging through it.

I'd gotten through pieces on Muslim feminists, celebrity teeth, and a mysterious concept called "traffic-stopping trousers," when I saw it, a column called "On Holiday," and under it, a headline: *Shipwrecked on Corfu! Meet four women who've turned their lives around by telling their men to sod off and seeking sexual freedom on this beautiful Greek island! By Kelah Morris.*

I was so surprised I dropped the magazine. It took me a few seconds to find the page again. I called Claire, the only SNiP whose villa had a phone.

"Better get over here," I said, scanning the page madly. By the third paragraph, the author was positing whether "P." would lose her postmarital virginity to "J.L."

"Oh, and better pick up Parker. She'll want to see this!"

chapter 25

PARKER

Just when things were starting to look like a normal vacation, replete with lazy, uneventful, sunny days that merged into one another with a sort of sublime indifference to time and place, this had to happen. Infamy. Semianonymous infamy, but infamy nonetheless. I could imagine Kelah's defense now: *Well, the names were changed to protect the, um, guilty, so I thought you'd be okay with it.*

Yeah, whatever.

In a frenzy, we'd hunted down the four back issues of the weekly magazine that contained the column. (*Flounce?* What were they thinking?) We'd had to make a special trip to Corfutown to do so. The whole time, I'd half expected a total stranger—the bus driver or the cashier, the drunken rugby team from New Zealand or the honeymooning Canadian couple—to lean over, smile slyly, and say, *Well, if it isn't C., P., and A.! You're P., right? Did you ever get busy with that J.L.? Come on, you can tell me!*

I read the final paragraph and sighed.

"I can't fucking believe this! I thought Kelah was one of us," I muttered.

"Well, you have to admit, that part about you getting blotto and waking up on the beach was kind of funny. Well written too. And evocative. It quite captured the essence of public intoxication, especially the part about the grains of sand in the cheeks. Didn't clarify what set of cheeks, though." Claire frowned.

"Not as funny as the part where you grabbed Sven's ass on the water banana," Anya said.

"It's not a banana. It's a doughnut," Claire corrected her.

"More like an éclair," mused Anya.

"I suppose you're right," Claire said.

"Will you guys please focus! Am I the only one who's a little concerned about all these details of our private lives being out there for the world to see? I mean, someone we know could get hold of this, and we'd be up shit creek! We come off sounding like sex-crazed maniacs. What if . . . what if I wanted to run for president or something?" Okay, that was a stretch. "I might as well take out a full-page ad in *The New York Times*: *Parker Glass became an inebriated misanthrope after her husband left her. Find out more, Thursdays at 8 P.M.!* Plus, there's something unethical about her studying us like that. I think it's weird," I said, trying to remember if Kelah was around when I went home with Supertongue.

Anya looked over my shoulder. "I like the way she describes Ethan—excuse me, E.D.!" She read from the July issue, mimicking Kelah's English accent: *"E.D. is a sinfully well-built Aussie with the type of shoulders you can only achieve through brutal physical labor during those long, hot summers Down Under. Or through the presumably harsh natural selection that takes place in a remote former penal colony"*—bit of a dig at Australia, there—*"plus, he's got a softer side and is that rarity among Generation X men—he really likes women! I think A. should go for it. I mean, look at the mother-in-law she'd get!"*

Claire and Anya nearly pissed themselves laughing. For God's sake, they were acting like sisters, not in-laws! Of course, their accounts were perversely flattering, in a way, what with Anya depicted as the Latina social progressive with a heart of gold, valiantly escaping clinical depression and a dreary life in San Francisco and finding true love in the Greek isles, and Claire, as Kelah's editor had put it, *telling her man to sod off* and relaunching her singing career with a half-naked, half-her-age lutist at her side along with a respectable Nordic admirer contingent. I, on the other hand, emerged as a hopeless neurotic with good color sense, bad taste in dogs, and a drinking problem. I mean, drug problem. Well, both.

"I think we should confront her," I said.

"Kelah?"

"Well, of course Kelah! Who else got us into this mess? It's not like we can assume this'll remain a secret. There are a lot of tourists here, and, besides, the Greeks are bound to discover the column too. They'll be excited that it's all about Corfu. Probably have her do play-by-play readings at Tony's. Sort of like a live *Sex and the City*," I said.

"What's *Sex and the City*?" asked Claire.

"Nothing. Tell you later." Anya waved her hand.

"I'm quite interested in what Ms. Morris has to say for herself. I'm calling a SNiPs meeting. Seventeen hundred hours at Tony's. Don't be late," I warned, which, predictably, caused my friends to laugh. Again.

Tony's was its usual charming, wilted self that evening. Its proprietor, who had apparently forgotten the dire state of his finances, was dispensing free drinks to a couple of girls who would not look out of place on a St. Pauli Girl six-pack. His ragged collection of waiters and busboys smoked on the terrace in full view of the customers—all three of them, not counting us—occasionally leaping up to execute a substandard hip-hop move. The crackly stereo was playing Abba's greatest hits. Claire and I had tried to influence Tony on this point, introducing him to concepts like ambience and twenty-first-century music, but he professed an unshakable belief in the eternal superiority of Swedish pop and '80s boy bands with predilections for fluffy blouses and false eyelashes.

"Tony, a round of the strongest stuff you've got and four shot glasses, please. And a beer chaser," I said.

"You plan to sleep on the beach again?"

"Booze," I said menacingly. He shrugged and left.

Anya and Claire joined me a minute later.

Then Kelah came in. She had on her usual uniform of baggy cargo pants and a tight tank, a strip of tan belly with a piercing peeking out. Her hair was gathered into four springy bundles. I wanted to tell her it was cute, but that seemed inconsistent with being the picture of indignant rage, so I stayed silent.

"Hi, kids. How goes?"

Claire and Anya widened their eyes at me. Apparently, I was expected to lead. So be it.

"Kelah, can you explain this?" I said imperiously. I laid the magazine down, folded along the crease so that her byline, and the sensationalist sludge that passed for a headline, could be seen in stark, magenta relief.

We watched her almond eyes narrow and then widen in shock. She grabbed the glossy and scanned the page, her mouth forming a little frozen moue of dismay.

"Well?" I prompted.

"No, I absolutely cannot bloody explain this," she said, "but I know someone who can."

"So you see? If we open up this wall and build a window here, foot traffic will be able to see people eating inside, instead of the back of the wall they see now. And they'll want to come in."

Tony nodded and I measured the dimensions of the glass I wanted to put in the taverna wall. We'd talked about the cosmetic stuff, the curtains, paint, seating arrangement, colors, greenery, and such, and had moved on to larger-scale changes I wanted to make.

"One of my brothers, he do construction. He can do the work for cheap. He owes me one for telling his wife he work here when he is really betting on poker," said Tony.

Was there no end to human beings' duplicity?

"Great!" I said cheerfully. "Now, let me tell you what we can do with these columns. . . ."

Two hours later, we'd agreed to a first phase of work that would open the place up, bring in more light, update the style, and improve the acoustics. Tony would pay for materials and construction; I would get free food and drinks and a moratorium on smart remarks about my sex life for the duration of my stay in exchange for my services.

"Bye, Tony. See you tomorrow." I was looking forward to ripping down those raggedy curtains. It was a little sensitive, since they'd been a gift from the mother of Nia Alexiou who ran the travel agency, who was the sister of Nick Somethingopolous, who was married to Patricia, Claire's American acquaintance, who ran the Dallas and had let Swedish Sven see her etchings. I'd learned weeks ago that the relationships of Pelekastritsa were intertwined beyond simple social incestuousness and required considerable concentration to navigate safely.

I retrieved Blakas from a sunny corner of the terrace and tucked him into the basket at the back of my scooter. I loved riding with him that way; Claire's son Brian had said we looked like cartoon characters from *Yellow Submarine,* which seemed weirdly right.

We putted along for about twenty minutes, through the small inland towns of Kinopiastes and Skripero. The breeze was sweet and gentle against my face and I thought suddenly how much Neil would like the empty, undulating hills, with just enough goats, lambs, stout old women, and whitewashed stone cabins to prevent monotony. Before I could even consummate the thought, the other realization seeped in—that I no longer had the privilege of wondering what Neil would think of anything. That happened a lot lately. My mind shifting with the speed of a butterfly, from the complacent mind-set of how things used to be to the prescience of pain and loss.

I turned off on a gravel road and tried not to fishtail for about ten minutes. The sun was clinging to the edge of afternoon when I got there—my ruins. Anya had told me about this place after Ethan brought her here. It was sort of off the beaten path, so I was rarely interrupted by tourists. Somehow, sitting in the middle of the mausoleumlike chamber, with its shaded, slightly damp, thick-walled silence, I was able to picture the exact changes I would make to Tony's Taverna. The dimensions of the rooms would rotate in my mind and I'd play with them, conjuring a leaf motif or a row of sconces.

I stopped, and Blakas jumped out of the basket and ran around happily, chasing bugs and urinating on everything in sight. I went inside and kneeled for a second on the cool earth. It felt sort of silly, but here I always felt the need to commune with the gods, great spirit, the Church of Kate Spade Disciples, whatever you want to call it. I figured it couldn't hurt to cover all my bases, now that I seemed to have hit rock bottom and was slowly inching my way up out of the pit. Since I had long ago lost touch with my own gods and was fresh out of proper liturgical vernacular, I drew upon my only recent spiritual touchstone: yoga.

"Namasté," I said quickly and stood up, brushing off my knees.

Suddenly, the already dim chamber darkened further.

"Ma'am, please step away from the dirt pile and stow your weapons."

Josh Lido stood in the doorway, silhouetted against the almost painfully blue rectangle of sky.

He came closer. In the dim light of the square hole in the wall, he could almost pass for handsome. I felt heat creep up my neck.

"Why have you been avoiding me, Park?"

"I'm not avoiding you."

"So when you see me coming down the street and do an about-face that almost causes you to run into a wall, that's just coincidence?" His voice was gentle.

"Yep." I busied myself packing up my notebooks. "Come on, Blakas."

"See, you're doing it again."

"Don't flatter yourself, Lido. I just need to be alone to work, and with you here, that makes three, counting Blakas and myself, and, as they say back home in the real world, *three's a crowd.*"

I tried to squeeze by him but he stayed put, solid as a kumquat tree. I felt my eyes rising to meet his. I swear he employs some sort of evil alchemy that makes me unable to tear my eyes away from his large, thickly lashed, brown ones. Bastard.

"It's because of that little kiss, isn't it?" he said.

Little? Ditto on the bastard. Times one hundred.

"Perhaps you have me confused with one of your junior-high friends," I said, aiming for haughty.

"Oh, come on, she could have passed for at least sixteen."

"I'm sure whatever you're doing with her is legal. In Sweden. Now, get out of my way so I can get some work done!" Blakas, that traitor, was wiggling madly in Josh's hands. Like mistress, like bitch, I suppose.

"Parker, listen to me. What happened is my fault. I shouldn't have let you think I was available. I shouldn't have flirted with you shamelessly all these weeks. And I shouldn't have taken advantage of your vulnerability when you're obviously on the rebound," he announced. The word *rebound* seemed to reverberate off the clay walls.

Quite frankly, I was stunned speechless. Somehow, his apology, his acknowledgment of his role in the proceedings, took the wind out of my rage-filled sails.

"It was shameless," I muttered grudgingly.

"What?"

"I said, what a shame you aren't less conceited." I overenunciated.

His mouth turned up at the corners, and those chocolate eyes bathed me in warmth. Literally. Like a bath.

"Does this mean I'm forgiven?" Josh said.

Too easy. "Has anyone ever told you you have absolutely no way with women?" I said sternly, still mining my hurt.

"Frequently."

"Well, maybe you should see a therapist for that."

"Believe me, I've spent so much time on the couch it's a wonder I'm not working for Levitz."

I could tell he was serious. His honesty further disarmed me.

"Well, that's good," I continued. "'Cause you're, like, a menace."

"Yep."

"You can't mess with people's minds like that."

"I know."

"I have enough to deal with without plumbing the depths of your maladjusted psyche on a daily basis."

"Of course you do."

"Well, okay, then. I guess we can call a truce," I said.

"So I'm forgiven?" he asked again. This time I nodded.

He came closer and touched my shoulder lightly. I tried not to wince with pleasure.

"I'm glad, Park, because you're one of the most interesting people here, and I think we could be friends." He waved his hand in the air. "Don't worry—not pseudo-platonic, me-always-trying-to-get-in-your-pants and you-getting-drunk-and-trying-to-kiss-me-because-your-loser-boy-toy-passed-out friends. The real thing. Like Laverne and Shirley—"

"Or Laurel and Hardy—"

"Or Batman and Robin."

"Billy Bob and Angelina?" I suggested.

"No way! They were married and broke up and hate each other's guts. What a tool. She's so hot."

"Of course you would think she's hot."

He snorted. "Don't you?"

"Well, yeah, but it's kind of tacky to say it like that after you've just admitted you took advantage of me with all your sexual innuendo and . . . horndogness."

"Horndogness? Oh, my. I'm terribly sorry if I engaged in any licentious . . . Horn. Dog. Ness."

I blushed.

He let me off the hook.

"Come 'ere, Blakas. Come on, boy. Yeah, that's a good boy. See Mommy? Isn't she cute when she's angry, boy?"

I watched Josh Lido's talented hands stroke my ugly dog and wondered what exactly had made him so "not available."

chapter 26

CLAIRE

Counseling your offspring on matters of a sexual nature is one of the more trying aspects of motherhood, I'd say. Sure, I'm okay on condom dispensing and looking the other way when my boys stagger home at dawn with goofy grins and other people's shirts on, but actual advice is a different thing altogether.

"What do you think I should do, Mum?" Brian said.

He had confided that his latest lover, Vincenzo, a visiting social-geography professor, had confessed to having a wife and children back home in Florence.

"Do you want the sounds-good-on-paper-and-makes-you-feel-better answer or the probably-correct-but-harsh-as-lye answer?"

"Harsh as lye."

"If you see this man again, run screaming in the other direction, delete him from your speed dial, curse his name to everlasting hell, blot him out in your address book, avoid everywhere you went together, and, the next time he calls, hang up and unplug the phone," I said.

Brian was quiet. "Lye? Are you sure? 'Cause it was more like, dunno, battery acid?"

I stroked his worried brow. "Bri, if he lies to his wife, he'll lie to you. Already is, in fact. You're better off without him. I say that with one hundred percent utter assurance. He doesn't know your worth."

"All my relationships end," he said flatly.

". . . so you'll be free to meet the right one."

"Or free to make a complete ass of myself again." He withdrew his hand, glancing at me apologetically. "People think queers are just about fucking everything that moves. Slithers, I should say. But, Mum, I don't know if I can stand the dating scene anymore! It's really horrible. I just want to meet a decent guy, someone halfway attractive, out of the closet, no wives or kids creeping around underfoot, not afraid of work himself, able to cope with a totally neurotic sporadically employed actor, and who knows the Kama Sutra like the bloody Bible. Is that too much to ask?" He smiled ruefully.

"Not at all. And if he knows the Kama Sutra like the bloody Bible, ask him if his father's single," I said.

"What about this one?" I asked.

"Too matronly," said Anya.

"Not sexy enough," added Kelah.

"Guaranteed to kill any living male's sperm dead in the water," Parker shot back.

"Is grotesque too strong?" said Brian.

"Christ! The show's in one hour. I can't do it! That's it—I'm not going on. It'll have to be canceled. Tell Andreas and Tony I'm sick. I think I am going to be sick anyway." I felt my throat close as if I had gulped bad-tasting medicine.

I was in the midst of a full-blown clothes crisis. I'd thought I was too old for such a thing, that it was the province of schoolgirls and recent university graduates prior to their first day at work. Wrong—it's the province of anyone who ever wanted to look like

a drop-dead gorgeous she-devil for one night and sing profession-
ally for the first time in two decades.

"Look, Mum. You've got to forget about these fussy styles.
They're just not you. You need to pare down, keep it simple. A
certain ridiculously well-known costume designer with excellent
taste in clothes and men who shall remain *nameless*"—chorus of
shouts begging for more information, which he soundly waved
down—"anyway, he once told me, play up your best two features
and hide the rest and you're golden. It always works."

"But what are my best features? I'm just an old Aussie housewife with stretch marks and, God help me, an extra stone or two,"
I cried.

"Boobs. Definitely boobs," said Parker.

Anya nodded. "And eyes."

"What about hair? You've got the greatest long red hair, Claire. I
vote for that." Kelah was resolute.

"Okay, she's my mum, so I don't want to be too outrageous, but
I'd have to agree with the girls: tits, eyes, and hair," Brian said.

"But that's three."

He shook his head. "Doesn't matter. It's the principle of the
thing." Brian rummaged through the pile of donated garments
and SNiP-member clothes on the bed, casting most aside and
laying a few select pieces on a small pile.

He handed them to me one at a time, explaining their various
virtues and downsides. "Try these on, Mum, and we'll see who's
the siren tonight at Tony's."

The bottle of wine on the chopping block was taunting me. I
waited till the waiters had left and the cook—Tony's sullen older
sister—had turned her broad back to me, and I slugged a glassful
directly from the bottle. A rivulet trickled down my chin and I
wiped it off. I was sure my lipstick was smeared and my eyes were
glassy with fright. Just the type of look to ensure a welcoming reception from a discriminating crowd of world travelers out for an
evening involving live music.

"You look beauty."

Andreas stood there, smiling at me. His teeth were very white in his tan face, eyes a pure hazel with a golden feline ring around the center. In my heels, our height was a match.

"Beautiful," I corrected.

"That also."

I smiled back fleetingly and tapped my foot on the floor. I knew he was making silly English mistakes to take my mind off my performance anxiety. Out there, in the main room, everyone I knew on Corfu and quite a few others were assembled, ready to witness my complete humiliation at the hands of a microphone and a wicked strings player who just might be congenitally deaf.

Andreas closed his hand over mine. His was warm and rough with calluses.

"Just sing to them like you sing to me, and they will be loving you. They'll love you like . . . like . . . cool water on a hot day! Like the dream woman they saw once in another city and they follow her but she turns a corner and is gone. Like those little chocolates from Belgium that are seashells . . ."

His lips brushed against my hand. Then they were on my mouth, and he was kissing me with the lazy assurance of a bee plunging itself into a nectar-filled flower. It felt so natural, I didn't bother to resist. His arm banded around my waist so I could feel his restless tiger's energy reverberating up between us. He kissed me one, two, three times before I lost count. I was drowning. Confused. How could I be floating and slipping under the water at the same time? How could one set of lips be so different from another? Was I a terrible person? Why was he stopping?

Andreas pulled back, held out his hand.

"Come on. It's time," he said.

I stared into the familiar face in the mirror. Flushed cheeks. Fine lines fanning out from wide, shining amber eyes. Strong brows arched in buoyant surprise. Hair a battle between brunette and red, auburn the winner. Silkier than usual from the moist heat. Smile threatening to explode. Euphoric fragments.

It had gone far, far better than I'd even hoped.

As soon as I got to the microphone, thanked the crowd for being there, introduced myself, everything came back to me in a glad rush. I've heard of—experienced—nights where things go wrong, and you slowly, inexorably, earn back the audience's trust with a well-practiced set. I've also had nights where everything that *can* go wrong *does* go wrong. And those uninspired evenings when you nail all the technicalities but lack that intangible something that moves the listeners to the edge of their chairs, then up into the air, tapping in time to the wild staccato rhythm the music and song bring to their hearts.

This night was nothing like any of those. It was one of those rare, cherished evenings where a calm sense of purpose, of mastery, settles over your shoulders like a velvet cloak. My slinky burnished-brown wrap dress skimmed over curves without bunching or clinging. I could feel it whispering against my bare legs, my calves tensing in sinfully high heels. Andreas and I had planned a set of lounge-y covers and original songs, and I played the femme fatale role to the hilt. Parker had slicked my usually unruly hair into a sleek Veronica Lake wave that fell over my eye when I dug into a chorus. My makeup was subdued but sultry, all glossy burgundy lips and smoky eyes. A light perfume. No powder. Why bother, when my face and body would dampen within minutes?

For an hour, I forgot about Gary, the massage therapist, Valerie, the boys, Andreas—forgot everything except the throaty timbre of the words in my mouth and the deep, dark current running between me and the crowd. I focused on a few, the way they teach you to—a pudgy boy with little interest in his beer, a kittenish young woman in a stringy top, my American friend Patricia, whose (forgiving) dress I was wearing tonight. And when Andreas and I finished the last of our encores, and the room slowly swam back into focus, the sound of glad applause ringing out against the taverna's heat-moistened walls, I laughed out loud at the feeling of it all. My body was so weightless, I could have drifted out the window toward the stars, purposeless as a breeze-borne dandelion.

"Come to bed." Andreas slid his arms around my waist. Together, we watched the stars wink out. It was that late—or early. His small flat was filled with books and music, string instruments from all over the world. Our clothes hung off them like discarded snakeskin.

For a moment no longer than a hummingbird's heartbeat, a snapshot of my former life, my *real* life, burst against the backs of my eyes. Compared to the way I felt tonight, it all seemed as cheaply fabricated as a T-shirt made in a Chinese factory. Just as quickly, I doused the thought; how painful it could be to develop expectations. To hope and dream.

Without speaking, Andreas led me away from the window, back to the thin cushion that served as his bed. I breathed deeply and unfolded myself before him; lean legs, strong arms, proud chest, freckled clavicle, hips and belly softened by the rigors of carrying three children. He bent over me. His forelock brushed against my thighs. I felt my mouth form a textbook, comical O of pleasure.

I told myself I expected nothing. And my inner voice whispered back a single word.

Liar.

chapter 27

KELAH

Shipwrecked on Corfu, August

C. relaunched her singing career in front of an appreciative audience of international wastrels at Tony's Taverna. Are you ready for this? The woman was fabulous. Fabulous as in why hasn't someone given this woman a recording contract fabulous. Fabulous as in with a chest like that, who needs a voice? Apparently, at least one young stud was watching (hint: he's been "instrumental" to her success), because C. disappeared for nearly twenty-four hours after the show and was spotted the next day wandering the streets of Pelekastritsa with the kind of smile on her face that can only be earned through ingestion of enormous amounts of high-quality chocolate or fantastic sex. On the day in question, the shop was said to be out of its usual supply of stale Toblerone. Hmm . . . P. and J.L. are back in each other's good graces after a few stormy weeks that included three public fights, two

*appalling disses, and a tussle over the last remaining table at
Tony's. The formerly fractious pair was spotted exiting a
remote cave with their faithful mutt, B., in tow. It's too early
to call it, but if I had to, I just might call it love. . . .*

I'd been published.

I wanted to die.

It's possible that I'm the only person ever whose work has appeared in *Flounce* who has hairy armpits. Who has not been depilated, exfoliated, or plucked. Good thing the photo Boz sent them is a face shot—no airbrushing necessary, though my skin looked suspiciously glowing and something was peculiarly white about my smile.

When Parker first laid the magazine on the table and showed me my byline, I'd thought it was some sort of elaborate joke. Unfunny, but elaborate nonetheless. There was a thumbnail photo of me, looking a bit dodgy with my hair all gelled into submission, fresh from a trip to the salon. I had on the perfect, smug, I'm-a-*Flounce*-columnist smile. Well, actually, it was the perfect Fee-pretending-to-grab-some-bloke's-arse-as-we-got-off-at-Covent-Garden smile. I remembered the day clearly. It was the week after Christmas and we had stopped at Marks & Spencer to return all the horrid presents we'd gotten. Jumpers with reindeer on them, pointed gift certificates redeemable for a style makeover, granny-size knickers, Céline Dion CDs. When I stepped out of the lift into the daylight at Covent Garden, a bird shat on my left shoulder. Boz insisted it was good luck. I was dubious. Under my photo, there was one page, three columns. My journal. Only not so much mine anymore. Everyone's who happened to speak English and had a pressing need to know What-to-Wear-to-Seduce-Your-Married-Boss or The-45-Best-Places-to-Meet-a-Financially-Solvent-Doctor-with-a-Huge-Penis. Whatever they paid per word, it wasn't enough to compensate me for the loss of dignity, that's for sure.

I called London from the telephone center. The booth was too small for all of us, so Anya held the door open so the others could hear everything. My rage was comical, something out of a cartoon, rabbits with smoke pouring out of their ears, coyotes with flames shooting from their nostrils.

I dialed the familiar numbers, adding on England's country code.

"Hallo? Boz, it's Kelah."

"How are you?" he said without a hint of wariness.

"When were you going to tell me?"

To Boz's credit, he didn't say, *Tell you what?*

"When you were done sniveling and acting the perfect bitch."

"I wasn't sniveling!" I whined.

Silence.

"Boz, just tell me—why'd you do it?" I whispered.

"Because you'd never do it yourself. You're so caught up in this rose-colored vision of what you think will impress your mother, you're absolutely blind to what's right in front of you. You've got talent, it's just not necessarily the type you imagined having. Most of us would give our left arm to have your talent. You should be grateful."

"You had no right!" I cried.

"What are you so up about? They liked it. They thought it was dead clever, Kay! And they're paying you—I've got a thousand quid for you. I can send a check. And they want more columns. I had to pretend I was your agent—"

"Agent," I repeated.

"Since when did you lose your bloody sense of humor, Kay? God, it's like ever since you went to Greece . . . no! . . . ever since Fiona sold her short story, you've been a bloody lunatic."

"Did it ever occur to you that it violated my friends' privacy? That people here might have an issue with that?"

"Did you ask them if they mind?" he countered.

"That's not the point—"

"The hell it isn't!"

"Look, this is really stupid. This is costing me, dunno, a pound a minute. I want it to stop. Now. Do whatever you have to do."

"Well, um, I kind of can't," Boz said. I pictured him in his horrible East End flat, slouched in the tattered lime-green chair with his *Mirror* crossword puzzle, oversize, holey-sock-clad feet crossed on the scarred table.

"I'm not arguing. I'm telling you. I will not be published in that . . . that . . . trashy . . . Jerry Springer-loving, beauty-product-promoting gutter swill!"

"Well, the problem is, you signed a contract."

"I didn't sign anything! You . . . you stole my identity!" I yelled.

"Okay, so *I* signed a contract. If you try to back out now, things could get complicated. As in lawsuits-and-barristers complicated. Look, why don't you just take a few days and think about it—"

"Bosworth Terrence Sutherland, I am not going to think about anything. Call them and get me out of it. That's it. End of story."

I hung up before he could answer. My hands were shaking.

Anya let me out of the call booth. Outside, it was obscenely bright.

"You okay?" Her wide, ebony eyes were sympathetic.

"Have you ever wanted to strangle someone? Literally strangle them?"

"Yeah."

"What happened?"

"Nothing," she said.

And that would have been the end of it, except for Davey.

On Thursday, Anya got a call down at the travel agency. She brought me the message during her lunch break.

"Kelah?" she called. I usually worked at night and slept till afternoon.

"Um," I said.

"Get up. I have a message for you."

Curious, I slipped on my cargo pants, which were about ready to stand up by themselves, and a faded Gap T-shirt Boz had left behind. His musty boy scent clung to it, which irritated me, but I couldn't seem to motivate myself to wash it.

"Hey," I said.

"Your friend Fee called for you at Nia's. She says you have to call her."

"Did she say why?" I was worried. What if my dad was in an accident? Or maybe one of Charlie's kids was sick. On the other hand, perhaps Fee had sold another story and wanted to brag a little.

"No, just that it was important but not life-threatening."

I thanked her and she waited while I threw some water on my face.

"How are things?" I asked as we walked down the narrow paths.

"Good. Ethan extended his ticket another two weeks."

"That's cool." I was apprehensive for Anya. How could these things end but in disappointment?

She must have caught my look. "It's okay. I know what everyone thinks. I'm not crazy." Anya hung her head so thick sheaves of shiny black hair obscured her face. "I know nothing's going to come of it. But it's nice to pretend. . . . I mean, it just feels so comfortable to let things go on. Before, I always had a clear reason to break up with somebody—or they with me, I guess was more common. How do you break up when you're not officially together in the first place? I don't know." She turned suddenly to face me straight on. "Do you believe in curses?"

"Curses, as in 'you will walk the earth in limbo for seven years' curses?" I said.

"Sort of."

I thought for a second. "No. Not really. Except in the sense that you might sabotage yourself if somebody curses you. Like a self-fulfilling prophecy."

Anya seemed to consider this. "I probably shouldn't be telling you this, because of the column and all—"

"The column's over," I interrupted.

"Well, I'm pretty sure I've got a curse going on," Anya said.

"Why?"

Anya's gaze slid to mine, weighing. "I did something, something bad, when I was fifteen. I've never told anyone," she said slowly, each word sounding as fossilized and sour as a jawbreaker candy.

"Anya, we all do bad things. That doesn't mean some god above hands us retribution." I was impatient. What had Fee called about?

"I killed someone," she said softly.

Then the words gushed out of her.

"That was quick," Boz said. He sounded like he was chewing on something gummy, toffee caramels or beef sticks.

"Yes, well . . ." My voice dribbled off.

"So, now you're saying you *want* to continue the column, and *don't* call the editor and explain that I'm not your agent, I'm just some evil bloke who *stole your identity,* and you're happy to keep accepting their money and writing a popular new column for the most popular women's glossy in England—"

"Okay, I get it! I'm sorry! I didn't know this would happen."

"Humph," he said.

"Boz, I'm sorry I yelled at you the other day. It's just, it took some time to get used to the idea." I swallowed hard and visibly shuddered. "I'm very grateful to you for thinking of me when you pinched my personal journal and sold it to England's premier women's magazine for one million pounds or whatever ridiculous sum you negotiated for me whilst masquerading as a literary agent—"

"Your sincerity astounds me."

"Well, what do you want from me? Before, I needed dignity, not money. Now I need money more, and I'm ready to negotiate. I'm not going to grovel," I said foolishly. *Grovel* might as well be my middle name. Kelah Grovel Morris, whore-writer of smutty, insipid travelogues.

Huge exhale. "How's Davey?"

"Okay. He'll be better when he makes bail and they let him out of Wandsworth."

"How did Fee find out he was in?"

"When Mum and Dad refused to pay, Davey called my old number at the flat, at Fee's. He didn't know I'd moved home, didn't even know I was in Greece. Fee took down the information and called me here." I felt a small ball of despair curdle up against the back of my throat. Oh, Davey, why'd you have to muck it up again?

"Kay? I'll bring the money down to Fee's and we'll go to court with him together, make sure his solicitor's on top of things, okay?"

"Oh, Boz, that would be brilliant. I was thinking of coming home myself—"

"Oh, no, you mustn't. It won't make any difference anyway. There's nothing you can do for him but get him out and get him into a treatment center. We can do that just as easily as you can."

"You're a good friend, Boz. The best."

"Oh, you'd do the same for me," he said without a trace of irony. Boz's only sibling, Mathilde, is married with three children, acts like she's ninety, and spends her days shepherding her sons to cricket and crocheting gruesome afghans.

"After all," he continued, "I've got a reputation to uphold as a high-powered literary agent."

"I'm your only client."

"*First* client. Big difference."

"First and last if Mum ever finds out. I can't believe you didn't think to use a pseudonym," I said.

Silence.

"Boz? What?"

Extended silence.

"Bozzie, does Mum know? She doesn't read that sort of stuff. I mean, avoids it like the plague. . . ." I was livid. Also, paralyzed. With something that felt like fear.

"See, it's sort of good you called, Kay, because I've got news for you too," Boz said.

"I'm disowned?"

"No, actually, your mum and dad are coming to Greece to make sure you're all right. They're terribly worried about you, see. In fact, I'm to show them where you are. We leave in . . . oh, Friday week."

With lovely cinematic precision, I hung up on Boz for the second time in three days.

chapter 28

~~~~~~~~~~~~~

ANYA

Some women who are unlucky in love are doomed to dateless celibacy, but that's never been my problem. I may not be down with one-night stands, red lipstick, or public displays of affection, but that never prevented a certain type—or types—of guy from checking out what I had in the pantry, so to speak. I guess you could call me a serial monogamist with a dash of Catholic Cinderella naïveté thrown in for flavor. Before Rick, there was Philippe. Before Philippe, Anton. True, there was a dry spell before I met Anton at that anti-English-only rally. But it was a short one, and I was still in recovery from losing my illusions about Tranh/Montel/Joey/Perry/Joaquín. With each successive boyfriend, my gilt-edged sense of marital destiny eroded a little more, so by the time I ate those sleeping pills that terrible May, I was thinking nonstop about bad luck, and curses, and how I could undo the most undoable of acts. I was ready to do some wacky shit. I was *loca en la cabeza,* and everyone knew it.

"Why you look so down, *chica?*" my little sister, Carilu, asked me as we walked down South Van Ness, going home from our annual Easter pilgrimage. I avoided church if I could help it, but somehow my socialist parents managed to maintain an expedient if uneasy Catholicism, and some holidays were nonnegotiable.

"I'm not down. I'm thirty-one and unmarried with no prospects. Big difference," I answered.

"So many guys like you, Anya. I'm sure you'll meet the right one soon," said my dear friend Carda, whose only adult love relationship had lasted eight weeks and was with a fifty-three-year-old married paraplegic who resuscitated broken CB radios in his garage and voted for Ross Perot. Carda could always shame me into rethinking my approach. Not that she did it on purpose. Maybe that's why I always invited her to mass.

"I don't know," I sighed.

"Well, I'd be happy with a date for Fall Fling. Just a guy who wants to have watercress salad and lemongrass bean curd at Chez Panisse and knows how to dance swing and will stay with me the whole night."

Carda knew better than to say, *Is that too much to ask?*, since, as often as not, it was. Parker's sister was an administrative assistant in the rhetoric department at UC Berkeley, a situation that, sadly, seemed to put her in daily contact with every overeducated, narcissistic, puffed-up, elitist, misogynistic boob in the San Francisco Bay Area. Each year, the College of Letters & Science had a dance so the geniuses and freaks who served on the university's faculty could pretend they were normal for a night, big players who could flirt and shimmy and vomit in the bushes with the best of them. It was one of those events destined to remain anticlimactic at best for someone in Carda's shoes, and quite possibly excruciating at worst.

"Oh, we'll get you a date, Carda," Carilu said confidently.

Carda looked doubtful.

"What about Emanuel, Anya? He's cute. Oh, yeah, and John Yamasaki, I could ask him? No wait, he's gay. Oh, no, no—that guy you brought to the party at Antoinette's. He was a great dancer.

Sanjay? Just because he doesn't want to settle down doesn't mean he wouldn't be fun for a night out," Carilu said.

"He just got engaged to Robin Flores," I said. I was there when they met, my date and my coworker, over the keg at Antoinette's. Robin was so tiny, she'd made even skinny, silk-shirt–wearing Sanjay look tall and courtly, like a prince.

"Oh," said Carilu, her pistachio eyes sliding away from me. I couldn't blame her. After all, the jury was still out on whether or not curses are contagious. I could be as inflamed with unlucky-in-love disease as a bout of influenza, and we wouldn't even know it till the spores floated off me and landed, like unmanned space pods, on the upturned faces of my loving girlfriends. There, whirring with indifferent efficiency, they'd set to work, dismantling the innocent dreams of their unaware hosts, forever ravenous.

I was showing Ethan my freestyle stroke. It was pretty awesome, actually. Johnny said I was ready to get up on the windsurfer board, but I wanted a few more weeks of swimming under my belt.

"Anya, that's brilliant!" Ethan yelled from the beach. "You look like what's-her-name, Janet Reno!"

I swam to shore and dragged myself out of the water. The sand was firm and grainy, like millions of small hands massaging my feet. I couldn't believe I'd ever been banished from it, forced to settle for a quick toe dip and a splash.

He wrapped me in a huge beach towel and hugged me.

"Janet Evans," I corrected.

"What?"

"I think you meant Janet Evans, the swimmer, not Janet Reno, the former attorney general of the United States."

"Oh, yeah." He smiled his don't-blame-me-I'm-just-an-Aussie-grin. At moments like these, if he told me he'd just flushed the winning lottery ticket down the toilet, I'd fling my arms around his body and squeeze. I could forgive him anything.

"So, what do you want to do today?" I said.

"Go to the beach. Get some food. Read?"

That's one thing I love about the Greek islands—everyone pretends deciding his daily schedule is a terribly weighty exercise, when, really, we all do the same thing, day in and day out.

"Okay," I answered happily. I wasn't working at the agency today.

We bought sandwiches from the stand at the end of the beach. Slabs of pale, seedless Greek bread, spread liberally with creamy *tzatziki* and stuffed with cucumbers, red pepper, tomato, avocado, and onions, drizzled with olive oil. Our favorite. Ethan spread our mats out, scooping out sand to accommodate our butts. I ground a long cylinder of mineral water into the sand and covered it with a shirt.

"Buen apetito."

We dug in.

For the next three hours, we swam, slept, snuggled, and talked. We called hellos to our friends across the sand and reveled in how much we belonged here, our little alternative universe. We agreed on such disparate issues as chocolate (Belgian dark), the Middle East (land for peace), and Kirsten Dunst's hair (red).

Predictably, the perfection of it all culminated in a giant, unassailable urge to pop the bubble. To test the glassy-calm waters. To spoil it all with a protracted, weepy confessional of the "I have something to tell you" variety. The type of admission you get in the eighty-seventh minute of movies starring Julia Roberts. The type that makes you think, damn, I was really starting to like her, she's showing some spunk, hey, what'd she do that for? No! Stop! What a *pendeja!* I felt it build up against the walls of my chest like a surge of floodwaters behind a dam. The compulsion blossomed into a hairline fracture, futile and valiant against the tsunami waiting to happen. I wanted to challenge the curse, dare it to raise its monstrous gorgon head, its moist-lipped, succubus mouth. Hey, *diablo,* I'll take you down, I'd shout. I'm going to drag you out to sea and leave you to flounder around while I do a mean backstroke all the way back to shore. This is the one who won't get away. This is the one I fight for.

"Ethan, I have to tell you something," I said weakly.

Hola, minute eighty-seven.

"I have something to tell you first." He looked deeply into my eyes. Then he pulled my hand into his. This was highly unorthodox.

I eased it away. "Seriously. Come on. I really want to share something with you."

"Nope. It'll have to wait. It's now or never for me, Annie." Then he laughed, the girlish, terrified giggle of a man who was about to throw something heavy overboard, like his male independence. You know those movies with Julia Roberts? This is what happens in minute ninety, right after the huge confessional in minute eighty-seven and just before the full-circle-camera-angle-pick-her-up-and-swing-her-around-so-her-highlighted-hair-twirls-around-in-the-unbelievably-ambient-light moment.

I started shaking.

"So, Annie? Yeah, all right. Christ, I'm shaking like a leaf. Okay. I've been thinking? We're getting along so well, you and I. But summer's ending, and you have to go back to San Francisco and I have to go back to Sydney, and, well, I know you're thinking about it, too, what's going to happen? And I've been thinking—oh, shit, I already said that—sorry, I'm nervous. Anyway, I was going to say that . . . that if you want to give it a shot, you and me, I'd like that. What I'm trying to say is, I'm willing to come out to California for a while, see how it goes for us. I wouldn't expect you to come to Australia, not with your family and your job and your apartment and everything. But I can talk to my dad, and I'll always have a job to go back to, and I wanted to see if you were interested . . . open to discussing . . . I mean, is that something you'd be amenable to negotiating—oh, God, I sound ridiculous. . . ."

"Only a little." I laced my fingers behind his neck. His eyes were the exact color of amber sap. I wanted to crawl in and lie there like a trapped bug, forever frozen.

"So, what do you think?"

Instead of answering, I smiled and let my gaze wander over his freckled shoulder, across the white crescent of sand that was

Lifada Beach. I didn't trust myself to talk. Also, there was a lump in my throat the size of Athens. He may not have reversed the curse, but he'd just poked it straight in the eyes. Hard. Was that all it took? A swift jab, fingers extended, elbows crooked, ninja-style? An ember of an idea burned deep and low inside me, sparking: What if the curse wasn't a curse at all? What if it was something in me? Something I'd made. A creature I'd fed and clothed and, yes, even loved. My very own child, squalling and spoiled. *Mi'ijito.*

What happened next is burned into my brain with the type of brutal clarity normally reserved for photos of famine victims and extraordinary natural wonders.

She approached slowly, leisurely. There was nothing sudden about it. One step in front of the other, the beach a long, grainy catwalk. People—men and women, Greeks and foreigners—stopped what they were doing and watched her predatory hunt, regarded those long feline legs scissoring up the beach, whispering against the silky bias-cut skirt. I could feel her eyes on us from a hundred yards away. Tractor beams. Hard blue rays, like lasers. The kind used by doctors to slit open hearts while they are still beating. The kind that promise to spill very little blood.

The woman everybody watched strode up to us as if we were interlopers on her private beachfront. Her delicate feet seemed to hit the sand in time with the gentle beat of Ethan's heart under my fingers, owning it. *Pluff, pluff,* went the feet in their strappy sandals, which somehow managed to stay on. The grains sprang away from her high arches as if in fear.

All of this I registered in a few wrenching seconds: blazing azure eyes, a sleek cap of chestnut hair, concave slimness, amused brows, a scimitar-shaped scar on one wrinkle-free temple. And, wrapped around it, a crisp grosgrain bow of a smile. A second later, I noticed the two other women who trailed behind her, somber and solicitous as bridesmaids.

"Well, Ethan, you certainly had me on the proverbial wild-goose chase! That bloke over at the taverna thought you'd be at Beach Murty-tissa-something, and the lady at the news agent's said you'd gone motorcycling. And for God's sake, whatever you do, don't say, *What are you doing here, Rachel?*" Her laughter sounded like a mirror breaking. "I'm here to see you, of course. So tell me, where the hell are you going to buy me a beer while we talk?"

chapter 29

〜〜〜〜〜〜〜〜〜〜〜

PARKER

"What do you think of this one?" I held the striped chintz against the wall so Brian Dillon could compare it to the solid.

"Nice. But maybe just a touch too corporate?"

I squinted at it, a technique that has inspired confidence in dozens of moneyed idiots. "No, you're right. It's got to go. We'll use the blue."

I was glad to have Brian around to help. With his background in theater, he was invaluable when it came to textiles and colors. I'm not generally one to perpetuate stereotypes, but you can't argue with the fact that you'll get better design feedback from a queer, legally blind eight-year-old than a fully sighted straight guy with an MFA from the Rhode Island School of Design. It's just my experience. Plus, Brian was funny and talkative and made the work go faster. He had two types of stories: those concerning men he wanted to fuck, and those concerning men who'd fucked him (equally distributed among the literal and figurative). Actually, he had three types, counting theater and television commercials he'd acted in. No, four: His parents' foundering relationship and his dad's refusal to accept that he was gay was an endless source of conversation. Interestingly, I found his assessment of the evil Gary to be more generous than Claire's, which I took as an indicator of the amount of time that had passed since the original betrayal.

I asked him what he thought Neil's rating was on the dirty-dog meter.

"On a scale of one to ten," I added.

"Ten being highest?"

"Yeah."

"I have to consider the fact that he did it within a fortnight of the wedding an aggravated circumstance. Adds, say, two points. Plus, the whole pregnancy thing. Definitely an eight. No, wait— the cow's Belgian, right? Nine. I went out with a Belgian once. Damn mongrel," he said.

I tended to agree. I'd somehow been hoping he'd merit an 11+, but, then, Neil *had* paid the mortgage for the summer, which counted for something, I suppose.

"Top five names for children of Madonna," Brian called out. He was painting the banquette. We'd developed this game to pass the time.

"That's easy," I said, thinking furiously. "Okay, not necessarily in this order: Ulysses, Rambo, Scooter Riot, Greer Scone . . . and . . . and Princess Diana!"

He glanced at me admiringly. "You're a genius, Ms. Glass."

"Thank you," I said.

Tony walked in.

"How things are going?"

"Good," I said. "See that hole? That's where your new terrace window's going to be."

"Are my brother's guys doing what they supposed to be doing?" He regarded the hole dubiously.

"Oh, yes, we're very happy with them." Brian and I looked at each other and smiled. There's nothing like ninety-degree weather and hard physical labor to make strapping young men take their shirts off for a needed rest.

"Parker, can I talk to you for a minute?" Tony asked.

"Sure. Just a sec."

I hung my paint-splattered shirt on a peg and paused to stroke Blakas's speckled back, which made him squirm with pleasure. I must say, it's nice to be loved, even if your only suitors are a drooling mutt and a hunchbacked Greek.

Tony motioned me into the kitchen, where Big Sister of Tony was busy doing obscene things to a ball of phyllo dough.

"What's up?"

Tony poured us both a glass of wine. "There's no easy way to say this, so I just say it. I might not be able to pay the bills on this place past this month! Things are even worse than I thought. It is a terrible thing! Terrible! This taverna has been in my family for two generations!"

Hmm. I didn't bother to tell him that was a shorter period than some marriages. Except mine, of course.

"Before my grandfather bought it, it was a cheap place that sold bad food and wine, but then he turned it around into something we can be proud of! Oh, Parker, I don't know what I am going to do." He put his shaggy head in his heads, and I found myself placing my hand lightly on his little curved shoulder.

"So we'll go to Plan B." I tried to sound cheerful.

"Plan B? What is Plan B?"

"What is Plan B? Tony, Tony, *Tony*. I'm disappointed. It's only the biggest damn party this little ole island chain has ever known!"

One of the games I've taken to playing on dark days is a pleasant diversion called Weak-ass Husband. I considered naming it Signs of Evil, but it sounded a little too Fox Network for my taste. Like something that might be hosted by John Walsh, complete with slo-mo, misty montages of stringy-haired white guys with jailhouse tats and beer guts running shirtless out the doors of trucker bars into flocks of waiting cops.

Weak-ass Husband involves plundering my memory for incidents that foreshadowed Neil's departure. Incidents I should have observed and documented but didn't. Character flaws. Asides. Clues. Tidbits. I scoured my personal history for these moments like a beggar grabbing at crumbs tossed by indifferent passersby. Some grasping part of myself demanded knowledge of cause: *Why* did Neil slip the neatly folded resignation letter under his boss's door and step on that 747 that harmless, pretty May day and fly business class to South America? *Why* didn't I get that Brazilian bikini wax like he'd always wanted me to? (Would an at-home landing strip have subverted his sudden need for global travel?) Should I have put on a more convincing act that I liked his sucky friends, like Carl, who once placed his hand on my ass during a *tapas* dinner, or Lee, who broke up with his girlfriend because she wouldn't get a boob job? Did I, in my blissful ignorance or criminal state of denial, miss a hundred little signs of connubial unhappiness? Or was life really as random and merciless as such an event would indicate? Come to think of it, maybe I should rename the game Weak-ass Wife, or at least Weak-ass Spouse, in the spirit of sharing.

These thoughts were weighing on me as I lay on the beach staring up at the stars with Blakas wedged against me. Most nights, they made me want to do something crazy, like put a hit on the Belgian or consume a lump of cheese bigger than my head. Tonight, I felt strangely . . . I don't know, content? No, too strong. Resigned? Too negative. Accepting, I guess. Familiar with the concept, at least. The idea that reconciliation of the Harlequin variety was not going to occur was no longer the horrifying, unacceptable suggestion it once was. Small granules of hope had begun to appear in my thoughts, sweet and tasty as chocolate chips in a smooth expanse of vanilla. I was free. I could do anything I wanted.

"Blakas. Let's do a list," I said aloud. "The Top Five Things Parker Glass Can Do Starting Now that Don't Include Neil Wentworth, Weak-ass Husband, 9.0 on the Dirty-Dog Scale."

Blakas buried his moist, freckled snout in my armpit and sighed. I took that as an assent.

We consulted for a while, Blakas and I. When we were done, the list looked something like this:

1. Rent chick flicks with impunity——Neil's list of criteria for choosing an acceptable movie rental consisted mostly of *don'ts:* Don't have a happy ending; don't contain the word *commitmentphobe;* don't feature Meg Ryan. The result is that we inevitably brought home movies with asteroids blowing human bodies into smithereens, Steven Seagal's brow furrowing under a flurry of karate chops, Flemish subtitles (possible early sign of predilection for Belgian coochie?), or a scantily clad Milla Jovovich. No more. In fact, as of this point, I was officially announcing a Milla moratorium. She may look like a long drink of Siberian runoff, but the girl can't act her way out of a Chechen bunker.

2. Have Molly and my sisters over for dinner during *Monday Night Football*——Personally, I can't think of anything more satisfying than burning an effigy of John Madden while mowing through five pints of Häagen-Dazs. (Howie Long will likely be spared due to Molly's shameful weakness for buzz-cut blonds in glasses.)

3. Visit Taveuni——If there's ever a time to be ravished by a three-hundred-pound saronged Fijian while eating fresh fruit, it's now.

4. Get to know Sharon Stone——She lives in San Francisco; I live in San Francisco. She has money and taste; I have design skills and a business card. She knows people; I know other people. Her ex-husband got bitten by a Komodo dragon; my husband dressed up as a drag queen in a kimono for Halloween. We both even have big oversize noggins. See? It's perfect. A match made in heaven. I was envisioning something like an artist–muse relationship with a little rich-patron–Cinderella thing thrown in, whereby Shar-babe would call me and snarl into the phone, "Park? Sooo glad you're there. You won't believe

what happened! I woke up this morning and *hated* the
entire west wing. Simply hated it. Can you redo?" Neil's
parents, who orbited the rich and powerful like tertiary
planets in a candy-colored universe chock-full of potential
clients, steadfastly refused to point any of them in my
direction. Apparently, helping me build my business was
too unseemly for people of their pedigree. I used to rage
about it to Molly. "For God's sake," I'd lamented. "You'd
think they all got where they are through hard work or
something!" "More like indentured servitude and selective
pimping for friends with breeding papers," Molly replied.
Neil professed to be proud of my skills, but he'd inherited
more than a drop of Jack and Jill's snooty classism. (Yes, it's
true: Jackson the Third and Jillian the First. You have my
permission to go barf now.)

5. Nightly masturbation——When we'd first started seeing
each other, starting on Molly's wedding night, Neil
approached the act of self-pleasuring with a delightful
sense of openness and more than a little perversion. When
he wasn't demanding that I stand over him bare-assed in a
miniskirt, he spun elaborate fantasies that involved me, a
magnifying glass, and a bottle of Château Lafite. But as
time went on, I sensed a change. Neil had started to regard
such activities as an affront to his manhood, the rise and
fall of blood to my nether region as a process he'd annexed,
a sport to be played out on his own private playground. A
fox hunt he was free to commence, but not I.
Consequently, our sex life had turned into our own little
version of the Big Bang, lacking the delicacy and slightly
aberrant whimsy that had drawn me to him in the first
place. You know those nights when you're just bone tired?
When the thought of waiting for your man to ram you to
completion in a cool sixty-eight minutes, when you can
buzz or tweak it over the edge in ten, fills you with despair?

Story of our week. Today? Finito. Now I was free to grind away at the old nub until cataracts encrusted my corneas and hair fell off my palms like Rapunzel. A veritable clit fit.

I stretched my hand as if to practice wrist rotation. Pretty decent.

Suddenly, Blakas barked once, rose to attention, and sped off into the darkness. I figured it was either Josh Lido or a homicidal maniac. Who else would be out here stalking me at this hour?

"Hello, Josh or homicidal maniac," I called.

"Hey, Park. What's going on?" Josh said.

"Planning my postdivorce masturbation strategy."

"Need a hand?"

I giggled. "Or three."

He grinned and lay down beside me on the blanket. I had pretty much gotten over the humiliation of his rejection. In retrospect, I saw the wisdom of avoiding an entanglement in my state, which was spelled R-E-B-O-U-N-D. Plus, there was something neat about having my own special friend on the island, apart from the SNiPs, that is. And Blakas.

We'd see each other every couple of days. Bike rides, sightseeing, working on Tony's place, meals. Good clean fun with the occasional dirty fantasy of him throwing me against a Corinthian column and relieving me of my chastity. We had reached the point where we could coexist silently and enjoy our fantasy lives, Josh and I.

We lay there for a while. The air was cool, but for obvious reasons I refused to snuggle against him. It was enough that he was there. Almost.

What I said next surprised me.

"Josh, sometimes I can't believe I'm almost divorced. It's frightening, the idea of going home. It is so not okay to be divorced at home. Here, it's okay to be single, because it's so"—I searched for the perfect word—"*surreal.* But at home, it's going to suck. I just know it."

"Yeah, well, being married to the wrong guy, that sucks too."

True.

"I don't think I'll ever be with anybody that way again. Like life partners. That scares me." The creamy darkness made confessing this easier.

I felt his breath pause before he spoke. "They say people who've been married once usually do it again, and the second time's better."

"What a bunch of bullshit. Where'd you read that, *Cosmo*?" I said.

We laughed.

"Yeah. It also said pink is the new black."

I shuddered. "Over my dead body. Look, I don't want to talk about me anymore. I'm becoming a boring old hag who can't stop talking about her relationship problems. Or lack thereof." I pulled the edge of the blanket over my bare legs. "So, were you in a relationship before you came here?"

He sighed. "Do we have to do this?"

"Yes. Otherwise, I'll hammer away at you until you give in. Or I might try to kiss you again."

He looked at me in mock horror. "Well, I guess I better tell you, then. My ex's name is Lauren. We met at an AIDS benefit a few years ago. She does PR for Macy's, which was sponsoring the event. I was with my friend Lizzie, who's a social worker. She does hospice care for people with HIV. She was speaking. I was unemployed at the time and was there for the free food. Also, there were supposed to be women parading around in underwear."

"Yeah. Um, philistine boy? I believe they prefer to be called lingerie models," I said.

"Yeah, well, whatever. As long as they're wearing those little lacy numbers. Hey! Stop it!" He reached over and planted my fist firmly in the sand. "So, anyway, Lizzie introduced me to Lauren, who was instantly overcome by my intercontinental charm, machismo, and command of underwear—excuse me, *lingerie*—culture, and demanded to go out to dinner with me. And that's it. We were together for about two years."

"Why'd you break up?"

"Different goals, I guess."

"Not *that* old chestnut. What does that really mean, 'different goals'? Doesn't everyone ultimately want the same things? Happiness, a decent job, a couple of bucks for shoes, good sex, and deep spiritual satisfaction?"

"I guess I just wasn't ready to settle down. She was. I got the old ultimatum and that was the end of the Josh and Lauren show."

Josh's profile was serene against the starry sky, but I saw his jaw clench a little.

"What else? That couldn't be all of it," I said.

He swung his arms back and latched his hands together under his curly head. His eyes were wet. They reflected the moon. Josh took a deep breath.

"No, it wasn't all of it."

I waited.

"Are you sure you want to hear this?" he said into the darkness. The way he said it sent a little oh-no chill down my spine. He sounded like he was talking to himself. When I didn't reply, he continued.

"My brother died of leukemia," he said softly. "I needed to deal with it my way. I guess I wasn't the Josh she'd signed on for anymore. That's what she said, that I'd changed so much she couldn't recognize me, couldn't help me. That I wouldn't accept help from anyone. So she left. I don't really blame her. I was pretty fucked up for a while."

He cleared his throat. "One day at work, my boss asked me why I hadn't double-checked this guy's name—this Japanese guy we were meeting with about a merger between two consumer-electronics companies. I'd spelled his name wrong in the PowerPoint presentation. Total rookie move, but what the fuck? At that point, I was barely capable of shaving in the morning, let alone spelling some dude's fucking unpronounceable name. I got up, in the middle of this meeting, and walked over to the window. It was one of those high-rises, you know? With those huge, black plate-glass windows? We were on the thirty-second floor. That high, you don't even see birds flying, just white space, air. I punched the window as hard as I could. There was like this hair-line fracture in the glass. Just this little fucking line that opened up and ran all the way up. We watched it while it cracked, right up to the top. Then I walked over to my desk, threw a couple of things in a box, my Las Vegas snow globe and a bunch of those miniature Post-its and a photo of me and Raphael from when we summited Mt. Shasta. I just walked straight out of there. Never went back. My hand was broken in fifteen places."

I realized I was holding my breath. I let it out slowly. I couldn't think of anything to say. Everything seemed hopelessly inadequate.

He turned to face me. "Park—"

"Shh! You don't have to explain. God. God," I repeated moronically.

"But there's something else I have to tell you—"

"Josh! I understand completely! Please, just be quiet. There's nothing to explain."

He started to argue with me, but then seemed to think better of it and his words dribbled into the night. Finally, when his trembling subsided, I leaned over and slipped my fingers into his, laced them through his knotty hair, felt the warmth of his skull under my hands.

"You're going to be okay," I murmured.

He squeezed my hand over our heads. Between us, Blakas growled in his sleep, chasing imaginary butterflies between waving fronds of grass.

chapter 30

CLAIRE

The day after the show, Andreas went to the mainland to visit family in Thessaloníki. I was relieved. What with Rachel showing up unannounced to stake her expired claim for Ethan, Anya retreating into grim stoicism, Parker and Brian madly trying to save Tony's Taverna from extinction, and Kelah's inadvertent but very potent column snaking its way into the very dankest corners of our lives, I wasn't sure I could handle the natural evolution of a love affair—or whatever it was.

The morning after. Who hasn't heard of it, lived it? But it had been about a hundred years since I'd had to do it, and I wasn't at all confident I would pull it off with any dignity or precision, let alone joy.

Morning. The first thought that came into my head as I lay, fuzzy and sublimely exhausted in the mess of sheets, was: Where did he learn that crazy stuff with his hands at the tender age of twenty-eight? Yes, to my everlasting shame—or thrill, depending on which second you caught me—I had had carnal knowledge of a person who was not even born when I lost my virginity. Did you hear that, Australia? *Not even born.*

The second was: Did adulterous acts cancel each other out, ethically speaking?

Then, a third: Quick, pull the sheet up over those stretch marks.

Andreas was gone. Just like in the romance novels, there was a gentle dip in the bed where his body had been, still warm, and smelling of sex and lavender. The overlay of strong Greek coffee percolating from the kitchen and the clanking noises of dishware told me I had a few seconds of privacy to spare, so I buried my head in his side of the bed and inhaled, keeping an eye peeled for intruders. Then I got up, wrapping the sheet around me, and hunted down my clothes. I suppose, if pressed, I'd have to confess I had envisioned a crisp white man's shirt casually slung over a chair that I would slip on, designed to just cover all the unfortunate areas while leaving a long expanse of bare leg. But as there was only a pair of Andreas's model-slim dungarees and my own soiled undies available, I threw on my own clothes from the night before, sans undergarments. Thankfully, I'd brought a casual skirt and tank with me, as well as a load of concealer for the inevitable black under-eye circles.

I slipped into the pillbox-size bathroom, peed, and washed up, tying my mass of hair into a sloppy topknot. My crotch felt as if it had independently visited the gym and gone five rounds on the StairMaster. I half expected to see it glowing from under my skirt like a scarlet letter.

I steadied myself and strode into the kitchen.

"Good morning," I said to Andreas. He was doing ten things at once and still managed to look calm. And mussed. And terrifically sexy.

"Claire." He put down the small, Turkish-style glasses of sludgy coffee and kissed me on the lips and neck.

Three hours and fourteen Kama Sutra positions later, Andreas left for the ferry and I went home. Out in broad daylight, my actions seemed less comprehensible. What would Ethan and Brian think when our affair became known?

In a daze, I smiled and waved at the townspeople I'd gotten to know on a hand-wave basis. The old man with the switch was in full form this afternoon, prompting shrieks from a gaggle of young women. On impulse, I slid into the dim interior of the Dallas. I hadn't talked to Patricia in several days.

Most of the bar's patrons were sitting outside enjoying the sunshine at this hour. An Irish waitress with a nose ring and a waspish waist carried trays of overflowing pints in and out the swinging doors. In the far corner, a boy in a football jersey played pinball, occasionally slamming the machine when the game didn't cooperate.

Patricia was wiping down the bar. Her frizzy hair was tucked into a bun and her eyes were tired.

"Claire Dillon. How are you? I wanted to tell you we really enjoyed the performance last night. You have a fabulous voice. Everyone said so."

"It was a good night. It can be hit-or-miss at my age. My voice was pretty out of shape."

She wrung out the cloth. "What can I get you?"

"Oh, I don't know. Mineral water? With a lemon slice?"

"Coming right up. Have you eaten? I can whip you up a toastie—tomato and cheese or ham," she offered.

I shook my head. Patricia pulled a hose from the bar and expertly arranged my drink. She placed it in front of me and came around to sit on the stool next to me.

"I tell you, if Nick doesn't give me that vacation soon, I don't know what I'm going to do."

"Are things, um, going better with you two?"

She nodded and waited for the Irish girl to draw a half pint and leave before speaking again. "For now, at least. I'll tell you one thing, that thing with Sven? I mean, it was nothing. A blip. Two times. Certainly nothing to compare to Nick's . . . stuff. But it made me appreciate things about Nick I hadn't noticed in years. You'd think it would be all about me feeling good again, and I guess to some extent it was, but the funny thing is how it mostly made me conscious of what I had missed. Everything this Sven guy wasn't, Nickie was. Before we started having problems. Solid. A good father. Attentive. Like the way Nickie used to rub my neck after work. And the time we all sailed to Italy together. And how he used to fall asleep in the library when we were in college and his sister Nia and I would take turns babysitting him while he drooled over his books." She smiled shyly. "He said he'd take me to Europe when the season's finished. We're going to leave the kids with his mother and go to Paris. Stay in one of those little pensiones near the Marais. Gorge on cheese and wine every night. See if we can, you know, get back on track."

The Irish girl came back with a drink order. Patricia threw her dishcloth over her shoulder and sighed deeply.

"Duty calls," she said.

I said good-bye and stepped out into the harsh sunshine. I thought about what she'd said, about reducing your world to wine and cheese and safeguarding the few memories of your husband that still bestow joy.

chapter 31

ANYA

Carilu, Tomás, and I used to play a game when we were little. We called it Disappeared. Nothing as conventional as hide-and-seek for the Soberanes kids. As far back as I can remember, *Mami* and *Papi* were involved in the plight of the Central and South American *Desaparecidos,* the good, sometimes outspoken sons and daughters who'd been snatched away from their families by the nefarious forces of struggling dictatorships and were usually never seen again. The mothers would come to San Francisco on awareness-raising junkets, scrawny women in black with shadows under their eyes as rich as coffee grounds. Sometimes they'd stay in our bedroom, mine and Carilu's, and we'd camp out in the living room, wrapping blankets around the dining-room table and chairs until we had an impenetrable fort. *Mami* would steer them through the front door. They were proud and melancholy, angry and near catatonic, tired and manic. They carried small cardboard suitcases and large photos of their missing, forever smiling children. They woke in the night unable to sleep and paged through the Bible, lamplight leaking under the crooked bedroom door. We listened to the stories at the community center or church the next day. Their Spanish was different from ours—faster, more mellifluous. Carilu, Tomás, and I had to pluck out the words that meant something, the really horrible ones: *beaten, raped, threatened, seventeen years old.* We pretended we were Sophia from El Salvador or Esteban from Colombia, cleverly evading our captors and floating out of the secret jungle camp on a raft woven from the leaves of banana trees. Sometimes we scared ourselves, so we'd have to beg *Mami* and *Papi* to let us sleep with them.

I couldn't help remembering now, as I sat behind the counter at Nia's travel agency. I felt as if I, too, had disappeared. Been disappeared. I saw myself on the beach two days ago in full color, slowly disintegrating into gray pixels as horrible Rachel's feet cut deeply into the sand, snaking toward us, leaching me from the scene with every step.

"Excuse me?" The kind-eyed Frenchman was holding his hand out.

"Oh, sorry," I said, and gave him his change.

"Merci."

Yeah.

The store was empty, so I went through the familiar ritual of turning the area fan toward my face, taking off my shoes, and picking up an English magazine. I tried to fight my way through an *Economist* article about Third World debt but kept seeing Ethan's face as he stood up, shedding me as neatly as if I were a pesky clump of seaweed.

Parker was livid when I told her.

"Fuck her. And fuck him, for that matter. You don't need that kind of bullshit, Anya. If he's not man enough to tell her where to get off, then maybe he's not right for you," she said hotly.

"I think he was sort of in shock." Parker's eyebrows shot up. "I'm not making excuses for him, but I have to be rational. When your ex shows up on a beach half a world away from home, you can hardly ignore her, no matter how it ended."

"You deserve better."

I shrugged. "If he wants to talk to her, I can't stop him."

"Yeah, but you can make it profoundly more difficult."

"Why would I want to do that? Like that's going to incentivize him to come running back to me? If we pick this thing up where we left off, I want it to be because he wants it to happen, not because he's settling or being browbeaten."

"Yeah, well, that may be true, but I find it highly disturbing that she comes bursting into the picture right when you two were about to take the next step. It's too convenient."

"When I first made the connection and figured out who she was, I had some crazy thoughts. I even thought for a minute that Claire hated me and had called Rachel and convinced her to come here," I confessed.

"No way. Claire's worried about what's going to happen, but she's very fond of you. You know that," Parker said.

"I know. It was just one of those split-second, irrational thoughts you have when everything you thought was going to be one way suddenly looks like it's going to turn out another way."

Turn out another way.

I turned the pages of the magazine, seeing nothing but a black-and-white blur. Without Ethan's love, without the bridge his presence in my life created, linking together my dreams and my future, I was a curiously pale, timorous version of my new self. In fact, I was looking a lot like the old Anya, the one who thought her love forecast was filled with skeletons.

I promised myself I wouldn't cry, wouldn't show how little faith I had in us to defy small obstacles like cosmic curses and poker-thin Australian pharmaceutical executives with sexy laughs. I would be evolved, not primitive.

"G'day," I said.

"*Hola,*" Ethan answered.

He looked so lovely this morning, I wanted to eat him. Tight khaki T-shirt and faded chinos that brought out his sherry-amber eyes and the auburn glints in his dark hair. Tattered backpack under his arm. Sandals. Peeling nose. Caring, if-you-were-a-lost-dog-I'd-stop-to-save-you expression.

He leaned over to kiss me as we sat down at a table in the far corner of Tony's terrace, but some moronic impulse caused me to turn my head and we ended up bumping foreheads, something that should never happen after the second date.

"How are you?" I said.

"Okay. How about you?"

Oh, fine. I don't mind at all that we're talking like this is a *pinche* job interview.

"Peachy," I said brightly. "I sold four round-trips to Athens yesterday and Nia gave me a bonus."

"Oh. That's nice." He seemed distracted.

Tony brought over our coffees and fruit. "I hear you have another woman over here, on Kérkyra," he said to Ethan with his customary lack of tact. He shook his head. "Why you want to complicate things when you have the most beautiful girl on the island right here I don't understand. It's—how you say?—going beyond me." He walked away, muttering to himself. For the first time in two days, I smiled and meant it.

"Don't mind him. He's an old woman," I said, grinning.

"Bloody nerve," he said sourly.

"So, what'd you want to talk about?"

Ethan took a swig of coffee and sat back in that ridiculously macho way he had, totally unself-conscious, knees splayed.

"We have to talk about Rachel."

I nodded.

"I had nothing to do with her coming. I hope you know that. In fact, I was pretty shocked she'd do something like this. It's certainly never been her M.O. in the past. She's always been the chased, never the chaser. Don't know why she'd start changing her methods now. Whatever I was offering a year ago is no longer on the table, in any case, and if it wasn't good enough for her then, I don't know why it would be good enough now."

I could think of a few reasons, ranging from dwindling prospects to biological clocks to good old-fashioned possessiveness.

"Anyway," he continued, "I wasn't happy to see her, but we have a history together so I thought I'd at least hear her out." He fiddled with the edge of his shirt, something I'd seen him do even in our comparatively brief courtship when he was about to drop a bomb. He raised his eyes to mine, and I felt my heart rate careen upward. "Rachel says she made a mistake breaking up with me. She wants to give it another chance. I told her she was out of her mind, but she said she'd had time to think about it and thinks she was mad to let it go. She blames it on work stress." Small smile. "Of course, it's out of the question. Water under the bridge and all that. I told her I was involved with someone. Someone I'm serious about. She listened to what I had to say, which is more than I can say she ever did when we were together. That's never been Rachel's strong suit, listening. Anyway, she says she can respect that. I said she'd have to. I asked her when she was going home with her mates, Martine and Nell. Said it was a shame they came all this way for nothing. And she said, well, they're here and put in for the holiday at work, so they might as well enjoy themselves. She asked me if it would make you uncomfortable, them being here. I said I'd ask you. I think she really felt bad about her friends, since they'd spent their own money on tickets and thought they'd find me accommodating and get a proper holiday out of it. Of course, I'll insist she leave if you have an issue with it. I don't see us having any unnecessary contact. It'll be like she isn't even here, I promise. The past year's been hard on Rachel, I think. Maybe she's even changed. I felt like she was being honest with me. She seemed genuinely resigned to what I was telling her." He cleared his throat. "So, what do you think?"

What did I think? I imagined the two of them sitting across from each other, much as we were now, Rachel's elegant hands grazing Ethan's arm as she leaned in to remind him of this or that memory, with a spoonful of her caviar chuckle on the side, her silky blouse parting over an expanse of creamy tennis-ball-size breasts and lacy bra. I tried to picture our life on the island with Rachel gliding into Tony's and the Dallas like a poltergeist, all smiles and rounds of drinks and wicked, insinuating charm. Couldn't he see how duplicitous she was? The idea that a woman like Rachel would pack her bag and fly to Greece on such a mission and accept defeat so easily and graciously was ludicrous. She would lie in wait like a scorpion, waiting for the perfect moment to sink her poisonous talons into our necks. *Dios mío,* if she thought I was going to stand by and watch while she swished that fancy tail back and forth and licked those pointy fangs, she had another think coming. Because I wasn't going to disappear. Not this time. I was going to live my life in full color, with Ethan by my side, and the SNiPs there to turn up my wattage when I was fading. Now that I'd tasted the seven seeds, rolled the pomegranate shells on my tongue, I was ready to spar with the devil to protect what was mine. Ethan may be blind to Rachel's cunning, but I'd be strong enough, all-seeing enough, for both of us. Not for me the clingy, needy possessiveness of the Vine Woman, who can only keep her man by ensnaring him with her grasping tendrils, prickly thorns, and pungent blooms. No, I'd stake out the boundaries of my wishes like the four corners of a fertile farm and cultivate those lush acres until they drew visitors like bees to pollen. I'd practice, repeat the blueprints for the person I want to be to myself like a mantra, until it was more than just a promise. Until I could occupy the skin of my dream self as sweetly as a caterpillar cocoons itself in its hopeful filaments. I would be—*am*—my own butterfly. I was ready to change. Ready to be my best self. For us.

I reached for Ethan's hand. "Well, I'm not thrilled with it, but I'm sure it won't affect us that much. We're so much stronger than that."

It sounded so good, I almost believed it.

chapter 32

KELAH

If Boz's new mission in life was to destroy mine, he was doing a damn fine job of it. The idea of my beyond-busy parents rearranging their frenzied schedules to travel to a remote Greek island and check up on me—images of crucifixion looming—was so alarming that I repeatedly awakened with my teeth clenched and fists curled in the days following Bozzie's announcement. It didn't help matters that the editor at *Flounce* wanted to move the column to a weekly schedule, and the additional money that meant for Davey's defense made refusing the work impossible. So I was writing my column like a demon and my erstwhile novel sat, moldering, under an Amstel beer can and a damp maillot.

On Wednesday, the SNiPs had our long-delayed meeting to decide the ground rules for the column. Sure, I could continue to write unimpeded, but I was willing to accept a few conditions in exchange for my continued (tenuous) position in my friends' good graces.

We met, as per usual, at Tony's.

"You did a beautiful job with the last installment, Kelah," said

Claire. "I'm sure it doesn't matter, but just so you know, Andreas didn't—what's it say?—'carry me up the mountain toward his aerie.' I fear if the poor man had tried to hoist this arse he'd have been set in traction in hospital."

"Editorial license. We all get smaller bums, bigger tits, biting wit, and honorary degrees at prestigious universities," I said.

Anya interrupted. "Can I say something? I think it's great that Kelah's been published. Sure, it's strange, maybe even uncomfortable, reading about yourself every week, and sometimes it does get a bit personal, but she's obviously doing something right and this is a great opportunity for her. I don't think we should mess it up. I mean, especially since she needs the money to pay Davey's lawyer. I guess what I'm saying is, we can try to establish guidelines, but it won't have the same . . . I don't know . . . *rawness* I guess is the word . . . if we try to control it too much. Not many people know it's us anyway. Certainly not anyone who knows us back home, so we're safe in that regard."

"She has a point," Claire said.

"True," Tony added. We'd brought him into our confidence because, well, he refused to leave the table.

"Parker? Thoughts?" I said.

"Well, I guess I'm the spoilsport, as always," Parker said.

Everyone laughed and made nay-saying noises. She waved us off.

"I guess the weird part for me is that the more outrageous we are, the more horrid Swedes we sleep with, the more drunken confessions at two A.M., the more sordid love triangles, the more singing debuts, the more naked jogs down Main Street, the better the material for Kelah's column, the happier her editor, and the more embarrassed we are. Inherent conflict of interest!"

"That may be true, but what that really means is, there's no point in limiting what Kelah writes about. It's all or it's nothing," Claire said.

"Who ran naked down the street?" Tony looked disappointed he had missed it.

"No one—yet," Parker told him. "And what about the third

parties? The people who aren't here to represent themselves. The E.D.s and the J.L.s. Not to mention the B.S.s," she finished slyly.

"Who's B.S.?" everyone said at once.

"*Boz,* people. The dear man who got us all into this mess. And how that plotline will end is anyone's guess," Parker said.

"Sod off!" I felt my cheeks burn.

"I'm just pointing out that our acquaintances have a vested interest in how they're portrayed in the column as well. But about the Boz angle—you better let one of us write that one if you want to retain a shred of integrity," Parker said.

"Nothing's going to happen with me and Boz. We've been friends forever," I said.

"I know!" said Anya. "I've got it. We'll review each column by committee—except the person that it's about has no vote. You only vote on other people's story lines."

"So I get to help decide whether Kelah mentions that you threw Rachel's laundry in the trash, and you get to vote on whether me kissing Josh Lido makes the cut?" Parker sounded dubious.

"That's it," Anya said.

"I like it."

"Me too."

"Genius."

"And for the record, I did not throw Evil Rachel's laundry in the trash. I did, however, pray for a bird to shit on her head while she was talking to Ethan," Anya said primly.

"That's actually good luck," I pointed out, remembering Boz's wise words outside Marks & Spencer.

"Well, then, never mind. I take it back."

And that's how we decided that, essentially, anything went, as far as cheesy, sex-obsessed, vulgar, embarrassing, and potentially libelous columns were concerned.

"Mum," I said weakly. "And Dad. Hi."

I lurched toward Candace and Charles and ended up pressed against my parents for a few uncomfortable moments. I was conscious of the wetness of my armpits and tried to hug my mother with my arms pressed closed so that I wouldn't get anything as unseemly as perspiration on her crisp rose-colored blouse. If you've ever tried to hug someone without using your arms, you know how challenging that can be. We ended up bumping our (nonexistent) chests together like a couple of underweight sumo wrestlers.

"Anything for your loving agent?" Boz asked, grinning like a demented monkey.

I gave him a huge bear hug and grabbed his ear lightly in my teeth. "You'll pay, fiend," I whispered against his temple, which smelled familiar, like damp cookie dough. Then I mentally shook myself. Who cared what Boz's temple smelled like?

"Lovely place, er, island," said Mum. She was fanning her glistening face with a rolled-up *Bookseller.* Perhaps she had placed an ad in the classifieds: *Disappointed highly literate mother seeks new home for writer of lewd sex column, a.k.a. disowned daughter unit. Housebroken and able to conjugate English and French verbs with ease.*

"Fantastic," Dad murmured. Dad's tendency to murmur is well documented, which doesn't make it any less irritating, as you often have to ask him to repeat himself, and the second attempt at communication tends to be loud enough to shatter eardrums.

"Well, since we're all in agreement about how great Greece is, let me show you to your villa. I got the hire car already, so we just have to load up. I'd better drive; I've gotten a bit used to the right side. Mum, want me to hold your bag? No? Okay. Everyone okay? This way, this way . . ."

"Kelah, slow down. It's not a footrace." Mum's face looked pained. I realized I was nearly running and tried to take slow, deliberate steps, which only gave me the effect of a reluctant bride trudging down the aisle.

"Kay, you're acting like a freak," Boz hissed as I swung all three suitcases off the baggage belt. I was pumped with adrenaline.

"Well, what do you expect when you railroad me like this?" I snarled back. "Mum, Dad, are you ready?" I smiled as sweetly as I could at them. Dad looked suspicious.

When we got outside, I stuffed them into the rusted yellowish Volkswagen Thing I'd hired from a seedy character in Corfutown. I had to slam the boot repeatedly to get everything in. Mom winced.

"We're off," I called out maniacally.

The trip to Pelekastritsa was uneventful, discounting the two stop signs I ran, the little old lady I nearly sideswiped, and that relatively inconsequential roundabout mishap.

Mum's good-bye at the hotel was curt. "I'm exhausted and so is your father. We'll just have salads in our room tonight. We'll talk about all the other business tomorrow."

I wondered if the mainland was too far to swim to.

I sought out Boz at dinnertime. He was back in my villa's extra bedroom, sewing his rucksack up with a piece of dental floss.

"Why'd you do it?" I moaned.

"Kay, they're here. They know. Get over your fine self already. I'm sure it'll go well tomorrow and you'll be well chuffed that they're here and you'll go home together like one big happy family."

"*Happy* and *family* are oxymoronic when applied to the Morrises."

"Well, at least give them a chance."

I snorted. "They're just here to make sure I haven't completely descended into iniquity, and I'm just here to talk about Davey."

"Suit yourself. What are we doing for food? I'm a bit peckish."

I fumed.

"Perhaps my agent can do his job and see that his artist and cash cow is kept in the style to which she has become accustomed," I said.

"What style is that? Bloody ingratitude?"

"Bloody pulchritude, more like."

"What in the effin' hell is pulchritude? Is that, like, a bad odor or something?"

I pinched the back of Boz's upper arm, something he abhors, and was satisfied to hear him yelp. "Your vocabulary is shockingly dismal, considering you're a product of the best public schools dirty old money can buy. *Pulchritude:* physical or moral beauty or excellence," I recited.

"Well, I'm still starving, and you're still pulchritudinous, so why don't we go down to Mirtiotissa Beach and get some of those grilled lamb bits and chips and yogurty sauce."

"Okay."

So we walked along the gravelly road and down the olive-strewn path to the beach. Our favorite place was little more than a shack with meat sizzling on a spit and a sweaty man in a bandanna slopping fixings and sauce into gyros. What it lacked in hygiene it more than made up for in price.

"So, Fee says you're going out with Marta's sister," I blurted out, and mentally kicked myself for violating the embargo so soon.

"Fee told you that? Hmm. That's interesting."

"What do you mean, interesting?"

"Oh, you know, the opposite of boring. Look it up. It's about three hundred pages ahead of pulchritude."

"Bozzie! Don't be a wanker. Come on, what's her name, Ina?"

"Inez. And before you start haranguing me, they're fraternal, okay? They don't look anything alike, so it's not at all weird that I'm working for Marta."

Hmm. Disturbing. Now I was dealing with a totally unknown quantity.

"So, what's she like, this Inez My-Father-Owns-Milano San Giacomo?"

"Nice."

"That's it? Nice?"

"Well, I could tell you other things, but you'd just be jealous or make fun of me, so what's the point? I'd rather just get our souvlaki and decide how we're going to deal with your parents tomorrow, since you think your darling mother is going to rip you a new one. Come to think of it, maybe me too." He handed the sweaty man some money and picked up one of the greasy, dripping masses of lamb and gave it to me.

I guess I should have been worrying about my familial forecast, but, instead, I couldn't help wondering whether Inez San Giacomo had glossy raven hair like her sister and whether Boz had lain with her as he had me, curving around her like a spoon.

"On the other hand," Boz continued, "people do surprise you once in a while."

The key word being, I suppose, *once.*

We don't go back to Jamaica very much. Not since Dad's parents died when I was eleven and twelve, respectively. Before that, we'd fly to Kingston every two years, entering the plane in dismal London rain during the holidays and disembarking into the West Indies' almost ridiculous sunshine. Dad was the archetypical local boy made good. We stayed at a hotel in town, but when we drove to Grandma and Grandpa Morris's house outside Negril, everyone waved and came out to talk to Isaac Morris's boy who went to England and became a doctor.

The year I was eight, Grandma Pearl had the first bout of the breast cancer that would take her life three years and eight months later. When we got to their house that first day, pouring out of the taxi Dad had hired at the airport, Grandma and Grandpa were sitting on the porch waiting for us, like always. But Grandma's normally plump arms and face were thinner, her glossy ebony complexion grayish, and Grandpa didn't try to argue when Dad said Charlie and Davey would carry the bags in for everyone.

Nobody told us she was sick; we just understood, the way kids understand the politics of school break and hoarding candy. Maybe it was the way my normally reserved father's eyes crinkled up when he complimented Grandma on her chicken ragout at dinner. Or the unexplained absences Grandma and Grandpa took every couple of days, leaving us alone to walk through the neatly tilled fields to the shop we called the ice cream shop, because that's all we bought there.

But what really resonates in my memory is that it was the visit when things got better between Mum and Grandma Pearl. I see now how awkward and ill-fated their relationship must have been: the proud, bossy Jamaican mama utterly in charge of her domain, a sorceress with her own loving brand of controlled chaos, yet just slightly diminished, infinitesimally dimmed, by the alien world her unexpected daughter-in-law trailed into her home like springtime pollen, the words and people and conversation of rich white people in London, England. And Mum: bossy and precise and maddeningly, conveniently bohemian; smart enough to never show the slightest condescension toward any of Dad's people or places, expert at displaying the sort of cool interest that cannot be faulted in its directness, and never, ever apologetic for having done the original unthinkable act: marrying a brilliant, talented, impoverished black medical student in a London courthouse. I think she felt that, had she shown a smidgen of self-doubt, a dash of regret, she would have been inundated with recrimination from all quarters. The line she walked with Pearl was particularly fine, a single thread pulled taut between the twin pillars of right and privilege. It was a game where weakness was measured in the fervency of dishwashing and well-modulated refusals of assistance. It was a game that nobody won.

We always ate lunch at the hotel and dinner at the house in Negril. After we ate, the boys followed the men onto the screened-in porch to smoke and talk about fishing and cricket, Dad's brothers and sisters, and the new resorts eating up the island coastline. Usually, Mom drifted into the living room then to read a magazine or a manuscript, her glasses pushed far down on her nose, red pen clicking against her short, square nails. Mom's was a kind of purgatory that nobody seemed to want to challenge. My aunts, if they were there, chattered with Grandma in the kitchen, while I sat in my chair fanning myself, swinging bare feet and listening to the music their voices made.

One night, we were the only ones; Dad's sisters were working at the hotel where they were maids. The men left and Grandma shooed me away with her dishrag so she could whisk dishes to the sink full of soapy water. The skin on her upper arms hung slack and her breath came in little pants.

"Grandma," I said. "Can I play with Daisy and Simone tomorrow?" My cousins lived three miles away, in the shadow of one of the bigger resorts.

"If your mama and papa say so, baby," she said.

Then Grandma Pearl slid down to the floor, as if she had succumbed to a pool of quicksand. Before I could still the tremor that alit in my veins, paralyzing me, Mum was there, grasping Grandma in her long, pale arms, easing her into a chair. Mum brought Grandma a glass of water and watched silently while she sipped it. The kitchen was so quiet you could hear the *plink* of leaking water torturing the floorboards under the sink.

"Oh, Candace," Grandma said. Her voice was thin. This was unusual; she usually didn't call my mother Candace or anything.

Then Mum did the most extraordinary thing. Without saying a word, she took the dishrag from Grandma's closed fist, migrated a stack of dishes from the greasy table to the countertop, and proceeded to clean Grandma Pearl's kitchen, scraping crumbs into the litter bin, sweeping the vinyl floor, scrubbing the tub-size, bean-encrusted black pot until the scratched metal showed through. Neither she nor Grandma spoke. I took their cue, listening to my heart slow down, watching Grandma breathe.

Outside, Grandpa Isaac did his bananaquit bird imitation and my brothers hooted with laughter.

chapter 33

PARKER

Josh slid his hand under my bikini top and pulled the string. I felt it trickle down between my breasts. I looked down and saw they were just like Heidi Klum's—brown and as round as Granny Smith apples.

"Turn around," he ordered.

I faced him, sitting Indian-style. Josh smiled. His canted incisor pointed straight at the pillow of his lower lip. Heat bloomed in my belly. Josh dipped his finger into the bottle of fizzy lemonade and lifted it, dripping, to my chest. He rubbed my nipples in little concentric circles, which felt fantastic. Then he bent his head and licked one. I pushed my hands into his wild thatch of hair.

"Sweet," he murmured.

Suddenly, Neil loomed over us. He had on black chaps and a steel-gray Gap pocket T with an enormous rainbow lollypop sticking out of the pocket. He was bare-assed and his hair was parted on the wrong side.

"Did you tape over *The Simpsons*?" he said accusingly.

I woke up.

My hands lay across my chest, benediction-style. My nipples were hard and my panties felt like someone had spilled chamomile tea in them.

"Oh, God," I moaned.

I hate this type of dream. No, actually, I love this type of dream. What I hate is the way you feel the next time you see the person you dreamed about. There's no way for them to know, but it always seems like their gaze is just a little too knowing, a touch contemplative for comfort. You're afraid to make eye contact, lest something furtive and guilty transmit itself from the recesses of your subconscious to theirs. You worry that extremely vivid sex dreams confer on the dreamee psychic abilities. You blush, stammer, and act like an ass. Not necessarily in that order.

I dragged myself out of bed and looked at the calendar I'd hung over the dresser. September 15. I knew it! Three years to the day since Neil and I bought the bed. Our handmade McRoskey Airflex mattress set with extra-fluffy pillow top was enough to make a cold-blooded mercenary fall to his knees and weep. When we'd slid our joint credit card across the counter to the angel-faced clerk—how could she be anything else, since she was sleeping like a goddamn baby?—I knew we'd be together forever. Nagging disputes? Ha. Petty disagreements? Inconsequential. Financial ruin? No problem. We had the McRoskey, and that meant permanence. When life got too brutal, we'd simply slide between our Egyptian cotton sheets, hunker down atop the individually weighted springs, and wait for peace to envelop us. It would be that simple.

One of the things I'd noticed as I took inventory of my life with Neil was that so much of my security had rested on things. Things bought together, owned together, disagreed over. Things that represented real pivotal moments in our relationship, and things that we'd acquired because we needed them in lieu of those types of moments. Things that made us laugh, and things that made one of us cry. Things that came from past lives and old lovers and lurked in the corners of our life like haunted dust bunnies. Things that represented the future, like the discount ticket booklet to Hawaii and Neil's baby blanket, carefully wrapped in tissue by Jillian the First the day after she'd finally accepted that Neil would not be entering matrimony with a Vanderbilt, an Astor, or at least a Hilton sister.

Things.

I could see now how much structure and purpose I'd derived from them. From the beginning, a lot of our closeness, Neil's and mine, was rooted in a compatibility based on taste and a kind of primal acquisitiveness. We loved early Madonna, Manolo Blahnik, and Eames. We deplored Trump hotels, fake tans, and Sun Valley. Ergo, we were perfect together. The fact that we arrived at our mutual good-taste destination on entirely different paths was immaterial, at least then. For Neil, taste was something that just came with the territory, like having a nanny and three middle names. For me, it was a reaction to the disorder of a household that reinvented itself every week around a new political candidate or bioengineered-fruit protest.

Now, instead of Neil and a lifetime-guaranteed mattress set, I had a foster dog and a bamboo beach mat that wouldn't survive the summer.

With typical prescience, Blakas chose that moment to rush into the room. My canine friend was a highly emotional creature. He always acted as if we were star-crossed lovers torn apart by unfortunate circumstances, reuniting after years of misery. His tail quivered and his raisin-colored eyes squinched up at the corners. His small barrel chest heaved, full of love.

"Blakas, you are the best," I said, rubbing his velvety ears.

He licked me once, ran outside, and peed hard into Mrs. Gianniotis's flower bed.

Molly e-mailed me on Wednesday. Something about landing a big client and calling her as soon as possible and being featured in

Dwell and world domination. I was so consumed by the final stages of Tony's redesign and party preparations I forgot to call. I got another e-mail from her on Friday.

> Hey, kid. Where are you? Stop. Need to talk. Stop. Call immediately. Stop. Major business development. Stop. I hope you got rid of that Ativan. Stop. It was making you nuts. Stop. CALL ME. Stop. Mol

I had to smile. It was a little joke we shared to punctuate important communiqués with telegram marks. I resolved to call her that evening—morning her time. For Mol, *urgent matters of world domination* was often code for where'd you put the stapler, or what do you think of cranberry red with military blue.

The rest of the afternoon slipped by quickly. Brian and I had just about finished the interior of the taverna. Tony's workmen had opened up a gorgeous window that brought light into every nook and cranny of the place. The upholstery had been replaced on all the chairs. The walls were a monastic white, the trim shining Greek blue. A thick arch of bougainvillea encircled the doorway. The floor had been fixed, with paver tiles cemented into cracked areas. I'd moved the bar around to the other side to open up the room, creating an intimate dining area to one side but a larger area that could be used for dancing. I'd shipped out all the dust-collecting tchotchkes and pared down to a few fine old Greek collectibles. The wait staff would now wear crisp white shirts or blouses with black slacks, except Tony, who would don a classic Greek key-pattern vest (we'd joked that he'd need a different color to match red, blond, and brunette). Brian had found a fabulous slab of black marble threaded through with white filaments at a flea market in town. We'd affixed it to leftover stone on the terrace and turned it into a beautiful tabletop overlooking the sea. We were so close I could almost taste the spanakopita squares we'd serve at the coming-out party.

I waved good-bye to Tony and the crew and hurried over to the

telephone center before it closed. I bought a phone card and
went through the usual rigmarole.

"Good morning. Glass, Ng and Associates." The latest intern
sounded hungry and vaguely Eastern European.

"Hi. This is Parker calling from Greece. Is Molly around?"

"Parker?" Miss Latvia drew my name out until it sounded like
she was ordering someone to park the car.

"Parker Glass, as in *Glass,* Ng," I said sharply.

"Oh, excuse me, Ms. Glass. I'll transfer you now."

"Peachy," I said to the Muzak. "And hurry up or you're fired."

"Park." Molly sounded relieved. "Where the hell have you been?"

"On a remote Greek island without a telephone or regular
e-mail access, redesigning a bankrupt taverna pro bono and having an active fantasy life but, sadly, no action as of yet."

Sound of papers rustling . . . "Well, yeah . . . oh, here it is. . . .
What did you say about a taverna? Never mind. No time. Okay,
Park, you there? Things are rockin' around here. You've got to
come home. I already reserved you a seat on Monday's flight.
We've got two new jobs starting and summer's officially over.
You're not going to believe who came through for us! Barbara
Bergman, of the Muff poodle, lawsuit-bringing Bergmans? Ap-
parently she's on the board over at the MOMA. And she hap-
pened to mention the work we did at a board meeting, and guess
who's just hired us to do their guest wing? Come on, guess!"

"Sharon Stone?" I'll admit it, all this talk of flights and clients
had me feeling sort of . . . well, odd. I figured if anything was going to get me home, it was Shar-babe.

Molly snorted. "I wish. Close, though."

"Danielle Steel?"

"Sadly, no."

"Danny Glover?"

"Cold."

"Robin Williams?" I was going through San Francisco's hand-
ful of celebrities with a fine-tooth comb.

"Better."

"I give up."

"Christopher Peña," she whispered.

I felt a shiver work its way down my spine, reminiscent of some of my wilder dreams of things Josh Lido might do to me with his tongue. If you were an ambitious young decorator on the rise, you didn't just say Christopher Peña's name; you *invoked* it. Christopher Peña was a television actor slash movie star slash Latino hunk slash political activist, recognizable to all but a few TV-less freaks, Shaolin monks, and my parents. Last year, he'd announced in an exclusive interview with *Entertainment Tonight* that he was renouncing Hollywood, giving up Hollywood screen goddesses, and moving back to his childhood home, San Francisco. Apparently, part of keeping it real included marrying a costar/supermodel who looked exactly like him (unbelievably gorgeous with Mayan cheekbones and central incisors you could surf on) and renovating a sinfully ornate landmark Victorian in the city's golden corridor off Alamo Square. Peña was occasionally seen about town, squeezing organic vegetables, eating at taquerias, and signing autographs for swooning men and women.

I did a quick approximation of what I thought was the Catholic self-crossing ritual. *Christopher Peña.*

"Good Lord," I said.

"She sure is," said Molly.

"Have that Latvian girl send Barbara Bergman flowers or something. To thank her."

"Already did. And she's from Tajikistan. Her name's Farangis."

"Does that make her Tajik or Tajikistani?"

"Who the hell knows? The first three weeks, I thought her name was Angus. She finally corrected me last week," Molly said. "So, what do you think? About this Peña stuff?"

"I think it's fantastic. Who's the other client?"

"Oh, nobody important."

My bullshit radar went into high alert.

"Molly, who *is* it?"

"Um, can we talk about this later?"

"*Molly, this call's costing me like ten dollars a minute. Who's the freakin' client?*"

"Jack and Jill," she said.

"As in Jackson and Jillian Wentworth, my in-laws," I repeated stupidly.

"Well . . . yeah."

I freaked.

"What *is* this, some sort of weird revenge? Like they're going to commission a fuckin' kitchen or something, skip on the bill, then hightail it back to New York? Besides, they never send me business. They think you grow a business by praying mightily for success on major Episcopalian holidays and air-kissing socialites at christenings. There must be some mistake," I ranted.

"No mistake, Park. In fact, they want to have the apartment ready when, uh, Neil comes home with the, um, baby."

"What do you mean, '*comes home*'?"

Silence.

"What are you talking about? Neil's in South America. That Belgian . . . creature—she's in South America too. And whatever evil grommet they spawned . . . *Are you saying they're moving to San Francisco?*" Horror spurted through my body so forcefully I thought I might faint. I bent over to jam my head between my legs. Somehow I'd never imagined that this could happen. When I spun nighttime terrors about Neil's affair and the Belgian Waffler's pregnancy, they always ended with the despicable duo ensconced somewhere in the Third or Fourth World with thatched huts and lepers. And hantavirus. Lots of hantavirus.

"Well, none of this is substantiated. I swear, I'd tell you, Park. All I know is that I get a call out of the blue from Jillian, and she says they want to be able to see their first grandchild, so they're buying a condo in Pac Heights for visits. And they want to redecorate. So, I'm being kind of snotty, and I ask her who referred her, and she says Neil. So I'm, like, *ohh-kay,* if that's the way you want to play it, lady. Maybe it's Neil's way of trying to make up for the mess he's made, in some incredibly inadequate and pathetic way? Like sending you business is the best he can do at this point? So

I'm, like, whatever, it's a good job, and I'll take it, you know? The only condition is that I manage the project. No Parker. That's why you need to come back. I need you on the Peña gig, lucky cow," she said.

My mind was racing. I realized suddenly that, over the past three months, a strange reversal had taken place and Greece had somehow become my home and my real home, San Francisco, had become my new escape route. If Neil and the Belgian Endive were to—Goddess forbid such a travesty—make their home there, I'd have to move. Far, far away. As in alternative universe or Arctic tundra far.

Like everyone, I'd had the mandatory what-if-you-ran-into-them-in-all-their-procreative-glory nightmare. In mine, I was inevitably in sweats, alone on a Saturday night, and cursed with a mountainous zit. We were at the local video store. They were flaxen-haired and glowing, their cherubic soon-to-be-bilingual offspring wedged into one of those arrogantly plush strollers that look like tiny SUVs. I was simultaneously flabby and anorectic, as a result of a diet consisting entirely of Laughing Cow cheese squares and See's caramels. My formerly peaches-and-cream complexion was tinged with yellow due to terminal liver damage. I smelled.

"Parker," Neil would say courteously, staring at me with pity welling in his crinkly IP-attorney-cum-aid-worker eyes. "This is my new wife, Juliette, and our little one, Moppet Without Borders."

I'd peer over the side of the carriage, careful not to spill my week's supply of Captain Morgan's and porn lite on the little munchkin. Before my eyes, the innocent babe would morph into a hideous gorgon, fangs springing into drooling projectiles, snakes curling from its Raphaelite ringlets.

But only I could see it.

"Aaagh," I wailed.

"Park? Park, are you all right?"

"Mol? Tell Peña I'll call him on Monday," I said bleakly.

"Does that mean you're coming home?"

Home. A nice concept, don't you think?

chapter 34

CLAIRE

Something strange has happened since I slept with Andreas and started singing again. Well, more than one thing, I suppose. First, I found myself shopping for undies that didn't look like adult-size diapers. (If you must know, I stopped short of buying the velvet thong and suspender set and settled on butter-yellow silk French hi-cuts.) And yesterday afternoon at the used bookshop I ducked behind the archaeology section with a worn copy of Anaïs Nin I was too shy to buy and devoured five stories before the clerk issued a discreet cough. (Have you read that bit about the schoolgirls and the little dog with the, er, long nose? Chrrrist!) Also, I find myself saying no to Ethan and Brian quite a bit more than usual. Sometimes it's just unimportant things, like let's-go-to-the-dairy-for-yogurt or how-about-a-walk-Mum. But as often it's the type of contact I would have jumped at back home: the entreaties to do their laundry while they keep me company from the kitchen (usually involving serious obliteration of what-ever I had prepared for dinner, lunch, or breakfast, or perhaps all three); the inquiries as to my availability to discuss whichever love interest/boss/friend/roommate/family member is currently carrying out a vicious and utterly deliberate campaign to ruin said son's existence. These days, airy refusals slip off my lips with almost frightening ease. After the first few such responses, they stopped staring at me with those wide amber eyes, startled and hurt and uncomprehending as lion cubs denied their dinner. They'd ceased pleading with me—*Oh, Mum, come on, what are you on about?*—and simply started shrugging their muscular shoulders and muttering about women and incipient madness and things beyond their control.

I know how I'm supposed to interpret this change. It's all part of my liberation, of course. No longer am I the Mother Vessel, the perfect urn for carrying the weight of my family's expectations. Now I'm Independent-Thinking Woman. My husband slept with a young tart and had the predictably poor taste to do it in plain view, so I did the only thing I could to retain my dignity: had an affair with an equally young, foreign strings musician with a proclivity for crisp white shirts and exposed chest. (I should also add, for the record, that he is quite swarthy, which, if I'm reading the literature correctly, grants me extra points in the piss-your-neglectful-husband-off-to-no-end category.) It's supposed to feel like the great equalizer, the exact cure for the rejection disease. Now that I've evened the playing field somewhat by sowing my oats in the greater European Union, I can expect to have the denial slip away, the wool lifted from before my eyes, the rose-colored glasses through which my former life was viewed slipped gently off my nose and left in the gutter to be crunched underfoot by teeming hordes of suitors, eager young men grateful for the opportunity to gobble up life at the altar of my greater wisdom and experience. When I opened my legs, the voices say, I also opened my mind. Hail to the Independent Woman! I shall emerge from the bed of my lover(s) sleek and delightfully self-absorbed, a creature of unerring instincts for self-preservation and pleasure. Like a cat. And we all know how cats treat their children, right? Long-nailed swats, serial abandonment, occasional cannibalism. Such fun!

The pressure to play the game, to rattle the saber, to buy the thong, is strong indeed. It's almost as if there's an unwritten rule book one must follow, or betray the sisterhood: *The Ten Commandments of the Adulterous Married Woman Who Has Sought Payback in the Greek Islands with Her Swarthy Underage Lover*:

1. Thou shalt no longer respond to antiquated, oppressive labels such as "Mum." Hereafter, thou shalt instruct thine offspring to refer to thee as either "Claire," "Ms. Dillon," or "Hot Pants."

2. Thou shalt refer to thy husband not by name but by epithets such as "sperm donor," "that man person," or simply "wanker."

3. Thou shalt purchase revealing lingerie in shades of red, black, or leopard print. Furthermore, thou shalt charge said lingerie to the wanker's credit card from an outlet easily recognizable as a purveyor of such objects, such as Victoria's Secret or Frederick's of Hollywood. If thou art feeling particularly energetic and creative—which presumably thou art, due to sudden influx of youthful, swarthy sex—thou shalt entice thy female comrade to telephone the wanker's home and pose as customer-care representative, inquiring as to the desirability of the suspenders to go with the recently purchased nipple-less bra and crotchless edible panty set.

4. Thou shalt procureth a "fun" job as a sex-toy manufacturer, professor of women's studies, real estate agent, or cruise-ship director, amassing great personal wealth and possessing gorgeous manicures.

5. If thou possesseth a passable singing voice, thou shalt sing immensely sensual duets with the young, swarthy lover, preferably in the presence of the wanker's business associates.

6. Thou shalt cosmetically alter thy lips, face, nose, stomach, breasts, or thighs to match as closely as possible the exact dimensions of Britney Spears and deny vigorously that thou hast altered them (except if thou must trade on secret in exchange for name of more highly skilled plastic surgeon for next round of "spa facials").

7. Thou shalt participate in inordinate numbers of extracurricular activities, with names including the words *club, swinging,* and *group*. Membership in clubs with high quotient of rich single men is encouraged. Not because thou seeketh a man, of course—how *beneath* a strong, independent, sexually liberated woman and owner of thong underwear—but rather because it reinforces how alive thou art, how in control of thy emotional state, how *committed* to the preservation of bird life throughout the greater Sydney area.

8. Thou shalt donate thy sweatpants and leggings to charity.

9. Thou shalt stop cooking.

10. Thou shalt not experience a milligram of regret as to above actions, as to do so would be tantamount to a total negation of self-pride and cause all women ever born anywhere to lose all their hard-earned gains and revert back to social status of eighteenth-century immigrant garment workers.

Indeed.

On the heels of this newfound reluctance to give as freely of myself as I had before, I found myself confused. And embattled. And assaulted by the agendas on all sides. On one side was the eye-for-an-eye brigade. The ones who believed the modern woman is supposed to feel marvelously unconflicted about her journey back to dignity through gainful employment and compulsive shopping. Or her search for self-actualization and sexual independence through actual cheap sex. Or her decision to buy—and, yes, even *wear*—thong underwear. Granted, there are women who don't agree with this view, namely my sister Valerie and the other two happily married women in Australia, and probably some nuns and the terribly ancient Corfiote woman who sells bags of olives to tourists for one euro and has been wearing black widow's weeds since her husband died fighting the Turks in 1897. These women have their own rule book, sort of like the Old Testament versus the New. Theirs would be called something like *The Ten Commandments of Women Who Wish to Never Have Sex Again, Especially with a Swarthy Underage Lover, Even Though Their Husbands Are Experiencing the True Meaning of Deep Tissue with Massage Therapists on a Weekly Basis:*

1. Thou shalt wear black a lot, with the exception of black garments designed by Donna Karan or any designer, or anything sexy or resembling an outfit. Black garments that are also shapeless are preferred.

2. Thou shalt reorganize thy responsibilities and interests to coincide exactly with those of thine offspring, so that thou art able to view removing the stains off soiled rugby jerseys with the same level of enthusiasm thou currently possess for vacations in Bermuda or winning the Tattslotto.

3. Thou shalt sublimate thine libido into scrubbing the mold between the shower tiles.

4. Thou shalt respond to potentially embarrassing marital transgressions by baking a pie or, in a pinch, a tart. Pies that are of prizewinning quality are encouraged. Homemade crust is encouraged.

5. Thou shalt cease to get massages.

6. Thou shalt cultivate an intimate relationship with thy mother-in-law that involves such activities as baking pies and poring through old photo albums that depict the

wanker as a child, before he took a shine to massage therapists practicing the Swedish or deep-tissue methods. If thy mother-in-law is dead, thou shalt cultivate an intimate relationship with thy favorite talk-show host or the various voices thou hast heard in thy head since the Incident.

7. When asked what one "does," thou shalt say thou art writing thy memoirs or researching thy family genealogy. Writing thy memoirs is not encouraged.

8. Thou shalt color thy hair using home coloring kits that do not effectively cover up gray or achieve enviable translucency or shine.

9. Thou shalt not travel to the following places: Greece (except for Athens), Caribbean islands, Antillean islands, Hawaiian islands, Polynesian islands, Latin America, Paris, Parisian suburbs, or the apartment complex where thy husband's girlfriend lives.

10. Thou shalt never have sex again.

The problem with all this, as I see it, is that Gary's sleeping with the masseuse doesn't cancel out my sleeping with Andreas. Not really. That seems to me a rather narrow moral and common-sense ledge to stand on, you know? At a springy forty-six, I know myself pretty well, and I don't see myself and my needs fitting comfortably on that ledge. The other problem is that I suspect I might have screwed some man silly even if Gary hadn't cheated on me. Sure, it may have taken a bit more work on my suitor's part—roses, dinners, poetry, sidelong glances, and a bit of those lovely gropings that seem to go by the wayside when you tie the knot, along with roommates, two-piece bathing suits, and holidays with one's mates. I'm not saying I'm racked with guilt exactly—more ambivalent than anything. I mean, I fully expected to be racked with guilt, had the old hair shirt ready, complete with nasty, itchy wool or something equally punishing (Astroturf?

Sink scrubber?). In fact, I'm more troubled by what I *don't* feel than what I *do*. That's what I'm getting at.

And as to the rule book? Well, my pies always were sort of mediocre.

Gary wrote me a letter.

When I picked up my post at the travel agency/poste restante/gossipmonger's that is Alexiou Travel, I could tell instantly that something was amiss.

"Morning," I said to Anya, who was behind the counter playing horse and rider with that chubby boy of Nia's.

"Claire!" she said.

"What?"

Anya's cheeks pinkened. "Oh, nothing. You're here for the mail, right?"

"I'm here for the post and to talk to you, of course. See how you're holding up." Rachel had slipped back into our lives like a favorite pair of earrings that had been lost, written off, replaced at great cost, and found too late. Ethan and Anya seemed to be weathering it fairly well, but one never knew.

"Oh, things are okay." Anya busied herself alphabetizing letters, paused. She looked at me straight on, her thick-lashed eyes glowing with something that looked close to pleading. "Tell me something, Claire. What did you really think of Rachel when she was with Ethan? What was your relationship like?"

I chose my words carefully. "Well, it was pretty average, I'd say. Typical Mum–girlfriend relationship. She was mostly working, and Ethan works long hours as well, so I'd see her on the occasional family holiday or birthday dinner. They were, you know, living together. I suppose we always got along, but it's hard when you see your own child unhappy with something. I mean, they didn't have a bad relationship that I could tell, just didn't want the same things in the end. But, as a mother, your first allegiance is always to your child, and in that respect, the people your children get romantically involved with are to be viewed with respect and no small amount of wariness. They have the power to make your lovely kid very, very unhappy someday." I laughed to try to lighten my words. "I sound like an old fishwife, don't I? Didn't mean to come off so negative. Long story short, I always liked Rachel and I think she liked me well enough, but since our relationship wasn't the primary one I'm not really capable of judging it."

"So she wasn't . . . diabolical?" Anya said.

I laughed. "No, maybe a little self-absorbed. Really, I don't know. You'll have to ask Ethan." As soon as I said it I realized the absurdity of the suggestion.

"On second thought, I take that back," I said.

Anya grinned. "You have a letter." She handed it to me. My home address blared out from the airmail envelope. Seeing it brought back all the new realities in a rush: singing, sex, our marriage, singing, Gary.

Sex.

"Oh," I said. Somehow, in my evolution into Independent Woman, I never imagined Gary initiating contact. It made everything seem so much more negotiable somehow. I wasn't sure I wanted that. Yet. I had gotten used to the whole indirect communication thing—Gary telling Valerie to ask me did I want to renew my subscription to Women of Substance gym; me telling Brian to tell Ethan to tell Gary that the spare scissors were in the third drawer from the left, underneath the spatulas. Somehow, I'd suspended disbelief and started to cultivate the notion that we'd float forever in this airy, impersonal way, like friendly but distant planets in a sprawling galaxy. The letter changed all that.

I took the letter, said good-bye, and walked home by way of side streets. One of the huge ferries that arrived daily from the mainland and other islands interrupted the horizon. It looked tiny and innocuous, a speck at the edge of the filmy bluish line that separated the brighter colors of sea and sky. I'd noticed that they never seemed to move. Yet the next time you glanced up, the ship would have relocated as if plucked up and set down again by an enormous hand, the details just starting to emerge from the blur, doll-size people sprinkled on the deck, engines churning ivory froth in two neat lines. The ferries always seemed a bit menacing, looming as they did, bringing new cadres of explorers.

I found a good spot on the town's single bench, between the Dallas and the launderette. The envelope was partly unsealed, as if Gary had written something he'd regretted, torn it open, amended it, and hastily pressed the damp edges back together.

> *Dear Claire,*
>   *It's terrible and strange to be writing to you care of a post office in another country, not knowing where you are. Especially knowing I sent you there. While I can't say this was the worst summer I ever had—when Ruth was born was probably worse for both of us—it's been a long, lonely road, Claire. Whatever unique hell you've imagined is going on at the house, well, multiply it, say, ten times, and you've about got it. . . .*

In spite of myself, I had to laugh. Perhaps my visions of crusty TV dinners had been close to accurate?

> *The reason I'm writing is that I want to tell you I've gone into counseling, or therapy I guess you'd call it. I know, I know—next I'll be reading your women's magazines and joining the bloody knitting circle—but bear with me for a minute. Here's what I've been working on saying: It's about time I take responsibility for my behavior, for who I am. I just wish I had done it years ago, before things reached the state they did. I have been extremely unhappy, and have only myself to blame. Now, don't go looking out the window to see if hell has frozen over—this really is me talking. But I've had a lot of time to think, more than ever before maybe, and I've decided I want to change. For you and for the boys—both our boys—but most of all for myself. Dr. Francetti—that's the*

counselor—*says I have to be open to trying new ways of communicating, new ways of doing things. And I am. I think. If you'll think about forgiving me—well, not forgiving me, I know that's too much to ask, but at least listening to me, giving us another chance—I will do my best to make sure you don't regret that decision. Dr. Francetti, Dina Francetti—yes, she's a lady doctor, can you bloody believe it?—is very good at her job. You'd like her, Claire. And I know she'd like you. (She already told me I need to stop worrying about being liked and get on with the business of sorting myself out.) I've thought a lot about what made me get involved with someone outside our marriage, have an affair, that is, and lie about it, too, and while I don't have many answers yet, I've been thinking that part of me was trying to provoke you into something, some reaction. I never wanted you to leave, never wanted to split, but you've always had a self-containment that I've never had. Maybe it was growing up with parents like yours, devoted people who taught you you could do whatever you put your mind to, or something. I don't know. I just know that I am ready to change if you'll have me back. Will you have me back, Claire?*

About Brian. When I told Dr. Francetti that I hadn't seen my son in seven years, five months, three days, when I heard those words coming from my mouth, I felt as if someone had punched me in the head. I felt sick. It's almost as if I'd been in fucking hibernation this whole time, for all the emotion I'd allowed myself to feel about our—what's the word she used?—estrangement. I still have a hard time with the life he's chosen for himself, and may always have a hard time with it. But he is my son, our son, and we can't waste any more time. What if he was taken from us, like Ruth was? I know you've lived with that reality for more years than I can imagine, and I am more sorry than you know for that. He's of my blood, and there's not much else in this world, is there, Claire? What else do we really have, but each other, our children, our dreams of something better? Whatever you want

me to do to repair the mess I've made, I'll do it. I swear. I
know I don't have much credibility with you, but believe me
when I say I've changed. Ask Val. We've talked a lot on the
phone and I think she understands where I'm coming from,
that I've really made a change, am working on changing, I
mean.

I'm sure you're wondering what happened to make me
undergo this sea change. I guess you could say I had a
revelation of a sort. I haven't told anyone else about this. Not
Dr. Francetti, not Stef, not Valerie. No one. But it seems right
to tell you, so I will. Here's what happened: I was walking in
the field behind the house. I brought Briggs, and he was just
running all over the place, chasing birds, enjoying himself. I'd
been taking a lot of long walks in the evening, after work.
Helps me relax. Anyway, I'd just passed through the trees back
of Murphy's place. The thing I remember noticing is that
there was no wind, nothing. I mean, usually there's a little
breeze in the evenings, the sound of leaves brushing against
each other. Something. But that night there was this stillness
to everything that made it seem like we'd stepped out of time
and walked into another dimension or something. I stopped,
and it felt like I was listening to something, that this whisper
came from all around me, not a voice but like a rustling. I
wasn't scared, but I didn't know what it was. And then Ruth's
name popped into my head. It was the strangest thing. I
wasn't seeing her, or what I would have imagined to be her,
just a name, a sense of her presence. But it's like she was older
than me, older than any of us. Just this amazingly wise, calm
presence. And I felt an incredible peace come over me. That's
when I knew I had to let certain things I was clinging to go. I
just knew. Later on, I felt sort of weird about it—it's
practically a ghost story, isn't it?—but I thought you'd
understand. I remember feeling terribly disappointed that you
weren't there. I wanted to tell you right away. And that told
me something too.

I think I'll just end here. It seems like the right spot. I love

you very much. That's what I want to say to you. That and
please come home soon.

> *Love,*
> *your husband,*
> *Gary*

I realized I'd been breathing shallowly and tried to let some air out of my lungs. There were people all around me, moving around, but it looked like a silent film, their movements jerky and soundless. My whole world had dwindled to the size of a love letter.

I felt the paper between my fingers flutter to the ground. Through my tears, I could see that the ferry had come in, had been relocated to the harbor by the huge, unseen force that governs such things. The island's newest explorers disembarked down the gangplank, walking the tentative walk of people seeing something absurdly and unexpectedly wonderful, of being given a license to hope, perhaps for the first time.

chapter 35
〰〰〰〰〰〰〰〰〰〰〰

ANYA

"What a moron," Parker said.

We were sitting on the beach, under an umbrella. Parker was trying to decide what to tell Christopher Peña tomorrow about the job. I was trying not to stare at Evil Rachel, who was lying between her minions, Martine and Nell, in a strip of pink Lycra that left little—nay, nothing—to the imagination. She had the sort of voice that shrieked "Look at me!" without even trying. A teasing, bantering tone and champagne-flute trill that carried all the way down the beach and back. A beach in Australia or Martinique. So far, she'd adhered to the agreement not to instigate trouble or talk to us. For all the good it did. Without even moving or talking, she was trouble. Provocation would have oozed silently from her pores—if her seemingly flawless flesh had any such human blemishes. Every time we saw her she'd give us a little princessy wave. Too smart to let her gaze linger on Ethan, she'd grant him the edge of her sharp cheekbone and a silky-smooth hip and plant her azure gaze directly on me. If she'd actually been pissier, had sulked or screamed or flirted or had a hissy fit, it would have been easier; it was her breezy acceptance of everything that scared the *mierda* out of me.

"Thank you for being so supportive and also constructive," I said to Parker.

We laughed.

"But so far you can't fault her for anything but having a perfect body and white teeth," I continued.

"The only women who wear that color pink are prostitutes and Pamela Anderson," Parker said.

"Maybe she thinks it's okay because there's so little of it."

"Could be."

"Oh, God, there she goes again," I hissed.

Rachel stood up, extended her long, lean body, and performed a series of deceptively casual stretches that showed us in graphic detail just how extensive that bikini wax really was. The shiny cap of chestnut hair swung cheerfully in the sun, seemingly impervious to dirt, salt, and dullness. Her bare breasts didn't droop or even bob—they saluted. *Chica,* I'm not kidding—if those babies were in the military, they'd get extra points for maintaining their upright bearing in the face of little things like gravity or nuclear war. Finally, Rachel ran down to the water's edge and jumped in, shrieking gaily when a group of young men surrounded her like roving sharks around a chum spill.

"Christ on a freakin' stick," Parker muttered.

"Don't take Jesus's name in vain," I said automatically.

Parker rolled her eyes. "Where's Hey-Zeus when a couple of nice, decent gals like us are being forced to watch live outtakes from *Debbie Does Downward-Facing Dog* on a public beach? Huh?"

I shrugged. Talking about her only made it worse. I wasn't about to let myself get obsessed with Evil Rachel. Besides, I had something other than Rachel on my mind. Before the forked-tongued one had swooped in from Down Under (literally— ha-ha), Ethan had asked me if I wanted him to come to San Francisco. If I wanted us to be together. Pretty simple question, and we still hadn't finished our conversation. Also, I still hadn't told him everything he should know to make such a weighty decision. I still hadn't told him my secret. And now the climate for such a confession was more inhospitable than ever. I'd sworn Kelah to secrecy, and she'd agreed to keep past transgressions out of the column. But I felt the weight of it like a sack of wet sand. That's the problem with secrets, you know? Once you start thinking about them, imagining how it would feel to make them, oh, not secret anymore, their weight and import become almost unbearable. Plus, in my case, there were mitigating circumstances—the curse. You see, I knew what it was like to live with the Love Curse. And I knew the cause of my petty miseries. But I didn't know what would happen if *yo lo chaste,* if I spilled the beans. Would the curse depart, rising up out of my body like a freed soul, wings tipped with stale gold? Or would it shriek its indignation, burrowing deeper into my future, gorging on my blood like a maddened deer tick? Was this my one true chance to free myself, or the biggest mistake I'd ever make? (Well, second biggest.) Would Ethan look at me one final time with those sweet, sexy eyes, tell me how sorry he was, and run screaming for the next flight to Sydney? Or would he enfold me in his arms, kiss my face, and bring his fist down, shattering the curse into a million bits? Maybe he'd buy a six-pack and order a pizza—all the better to watch *Mi Vida Loca.*

"Would you look at that?" Parker said.

"Hmm?" I was still lost in thought.

"G-string. Miss Can't-survive-without-attention-for-more-than-five-minutes." Parker pointed to a dappled speck out near the floating raft. It seemed to be waving.

"What's she doing?" I said. Without my glasses or contacts, I was all but useless.

"Oh, waving and yelling something. I guess the Italian racing team wasn't enough for her. Now she's got to summon the whole beach to come feel her up."

I squinted but couldn't see anything. "Could she really be hurt?"

Parker shrugged. "Yeah and I'm going to sleep with Christopher Peña." She flicked some sand off her knee and grinned at me. "Okay, bad example."

Next thing we knew, Evil Rachel's minions jumped up from practicing their Satanic verses and started yelling.

"Help!" screamed Martine or Nell. "Our friend's drowning!"

"Omigod, she's out there and something's terribly wrong," shrieked the other one.

"Somebody do something!" they wailed in unison.

"Oh, my goodness, oh, shit, cor blimey, aye, matey, Rachel's dead, her boobies popped," mimicked Parker in an atrocious Aussie accent, a shade too loudly.

"Hey, I think she's really hurt," said Graeme, a permanently blistered, permanently stoned, ginger-haired Scot. He stared out from the shoreline. We could see he had no intention of sacrificing a joint to make a heroic rescue. He took a long drag and sat back on his heels to watch the action unfold.

I sat up a little straighter, feeling that shot of adrenaline you get when something freaky happens. Who was going to deal with this? I could swim now, but certainly not strongly enough to save someone else, not to mention that I couldn't see two feet in front of me. Not to mention that Evil Rachel was my nemesis.

Before the thought was even completed, a long tan blur streaked toward the water, arcing into the petite waves with Olympic precision. Strong arms windmilled through the turquoise swells, churning out purpose with every round.

It was Ethan.

"Oh, for God's sake, what crap," muttered Parker.

"What's happening? What's he doing now?" I said. How irritating not to see anything.

"Well, he's almost there. . . . She's out there near that sandbar on the way to the diving raft. He's got her. . . . She's struggling—ungrateful little hussy. He's got her panties around his head—just kidding—good God, her legs are around his neck. . . ." I made a choking noise and Parker actually winced. "Sadly, that part is true. Okay, he's bringing her in. He's swimming back to shore and the evil one's kind of tucked under his arm on her back. David Hasselhoff always did that on *Baywatch,* yeah? Well, I guess it was his stunt double. Anyway, ooh, they've hit the shore. Oh, God . . . yick," Parker said.

"What?"

"Well, she tried valiantly to stand but Little Miss Helpless just couldn't manage it, and now Ethan's picking her up and carrying her to shore. Blech. This is too gross." Parker lay down on the mat and threw her T-shirt over her face in protest.

In spite of myself, I stood up to watch. Gradually, a shape materialized onshore. Water streamed off Ethan's shoulders, plastered his auburn hair into a seal's cap. Not made for water, his cotton shorts sagged, exposing the tender curve of iliac crest jutting from his hips, the corded muscles of his straining abdomen. Evil Rachel lay supine in his arms, reclining almost comfortably, and certainly familiarly, chestnut head thrown back, white throat prettily bared, boobs peaking five inches from Ethan's face like ramekins of whipped cream. Her delicate foot even dripped a little blood daintily onto the sand, without so much as marring their (scant) clothing. Color bloomed in her angled cheeks, framing the Cheshire cat smile, which was turned toward Ethan at full wattage. It was like the *pinche Blue Lagoon*.

"Those are definitely fake!" Parker crowed, upright again. "Normal boobs don't stand up like that when you're lying down. They flatten out, like pancakes!"

"*Dios mío*, it's the curse," I burst out.

"What curse?" Parker answered.

I ignored her and concentrated on imbibing every detail of Ethan and Evil Rachel's watery, cinematic exit. He laid her gently on her beach mat. The guy who rented beach chairs was already there with a first-aid kit and was removing bandages. Ethan leaned back on his heels. I could see his chest working in and out, as if he had just made love. Evil Rachel kept his hand firmly grasped in hers, linked by the forefingers. I could almost see their old bond reasserting itself, the fates showering them with sparkly, fated *rightness*.

"Hell, Ethan, you always did have good stamina," Evil Rachel said, her throaty voice made dizzyingly raspy by swallowed sea. "I guess this means I'm yours to take care of. Isn't that what they say when you save someone's life? That you have to watch over them? And isn't it for forever or something?"

There are three kinds of fated relationships. The first is forged on shared good fortune: high-school sweethearts with lockers assigned next to each other; airline passengers with fortuitous layovers in benign locations; truants whose lives are turned around by the star-crossed guidance counselor filling in for someone on maternity leave.

The second type is carved from the stony masses of tragedy or misfortune. It is much more powerful. We've all seen footage of disaster survivors—people who walked or were carried away from downed airplanes, from torched buildings or twisted car wreckages, abusive husbands or animal attacks. On *Sally Jessy* or *Maury Povich,* tough grown men from the heartland sit side by side like shy lovers, gazing into each other's eyes with the kind of devotion they normally reserved for the Sooners or Old Milwaukee. They say things like, "If Bob hadn't saved me, I'd never have lived to see my son grow up! He may be black, but he's my brother, man! He's my brother!" They embrace awkwardly, reaching around their scars. They cry.

You don't mess around with this type.

There's a third kind too. Not the kind that you talk about, the kind that ends well and, as the years go by, is taken out and passed around by loving hands, the kind whose shining patina is honed by sheer gratefulness and mutual gladness. No, the last type comes from somewhere else. It's the dark, deadly version of the second type. It's the crimson tie that pulses between the drunk driver and his victim, the battering husband and his wife, the molester and his survivor.

The sinful lover and his accursed beloved.

Between them is an umbilical cord that never gets cut. I know all about it. I still have one, leaking out from my belly, back to that railcar flat in the barrio, tugging me back to reality whenever I try to fly too high, too far, too fast.

chapter 36

PARKER

"Is Mr. Peña there, please?" I said a little haughtily, as if I rang movie stars every day.

"Who should I say is calling?" the no-nonsense, middle-aged Latina voice at the other end said. I conjured sooty hair, thick waist, a ledgelike chest.

"Parker Glass of Glass, Ng and Associates."

I prayed for Greece's notoriously fragile phone system to do right by me this time. After an appalling two minutes, which I spent counting long-distance charges and trying to overhear what was going on in his house, he answered. The One True God: Christopher Peña.

"*Christopher* speaking," he said, pronouncing his name the Spanish way.

"Good afternoon—oh, I guess it's morning there, sorry—I mean ... anyway, this is Parker Glass, Molly Ng's partner. Just touching base with you about the guesthouse."

"Well, it's nice to meet the elusive artist at last. You do excellent work, Ms. Glass." His voice was deep, ethnic, and mellifluous, his vocal cords cello strings dipped in liquid sex. I felt a silly quivering jellify my knees and swallowed.

"Thank you. We're very grateful for Barbara Bergman's referral. I'm looking forward to seeing your home. Based on what Molly said, I think we can produce some outstanding designs for you. Hey! Ouch!" I turned around and there was Josh Lido, grinning. The nut had bitten me on the neck! I did a quick triple prayer for forbearance, Josh Lido's premature death by alligator attack, and Christopher Peña's hereditary deafness.

"Please excuse me. I've been attacked by killer flies," I said calmly into the phone. Blakas jumped into Josh's arms. I stared at them both in what I hoped was a menacing fashion and ran my finger across my neck. *Die!*

"Molly said you were in the Greek islands, I think it was?"

"Yes, just a little needed vacation."

"I keep a villa in Kárpathos, kind of off the beaten track. Do you know it?" he asked.

"Lovely," I murmured, which is what I would have said if he had mentioned a harem in Attica, child porn in Bombay, or group sex with a herd of goats. I mean, *villa in Kárpathos?* Damn. I started imagining my new life flitting around the globe as Christopher Peña's decorator of record. I really should brush up on my Spanish. Be part of the inner sanctum. Parker Glass, designer in residence and token *gringa*. Sort of like the Godfather's consigliere of interiors. Perhaps Anya would give me lessons?

"My wife and I stay there when we're not at the Costa Rica house," he continued. "Although Marisol really prefers a cooler climate. The Aspen and Sun Valley places could use a lift, come to think of it," he mused. I almost creamed my panties. And to think I thought ye olde work ethic had gone south with my dear husband!

"All in good time, Mr. Peña." I just skirted smarmy. Josh made vomiting gestures. I poked my fingers toward my eyes in a backward V, which is Soprano for *I've got my eyes on you, mister.*

"Oh, please call me Chris," he said.

"And you must call me Parker." *As long as you call me!* I almost said, and thankfully managed to choke back at the last second.

"Parker as in Parker Stevenson?"

"I was precocious."

"Clearly."

"You don't want to know my real name."

"Maybe you can tell me sometime."

Dirty dog! Flirting shamelessly, and him newly married!

"I'm sure we'll be too busy to discuss such things," I said snottily. He chuckled. Why is it that powerful, successful men just want to be abused? "Anyway," I continued, "what we really need to do is nail a start date. Why don't you tell me what you're thinking?"

"A week from today?"

I gulped. Me. In San Francisco. Home. In seven days. Potentially sharing a city with Neil and the Belgian, whom I might actually run into. Note to self: Convert to a religion that requires an extensive modesty headdress.

"Perfect," I lied. "Will you be our contact for the project, Chris, or perhaps your wife, or a manager. . . ."

"It will be me, for the most part. Marisol's shooting in Vancouver at the moment."

"Well, I guess I'll see you then. I'll familiarize you with our process, ask you a bunch of questions, and get to know your tastes and your home. How's that sound?" I said moronically, as if I was selling Christopher Peña a subscription to *USWeekly* or trying to get him to join my church. Dimwit!

"Sounds good. Oh, and Parker?"

"Yes?"

"You have a lovely voice. Did anyone ever tell you that? Very mellifluous. I guess I'll see you next week."

"Good-bye," I choked.

For a second we were awash in mutual mellifluousness. Then he was gone.

I turned around and smacked Josh in the forehead.

"Hey! What'd you do that for?"

"For nearly ruining the most important client call I've ever had!"

"Oh, was Tony acting up again?"

"If you must know, that was Christopher Peña."

"Of the San Francisco Peñas?" He smirked.

"Come on. We're lucky to have snagged him. No thanks to you," I added.

"So does this mean you're going home?" Was it my imagination or was there something unhappy in his voice? An almost imperceptible tinge of disappointment?

"Looks like. Of course, I want to wrap up Tony's in the next day or so. And we've got to get ready for his big opening party. It's next Saturday."

Claire, Brian, and I were having lunch with Tony to discuss the grand reopening party.

"Are you sure about the flyers? Won't you get a lot of, you know, pissheads? Sorry, Mum," Brian said.

Tony shrugged. "Pissheads with money, who care?"

I shook my head. "No, Brian's right. That's the difference between old Tony's and new Tony's. Better clientele, a more upscale crowd, people who actually appreciate your good food, more people from the resorts coming over for cocktails and dinner. It's a longer-term strategy. Oh, and quality entertainment." I smiled at Claire.

"Ancient entertainment," she said.

"Goes with the Greek theme, like archaeological artifacts," Brian said.

"I'd better watch out, or they'll put your old mother in the museum," Claire said, but her amber eyes were shining and, truthfully, she looked ten years younger than I did, at least since I found out about Neil's plans to return to San Francisco.

"Tony!" Anya's nemesis, Rachel, and her henchwomen were at

the door, all tarted up, depilated, highlighted, and miniskirted. They looked like frickin' Destiny's Child.

Tony took in the expanse of bare, tanned flesh and grinned his wolf's smile. "Be back soon," he said.

We watched his departing hunched back.

"And that, my friends, is why this is all for nothing," I said wearily.

Brian reached for my hand. His was large and warm and felt wonderful. For a millisecond, I allowed myself to fantasize that he was straight and interested in me. "You're lovely, Park. The party's going to be a beaut, and you'll save Tony's business in spite of him, and everyone will want to pash you."

I laughed and squeezed his hand. "You should be proud," I told Claire.

"I am. Not a bad product for an ol' cheese, eh?"

"What's *pash*?" I said.

"Snogging."

I raised my eyebrows.

"Making out, for the younger set," Claire said helpfully.

"Ah."

Rachel and her friends settled at a nearby table, one I'd painstakingly applied resin to myself, over a variety of Greek paraphernalia: coins, fishing hooks, photos, and other collectibles. She waved at Claire and Brian and they waved back.

"Never liked the cow," said Brian.

"Oh, Bri, that's not true. I distinctly recall you and she going to see films together and doing a bit of shopping and such when Ethan couldn't be bothered," said Claire.

"Suffered like hell, every minute of it."

Claire rolled her eyes.

"Well, the important thing is, what does Ethan think of her now?" I said, recalling the scene at the beach.

Claire and Brian looked worried.

"My brother may be ridiculously good-looking," said Brian finally, "but he's not stupid."

———

The beach was deserted.

It was sunset, and everything was bathed in thick light the color of marmalade. The kind of light that makes you feel elemental, timelessly beautiful, existentialist, wise, and various other elusive things. The kind of light that feels like it would burn you to bleached white bone if it wasn't filtered through the moist and salty air. The kind that makes you feel clean. I liked to be out here at the tip of the day, digging my toes into the firm sand, slipping off the edge of the tiny landmass I'd landed on. If I squinted into the sun, curled my feet under the briny water, I could reimagine myself into a creature as weightless and opportunistic as an airborne spore.

I threw Blakas his stick with arrhythmic rightness, enjoying the splash of the knobby wood, the dog's fevered growls of joy, profound in their solitude. Out here, because of some mysterious alchemy of land and water, I could achieve a sort of "four corners" of the soul; I was at the same time less Parker Glass, thirty-two-year-old soon-to-be-divorced high-class junkie, and *more* Rosie Meadow Glass, soon-to-be-divorced funny girl and eater of baklava.

Edges aren't the stark endings you think they are. Right here, where this stubborn rock jutted out into the tepid Mediterranean, there was no sharp drop-off, terrifying in its finality. When you played along the edge, got to know the fine grains that made up the buffer zone between the elements, drove your toes into the silty confection underneath, you discovered a whole world of blurred boundaries and indecipherable identities, constantly reinventing itself. Neither deep nor shallow, sandy nor muddy, warm nor cold, the water's edge was an unownable gift that refused to belong to anything, or even to have a name.

Here's what I've learned: When you stand at the lip of something, you're already there.

chapter 37

KELAH

Shipwrecked on Corfu, September

*What does it take to get somebody's attention around here?
Apparently, a near drowning and a serious fanny wax. Yes, it's
true. R. raised the stakes this week, with a topless dive that
had E.D. hurling himself into the waves to save the poor
thing from sure, um, sunburn, while A. watched helplessly
from the shore. C.'s worse half clogged the post with
sentimental blatherings that showed his new therapist had
definitely earned her eighty quid. And P. drowned her sorrows
over J.L.'s platonic tonic with a Hollywood actor so famous, I
don't dare use his initials, for fear his fancy barristers will
come after me and this magazine. Something tells me those
two are made for each other. Oh, there she is now....*

"Unbelievable," I whispered.

"What?"

"I said, *unbelievable*."

"Not really, Kay, your work is really good. Fun, but good," Boz said. He resumed snipping his fingernails with a Swiss Army knife.

I flipped the letter over, to see if there was something on the back, like a line of text reneging on everything on the front side, but there was nothing except the indented seal of McKinney House, Publishers, Ltd., and some posh gold-leaf letterhead.

I was holding a letter from a perfectly respectable publishing house in England. They'd read my columns in *Flounce* and liked them. They wanted to turn them into a book.

A book.

I grabbed Boz by his flimsy lapels. "Bozzie! This is incredible! How'd you do it?"

"I didn't do anything." He looked frightened.

"But they're offering me a twenty-thousand-pound advance! And I didn't even do anything! Somebody must have done something."

"Well, you wrote a good column, which everybody's been trying to tell you for weeks now."

"Do you think my mother did this? Had lunch with one of her friends and coerced them into it?" I pleaded.

Boz raised his palms to the sky, as if to ask what he'd done to deserve this. "Kelah, your mum's come to terms with it but I don't see her getting involved like this. A bit mad, that."

"Maybe." I wasn't ready to admit anything close to pride, lest I be instantly struck down in the bloom of my brilliant youth.

"Not maybe. Really."

I thought for a moment. "When do you have to go home, Boz? Aren't Marta and, what's her name, Inez, waiting for you?"

"Marta's on holiday herself in Ibiza. I'm going to stay for the party next Saturday if I can crash on your floor. Coffers are dry, I'm afraid."

"Yeah, sure," I said absently. Could it be true? Could it be that easy?

Suddenly, the room blurred and I felt hands gently lowering me to the chair. A strange and beautiful image materialized in my mind's eye, of me, still a schoolgirl, throwing an armful of toy blocks into the air, where, instead of falling, they hung, as hopeful as balloons, coyly orbiting one another. My future was written on the sides in Asian characters. All my futures. The sensation of childlike wonder was so strong I could almost feel the blocks in my hands, the awesome simplicity of pure yearning. Without knowing why, I put my head in my hands and sobbed. Boz didn't say anything at first, just stroked my head with his long pale hands while I breathed raggedly.

"I know, baby," he said after a minute. "It's lovely, isn't it? It's so lovely."

The Talk, when it came last week, had been a total surprise.

By the time Mum, Dad, and I sat down in a quiet corner of Tony's to discuss my life, my future, my column, and the attendant embarrassment it brought to Clan Morris, I had worked myself into a state of defensiveness heretofore undocumented.

Tony was in rare form.

"Hello, gorgeous," he'd said to my mother when we walked in. Before she could protest, he slipped her cashmere jumper off her shoulders and frankly assessed her china-blue eyes and still-pert chest. "I can see Kelah has your . . . nose," he said without taking his eyes off her tits. I expected my father to bristle but he just laughed.

"Doesn't she?" Dad said, and we all went into the dining room.

"That's my *mother*!" I hissed. Tony just shrugged and made one of those ubiquitous Mediterranean hand gestures that seemed to translate as *God made me a simple creature and I'm going to stare at your tits no matter what, so why don't you just relax and wiggle your bum a bit more.*

I snuck off to the loo as soon as I could justify it. Parker was in there applying lipstick, smoothing down her already smoothed dark hair, and muttering something unintelligible about Josh Lido and the movie star Christopher Peña.

I waved weakly and stared at myself in the mirror. Except for two rosebud-size flares of feverish color in my cheeks, I was greenish. There was a souvlaki stain on my shirt. Shit.

"Tony tried to pick up my mother," I said.

"Did he do that tit thing?" Parker lowered her eyes to my puny ones and gaped exaggeratedly as she said it.

"Yeah."

"Fuckin' A," she said, shaking her head sadly.

"Yeah."

"How you holding up?"

I scrubbed futilely at the stain. "Not bad."

"You look a little . . . I don't know, stressed."

"You could say that." My palms were damp. Was child abandonment a punishable crime if the child in question was twenty-five years old?

"Not to be freaky or anything, but do you want something to calm you down?"

Parker opened her purse, took out four prescription pill containers of varying heights, and lined them up on the counter.

"Friends don't let friends talk to their parents sober," she said.

"This is so *Valley of the Dolls*."

"Except for the sex part. Look, do you want to try one of these? They're absolutely harmless. These little guys just make you feel a little sleepy. And these big blue ones are good for when you're really nervous. I always take a halfsie before client meetings. You're totally present, except things that would normally upset you are, like, oh, more manageable, I guess. These ones are Valium. Oh, and these are kinda fun. Have you ever smoked hash after you've had a whole lot of nighttime cold medicine and a tequila shot?"

"Can't say that I have."

Parker frowned. "I'd stick to these." She handed me a slippery sky-colored capsule. I popped it in and washed it down with water.

"You're not allergic to MAO inhibitors, are you?" she asked.

"What's a meow inhibitor?"

"Well, most people aren't," Parker said briskly. "Good luck."

She gave me a little hug and disappeared before I could query her about hallucinations or heart palpitations or spontaneous combustion of the cerebral cortex.

"Okay," I said to the girl in the mirror.

My parents were sipping red wine when I got back.

"We thought you'd left," Mum said, but her cheeks were pink and her shirt was slightly askew so that one of her silky bra straps showed. Pissed? Mum? What could this mean?

"Your father and I wanted to talk about this column of yours." Mum burped discreetly into her hand.

"Okay."

"It's really quite extraordinary, isn't it?" Mum continued.

"Um, yes." I decided at that moment: To keep the peace, whatever she suggested—up to and including massaging the Queen Mother's bunions—would be treated as the right, the only, way.

"The other day your father and I were at the symphony—what was it, Charles, Mendelssohn?—and some young women were talking about it during intermission. Your column! *Addicted* was the word they used. Simply addicted . . ."

I covertly spit my fingernail onto the floor.

". . . and then there was that story on it in the *Times,* about the next generation of English columnists. And you, right beside Estella Sykes and Jewel Goldstone!"

I realized I was grinning like a fool and tried to stop, but everything seemed suddenly, hysterically funny. Mum trying to make me feel better. Dad with that piece of calamari stuck between his two front teeth. Not being presented with papers forfeiting my inheritance. Boz shagging bloody Inez San Giacomo in the bloody stacks. My head felt like a big, lovely, fluffy pillow. I barely resisted the urge to puff my cheeks out and dance in my seat.

Mum leaned forward and took my hand. We looked like a fucking Benetton ad, except for my shirt stain, of course. I've always liked those ads, especially the one they killed in America because they can't deal with sex. You know, that one with the big black horse with the enormous willy about to mount the big white horse. . . .

"I realize I've been overly harsh with you in the past, Kelah," Mum said. "I know you don't think I worry about such things, but I really do, more than you know. In fact, I've often regretted what I said to you that day, about your work. I was only trying to spare you pain, you see. But, thankfully, it looks like I was unsuccessful. What I'm trying to say is, we're proud of you. Really, really proud. You're a stunning success, and we want you to know we'll do everything we can to help you navigate through this process, your father and I. Won't we, Charles? Charles!"

"Yes, of course," Dad chimed in. Apparently, even research-oriented endocrinologists are doctorly enough to wake up instantly.

Tony refilled Mum's glass and winked at me.

"Tony, did you know I'm a stunning success?" I slurred. Was that pillow-tamped voice really mine? Sweet baby Jesus, those pink tablets were *deadly*.

"Yes, someone say that," he said.

"Bloody right."

"Tony, will you bring us the best bottle of champagne you have?" Dad said.

Tony leaned over and whispered something in Dad's ear.

"Well, how about another bottle of that red stuff? I want to celebrate with my girls."

Tony's head dipped a second time.

Dad looked exasperated. "Well, I'm sure a bit of ouzo will do, then."

Tony scurried off. Dad put his arm around Mum. They both smiled at me hugely, as if someone had entered us all in *Survivor: The Ultimate Gigantic Smile Edition*. The Kelah floating above the table thought we looked almost normal. And happy.

"Was it just me, or was that Tony fellow staring at my tits?" said Mum.

chapter 38

CLAIRE

 "You're not serious?" said Parker.

Kelah nodded.

"You fell asleep? Right on the table at Tony's?"

Anya laughed. "Did you give her one of your mother's little helpers, Park?"

"I always recommend taking a halfsie. Didn't I say to take a halfsie?"

"Well, it felt like a wholesie sort of night," said Kelah.

"Oh, Park, you didn't!" Anya.

"Did." Parker.

"Sure did." Kelah.

"But what happened with your parents when you told them about the book?" I said.

Kelah's hazel eyes sparked. "Mum's going to help me with the foreword. She knows the editor. I'm off the hook. There must have been something in Tony's rotgut, because they even agreed to give Davey another chance, get him into rehab up in Scotland, where he can't get out with any of his mates."

"That's great."

"We're *so* happy for you, Kelah!"

"Fantastic."

"So, what's going on with you, Claire? You've been sort of quiet," said Parker.

"What did Gary's letter say?" added Anya.

"Letter?"

"Ooh, tell."

I shifted so I could catch the last rays of the sun setting over the hills. My waistband felt tight. In the spirit of self-improvement, I pushed away the plate of Greek pastries Tony had brought over.

"Well, Gary's done the unthinkable and got himself into therapy"—oohs and aahs—"and he wants me to come home and give him another chance, he says. I don't know what to think. I've changed. I'm not at all sure he'd want me if he were to meet me now," I laughed.

"What about Andreas?" Anya's onyx eyes cut through me.

I shrugged. It was impossible to explain the delight of the zipless fuck to the new generation, as they hadn't had to work for it. "This old lady has no expectations one way or another. I don't even know if I can fall in love anymore, at least with a man. Fall in love with myself, my singing, more like. Anyway, it's not really on my mind. I'm just trying to figure out if marriage is really what I want anymore. And if someone can change that much in a single summer. It's like, I've gotten over the worst of it with Gary—at least I think so—and do I really want to go back there? It seems so much safer to just slip away, rebuild, buy a little duplex in Sydney, be close to my boys, maybe perform once in a while. I'll take holidays in the tropics and become one of those eccentric mothers with small dogs in my purse and too much mascara."

They were quiet for a moment. It was not a picaresque life I'd drawn.

"But one of us has to provide Kelah with a happy ending!" Parker said finally.

"No guarantees here," I said lightly.

We looked at Parker. She snorted.

"All I've got are a few Christopher Peña fantasies and a stack of divorce papers waiting for me."

We looked at Anya. She shook her head.

"The curse," explained Parker.

"Oh, yeah."

We looked at Kelah.

"Simple sanity's quite enough for the time being," she said.

"Thank you, everyone!" I called to the clapping audience, and put the mike back in its holder. Thanks to Parker's face-lift, Tony's was now attracting patrons from the resorts on the other side of the island, even though the grand reopening wasn't till next weekend. He'd even managed to wangle a spot on the Hellenic World Music Festival circuit. The festival, which lasted the summer and was held in small venues throughout the islands, was designed to showcase local and imported music talent. I was the import; Andreas was the talent.

I made eye contact with Andreas, whose sleepy gaze seemed to be a little less drowsy than usual tonight. I tilted my head to show I was going to leave. He motioned that he was going to stay awhile, and I felt a frisson of desire in my belly that just as quickly dissipated. Singing again was terrific, but exhausting. I'd forgotten how athletic it was, the emotionalism and the physicality of it. The gratification was immense, though, beyond what I'd imagined after all these years.

I grabbed my cardigan from the hook in the kitchen, said good-bye to Tony's sister the cook and the busboys, and drifted out the door.

"Excuse me. Claire Dillon?"

I turned. The man in front of me was about my age, give or take five years, gray around the temples, and pleasantly crinkled around the eyes. He wore a splendid white linen shirt and conservative trousers. Discreet gold glinted at his neck and wrists. He was with a woman about ten years younger, all blond highlights and the kind of tan that takes effort. Her gold was a bit more present.

"Yes?"

"I'm Taylor Black and this is my wife, Charlene. We really enjoyed your performance. You have a very special voice, you know."

"Well, thank you."

He dug into his wallet and pulled out a card. "I'm vice president of A&R for Muse Records." He handed me the card, which was embossed with a shiny electric guitar. "This festival's a hoot. We saw a band last night from—where was it, honey?"

"Cyprus," she said in a soft southern twang.

"Right. So this band from Cyprus, they played this sort of gypsy mambo stuff on olive barrels. Olive barrels!" He shook his head, marveling, I suppose.

Taylor Black leveled his hard blue gaze at me. "Sometimes I get a feeling about an artist. Twenty-five years in the business, my feelings are usually right."

"Um," I said, hiding a yawn under my hand. Ah, bed. Had I changed the sheets recently?

"This is one of those times."

Suddenly, I understood. "Oh, absolutely. Andreas, my accompanist, is an incredible musician. He speaks English, you know. Would you like an introduction?"

Taylor Black's eyebrows shot up. "Well, no, sweetheart. Actually, I'm talking about you."

"Oh . . ."

"Do you have a demo?" he said.

The only thing I'd demo'ed in the past twenty years was a new Hoover.

"Not with me," I said, which wasn't exactly untrue.

"Well, Charlene and I are goin' to be on the island—where are we, honey?"

"Corfu," she said.

"Right. We're here until Sunday, then off to—where we goin', honey?"

"Santorini."

"Right. Charlene wanted to see Greece, and I wanted to hear music, so here we are. Anyway, I like your sound, Claire Dillon. It's fresh and classic at the same time. Sounds like you've had classical training, am I right? Thought so. Anyway, there's something you do, and it's bringing a folksy thing and a country thing and maybe even a little bluegrass thing, like Dolly in the old days, and I guess now, with her new album out, it's bringing them all together in a unique way. I want to get you in the studio and hear more."

He paused and cocked his head, as if waiting for me to fall into grateful groveling.

"But I'm Australian," I said stupidly.

"Australian, huh? Well, that's okay. Is that the one next to Louisiana? Ha! Just kidding. We Yanks may be a little isolated, but we're not without a sense of humor. Now, I've got to get this little lady home, 'cause I promised her I'd take her shopping for some genuine Greek leather tomorrow. You can call me on my cell. It's GSM, works anywhere."

"Okay, Mr. Black," I said.

He looked pained. "Taylor, please. And may I call you Claire?"

"Sure."

"Bye, then. Call me before the weekend."

"Bye."

Then they were gone.

I hummed to myself as I brushed my hair out. The very air seemed to crackle with energy. I had gone over the conversation with the music executive, Taylor Black, over and over, looking for some fatal flaw, the obvious giveaway that he was a fraud, or I was a fraud, or the whole thing was just a dream. Of course, I knew nothing was likely to come from it—as if I'd even get to America!—but it was fun to fantasize for a little while. In my wilder imaginings, I was given a first-class ticket to Nashville on Qantas, whereupon I spent the flight sampling champagne, lounging behind the sort of black-lensed shades employed by international celebrities to keep overly aggressive fans at bay, and generating an air of impenetrable mystique. The label would send a driver to greet me—three hundred pounds of pure Samoan muscle fluent in six languages and four martial arts (for my protection, of course)—and I'd be asked to settle in at my (five-star) hotel, which was adrift on a sea of (rare) flowers, (exorbitant) chocolates, and a (handwritten) letter from the president. Of the record label, not the country, silly.

Tonight, I was to meet the SNiPs at the taverna. There was a slight tinge of sadness now. The summer was officially in its death throes, and no one knew quite how to deal with it or what the future held. We'd all be gone in a matter of days. Most of us didn't even know what we'd be going back *to*. It was all a bit unsettling—and, yes, for some, exciting. But what I felt mostly, you see, was grateful. Grateful I'd had the chutzpah—Parker taught me that word, isn't it great?—to leave Australia and Gary for the summer, to take a lover, to sing again. To figure out which pieces of my family I could hold together even as others came apart.

And to do it all in front of my two nosy, adorable sons.

I grabbed my purse and headed for the taverna. For the first time, there was a slight nip in the night air. A few of the discos had even shut their doors for the season, their owners going back to the mainland for the winter. The rest were staying only a few more weeks, trying to squeeze the last few tourism euros out of the summer holiday.

When I got to the entrance, which Parker and Brian had made quite beautiful with its bougainvillea arch and crisp blue Dutch doors, Parker, Anya, and Kelah were standing there.

"Let's go on in," I said.

"Actually, we were thinking of eating at the Dallas," Parker said.

"The Dallas? Are you crazy? You want to live on beer and toasties?"

"For a change, that's all." Anya's normally fluid tone was near plaintive.

"What's going on?" I said.

"Not much. Tony's is just kind of crowded tonight and we don't feel like waiting." Kelah fiddled with her ratty rucksack.

"Tony's had a table held for us since June," I pointed out. "And you're starting to alarm me. Next thing you'll be telling me Gary's in there with the massage therapist. Now, come on and let's get some calamari and a nice fish."

I slipped by them and took in the room, which was only half full.

"I don't know what you were worried about, unless you've decided you need a half dozen tables to hold your nightly beverages—"

Then I saw them.

It was so predictable, it should have been printed on my fortune cookie: Confucius say your husband will cheat, you will take a lover on an exotic Greek island, revel in newfound sexual bliss and overwhelming self-love, only to end up abandoned for greener pastures/slimmer thighs/fatter wallets. In my talk with my American friend Patricia, I had conveniently omitted the ending of *Shirley Valentine,* the Pauline Collins film that had propelled me here in the first place. At the end of the tale, our heroine impulsively decides not to go home to her dull English marriage, returns to her Greek villa ready to reunite with her summer tryst, and encounters her "brokenhearted" lover, Tom Conti, already embarked on his next conquest, a mere hour later. Surprise! Time for one of those instructive movie moments when *Things Are Revealed to Be Not Quite What They Seemed.* Time for our heroine to experience her *Self-Actualizing Revelation Springing from Disappointment and Ending in Self-Acceptance and the Desire to Become an Independent Mediterranean Tour Operator.* Time for the *Feel-Good Movie of the Summer to Stake Its Claim.* At least old Tom had had the decency to look abashed, though, his hound-dog eyes and large nose pulling his face downward into grim resignation: *What you see is what you get,* his face seemed to say. *Don't elevate me into something I'm not.* Showing the sort of plucky courage that has catapulted many a female film heroine into the annals of chick flick history, Pauline shrugs her shoulders and settles down to the business of living happily alone, which was, of course, what she really wanted in the first place.

I should be so plucky.

The woman with Andreas was thin, dark, and Italian. Don't ask me how I knew this; it was just something I gleaned instantaneously, like one would an oncoming cold. They were already lovers; that was also readily apparent. The inexorable propulsion of their bodies toward each other, held tantalizingly in check, conveyed the heady days of successful conquest, with none of the weary familiarity of the long-term mated. Her forgotten cigarillo poked out from between red-tipped fingers, unsmoked. Their conversation must have been compelling—or her perfume especially intoxicating—so close to her sleek head nestled Andreas's shaggy one. She wore very tight black jeans and a plunging top that showed a little crepey chest, a gold cross, and enviably petite, pointed breasts. She was my age, mid-forties. Somehow that seemed terribly unfair: Why couldn't he flee the coop for the irresistible, yet utterly comprehensible, temptations of younger flesh? Why did my replacement have to make me realize I'd been his summer fetish instead of his lover?

Then: Wasn't it better to be somebody's fetish than nobody's fetish?

And: Hadn't I fetishized him too? Come on, just a wee bit?

Plus: Who cares, I'm going to be a major recording artist in America.

Finally: I'm still married. Sort of.

I sighed and gathered my wrap around me. The SNiPs swarmed behind me like a protective posse, ready to leap into action if I uttered the word. I could feel them bristling with indignation and resolved to deliver unto them a Feel-Good Moment of my own.

"Come on, ladies. It's not the end of the world," I said firmly, mentally saying good-bye to my summer satyr. "At least I got to buy some new underwear."

chapter 39

ANYA

I called Carilu today to keep *Mami* and *Papi* from calling me. A preemptive strike.

"*Hola,*" I said when she answered the phone in San Francisco.

"Anya? *Chica,* where the hell have you been? *Mami*'s saying novenas for your ass, girl. She thinks you done yourself in and went to the angels."

"No, I'm right here."

"Well, she was worried. *Papi* too. You should have called earlier. When are you coming home?"

"Next week." There. I'd said it. I let that sink in.

"You want me to pick you up? I can borrow Tomás's car. What day are you coming? There's this new club, Cartagena. Girl, you are so going to love it. On Fridays they have salsa, and on Saturdays they have world music and they play this kickin' Indian shit. It's *la cagada,* all these Indian guys, computer programmers from like Sunnyvale and shit, waving their arms all over the damn place. There's this DJ, he's so fine. Dark, I think he's *Salvadoreño.* He's got a tattoo of a tiger on his back and he smiles so sweet—

Hey, pendeja, *turn that down, I'm talking to Anya!*—What was I saying? Oh, whatever. Anyway, did I tell you Carda got a date for that dance at Berkeley? She's going with Sanjay. He's taking her to Chez Panisse, the restaurant, not the café."

"I thought he was engaged to Robin Flores."

Carilu blew air out through her teeth. "Girl, you missed everything! They broke up in August. They'd already booked the Maritime Museum for the reception and everything! Turns out Robin was cheating on him with her ex, that *pendejo* from Excelsior with the parrot? Don't know how she can choose him over Sanjay. That bird is so noisy, always squawking and shit. Anyway, I waited a few days, then called him up and asked him if he wanted to take my friend Carda out, and he said sure."

"You've got big ol' *cojones, mi hermana.*" I giggled.

"You want to date in San Francisco, you got to grow 'em big and brass."

"Can I ask you something, Lu?"

"Yeah."

"If you met a guy on vacation, a really sweet guy, would you try to, you know, keep it going?"

"Dios mío, *Anya's doing some Greek guy!*" Carilu screamed.

"Lu! I'm not *doing some Greek guy,* for your information." I hesitated. "If you must know, he's Australian."

"*He's not Greek, he's Australian!*" Carilu yelled to someone. "What? How the hell would I know?" She came back to the phone. "Diana wants to know if he looks like Crocodile Dundee."

"No, he doesn't look like Crocodile Dundee! He's tall, and good-looking, and likes Italian movies, and has his own construction business, and wants to get married—"

"*Anya's getting married!*" Carilu shouted.

"Carilu Anna María Soberanes! I am not getting married! Will you shut up and listen for a minute, *please?!*"

"Sorry."

I explained the situation with Ethan, up to and including the intrusion of Evil Rachel. I told her about Claire and Kelah and the column in the British magazine. I didn't tell her about the Love Curse or my secret; that would have been too much.

"Di, get me my Dew, will you?" Carilu always focused better when she had her thirty-two-ounce Mountain Dew close at hand. "So, let me get this straight. You and Alan—"

"Ethan."

"Okay, *Ethan*—girl, can you pick 'em any more *gringo*? He sounds like he just fell off the damn *Mayflower*—anyway, you and Ethan actually talked about moving in together? In San Francisco?"

"Well, we started to, and he started the conversation, not me, but that's when his ex-girlfriend showed up, and things have been sort of weird between us since then."

"Understandable. But, as I see it, also immaterial." Oh, good, Carilu was getting polysyllabic: Whatever toxic wire-you-to-the-eyeballs shit they put in that Mountain Dew was starting to kick in. "See, all that matters is what you're working with *now*, as in *today*. You got to lay it on the line, girl. You got to tell him what you want. And you got to ask him what he wants. That's it. You have four days to make it happen. You got to go balls out and just go for broke."

"That seems sort of . . . risky, doesn't it? What if he feels pressured?"

"Well, there's no return without risk. Isn't that what that *pendejo* Montel used to say, when he was trying to get *Papi* to give him all his money to invest? You think you can get what you want by waiting around for angels to come down and hit you with the magic love wand?"

Hmm. How did she know that?

"I know you, *chica*. You want it to be all clean and sanitized and shit. You want some big white knight to come charging out of nowhere and sweep you off your feet and then vacuum it up afterward. You want to keep your hands clean. You think if you push you're messing with fate, that it isn't meant to be, right? That if it happens and you're all passive and shit, that's proof that it's got God's big fat blessing, *sí*?"

"Sort of," I whispered.

"Well, you got it wrong, girl. Love is a big fat stinking mess from beginning to end, and you got to forget about dignity and destiny and crap like that and fight if you want to get what you want." She slurped from the soda straw. "It's you wrestling with your demons, Anya. Got to wrestle them bitches to the ground. Don't go balls out and you'll never know, will you? Go balls out and get the answer you want and then you have a new set of problems! God's really funny that way." She chuckled.

"Lu, how'd you get so wise in one summer?"

"Girl, I've always been wise, it's you who's finally noticing."

The sea had cooled and grayed as the summer days shortened, deepening into opaqueness like the eyes of someone with a secret. I stood shivering in thigh-deep water, the ripples kissing my pubic bone, darkening my now-faded black bathing suit. Thin clouds stretched across the sky. It was neither warm nor cold, exactly. I tried to gauge my mood and found it a twin to the weather: neutral and stoic.

Johnny held the slick white board by the tip. "The wind is come from that way," he said, gesturing down the beach. "It try to blow you back on the sand. You know where to hold the rope now?"

"I think so."

"Go now."

I thrust myself on top of the board, scraping my knees across the surface made sticky from no-slip tape. I crouched, peering out, my old habit of scanning for nefarious sea creatures alive and well. The sailboard bobbed back and forth, raising and lowering the horizon like a teacup.

"Ugh. This is hard."

Johnny treaded water next to me, looking like a brotherly seal with his hair slicked back and his green eyes telling me I could do this. I grabbed the neoprene-covered rope and leaned back, trying to find the wind. What was it Johnny had said? To let the breeze pull you around so you didn't have to use your back. My thighs were trembling with fatigue already. Suddenly, a huge gust yanked the sail, with its ten-foot mast, out of my hands. Or, more accurately, out of one hand. I clung with the other, my feet fighting for purchase on the slippery board. Then I sailed through the air and landed in the water. I dove underneath the surface in a swirl of green just in time to avoid the crashing mast. When I surfaced, all I could hear was the thump of the sodden sail against itself and water dripping from my ears. I'd already blown a couple hundred yards from Johnny's outpost. He waved at me to get back on.

I scrambled up, glad to be out of the water, and hitched my bathing suit out of my ass. My heartbeat resounded loudly in my ears.

"Come on, Anya, you can do it," I said aloud.

Anyita, isn't this fun? said the Voice. *I miss our conversations,* querida. *You're always with that Ethan. He must be something. I'm so proud of you. Did I tell you that? We always think the familiar's so much safer than the unknown, don't you think? And we're always wrong. But not you. Not this time. Things are going so well,* querida. *Are you going to tell him what you did that spring? Are you going to tell him why you can't give him what he wants?*

I ignored the Voice and repeated the process, closing my eyes this time to try to feel the urging of the wind at my back.

The first thing I noticed was that the hut where you rent lounge chairs had launched itself back along the beach and was receding, shrinking rapidly into an outhouse-size structure. Then I felt laughter bubbling up in my chest. It poured out into the salty wind before I even knew why, trailing behind me in a wake of giggles. Every muscle in my body was flexed, bouncing as if I was a nameless *pelícano* resting in the troughs of waves between food runs. Salty mucus trickled over my upper lip onto my tongue. My eyes burned.

It was wonderful. Flying.

You know when people say they experienced something cataclysmic, something that *changed their lives forever*? That's always puzzled me. It's like before whatever it was happened, they were another person, meandering down a yellow brick road toward a totally different fate. The life-changing thing, it's not an obstacle or a jump-start, a bridge or a trench lying across your path of life. The way we tend to think about these things, it's a meteor. It hurtles in from outer space and knocks you off your path completely, catapults you out of your natural orbit so that you plummet back to an earth as foreign as one populated solely by apes or cockroaches. How weird is that?

What really bugs me about this is it presumes a foreknowledge of future events we have no way of having. How do we *know* our original future was different at all? Maybe there's more than one path to the same destination. Or maybe the road forks, diverges, comes together again. Maybe the child who loses a parent too soon, channels his grief into art, and becomes a successful painter would have been a painter anyway. Maybe he would have picked up the brush at eighteen instead of eight. Maybe he would have lost something or someone else and *that* would have crystallized whatever redemptive talent lurked inside him into art.

Maybe there's no right answer, just choices. Maybe life's just another example of mix and match.

If I hadn't grabbed at the tangy poison fruit that was offered me that overbright spring day under the shade of a lemon tree, hadn't greedily gulped it down like it was honeyed nectar and I was forever thirsty, would I still be invisible today? Would I still feel like a ghost haunting the edges of my own life because I'm missing something essential, some crucial piece that slipped into oblivion centuries ago, before I was even born? I don't know. All I know is, something I needed desperately was taken from me, ripped away by someone with his own missing piece. Someone who, kneeling before *La Virgen* surrounded by a thousand weeping candles, asks himself the same question, even now.

chapter 40

〜〜〜〜〜〜〜〜〜〜〜〜

PARKER

They came today.

Divorce papers are a curious thing. Assuming you're not Prince Charles or Steven Spielberg or Madonna or something, it only takes a couple of sheets to *do* the deal, but it takes *hundreds* for even us mere mortals to undo it. Doesn't that seem a bit backward? It seems to me that they should put you through the bureaucratic ringer *before* you agree to merge life, love, and liquor cabinet. Afterward, if your beloved takes a fancy to an endodontist from Antwerp or a bricklayer from Brussels, there're no progeny involved, and you're both in agreement about the (nonexistent) future of your relationship, you should be permitted to end it with a brief form on the order of a gym membership or video-rental agreement. I mean, shit, you're already traumatized enough without the added stress of paging through hundreds of paragraphs outlining your character flaws and why the Karim Rashid planar chair is better off with *him*. Not only that, some enterprising young paralegal at my lawyer's firm had decided the trauma package would be safer traveling overseas rolled up in a poster tube, which left the novella-size stack looking ironically tumescent—like a phallic telescope set to focus backward on all the mistakes I had made.

I'd been warned not to feel overconfident about my recovery. *You just think you're getting over him,* my thrice-divorced college roommate Darcy had written, *but that's because you haven't gotten the papers yet. When Kev's papers came I signed them, mailed them, drank a bottle of Bonnie Doon dessert wine—it was left over from a dinner party, okay?—and cried so hard I had to put hemorrhoid cream in my nose to breathe. I took all the leather jackets Kev had left in the walk-in closet, doused them in gasoline, and burned them in the yard. Even the vintage Members Only. My eyelashes took a hit but it was worth it to see his face when he came by to get them and there was only barbecue left. Anyway, don't take it too hard, Park— think how much you'll save on waxing without a man in your life.*

Ginger Lyons, my mentor from the job I'd held before Molly and I went indie, had a different view: *Don't sign anything, Parker. When the papers arrive, just throw them away and pretend you never got them. Do that at least three times. Maybe that'll give Neil time to get his head out of his ass and start kissing yours. He'll come around; they always do.*

Ginger was an inspiration. Or she was certifiably insane. Opinions of her tended toward the subjective. She and her husband, Dane, had five-year-old twins and a rock-hard post-nup. Dane had tried to leave after he found out she'd had an affair with her kickboxing instructor, but Ginger had dug in her Jimmy Choo heels, calmly pled postpartum insanity, and waited for the twins' beatific power to work its magic. Now Dane believes she took a jab from the boxer because he (Dane) neglected her emotionally and spent too much time in their rec room playing foosball, and Ginger gets the house and a stable full of prizewinning racehorses in Virginia she's never even seen, let alone currycombed, if he departs again.

Miraculously, my own feelings were closest to Leo and Sue's, with whom I'd rarely agreed about anything more complicated than Bette Midler's performance in *The Rose* and the right soil for tomatoes. *Dear Rosie,* they'd written on mud-brown hemp paper, *your divorce attorney called us to find out where she could mail you the papers. We thought it would be all right to give her the post office box. We're glad to hear you're feeling better about things. There are forces bigger than us at work in the universe, sweetie, and you just have to trust in them sometimes. Signing those papers is going to open the door to the next (magical!) phase of your life, Rosie Meadow, and we'll be there to help you. We love you!*

My parents are the only adults I know besides a few *Lord of the Rings* aficionados who still use words like *magical* to describe life. Actually, they really are inspiring. In terms of their marriage, that is. And even I can see that they are in no way responsible for the fact that Neil had an early midlife crisis and took a runner. In fact, it would not surprise me one bit if Mom or Dad called up Neil or even Jack and Jill and gave them an earful of hippie invective: *Leo and I just want you to know that you suck. Peace.*

"I'm all alone," I said out loud, testing the sound of it. It sounded okay, like a song you really like played with a little more flourish and a little less exactitude by an enthusiastic cover band.

Blakas had the decency to whine.

"Tony?" I called. I couldn't understand why he wasn't out here; in all the weeks I'd been coming to the taverna, I'd never seen him leave the premises, barring the condom episode. (Basic professionalism and hygiene aside, there's something thoroughly staggering about a hunchback with a neo-'70s mullet bursting out of his on-site apartment asking passersby for condoms, his modesty protected solely by a D-cup brassiere.)

I wandered into the kitchen. Tony's stolid older sister, who had the unlikely name of Aphrodite, was sitting on a box of tomatoes, crying.

I approached tentatively. For all I knew, the woman had just discovered that the Greek islands were running critically short on mustache remover. Such things have been known to cause un-predictable behavior in the hirsute.

"Aphrodite? Is something wrong?"

She raised red, rheumy eyes to mine. We'd barely spoken five words to each other during the renovation, and I was surprised to see that her hazel eyes were thick-lashed and quite beautiful in the porridgy face.

"Tony is dead," she said.

"What do you mean? Where is he?" I glanced around, half expecting to see his tiny, twisted body laid out on the butcher's block as if in a makeshift morgue, primed with garish makeup and ready for viewing.

"My brother, he is dead at me!" Aphrodite said with gusto this time, accompanied by an uppercut fist.

"Aphrodite, I'm not sure if I'm understanding you correctly. Is Tony *dead* as in no longer breathing, or did Tony do something to anger you?"

"Dead!" she shrieked this time. She accompanied the shriek with a complicated set of hand gestures I presumed were Greek Orthodox in origin and clearly portended doom for the object of their ire.

"Aphrodite, what did Tony do?"

"He sell taverna!" she wailed.

"*This* taverna?" I was hoping that, unbeknownst to me, Tony operated another establishment on the other side of the island: Tony's Taverna Too.

"He say he out of money and want to go Hollywood to be in movie business. He no want make restaurant anymore. Taverna is in our family *two generations*!"

Considering their rich history, these Greeks had an appalling lack of respect for time.

"Tony sold the taverna?" I repeated dumbly.

She sniffled loudly. "Not yet. He—how you say?—*hired* it. He write the newspaper. It is terrible thing. Terrible! I work in the taverna all my life. There is no husband, no baby, just cooking for my friends, the tourists, coming every summer to see us. What I do now?" Aphrodite dissolved into sobs, her man-size hands with the faint arcs of garlic and tapenade under the fingernails covering her face.

I patted her shoulder. Under the housedress and apron, it felt like an overdone pot roast. "Aphrodite, I'm going to talk to Tony about this. I don't think he's giving the renovation a chance. I know it's the end of the season, but next year I think you'll see a big increase in profits. I can convince him of that."

"You help me?"

"I'll try."

"Good." She raked her finger under her runny nose. "Otherwise, Tony is dead at me!"

I left Aphrodite to her mumblings and located Tony on the terrace. He was sipping a glass of retsina and filling out naked-girl postcards to the summer's conquests, which would end up sprinkled throughout some of northern Europe's quaintest, coldest villages.

"Aphrodite's pretty upset," I said.

He shrugged. "What can I tell her? It is my business. I try to keep it going, but I'm tired of it. I can't keep it going just because she work here."

"Are you really going to L.A.?"

"My brother Giorgos, he is movie producer in Hollywood. He sleep with Cameron Diaz. Or maybe he has lunch with James Cameron? I don't know for sure. He say it all just lunch and parties and putting the money people with the other people. Pooft! Easy. We go into partnership together and make big movies. No more headache and drunk tourists."

"Do you have a buyer for the taverna?"

"This man, he own hotels on Crete and Ios, he want to buy it maybe."

"But won't he just knock it down and build another hotel? You've got a great view, Tony! They won't keep the taverna going!"

His sloping shoulders inched up again. "It is not a problem.

What can I do? I can't afford another summer like this one. I appreciate everything you and your friends do for me, nobody ever do anything so nice, but it just something I want to do."

"Well, at least go talk to Aphrodite."

He glanced toward the kitchen. "Did you see any knife in there? Earlier, she threaten me with a big one."

"I think she's calmed down a little," I lied.

He sighed and hopped off the stool to go comfort his sister. On the way, I saw him grab a meat mallet off the rack. When it came to sibling relations between Tony and Aphrodite Stanislopolous, nobody ever said they weren't tender.

"What flight are you on?" Josh asked me.

I read him the itinerary. I knew better than to ask what his exact plans were. He'd been deliberately cryptic about both his departure date and his destination: Beyond the fact that it was somewhere in California, I knew nothing.

We sat in silence for a while, munching these petrified, salt-encrusted pigskin chips I wouldn't have fed a dog back home. Once in a while, Josh tossed a tooth-marked Frisbee to Blakas, who wrestled with it at the water's edge.

Covertly, I stared at Josh's profile while I pretended to take in the horizon. Naturally tan, the summer had toasted his skin to a deep, surfer-boy chestnut. A few darker freckles sprinkled his forehead and the bridge of his strong, arched nose. I could see now that the lines bracketing his wide, mobile mouth spoke more of laughter and self-effacing amusement than the hedonism I'd first inferred. He had a nervous habit I found rather sweet, where he picked at the tufts of hair sprouting from his knuckles. Some sensible part of me knows that fact should scare and repel me, which is just a sign of how much I have drifted this summer from the things and beliefs I used to hold dear. Things like not even speaking the name *Birkenstocks* aloud and rationing my lifetime supply of Vicodin. I realized Josh's visage was as familiar now as a much-loved blanket and that somehow we'd gotten to the point where we could reference past moments in our shared history. It was almost as if we had an actual Relationship, but without the downsides (co-food shopping, in-laws, birth control) and one small upside (sex). My eyes traveled to his nape. His curls were clumpy and long. He needed a haircut. A glimmer of an idea formed. . . .

"Josh, can I cut your hair? You can't go back to civilization looking like that. You look like a cross between Tom Hanks in *Cast Away* and a rotten coconut."

"Thanks," he said. "What are you going to cut it with, a broken pork rind?"

"Nah, I've got manicure scissors in here. . . ." I dug around in my purse. "See, all ready to go. I'm pretty good. You'll come out looking like you just got out of the sa-lon." I pronounced it "saa-lawn," which cracked us both up for some reason.

"Is this like some kind of makeover? Do I have to get new clothes too? Maybe a nose job or something?"

I pretended to study him. "Maybe a back wax."

"Do I have a hairy back?" He tried to lean over at an impossible angle and check it out, which prompted Blakas to think Josh was playing and lunge at his head.

"Ow!"

"Down, Blakas!" I called uselessly.

Josh pushed Blakas firmly to the ground by the neck until he calmed down. I knelt behind Josh and fluffed his hair around the way I'd seen Vidal Sassoon do it on TV.

"So you want to do it?"

"Sure," he said.

I took out the scissors. "We'll just neaten it up in the back and over the ears, leave the length on top, okay?"

"Don't cut it too short. It shrinks up a lot."

I braced myself in the sand and started snipping. My thighs were pressed against Josh's back, which wasn't really hairy at all (unlike his chest, which had a nice Brillo-y thatch). His back and ab muscles were dense and rippled, built for lying down on like my McRoskey's mattress. His hair gave off a more-than-pleasant arboreal aroma. I wanted to bury my nose in it and roll around, like Eve in the Garden of Eden. His threadbare board shorts gapped a little at the base of his spine. The little knobs of it poked bravely out, pointing a trail down to his ass, which I could see was round and deliciously grabbable. We were so close I was practically straddling him. I felt blood rush into my cheeks: This is what happens when you spend the summer surrounded by red-blooded males and retain your chastity. This is what happens when your fantasy life and your real life become interchangeable.

This is what happens when you pretend you're satisfied with a platonic relationship with the most fuckable guy in the hemisphere.

"There," I said. "Turn around."

I checked him out from all angles and pronounced him finished.

"Here. You can look in my compact." I took out my mirror and flipped it open for him. Josh held it over his head. He twisted this way and that, vogueing a little for Blakas's and my benefit.

"I feel so hot, almost like Christopher Peña's guest room," he said after a moment.

My traitorous finger stroked his stubbly cheek. "You look great," I murmured.

He leaned harder into my hand.

I sort of fell into his lap.

Blakas twitched in his sleep.

The ferry horn sounded.

We kissed.

Before you could say *multiple orgasm,* Josh had me on my back and was nibbling me everywhere. One second his mouth was on my neck; the next, he'd migrated to my stomach, having pushed my shirt up to my neck. He bit me on the arch of my left foot and cupped my butt in his hands under my skirt, squeezing as if it were ripe fruit. I felt the dense weight of his body molding mine and the woodsy, cherry-blossom-tree smell of him soaking the layers between us. I felt him straining against my belly, trying not to come, and it made me want to run to a synagogue and thank everybody I'd ever known. In his hands, my flesh took on a life of its own, quivering with the veracity of a plucked violin string. Something in me released and I felt glad tears slip down the sides of my face, mingling with the salty sand. I wanted him inside me so badly that everything but this moment dissolved into a benign, insignificant blur. I knew what was going to happen next. It was the first time in months I could say that with impunity, and it almost made me weep with relief and gratitude.

As our tongues twined together and we began the prefuck tango, I wondered what Josh was seeing in his mind's eye. I had heard that men are more susceptible to visual stimulation than women, so I always imagined a montage of juicy snapshots flickering in their minds—succulent breasts, damp collarbones, parted thighs, briny wetness—an orgy of sexual images coming together in a sort of sensual feast. I guess I have the textbook female psyche, because all my desire generally agglomerates into a laundry list of words, the key ones being *DON'T STOP* and *RIGHT THERE*.

"Yes!" I shouted into Josh Lido's neck.

Suddenly, he leaned back on his heels. I felt bereft without his weight, the very air between us a rebuke. For a second, I was convinced he had moved away in order to facilitate ripping my undies off and fucking me rotten, and the thought made me squirm with glee. I couldn't help but compare it to last time. Then he'd been gentle and I'd been the aggressor. This time, I reveled in my passivity: If I didn't initiate anything, I couldn't make any mistakes, could I? I would win, win, WIN!

"Oh, God. Parker," he mumbled, and slid off me.

"What's wrong? No, no, stay there. Josh! Josh?"

"This doesn't feel right."

"Yes it does! It feels . . . extraright, perfectly right, just right," I babbled. I didn't even bother to regain my modesty, just lay there like a slutty schoolgirl who'd given it away behind the baseball diamond.

Or not.

"We're so good together. It seemed like you felt that way too," I said. I was starting to cry, my beautiful prospective fuck disintegrating like sugar crystals in hot tea. "I love being with you." Sob. Weep. Wring hands. "Why are you doing this to me?" I yelled.

He clasped his head in his hands. "Parker, I am so, so sorry. I'm such a fuckup. You are so beautiful. You don't deserve this."

"Then why won't you just let it happen?"

He gave me his profile. "The thing is, Park, I'm . . . I'm just a really sad person."

I took his hand and guided it to my breast, feeling my belly tighten as his fingers inadvertently explored its curve.

"No, you're not. You're a normal person who's had something very sad happen to him," I said.

"The way I feel, I don't know how to describe it. It taints everything. I can't get close to people, can't sleep with you even, because it feels like it's going to, I don't know, seep out of me and poison us. It feels contagious, like the flu." He turned to me and I felt his hand sweep my hair off my hot, moist neck. His fingers dug in, bracing. "I feel like it's wrong that I'm here with you, when Raphael will never be with anyone again. It feels like I'm killing him a little more every time I do this. When I think about him and it hurts, he's closer, close enough to touch almost. I can see his eyes sometimes, hear him talking, I have all these memories of us together. They look like films . . . but it's getting hazy, and I don't ever want to lose that. When I make love to you, when I laugh at some stupid thing in a movie or a book, or even just like the taste of something, it feels like I'm losing more of him. I'm not going to fucking lose him again, Park. I can't," he said fiercely. He got up and brushed the sand off his shorts.

"If I was going to be with anyone, Park, it would be you," he said. Then he turned and walked away. I sank into the earth, hugged Blakas to me, and let myself keen for a while, the kind of purposeful keening that leaves you too depleted to grieve.

chapter 41

KELAH

Shipwrecked on Corfu, September

*Men are pigs. A common-enough assertion. But is it
accurate? Maybe men aren't pigs at all. Maybe they're lizards.
Or sheep. Opinions around here are leaning toward the
reptilian. . . .*

"Wait. Stop," I panted.

Boz jogged in place while I bent over at the waist, trying not to
vomit. After a minute I was fairly sure nothing was coming out
and I tried speaking again.

"Remind me. Why we're. Doing this?" I panted.

" 'Coz we're flabby English with smokers' lungs and love handles," Boz said.

"Bloody. Cheek. I only smoke. Six a day. And I don't have any.
Love handles."

"You don't have the love handles *because* you smoke enough to
kill your appetite. So now that we're quitting, we've got to get in

shape. Got to train." Boz leaped around, punching an imaginary sparring partner. His knobby knees and exuberant hair made him look like a possessed scarecrow.

I was wary of self-improvement. Never did much for me. I mean, what is it really, except a reminder of the myriad ways in which one doesn't suffice? Also, I suspected that the origin of Boz's jogging and punching frenzy was female, raven-haired, dark-eyed, and at this very moment wallowing in Kierkegaard in one of the university's danker libraries. Why should I get fit on Inez San Giacomo's account? On anyone's account? In fact, why should I let Boz get fit on her account?

"Trying to get fit for Inez?" I couldn't help myself.

He grinned. "Sure. With all the shagging that bird requires, I'd be a fool not to. Otherwise, I'll have a heart attack."

"That's lovely, Boz. But maybe she'd be happier with David bloody Beckham if raw athleticism is what she wants in a man."

"You're trying to provoke me so we don't have to finish."

I glanced at my watch. "I must be doing something right, since I just wasted ten minutes." I was starting to be able to speak normally again.

Boz grabbed me and pulled me up. Instinctively, I reached toward him. Then he reared back and smacked me in the bum hard enough to bring tears to my eyes.

"What'd you do that for, you dumb git?" I shrieked.

"You know what your problem is?"

"Abusive friends?"

He shook his head. "You cling to ideas of yourself nobody else believes in anymore, and you're afraid to try anything new."

"Pop psychobabble. You sound like Parker."

"No, really. You're also afraid of success."

"I suppose that's why I'm writing a leading column and publishing a book?"

"You're doing those things in spite of yourself, not *because* of anything positive," he said stubbornly.

"Where'd you get that idea, Oprah? No, wait. You've actually been pursuing a PhD in clinical psychology when we thought you were at the Sticky Wicket, and you're doing your thesis on the psychopathology of half West Indian doctors' daughters who chew their fingernails?" The Sticky Wicket was the local pub, a damp cave that smelled of Guinness, nervous men, tarty women, and parquet floors that had never been touched by natural light.

"Hey, don't kill the messenger."

Boz jogged off down the bumpy footpath.

"And how'd we end up talking about me, anyway?" I called.

Boz wagged his fingers and turned around, hopping backward. "Trade secret. But it sure got you off the subject of Inez, didn't it?"

We spend so much time ruminating on how others disappoint us that we devote very little to the times they grant us their unique generosity and strength. But the really delightful thing about other people surprising you is that it makes you believe you just might be capable of surprising yourself.

After the dinner with Mum and Dad, I waited for our new-found, magical acceptance of one another to dematerialize, for reality to encroach—for time to prove that one night of rapport was the exception that proved the rule. The next day, I'd awakened enveloped in an unfamiliar feeling. I ran my hand over my drowsy eyes, trying to give it a name. It wasn't until I stood at the gate watching Mum and Dad board the plane back to London that I knew: It was contentedness. Somehow, viewing them as fallible, as human in the most universal sense of the word, had given me the impetus I needed to step away from viewing my accomplishments and myself as synonymous. Okay, start stepping away. *Okay*—prepare to think about stepping away. For the first time in a long while, I *wanted* something that didn't have anything to do with adding to my curriculum vitae. I wanted to feel right in my skin. I wanted to get on with my parents because I *liked* them, not because they were, well, my parents.

At the airport, Mum had held me to her tightly.

"I'm not letting you squirm away this time," she said.

"And I'm not letting you either," I answered.

We drew back. Dad was grinning at us.

"Don't think for a minute I'm going to let you turn this into a Kodak moment," I told him.

He ignored me. "I never noticed it before, but you and your mother do the same thing with your hands when you're thinking about something. That thing with the fists," Dad said.

"All the Grant women do it. It's a sign of intellectual depth," Mum said, smiling.

Then I got a wholly unexpected and quite embarrassing lump in my throat.

"I'm so glad you came—"

"We are too—"

"Stay as long as you want—"

"Come home soon. We miss you—"

Things went on like that for a while. When they left, I watched the plane tilt and rise through the dirty windowpane. After a minute, when the jet had gotten paper-airplane small, I backed up. I could see my reflection in the glass. I hardly recognized myself, but it didn't matter: I was pretty sure the girl in the glass was going to be a friend.

chapter 42

CLAIRE

I took a deep breath and pressed my palms against the sides of my skirt. They were damp and I didn't want to give my anxiety away. It was one thing to wave casually to Andreas when I passed him in the street or in town; it was quite another to come to his door, risking an encounter with my Roman replacement, and ask him for a favor.

I wanted him to accompany me for my demo CD. I'd found a studio we could use in Athens. All we had to do was take the ferry there, record the original songs and covers we'd played this summer, and go our separate ways. A cool forty-eight hours is all it would take, quick enough to get us both back for Tony's grand reopening this weekend. The request was purely professional. My concern? That Andreas would see it as a transparent attempt to wend my way back into his bedsheets. Not that I should care, but that was one thing I'd noticed about Mediterranean men in general—they had a rather primitive and inflated notion of their importance in a woman's schema.

Perhaps it had something to do with living in a tourist destination, but the Greeks especially seemed to have a unique ability to cram an entire relationship's worth of drama into whatever time slot was available. Going to Mykonos next week? No problem: We'll meet on Monday, consummate on Tuesday, wallow in happiness on Wednesday, get sick of each other on Thursday, and break up on Friday. See? It's no problem. You'll even have a day to get over the despair of my abandonment, before the ferry leaves.

It was not unusual to see a young couple who had swayed in each other's arms the night before shooting poisonous glances at each other the next night as they forged new alliances, the man flicking his hair over his eye as if to say, *I know how much I hurt you, but I just can't resist temptation.* The men cultivated a James Dean-ish persona, alternately vulnerable and dangerous, pretty pseudo-whores whose currency was female attention. What they didn't understand is that the women were, by then, dredging beer-addled memories for the name of their most recent conquest and wondering what the men of Turkey thought of condoms.

It was comical, really. I could imagine Andreas after I'd asked him, awareness dawning in the sexy, tilted eyes: *What do you mean, you only wanted me for my C chord?* But it was a risk I had to take if I wanted to get something decent off to Taylor Black before he forgot about me; before a younger, blonder voice sang its way into his memory. I'd been given a one-in-a-million chance to grab a power broker's ear and warble into it, and I wasn't about to waste it because of a few hurt feelings and a two-hundred-dollar lingerie bill.

I rapped smartly on the door, hoping he wasn't in his usual state of undress.

The door opened and he was standing there, rubbing sleep from his eyes.

It was four P.M.

"Claire?" he said sleepily. Then the eyes widened and something seemed to jolt him into full consciousness. "*Yasu, yasu,* come in. Come in. It is good to see you." He leaned forward as if to kiss me. I offered my cheek. He smiled nervously.

His usually languid demeanor was a bit jittery. Understandable, since I'd broken the rules, right? By this time, I was supposed to have either moved on to a new lover—perhaps the local high school had a candidate?—or sailed off, back to my husband/job/real life.

We sat down on the couch.

"How are you, Andreas?"

"Er, good?" He looked at me expectantly. I decided to jump right in. Then I realized: He must think I'm bringing bad news. Good Lord—maybe he thinks I'm pregnant? The thought almost brought on a fit of giggles, but I put my hand over my mouth and swallowed them.

"So, Andreas. Here's the thing. The other night, after we performed? Well, an American music executive approached me. He wants to take a demo of me singing back to America with him and possibly consider me for a recording contract. Do you understand?"

"Yes, of course. That is wonderful!" Andreas looked so relieved, I could only imagine what he had been thinking. Twins?

"Since I don't have a demo, I was wondering if you'd be willing to record one with me? I figured, since we've been performing together all summer, it would be a shame to start over with someone else. Also, with these types, you have to move quickly or they'll forget about you. We'd have to go to Athens. Of course, I'd pay for everything. Ferry, hotel, and studio time. What do you think?"

"I'm very happy for you, Claire." He moved closer on the sofa, stroked my arm lightly. "When I first hear you, I think, She could be famous singer! I am very pleased to record the demo with you in Athens."

I grabbed the wayward hand and placed it firmly on the arm of the couch. "Thank you, Andreas. That's a relief. I'm sure we'll make brilliant recording partners. You may want to tell your girlfriend you'll be gone for a couple days. I hear these sessions are all work and not really much fun. We're likely to not leave the studio except to sleep. We'll be too exhausted to be good company to anyone," I finished, staring intently into his eyes.

The sexy, tilted eyes of my former lover darkened slightly with something that might have been respect. Then again, as with all infants, it could have just been gas.

On Wednesday, Taylor Black called me from Santorini on his cell phone that worked anywhere. I could easily imagine the super-charged music executive strapping on a helmet and space suit for takeoff to Mars, Charlene glowing next to him like a blond candle in matching silver lamé. *Call me,* he'd say, as his cheeks wobbled at five hundred Gs. *We'll do luuuuunch.*

"Miz Claire?" he barked.

"Yes, this is Claire Dillon."

"Taylor Black here."

"Oh," I said. I was still waiting for someone to nudge my shoulder, wake me up, and tell me it was all a dream.

"You set up that demo yet?"

Yes, sir, I almost said. Then, "Actually, I'm going to Athens this afternoon with my accompanist. We'll be done by Friday. I'm to FedEx it to you—"

"Care of my office in Nashville. Address I gave you. Send it to my secretary, Sharleen. She'll know what to do with it." He pronounced secretary *sekra-tree*.

"Charlene?" These Americans were so confusing. I pictured Nashville as a puddle of a city, teeming with identical honey-tressed fembots with generous husbands and big jewelry. The Charlenes.

"Heh, heh. It's *Shar*-leen, with an *SH*."

Oh.

"Miz Claire?"

"Yes?"

"I have a good feeling about you. That means you're more than halfway there. You get my drift?"

"Yes, I . . . get your drift, Taylor."

"See you in Nashville, honeypie."

I stared at the phone for a while, listening to the soothing buzz and letting the giddiness tingle down to my fingertips. Honeypie Dillon. Not bad. Not bad at all.

I wanted to kill the one with the sideburns and unblinking lizard's eyes. Slowly and as painfully as possible. With a nail file. Or perhaps a particularly sharp toothpick. But first we had to finish. Then I would kill him. After I got some sleep and a decent meal. Oh, and called Brian and Ethan to let them know I was alive. And soaked my feet. Twice.

Ugh.

Lizard Eyes gave me the signal for the 486th time and messed with the dials on his panel. I made eye contact with Andreas, who smiled lazily and gave me his secret shoulder shrug. The one that I used to think meant he was mad with pent-up lust. For me. Now I could see it meant something else. Like calamari might be nice tonight. Or it's a bit warm for September.

Nervous sweat pooled in my armpits and trickled down the small of my back. Now that we were on our second day of taping, I had revised my vision of first-class international travel and Fijian bodyguards and chocolates nested in damask-swathed pillows like little pearls, waiting to be popped into my glossy mouth. These images had been replaced with those of harridans rasping tired country ballads at dive bars and guitar cases crosshatched with battle scars, lying open at busy intersections, hunched over a paltry few discarded coins. Anxiety and exhaustion had my vocal cords so worn I'd be lucky to get a job singing the national anthem at a children's rugby match. Or maybe I was just out of practice and couldn't rate my own performance. It certainly was different from singing live, when you had the audience's faces in front of you, a dozen meters set to ring if you slipped off-key or faded out. I closed my eyes and tried to visualize sweet sound spooling out of me, a toffee bar melting into caramel rivers in the sun, the way it felt when I trod the warm water on Mirtiotissa

Beach. I pulled my headset over my ears and let Andreas's guitar dance its way into my heartbeat.

This time, I found the thread I'd been searching for and let it guide me, weaving in and out of the emotional crevices of "Shake It, Don't Break It," a song I'd written during a low point earlier in the summer, before Ethan and Brian arrived and I still considered a day without a revenge fantasy something to tell my friends about.

Afterward, I knew we were done, because Lizard Eyes blinked. Just once, but I was pretty sure I saw it. I must have been right, because the other man, the one with the abundance of chest hair, turned everything off and leaned back in his chair. We all shook hands, I filled out a stack of traveler's checks to the studio, promised I'd keep in touch, and then Andreas and I stood outside in the fading daylight while busy Athens choked and belched its way through its noxious rush hour. There was something surreal about it all. I think the combination of being away from cities all summer, plus the alienness of Athens, plus seeing Andreas so out of context and somehow diminished by the feverish backdrop around us, had left me feeling rather floaty and sleepy. Not to mention that I had in my hand a thin slip of a disc that was headed toward Nashville, Tennessee, U.S.A., to the waiting—and I'm sure frightfully manicured—hands of Sharleen. Truly, life is strange.

"Do you want to get some dinner?" I said to Andreas.

"Oh, yes. We can go to my cousin's restaurant. It is near the Parthenon."

We started off down the frantic thoroughfare, our progress halted every few minutes by snarled traffic or a driver screaming Greek obscenities. Ahead of us, the huge structure rose up from the maze of streets, glimmering in the slanted haze. I hadn't expected it to be so thrilling, so stubbornly integrated into Athens's modernity. I guess I'd always thought such a thing would be kept carefully separate, sheltered from the ugliness of daily life and its banal betrayals, hidden behind the plush curtain of antiquity. I had always thought that surrendering that which is special to public referendum squandered its specialness. I was wrong.

"So, what do you think?" I said finally, not sure what I was asking exactly.

Andreas shrugged, but he looked content.

"I think it is likely that something good happens," he said.

Strangely, I did too.

chapter 43

ANYA

I pulled my head away from Ethan's crotch and gagged down what was left of his, um, *stuff,* while he was still flat on his back, unaware of anything but the pulsing afterglow emanating from his *pito.* I filled my lungs with great gulps of air. I swear, spending time down there is like being stuck in an Amazonian rain forest: high humidity, thick shrubbery, and it's better to leave some stones unturned, because you never know what kind of nasty you might find underneath. After I'd wiped the corners of my mouth on the starched sheet, I crawled up beside him—something I'd never managed to do with the dignity and aplomb that was outlined in *Cosmopolitan*—and let him wrap his arm around my neck, pulling me to his chest, cozy with the knowledge that I had sacrificed so much comfort for his love. Who knows? Maybe they even think we like it.

We women like to think we are so evolved, so past using sex as a bargaining chip or a furtive distraction. But as far as I can tell, our bag of tricks hasn't benefited from a new item since Frederick's of Hollywood got the bright idea to cut the crotch out of panties.

When our husbands ask us about the unexplained charge on the joint credit card, twelve hundred dollars bestowed upon the needy clerks at Coach handbags or Sephora cosmetics, we grin slyly and glance at the kids' closed bedroom door before stepping out of our skirts, confident in the accoutrements of prior largesse (lace balconette bra and thong panties; thigh-grabbing lace-trimmed stockings; terminal subscription to the Jenny Craig diet plan). When we anticipate our beloved's randiness falling at an inopportune time—parents visiting? hosting Christmas dinner? early flight to New York?—we cleverly execute a preemptive strike, delivering an energy-preserving quickie or hand job that will cause him to think twice about requesting further ministrations in the coming days (or *not,* as the case may be).

What I really wanted was to talk to Ethan about our future. To pick up our conversation where it left off ten days ago, when it was incinerated by the fiery breath of Evil Rachel's greeting. But every time I opened my mouth to begin, some pointless banality came out. I waited for the "right" time with the electric patience of a rattlesnake, but the moments that presented themselves were stunning only for their wrongness.

Case in point: two days ago. I'd finished my shift at Nia's and was locking up for the night when Ethan pulled up on his motorcycle and surprised me.

"Hop on," he said.

I slid into place behind him, something about the practiced naturalness of it nearly bringing tears to my eyes. His neat waist warmed my hands into stillness, a human muffler. My teeth were even with the wing of his shoulder blade, his sweater rough against my cheek. Experimentally, I conjured myself zigzagging home from work in San Francisco, shuffling through the barrio's windswept piles of trash, chicken bones, used condoms, syringes, and rotting newspapers, and wanted to scream. I needed a steed to bear me home, above the detritus of life's ugliness. Steeds came with knights; I needed a knight.

We drove to the monastery we'd gone to on our first "date," after he'd picked me up at the beach. We laughed about that now, our first, shared relationship joke. How he'd lurked around Johnny's sand-locked outpost, fully dressed, feeling like an ass, and how I'd assumed he was there to plumb me for information on Parker and gone all snappish on him.

Ethan parked the bike and I slid off, careful to avoid the exhaust pipe, which I knew from experience could sear a Coke-can-size circle onto your leg. I slipped my hand into his and we entered the part of the complex that had crumbled into delicate disrepair. He sat down on a bit of wall and I sat on his lap, clasped my arms behind his neck, tried to gauge our odds in his eyes.

"I'm sorry," he said.

"For what?"

"Rachel. Coming here. Ruining your holiday."

"She hasn't ruined anything. On the contrary. It's given the SNiPs something to do when we're not eating calamari. Ripping her to shreds—it's like a new sport or something."

He laughed and stroked my hair. "That's what I love about you, Anya. You've got this angelic quality about you, but inside there's a firecracker. You're a bit of a bitch, aren't you?"

"A bit." If you only knew, *querido*.

Then everything seemed to halt, to coagulate into empty wisps of space around us, so that the filament between us fairly hummed with expectancy. We were wholly focused on each other. In the groove. Supremely attuned to whatever addictive rhythm the combination of our unique selves produced. It was the moment. It was time. I recalled Carilu's advice from the other day: Fight for what you want. Be a fighter. Don't go down weak, and don't expect love to be clean.

"Ethan," I said. "Ethan, I want—"

His eyes drove me on, silently mouthed *yes, yes, yes.*

"I want to tell you . . ." No. Too whiny. I began again. "Ethan, in a relationship it's important to start off on a strong foundation, which you obviously know, as you are in construction. . . ." Construction? *Dios mío!* Anya Graciela María Soberanes, surely you can present a better metaphor than that.

Ethan took my hand. "Anya, it's okay. I think I know what you're going to say."

"You do?"

"Yes, and you don't have to worry. I know we never finished talking about our plans, but I want you to know my feelings haven't changed. I still want to come to San Francisco with you. I just have to go home first and sort a few things out."

"But—"

"I know when Rachel first came I acted like it didn't mean anything. But the truth is, in spite of what I said, it was hard not to imagine what it would be like to get back together with her. She used to mean a lot to me, and I wondered if I had made a mistake. I didn't wonder very long. But it was there. The thought, I mean." His eyes fluttered away from mine for a second. With a start, I recognized the look on his face: a mirror of Rick's when he did, finally, tell me he was leaving me (to date Mindy-Mandy, no less). My heart executed a sort of Greg Louganis-style dive, plunging down to my feet and flipping along the way. I kept my face in what I thought was a neutral pose—that is, not blatantly suicidal—and waited for him to finish. Perhaps my radar was off? Perhaps that intimate smile on his lips was a trick of light?

"But when Rachel kissed me I knew it was completely dead between us. I didn't feel a thing. And she was trying pretty hard." Ethan smiled beatifically, the kind of smile that indicates the smiler expects his revelations to bestow serious martyrdom. The kind of smile that says, sure, I kissed my ex, but it was no big deal. Men! I couldn't decide whether I wanted to slap him or kiss him myself.

"Well, I'm glad it didn't do much for you," I managed to murmur. Inside, the diving pool was churning. How much does it take to trust someone? Really trust him? What's he even *doing* kissing his ex-girlfriend *gringa* fake Gucci *ho*, and why does he have to tell me about it? Why do we always need to turn relationships into the damn confessional when there's a perfectly good place for that? Why do we even bother with this relationship *mierda,* when there are plenty of good things in life, things like ice cream and animal rescue and *novelas.*

Also: Did this qualify as overreacting?

"So what did you want to tell me?" Ethan asked innocently.

I stared at him, trying to absorb his essential goodness, reading leftover pain and yearning in the creases around his almond eyes. The wing-beating bird forever trapped in my chest struggled to free herself, and I imagined myself wrapping my hands around her, forming a safe house so she could be still, the way bird handlers do when a fierce, fragile creature escapes its cage. Suddenly, the will to do battle, to give Ethan the tools of my own potential destruction, to unseat the delicate balance we had achieved, left me. Even the image of the kiss he'd shared with Evil Rachel ceased to cause real pain, leaving just a tiny sting, like the site of a vaccination the next day, pinpricked with a little nimbus of bruising around it.

I took Ethan's hand and answered his question. "Nothing much. I guess I was thinking . . . do you think you'll want to live in my apartment, or look for a new one?"

And that was the end of that round.

The next one ended when Claire came back one day early from Athens, full of stories.

Another was cut short by the untimely intrusion of Evil Rachel, who had somehow "stumbled" onto our hiding place with her latest squeeze, a Dutchman who looked like the James Bond bad guy with metal teeth.

Then there was that little food-poisoning incident, which left me feeling on the weak side.

And so now, today, instead of spilling secrets, my mouth finds itself occupied with other things. And I won't tell you to get your mind out of the gutter, *chica,* because that's where the biggest deals, the most elaborate cons, always go down, right? In the gutter.

part two

THE PARTY

chapter 44

~~~~~~~~~~~~~~

PARKER

In the last few days, in between preparations for Tony's party and paroxysms of despair at having to go home and face my (*Encyclopedia Britannica*) of problems, I've had some pretty weird and unseemly thoughts.

These include:

▣ Why did Josh Lido's brother have to die?

▣ Why did Josh Lido's brother have to die before Josh and I had sex?

▣ Are there some men who just don't understand the concept of burying their grief in reasonably hot interior-designer pussy?

▣ Did Neil hang up the Belgian's lederhosen—or whatever they wear over there (Trappist cloaks? French fry pasties?)—the first time he fucked her?

🔳 Should I give away my favorite size-six Earl jeans and get a size eight, or just skip straight to relaxed Dockers?

🔳 Would Blakas shit in my Kate Spade black noel weave luggage if I tried to sneak him past customs?

🔳 Would the San Francisco district attorney charge me with felony murder for slipping something like, say, hemlock in the Belgian's and Neil's Peet's coffee?

🔳 Would Christopher Peña still let me design his kitchen if I had a felony murder conviction?

Not to mention the, ahem, rather unusual atmosphere surrounding the biggest event of the season, the year, perhaps even the island's history. (Okay, recent history, but that whole Peloponnesian war thing is, like, *so* antiquated.) Aphrodite—the goddess of lamb shanks, not love—had elevated her feud with Tony to a level of ire rarely seen outside of the *Godfather* movies. When he entered the kitchen, she left it, pausing to dramatically slam her cleaver into a hunk of raw flesh quivering on the cutting board, her heavy-lidded gaze leaving no doubt that the hapless hamburger was a glistening substitute for Tony's heart. When some poor cook happened to say Tony's name aloud, a globule of spit would sail into the corner of the tile floor, hygiene be damned. Aphrodite was nowhere near ready to forgive her brother his treason, and, consequently, the rest of us labored under the incongruous condition of preparing for a party originally conceived as a celebration, now a wake, in the face of a deadly familial discord that could net any one of Tony's staff a loogie on the shoe or a cleaver in the medulla.

Knowing that he'd used up his nine lives with me, Josh slunk around the fringes of Pelekastritsa society, avoiding old haunts and biding time until his flight left next week. It's not like I was angry at him per se. That would make me a heartless shrew, no? There was just the overwhelming sense that we'd hit our courtship's expiration date, the critical threshold by which one must, in the words of my Grandma Ivy, shit or get off the pot. Some things need to happen while there's still blind momentum pushing you forward, because the risks they entail are so great that if you stop to think about it, dawning logic will ensure you retreat from the object of your desire like a war criminal fleeing to Argentina. Our statute of limitations for consummation was officially up, and seeing each other now just highlighted how foolish our expectations had been and how stupid we were to expect intimacy and healing from a place where women dance barebreasted on bamboo mats and men wear cinched belts with Mossimo buckles. Seeing Josh made me feel like that carton of milk you come home to after a weekend away. The kind you sniff and wrinkle your nose at when its sourness smacks you in the face. The kind you consider spooning into your coffee the next morning anyway, in spite of its expired use-by date, because you're exhausted and fresh milk exists only in some alternate universe, a place where long weekends are actually energizing and dairy cows untainted by recombinant growth hormone spew frothy cream into your latte while your husband massages your neck and stays married to you.

But there were other things to do besides sit around and feel sorry for my (celibate) ass. Outfits to plan. Lights to hang. Dented mopeds to return. Mustachioed sisters to defuse. Fabulous parties to execute.

Business as usual.

"*Opa!*" we all shouted. Tony, Claire, Kelah, Boz, Anya, Brian, Ethan, and I, as well as a half dozen of Tony's employees, stood outside the newly minted door of the taverna. The party preparations were finished. We were ready.

"This call for a toast," said Tony. He pulled out a bottle of Greek table wine and filled everyone's tumbler glass with ruby liquid.

"I like to thank Parker first, for all she do on this place. I am some ungrateful guy, to go to L.A. now."

"Put me in one of your movies and I'll forgive you," I said.

"Only if you sleep with producer," Tony grinned.

A chorus of groans ensued.

"Dirty dog."

"God, Tony!"

"Hollywood's perfect for you."

"Hollywood's too good for you!"

"Quiet, everyone!" I said. "Does everyone know what they're supposed to be doing? Claire and Andreas are setting up in that corner. Ethan and Anya are on lights. Brian and I are picking up the flowers in town. Tony's on food"—I glanced at my gnomelike friend, who seemed to be sharpening his bicuspids on a piece of leather that resembled a whip handle—"unless Aphrodite kills him, in which case I'm on food. Boz and Kelah, you're picking up the balloons at Nia Alexiou's at six P.M. Any questions?"

One of Tony's busboys, a kindly, jug-eared fellow named Nico, timidly raised his hand.

"Yes?"

"Aphrodite, she give me message for Tony." Nico's eyes cut apologetically at his boss. "She say, she turn refrigerator up to eighteen degrees last night, so all food rotten for party. I not believe her, but when I come early I check and, yes, all the food stink like dead fish. I don't want to make you angry," he said meekly.

"What? I kill her!" Tony screamed, shaking his child-size fists in the air. He issued a few more choice curses, something about never closing one's eyes at risk of death and illegitimate children with horns.

I tried to remember what my mentor, Ginger Lyons, always told me about focusing on the positive with clients when things go wrong. That's probably what she did when she had to tell her husband, Dane, about the kickboxer. It's not so bad, she might have said, look what it's done for my roundhouse.

"Okay, what was in there?" I said, adding my own slightly less inventive curses to Aphrodite's head.

"Souvlaki, moussaka, dolmas, tzatziki, pita, baklava . . ." Nico went on to name a feast of Greek goodies.

"Is everything spoiled?"

He shrugged. "Maybe not all. I check."

"Okay, change of plan. Nico and Tony are going to check everything. Whatever needs to be replaced, I'll go pick some up somewhere." I didn't mention where I'd get it—Sunset Over the Parthenon, Tony's archenemy taverna over the hill in a neighboring village.

I grasped my watch. Silently, the others did the same.

"Meet back here at eighteen hundred hours. Oh, and try to wear something halfway decent," I said.

Fuck, fuck, *fuck!*

As the one who had driven Tony's redesign project to completion, I was also de facto party planner, sous-chef, and in-house psychotherapist. Luckily, only the souvlaki and the moussaka were deemed truly unsalvageable, so I'd elected to pick them up after getting myself ready for the big night. We expected upward of two hundred fifty people, after all, some coming from as far away as Athens and Crete (well, okay, three from Athens and one rumored Cretan—local cretins were all accounted for). We'd occupied some of the street outside, setting up white plastic tables under colorful cloths, to handle overspill. We could not sacrifice even a bite of food. I'd called the Parthenon people and begged them to prepare party trays. I had to bribe their silence with invitations to Tony's grand reopening and a promise to get them autographed photos of Christopher Peña. My ability to withstand work stress had atrophied over the long, lazy summer, and I was a wreck. Also, the whole town was coming, so I would doubtless see Josh there. Not to mention that Blakas, whom I'd scrubbed to snowy, speckled perfection yesterday for the party, had rolled in something both vile and staining, so that his formerly white coat now had a grayish, sticky cast, and he smelled like day-old tandoori.

Now it was too late to resurrect Blakas's sheen, but I could do something about myself. I stripped down to my bra and

underwear and checked myself out in the bubbly full-length mirror Mrs. Gianniotis had propped up for us when we'd outlasted
even the Greek vacationers. At the beginning of summer, the
Parker Glass in the mirror had been waifishly thin, white as milk,
and smudgy-eyed on endless cocktails of muscle relaxants and
despair. I tried to see myself as others now doubtless did: a
decent-looking woman, early thirties, definitely not fat but not
the picture of deprivation either. Steel-blue eyes that had seen
some living made brighter by a light toasty tan. Shiny black hair
that had grown beyond the confines of pricey layers into a loose,
sexy, unself-conscious mane. A hint of a smirk, frosted with hopefulness. Healing scratches marring forearms and shins, perhaps
from hiking through bushes or playing with an uncontrollable
mutt. Long, lean legs with feet rough enough to take me across
town barefoot. Unpainted nails. I took inventory and decided to
maximize one of the benefits of my ten-pound weight gain:
boobs.

Fifteen minutes later, I was ready to jump on the moped and
go. I'd settled on a halter top the diaphanous blue of a predawn
horizon. The airy color brought out my eyes and smooth shoulders. The deep V in the front showed enough cleavage to lose a
dime in. I needed to feel tough tonight rather than ethereal and
feminine, so I'd paired it with my outgrown Earl jeans, which I
could still tug over my hips if I skipped dinner and took a long
pee. The button no longer closed, so I'd pulled a studded leather
belt around my waist left here by one of our former housemates,
a Harley-riding Dane. I threw on fuck-me—actually, more like
fuck-*you*—spike-heeled booties I hadn't worn since June, and the
effect was rather impressive: With my party planner's notebook
and Tony's huge, jangling key chain hanging from my belt, I
looked like the offspring of Keith Richards and a high-school cus-
todian. No proper hairdo would withstand the moped ride, so I
left it thick and tousled. At the last minute, I grabbed a loquat
flower to pin behind my ear. MAC Viva Glam lipstick, of course.
And a bucket of Issey Miyake.

"See you in an hour," I called to Anya, who was showering.

"See you," came her voice, muffled from the water.

Blakas ran up to me, wriggling his firm little butt with doggish excitement.

"Peeew, you stink. Are you ready to go?" I asked him. Then I realized something was missing. Ah! I dug around in my jewelry drawer and pulled out a miniature version of my studded belt. The Dane's belt had been so long on me, I'd actually cut off a piece and attached a buckle. I clasped it around Blakas's neck and surveyed us. I thought we looked excellent: two tough bitches— okay, a bitch and a warlock—off to conquer the world. Then, to ward off the headache that was threatening to explode in my retinas, I grabbed my blue pill case off the counter and swallowed two aspirin. Just to be sure, I tossed back two more; it wouldn't do to come down with a migraine when Tony needed me to ensure the success of his final send-off.

"Let's kick some ass," I said. I swung my jeans-clad legs over my hog—I mean, moped—and tucked my purse into the basket. Blakas rode bitch. Experimentally, I spread my thumb and pinky out, middle fingers folded down, in the universal sign of rockin' belligerence.

Just an experiment, of course.

chapter 45

KELAH

Shipwrecked on Corfu, September

It's coming. We never thought it would. The end of summer. Last night, the four of us met at Tony's for drinks and were crying by the end. I know what you're thinking. Crying? Over holiday friends? It's just that there's something extraordinary about knowing someone's seen you at your worst as well as your best—and stuck around for the lift.

I'd been wondering what would happen to my column when the holiday ended. Writing about the misadventures of four women spending the summer in Corfu was all well and good, but we had to go home sometime, right? Predictably, my editor, Joan, had swatted my concerns away like pesky gnats whenever I'd raised the subject. Now that I was counting the remainder of the holiday in days instead of weeks, she had shifted overnight from blithe indifference to diet-pill-marinated hysteria. I'd tried to calm her down by suggesting ideas, which turned out to be exactly the wrong approach.

"Human-rights violations? The global sex trade? The sordid side of holiday travel?" I'd blurted out the other day on the phone. I had visions of co-opting my column for the kind of real reportage that merits Pulitzer prizes and invitations to speak at the international conference of Women Against the Enslavement of Women. Not having met Joan Vance in person, I could only imagine what sort of rotting Sloaney monster was sitting on the other end of the line. I refused to let Boz shatter my dread illusions, as my sharply drawn fantasy picture of scarecrow hair, carnivorous bloodred lips, dancer's posture, shriveled cashmere twin sets, posh moans, and a necklace of contributors' scalps provided many hours of prolific writing.

"Don't be ridiculous," Joan said when I broached my ideas. "This is *Flounce* we're talking about, Kelah, not Amnesty International's bloody newsletter."

"Um, lifestyles of the rich and inbred?"

She laughed, a gummy drumroll of phlegm and wads of chewed-off lipstick. "We could get you into my mother's Tea and Thimbles group. Honestly, they'd be really chuffed."

"How about what it's like to readjust to regular life in London after a summer of swarthy sex?"

"Closer."

"Where singletons find sex from Devon to Dover?"

"Possible."

Suddenly, I saw Bozzie's clear gray-blue eyes, the way he'd looked at me when I'd screamed at him for sending my journal to a magazine and bearing my parents to my Mediterranean doorstep. And the most perfect idea crystallized, one Sloaney Joan would not be able to resist.

"What about unrequited passion? What about deep, lifelong love that never dies but never gets consummated either?" I was getting excited now. "All the experts say relationships last if you're friends first, if you stay friends. But what's the real story? What if

I find couples that are at all stages of friendship becoming love? What if I follow their relationships for, say, a year, see who makes it and who doesn't? See if lovers who claim to be friends have a better chance of success than anyone else?"

Silence at the other end, punctuated by the sharp sawing of a nail file and that incessant cough. Canines like flinty Indian arrowheads descended into my field of vision. Was the mad bitch sharpening her teeth? Then, "I like it. Write up a proposal and have it in my e-mail by Monday."

"Tuesday. I don't get home until Monday."

"Whatever. Oh, and Kelah?"

"Yes?" I was already pondering angles that would get me into Inez San Giacomo's door. Trustafarian cow. Had to make sure Bozzie knew what he was getting into.

"Say hello to Bosworth for me."

"I can't believe Tony's selling the place, especially after all the work Parker and Brian put into it," I said to Boz. He was painting his toenails pale blue to match his vintage 1950s bowling shirt for the party. He'd borrowed the vile stuff from Parker.

"Dunno. If a man wants out, he should get out. Life's short and all that," he said.

"Yeah, I guess." But still. It was hard not to be nostalgic about Tony's. Something in me wanted to preserve it all in a plastic time capsule, like an enchanted snow globe, so I could take it out and look at it when I needed reminding. Of who I was. Kelah B.P.— before publication.

"So, what are you wearing tonight, luv?" Boz said.

I sighed and studied my standard uniform of ratty tank top and faded cargo trousers. I couldn't remember the last time I even wore a bra. The last one in my possession had been sacrificed for its underwire under stoned Graeme's careful supervision, to make a DIY water pipe.

"This."

Boz's thick eyebrows pulled together. "Bollocks. You look like the sale rack at Oxfam."

"Maybe I want to look like bloody Oxfam. Oxfam chic. Oxfantastic. Oxfandango!" I laughed and danced around as if on the runway. He did not react. "Hey, Bozzie. Not all of us are out to parade our tits around and get shagged, you know."

"In that getup, you'd get rejected by a prison block."

I feigned disappointment. "Really? Not even, like, the mad rapist would want me?"

"Come on. Surprise yourself. Think of it as a costume party. Parker wanted us to look smart for the glitterati. Do it for Tony," he said in a dead-accurate imitation of our favorite scene from the American classic *The Outsiders,* where a young, hunky, gunshot Matt Dillon crawls through the street moaning, "I did it for Johnny."

Damn. He always knew how to twist my arm.

"Fuck. All right."

So I slunk off to the closet to assess my pitiful wardrobe. Boz was right. It ranged from transparently rebellious juvenile to dead nasty to macramé-ish, naff horrors. Seeing my paralysis, Boz came in and grabbed a few items from the rack and off the floor, occasionally dropping a choice epithet highlighting the item's dubious pedigree. I sat on the bed and daydreamed about future iterations of my column: "Life as a Bitch" or "What if You *Hadn't* Married the Wanker?"

"That goes on top," he said, pointing to a scrap of something silky on the bed. "And one of those on bottom. Make sure you show some bum. And hurry up, we're to pick up the balloons"— he checked his watch—"fifteen minutes ago."

Boz banged on the door. "Kay, hurry up. We're late."

I hunched over and tried to check myself out in the only mirror we had—a broken Amstel Light coatrack scored by the fingernails of countless sods pawing for their jackets. I was pretty sure my arse was exposed, based on the amount of airflow down there, but couldn't be sure.

The door thumped again. "Kelah!"

"Okay, okay. I'm coming."

I took a deep breath and opened the door. At the last second, some deviant instinct had led me to extract my ancient tube of Boots tinted lip gloss and smear it on my mouth. And rub a little on my cheeks. And brow bones.

And, fuck it, cleavage. Well, what passed as such on me. The Netherlands, more like. Or the Sahara. Which, I now noticed, had glitter on it. Glitter!

"Well, here it is. Frankenstein," I said, and threw the door open all the way.

I felt Boz's eyes sweep down, trailing red-hot embarrassment in their wake, from my curly mop, which I'd left mercifully alone, over my tarty makeup, past my silver-hooped earlobes, down my neck to my chest area, which was swathed, gypsylike, in a long, wide silk scarf knotted in the back, leaving my shoulders and back brown and bare. I had on a denim mini and sandals, the only shoes I had except trainers. The mini was a mystery: I had no idea how it got in my closet, or why it was so frightened of my cricket-ball knees it had to crouch, trembling, somewhere around my crotch.

"I think we'd better avoid prisons and working harbors, for the time being," he murmured. Then, while my heart began a hot staccato mambo in my chest, Boz bent down and kissed me, quite chastely, and quite unfortunately, on the cheek.

chapter 46

∾∾∾∾∾∾∾∾∾∾∾∾∾

CLAIRE

I'd made a decision.

With my departure from the island counted in hours instead of days, I knew I had to come to some conclusion about my next move. Back home, I'd just slip into complacency, the familiar glove fit of life with Gary, club meetings and bridge parties slotted into our days neatly as sweaters in wardrobe bags, errand-running, space fillers constructed to obliterate memories of unconsummated dreams and unspoken regrets. It wouldn't be altogether miserable, of course, just unbearably wrong. I was like Eve in the garden, and having tasted the forbidden fruit of life without melancholy, without spun-sugar lies and wilting facades shielding seething interiors, I couldn't settle for the life we'd had before. The prospect of Ethan moving to California to be with Anya left an even greater hole gaping in the fabric of our family, though he was certainly leaving for the best of reasons. With no promises that Gary and Brian would, in fact, reconcile, I felt as if the few threads that had held us together were snapping, one by one.

And so, I would tell Gary I was moving out.

There was a time when a letter like the one he'd written a few weeks ago would have made all the difference. And it did give me pause. It certainly added a patina of sadness to what was predominantly relief. But—and in my more honest moments, I saw this as the fundamental driver it really was—the truth was, I was selfish enough to think I could choose my pain, and the pain I wanted was the pain of risk, of taking chances again, of flirting with strangers in a bar, or sending a CD with my voice on it to an American music executive with a Rolex and two women named Charlene in charge of his life. And to hell with the pain that would cause anyone else. I knew it was arrogant, maybe even ridiculously deluded, to think this summer was any indication of how I could and would live my life back in Australia, but I clung to it like a seabird soaring over rough water with a thrashing fish in its beak; I was more than willing to incur a few slashes if there was even a remote chance of a meal at the end of it. I realized that, without even knowing it, I'd been steeped in a culture of sly self-deception: Always play your decoy hand so people won't get the chance to see you fail at that which is closest to your heart. Hold on tight to whatever you have, even if you don't want it, because someone else might. Dream big and act small. Self-deprecate. Smile. Smile bigger.

I'd tell Gary it was for the best, that a trial separation would give us both time to figure out what we really wanted. He'd volley back that the summer had already provided that. I'd sketch a picture of the pain his betrayal had caused me. He'd show me how he was ready to redraw himself in a new image. I'd confess I'd slept with another man this summer. He'd stumble back, dazed. I'd knock him down with the recording-contract uppercut. He'd cry out for proof. I'd show him my tarty undies. He'd faint dead away.

Well, maybe not quite like that.

I needed to put it out of my mind for a while. While not the celebration we'd all intended, tonight's party was still the culmination of an incredible summer, and I wanted to relish every minute of it. Gary and I had plenty of time to make each other miserable, back in Sydney.

"Claire, you look beautiful," Andreas said.

"Thank you," I said, and meant it.

It's funny. Not too long ago, I would have responded to such a compliment with sidesteps and demurrals on the order of "Are you blind, man?!" "This old thing?" or just embarrassed silence. It's not like I was currying compliments now or anything, but something fundamental had shifted inside me, so that I felt not only deserving of such observations but also pleasantly unsurprised. They were not so much rare jewels as fallen raindrops during the wet season, iridescent and appreciated but expected nonetheless.

Concurrent with my newfound confidence, I spent less time agonizing over what to wear when I was performing, and still managed to look, I believe, better than Old Claire. Tonight, I'd thrown together a gypsy-style costume that reflected my mood, both romantic and nostalgic. I'd knotted a man's crisp white shirt at my waist, the sleeves rolled up to mid-forearm to expose a set of hand-punched leather bracelets Brian had given me as a gift. My skirt was long, crinkled, and dotted with flowers. The SNiPs had pronounced it dowdy, but that was when I'd insisted on wearing it with a long tunic. I think it would pass muster now. I'd unbuttoned the shirt as low as I could go without embarrassing myself, and one of my pretty new bras—red lace, if you must know—peeked out. A simple, wide, tooled-leather belt lay low on my hips, matching my gladiator sandals. A river of gold baubles spilled into my cleavage and from my ears, and I'd wrapped a gorgeous Hermès scarf Patricia—my clothing fairy godmother—had given me around my hair, which gave me a rakish air. I brushed my hair until it shone red and made up my eyes to look dusky and, I hoped, mysterious. At the last second, peering at the female pirate in the mirror, I'd impulsively switched my wedding band to my right hand. All the better to slay dragons.

And remove the last visual vestige of my married life (barring the crosshatched seams on my stomach and thighs, of course).

Andreas sidled up to me. I don't know what happened to the latest girlfriend. Moved on, I suppose. To Barcelona or Berlin. Johannesburg or Jenin. Somewhere terribly exotic where her husband would avert his gaze and she'd tilt those knowing sloe eyes toward another gilt-skinned boy. Wherever she was, Andreas had let it be known his interest in me simmered again. Low simmer. Somehow, the events of the past few days had restored whatever pliant-goddess-behind-impenetrable-fortress quality had attracted him to me, Claire Dillon. I wanted to say I was completely immune to his charms, that I, too, had moved on, but that would be a lie. I mean, true, I'd accepted and even endorsed our evolution to the status of former lovers and current business associates. And I'd done my best to see him through narrowed, extracoital eyes: to view his slim hips as needlessly swiveling, the moss-green glance as affected, the butterfly caresses as contrived. But there's something about clean-slate acceptance of your circumstances and the persons who wrought them that opens up a whole new can of squiggling options, including harmless flirtation and meaningless good-bye sex. Come to think of it, weighing my options was almost better than the sex itself. It made me feel as flinty and powerful as a granite wall. (I'll stop the metaphor there before I get into the inevitable chipping, cracking, and gouging comparisons.) Suffice to say I had little to gain by demonizing Andreas, and, remarkably, I felt little need to.

"I can ask you something, Claire?" he said.

"Of course."

"If your CD, it is accepted by Nashville"—despite my explanations, Andreas persisted in thinking of Nashville, Tennessee, as a company—"you think you might, maybe, tell them who is playing lute and guitar?" His long-lashed eyes swung downward. I realized suddenly that his awkwardness wasn't artifice: Asking was very hard for him.

I clasped his rough fingers in mine. "Yes," I heard myself saying. "Because it would be the truth, wouldn't it? I wouldn't have it any other way."

chapter 47

〰〰〰〰〰〰〰〰〰〰〰

ANYA

I'm going home. Tomorrow. In a mere two weeks, Ethan Dillon's joining me at *Casa Soberanes*. For those of you who've missed the last three months, Ethan's my boyfriend. We're not officially engaged yet, but we've discussed our desire to tie the knot with someone generally regarded as normal, have enough beautiful children to populate a rugby or *fútbol* team, and build a home together. Ethan is considerate, progressive, quietly funny, Catholic by birth if not sensibilities, predominantly truthful with himself and others, and so good-looking, I sometimes have to douse the flames of real fear when I look at him. Like me, Ethan's been burned—scorched, more accurately—by past relationships. His mother is a one-in-a-million woman I consider my friend. Plus, he tells me, often and with just the right amount of dazed wonder, that he loves me. Loves me enough to resign his position in his father's company, which he helped build, to abandon the house he'd been assembling in Australia for years and everyone he knows in the world, and give life a shot in San Francisco, where he'll be subjected to scrutiny and harassment on a par with that of the Inquisition, cut adrift in a sea of *tías* and *primos* and *hermanos* who will ask him repeatedly if he knows Nicole Kidman, discuss his faults in Spanish right in front of him, and raise their eyebrows if he refuses a second helping of grilled calves' brains.

This should fill me with joy, yes? After all, in the words of Publishers Clearinghouse, I WON! I should be swinging from the damn rafters, bleating like a girl band at the Emmys, slyly starting the wedding-venue search.

Alas, no.

What I actually feel right now is dread. Prickly, paralyzing, throat-tickling, stomach-acid-spurting dread. You see, tonight is the night when I tell Ethan that I've been lying to him all this time, lying to everybody, in fact. Tonight I have to tell my dream husband I'm not the Anya he thinks I am but, rather, a darker, muddier version of myself. Smeared. Shadow Anya. The real Anya. Anyita. The hastily written epilogue of the girl who leaned against a row of canned beans and gave away the single internal puzzle piece she needed to survive life intact.

Because I've run out of nights. Each day of summer, I peeled another day off the calendar in my mind, the terrifying rip of it echoing in my head like a late-afternoon thunderclap. I never, never thought I could hold it inside myself forever. The secret was a cold, dead weight inside me, pinning me to my own ocean-floor shadow even as I spun my arms toward the surface. Telling Kelah took up some slack in the oily rope of deceptions, left me floating free for a few oxygen-gulping seconds. Then the anchor came down again, tumbling me toward the bottom. Every time I hit, shock waves flowed through my body, jarring loose my resolve.

Tonight.

I watched from the window as Parker and Blakas putted away on her scooter. The last few days hadn't been easy for my friend, and, although we come at our problems differently, I admired her attitude. When life gave her the finger, she just leaned back and unfurled hers right back at 'em. The one thing I was sure of is that our friendship would survive our relocation to real life. Week by week, we'd inched toward each other, flirting with each other's repertoire of comedy, personal fables, defenses.

I ran my hand down my hair, which reproduces itself like rabbits and hadn't been cut since spring. It hung wetly against my back nearly to my waist. I wanted to do something different tonight. Something to give me courage. That meant no boring jeans, hippie skirts, caftans, flats, or earth-mama jewelry I'd picked up from the pitifully poor undocumented workers manning the stands near my home. That meant nothing I currently owned.

I opened Parker's closet, which was a veritable *Vogue* magazine of perfect clothes that seemed as alien to me as a kimono. She'd tossed me an offer to borrow something weeks ago without a trace of falseness. I'd just thought she was crazy. I mean, we weren't even remotely the same size. Next to her slim hips, my haunches resembled the hindquarters of the Budweiser Clydesdales. Okay, I've been swimming a lot, so baby Clydesdales.

Without thinking, I detached a fiercely tailored red suit from its fluffy hanger. I have no idea why Parker had brought such a thing to Greece, but I knew I wanted to try it on, even though it wouldn't fit. I pulled the skirt up over my hips, surprised to feel the zipper creep halfway up its track. The jacket's buttons strained but held. I slipped my feet into nasty-girl stilettos and wobbled over to the mirror.

Turning around, I stared at my butt, startled to see I had a waist and plenty of shapely tan leg showing beneath the slit skirt. The jacket nipped and tucked in all the right places. I did a little dance, then stripped down, hung the outfit up, and laid out all the sexy, sexy clothes Parker had worn all summer. I didn't allow my excitement to get the better of me, and carefully—reverently—pressed everything back on its given hanger or into its tissuey nest. I tried on exactly eighteen articles of clothing and loved every minute of it. Even my stomach full of dread stabilized a little. Apparel antacid.

Fifteen minutes later, I stood straight and tall in the doorway,

waiting for Ethan. I had on Parker's heel-skimming, lightweight
denim coat, faded to the hue of morning sky against my brown
skin. Underneath, an ivory camisole edged with the tiniest strip
of lace and white—white!—hip-slung capri pants, strung through
with a turquoise and silver belt. My own Mexican jewelry glowed
turquoise against my knuckles, wrists, ears, and neck. My feet
were enveloped in the most ridiculous, inappropriate mules to
grace Corfu, three-inch-high jobbies with assertive little triangles
for heels and the slimmest bondage across the toes and ankles.
I'd parted my thick hair down the center, slicked it down with a
ton of Parker's expensive pomade, and woven it into long braids,
which I'd twined into a weighty, gleaming bun at the nape of my
neck. I had on genuine Lancôme mascara, my own sandalwood
essential oil, and glossy red lipstick. I looked so freakin' hot, I
couldn't help but feel giddy and brave.

Ethan pulled up a minute later. He stared at me from his bike.

"Beaut," he said, and kissed me hard. I closed my eyes and
tried to memorize it. What if, looking back, this was the last time?

I came up for air. "I have to stop by Nia's. I left the lights
there."

He nodded and we sped off into the night. Stars were just
starting to sprinkle the eastern sky. I shut my eyes against the
wind, which was doing its best to tear my Lancôme from my
lashes, and let each sensory experience irrigate my memory bank:
Ethan's warm, cinnamon-smelling back, the moldering fruit
trees, briny wind, shy moonlight.

At Nia's, I jumped off and told Ethan I'd be right back. I even
gave him a little waggle to show him I knew he was watching
my *culita*. Inside, I picked up the bag with the twinkly white
Christmas lights I'd set near the fax machine. At that moment,
the whirring creak of the fax started up. I waited till the slick paper had wound its way out and plucked it from the tray. It was the
passenger manifold for tonight's mainland ferry. Nia knew someone in the Athens office, yet another Alexiou cousin, and he faxed
her lists of passengers getting off on Corfu, so she could spread
the news of their numbers to the *abuelas* who waited at the docks

or the bus station, hoping to rent their rooms. I didn't think anyone would be going there tonight, what with the party and all, but
Nia might want it on her desk first thing in the morning, since the
latecomers often found the grimmest accommodations the first
night and relocated the second.

My eyes fell on the sheet in front of me as I set it on Nia's
stack of papers. Two names, five slots away from each other,
popped out, glaring impossibilities in a sea of unfamiliar people. I
nearly dropped the bag, and my already thready heartbeat kicked
into race-car gear. I stumbled toward the door in my heels, lost a
shoe, grabbed it in my free hand, and hopped outside. I launched
myself onto the back of Ethan's bike like my ass was on fire.

"Drive like hell, *querido*," I panted into his ear. "We have about
ten minutes to avert total disaster. Twice."

chapter 48

~~~~~~~~~~~~~~

PARKER

People were already milling about the taverna when I arrived with the food. I swung my leg over the scooter and jogged up to Tony. Blakas trotted after me, polishing his chops.

"*In back!*" Tony hissed, while his henchmen started plucking boxes off the scooter and carrying them in.

"Is there food out? Drinks?" I said.

"We do fine now. But I very glad you here." Tony kissed me on both cheeks and laid his hand casually on my ass. I removed it. He put it back and grinned his toothy munchkin smile. "You are okay, beautiful girl? You look a little . . . white?" he said.

"Pale," I corrected. Actually, I did feel light-headed. Must be the headache. Or maybe I was just hungry. "I'm fine. Let me work the room and then we'll sit down."

I slipped inside and stood in the corner of the vast dining area. The moment when you first study a space you've designed when it's fully functioning is a heady one. The taverna seemed to glow from within with hundreds of candles, lining the walls, atop tables, and surrounding windowsills. Lights twinkled on the terrace deck, though I thought the strands seemed a little scant. Had Anya and Ethan forgotten to pick them up at the travel agency? I looked around but didn't see either of them. Later. Claire winked at me from behind her mike. Gorgeous outfit. Tell her later. Claire and Andreas were starting out with dark, sexy lounge favorites. After the first round of hors d'oeuvres and drinks, they'd segue into Greek dancing tunes and the foot-stomping pop-country and folk she excelled at. Blue and white balloons, the colors of the Greek flag, huddled under the high ceiling. Thank you, Kelah and Boz. I closed my eyes and felt the energy of the room hum through me: laughter, glass clinking, throbby music, burning wicks. Satisfaction, thick and molten hot, trickled down to my belly. Good. A job well done. We'd seen Tony off in style. I still had the touch. Hopefully, Christopher Peña would think so, too, when we met in—damn—two days.

My eyes fluttered open. Someone who looked a lot like Josh Lido was standing ten feet away, his eyes locked onto mine. Then I realized: It *was* Josh. His eyes were dark with ... something ... and his shoulders curved forward as if he was going to launch himself in my direction. He looked different. Harder. The corners of his full mouth, normally tugged upward, stretched into a taut line. I realized he was wearing a crisp gunmetal dress shirt and slacks. My eyes dropped to his feet.

No thongs.

For some reason, that scared the living shit out of me.

He moved closer. My head felt too big on my neck, like a broken daisy. I spun around and slammed into an old Greek lady in a black nightgown.

"Diabolos!" she rasped. Her gnarled finger tapered into a fish-hook. Her nails were black.

I backed away quickly and zigzagged between partygoers, aiming for the kitchen. I could hide in the meat locker. Or maybe the wine cellar? Laughter bubbled out of me involuntarily and I slapped my palm over my mouth. I looked down at my other hand. Strangely, I saw two of them. Someone was singing "She's a Brick ... HOUSE," which seemed a little incongruous.

Ah. Butcher's block. Cool. I stretched out and kicked my boots off. Maybe I could just catch a few winks. Nobody would notice, would they? Nico whisked by with a tray of pita sandwiches and did a really cartoonish double take, Elmer Fudd in an apron.

"Hi!" I waved at him from the prone position.

"Parker!" Anya ran through the doorway. Her eyes were enormous. Her nostrils puffed out like a galloping horse.

"I'm sleepy." I tried to get comfortable, but Aphrodite's machete handle was sticking into my ass.

"Parker!" She came over and shook me. Now, why would Anya do that? Anya was the nice one. Pushing people around was my job. "Parker, you've got to listen to me!" Her huge eyes narrowed to slits. "*Dios!* Did you take something? Tell me, did you?"

"Just aspirin." Right? Something about those little vomit-colored pills tapped at my memory.... Come to think of it, my headache was still hammering at the back of my eyes....

"Okay, you've got to pay attention now. I have to tell you something. The ferry that's coming in tonight—"

"Anya, you look so pretty! I just want to tell you that." I tried to lift myself up by her lapels, and she almost fell on top of me. "You can have the coat. Looks better on you anyway." I spotted a pile of grape leaves on the counter and stuck two behind my ears.

"Look, Caesars Palace!" I sang.

"Park! Shut up! Look into my eyes, okay? No. Not over there. Here! That's right. You have to prepare yourself. He's going to be here—"

But I never heard the rest of what Anya said, because at that moment he stepped through the kitchen doorway and everything simply stopped. Sound, sensation, the swirl of people's words, all ceased to exist and the world tunneled into a single image, framed by four planks of pine: a man's chino-clad legs, chest, shoulders, head, face, shock of hair.

Mismatched husky-dog eyes.

"Neil, you shit," I managed before I passed out, grape leaves fluttering like monarch butterflies across my shrinking field of vision.

I smelled it and knew, even before I opened my eyes.

Hospital.

There's an odor exclusive to hospitals that cannot be reproduced elsewhere. Something about the unique combination of disinfectant, blood, puke, urine, Styrofoam coffee containers, and pure adrenal fear produces a cauldron of anxiety in me that few other circumstances can. On the unfortunate instances that I have been required to step through the ominous sliding doors into the seafoam-green zone, I am notorious for not rising to the occasion but rather sinking into a quivery, whiny, gelatinous, demanding, low-rent version of my usual self. I used to attribute this antipathy to impatience, to my singular ability to tough it out alone (with the help of a few muscle relaxants strong enough to fell a rhino, of course).

Now I know better.

"Aaaah!" I moaned in fear. I conducted a quick inventory of all pertinent body parts. Physically, I felt completely fine, excepting a few pinpricks here and there. But then, that's always the way it is before they level you with a prognosis of necrotizing fasciitis, exploding internal organs, engorged brain tumors, and three months to live.

I opened my eyes to stark whiteness and two unexpected heads.

On one side of the starched bed was Neil Wentworth, cheating goatfucker husband unit extraordinaire.

On the other side was Josh Lido, maniacal mindfucker summer nonfling extraordinaire.

Blakas was curled up on my feet (such are the benefits of medicine in the Second World). When he felt me struggle to sit up, he torpedoed into my chest like a spiraling football. I tucked him under my arm protectively. At least one of us was shaking so hard I was tempted to call the nurse for a bedpan.

Neil and Josh glared at each other.

A third face loomed, pale and worried. Anya.

"I tried to tell you, Park, but you were kind of, you know . . . out of it. Well . . . I'll be outside if you need me." She squeezed my arm and slipped out of the room.

I closed my eyes again, willing my demons to dematerialize. Maybe this was all a bad dream. Maybe Neil had just forgotten where he'd put the Cock of the Walk Love Harness and needed assistance. Maybe my drug habit had finally caught up with me and my brain resembled Swiss cheese and this was an extremely elaborate hallucination.

Maybe hell was cooling under a thick sheet of ice.

"What's going on?" I said, finally, focusing on the plasma bag that was—egads!—sluicing liquids into my arm. Disgusting.

"Parker, we need to talk," said Neil. Shakily, I let my gaze drink him up: tan face, hair longer and blonder, familiar blue and green eyes troubled and heated, conch-shell necklace(!), wedding ring . . . on?

"So do we." Josh crossed his arms over his chest. He looked bizarre, like a plucked chicken. Then I realized: He'd shaved. Like, with a razor. Face, not chest—this wasn't a male burlesque. Yet.

Neil turned on Josh. "Lido, this has nothing to do with you."

Josh laughed. The column of his throat was long and very brown (all the better to hide bite marks). "I could say the same to you, Wentworth. Isn't that Belgian chick supposed to be popping your pup just about now?"

"Go fuck yourself." Neil stood up, his hands rolling into fists.

"Parker's sick. Why don't we take this outside?" Josh smiled. At that moment, he looked feral and primitive, like he wanted to rip out Neil's throat. With his teeth. I was, I'm ashamed to say, a little turned on. I felt the rubber tube snaking its way into my privates do a little dance.

"Stop it! Both of you! God, this is like a fucking *Melrose Place* episode," I said.

"What's *Melrose Place*?" they said in unison.

"Why do I bother?" I moaned. I looked at both of them. Neil's face was flushed. Josh bounced on his toes, ready to pounce.

"Whatever you have to say, you can say it here. I'm not going any-where with this goddamn IV anyway." I lay back on the stiff pil-lows. This was getting fun. I felt stimulated and faint at the same time. Like an eighteenth-century heroine with the vapors, watch-ing suitors spar over me with my loyal hound at my side.

Neil picked up my hand. Blakas growled. I shushed him. "Parker," Neil said meaningfully, twining our fingers together in the old, familiar way. His eyes cut warningly at Josh, then focused back on mine with laser precision. The arctic encasing around my heart melted marginally, and I prayed for a superhero or guardian angel to burst into the room, cape flying, and remind me that this is how they destroy your defenses, this is how they— kapow!—*eat your brain!*

"I think I've made a terrible mistake," Neil said. He massaged my hand, and I felt my insides shudder at the raw intimacy of what we'd been through together: steamy sex, courtship, redeco-rating, cohabitation, redecorating, eleven days of marriage, steamy sex, betrayal. "Parker, I know what I've done is unforgivable, but that's exactly what I'm asking for—forgiveness. I asked Juliette . . . I asked her to leave. It's over. The baby, it wasn't mine. All this time I thought . . . what I'm trying to say is, actually, ask for, is, will you give me a second chance? I want . . . I want us to put things back together. The way they were. I know it's too much to ask, but I want you to trust me again."

Josh muttered something under his breath that sounded suspi-ciously like "What a tool." Blakas and I sucked in our breath. Neil lost it. He rounded on Josh with the ferocity of a typhoon.

"You've got a hell of a nerve even being here, you sick son-ofabitch! How long have you been following my wife? How long?" He loomed over Josh. His voice was low and menacing. "I don't want you anywhere near Park. You hear me? I want you gone."

"Why don't we let her decide that?" Josh said quietly.

Something dawned on me then, a little spark of shock. "Do you two know each other?" I said. I stared into Josh's eyes, and for a second I thought I saw a flash of deep regret there.

Neil snorted. "This fucking freak is stalking you, Park! We

worked together at L&G! I have no idea what he's doing in your hospital room, but I intend to find out if I have to beat it out of him."

"Is it true, Josh? You knew Neil?" My mind was whirling.

"True, but irrelevant." Josh's voice was clipped.

"Oh, that's rich. Tell her how you saw her photo on my desk, you goddamn psycho," Neil said.

"Wentworth—"

"Tell me!" I cried.

Josh sighed. "Okay, but first he has to leave." He pointed at Neil.

"No fuckin'—"

I interrupted my soon-to-be-ex-husband with a patented Glass don't-be-a-prick eye jab. "Just give us a few minutes, Neil."

"I don't think you should be alone with—"

"Neil."

It's amazing what a few intravenous tubes and a stack of divorce papers will do for a man's spousal devotion. Shooting death stares at Josh, Neil backed slowly out of the room. Josh came and sat on a stool next to the bed.

"Hey."

"Hey," I answered.

Josh leaned forward as if to brush my hair back off my forehead, then seemed to think better of it. His fingers plucked at the creases on his (surprisingly well-fitting) slacks. Except for the ping of various machines and Blakas's contented low growl, the room was silent.

"This is worse than the time I had to tell Annie Cartwright I didn't want to be exclusive any more," he said after a moment.

"Oh, was she the one before Lauren?"

Tiny smile. "No, she was the one the summer before sixth grade."

"Budding ladykiller. What'd she do, cry?"

"Actually, she was glad. She told me she'd kissed Dougie Westfeldt at the skating rink and that my hair was gross."

This was so delightful, for a second I almost forgot I was enraged, in the hospital and ten pounds overweight.

Then I remembered my dignity was at stake and tried to look stern. "Josh, whatever you have to say, say it."

"Okay, but promise my you'll hear me out?"

I wasn't sure I should be pandering to stalkers, even if they had charming slanted front teeth and buns of steel, but I said okay anyway.

"I haven't been entirely truthful with you, Park," Josh began.

"Really? I always thought our relationship was built on a foundation of truth and honesty," I said, and immediately regretted it. "And pork rinds," I added, trying to redeem myself.

He had the good sense to ignore me. "I'm sorry about all this."

We stared at each other for a few seconds. In his eyes, I saw lots of good stuff: regret, longing, conviction, anger, and a pinch of lust.

"I did work with Neil at Liebman, Grizzutti. Not closely, but I'd go by his office, see your picture on his desk."

I tried to imagine Josh in a suit and tie and failed.

"I was a trial lawyer until Raphael died. Then it's like I told you. I quit. Floated around for a while. The first time I saw you was at the Christmas party two years ago. I was with Lauren then. You had on tuxedo pants and this kind of man's vest. All the other women were wearing dresses and stockings. They looked like they were trying too hard, next to you. You were talking to people, and every time you laughed, you sounded like a donkey. For some reason, that laugh stuck with me. I couldn't believe you could be so unself-conscious. I remember thinking, There is the most beautiful woman I'll ever see. It wasn't something I thought about. It was just something I knew. I wanted to know you, that's all. But I was with Lauren and you were with Neil, so I just ... you know, lived. Did what I was supposed to do. And later, tried to deal with Raphael, not very well, I suppose."

He moved closer to the bed, and I felt Blakas tense with anticipation. "Then I heard through the grapevine that you and

Neil had broken up, and I knew I had to meet you. So I came here. But I knew what it would look like ... weird, you know? So I tried to figure out a way to tell you, but it never seemed like the right time. And then when things weren't working out between us—"

"Working out ... *what*?" Neil, who had apparently (and quite uncharacteristically) been lurking at the door, exploded back into the room like he'd been shot from a cannon. His face was the hue of a Roma tomato. I felt his pain momentarily, then that feeling was replaced by an even stronger desire—that his loving memories of me watering the hydrangeas and tucking our duvet in be replaced by one of me sitting astride his hairy-thighed coworker with my breasts doing a triple-X Lindy hop.

I gave him the patented Glass palm-in-the-air treatment. He shut up. Aside from the whole cheating on me and knocking up the Belgian thing, he was very well trained. And I wanted to hear this.

"When things weren't working out, there didn't seem to be any reason to tell you. I didn't want to hurt you more than I already had. I thought I'd just slip away, and you'd go back to San Francisco and start over again. And, hopefully, things would be better. For both of us."

I would like to say that I was in shock at this revelation. But it actually explained a lot about our dynamic this summer and what had happened. Or not, as the case may be. I'd always felt like I knew Josh, and he me. Maybe that's why everything that had transpired between us seemed so weirdly, prematurely intimate, so utterly comfortable—and so alarming. This information was simply the missing puzzle piece clicking into place.

Clearly, I was expected to say something. "Josh," I started, then hesitated. "Can you give me and Neil some time alone? I need to think about this."

"Of course," he said quickly. He got up and headed for the door. His shirttail had come loose. With a pang, I realized I knew what he looked like underneath, that little trail of peachy fuzz marking the small of his back, the corded abs encased in a tad too much beer flesh, the hard little ass . . .

"Parker?" Josh had stopped at the door.

"Yes?"

"I just want you to know . . . this wasn't a game for me." Josh stood perfectly still. "I've been in love with you for a while now." Then he was gone.

Oh, boy.

My room at the hospital had a breathtaking view.

Breathtaking, that is, if ships' innards were your thing. Thankfully, where there were cranes there were stevedores. In between feedings and sponge baths by a succession of Greek hausfraus, I watched young sweaty men in sailor suits swab the decks. Not entirely unpleasant. Also a nice metaphor for my own state of mind.

They'd told me what had happened. Apparently, I hadn't taken aspirin, as I'd thought, but, rather, four powerful antianxiety tablets. Thankfully, they hadn't had to pump my stomach, but they wanted to keep me under observation for a day. With Anya's help, I convinced the doctors it was an accident and I didn't know how those nasty things had gotten into my aspirin pill case. (It wasn't hard because, truly, I didn't, which probably spoke more to my tenuous command of my faculties earlier in the summer than now, when I was sober enough to remember the location of my rainy-day narco-friends.)

Naturally, the trials of the day had left me exhausted and just a little bit punchy. There was a while when it was kind of touch and go, when I'd forgotten what was really important to me and felt myself pulled, as if by magnets, to that which promised the cheapest, simplest vindications. But then I'd sucked it up and thought about what I'd learned the last three months. Thought about what I really valued in life. About promises made. Thought long and hard. And, in the end, there was really only one choice to make.

I heard a click as the door opened. Then my bedside curtain shifted and he was there, smiling. His vagabond grin altered his whole face, took what was somber and turned it into something hopeful and redemptive. Blakas stirred beside me, yipping dreamily. Then my man came to me. I scooched over and he lay down in the bed next to me, our legs entwined. We fit perfectly. I buried my face in his neck and inhaled the familiar smell of him. He traced my face reverently, as if he'd never seen me before and couldn't believe his good luck. If there weren't laws against such things and the overdose hadn't dulled my appetite, I would have nibbled his cute ears off, he was that delicious. Suddenly, I knew why Zeus had made Persephone return to Hades after she'd tasted the pomegranate seeds. Made her live with her mistakes, which maybe weren't so bad after all. Smart guy, that Zeus.

"What's this for?" he asked, holding my remaining tube.

"Pee."

To his credit, he didn't wince. "Do you need it?"

"Probably not."

He rolled carefully on top of me. I wiggled the tube out, which was not too fun. After we waited a minute to alleviate our shared fear of a urine tsunami, he reached out and pulled the curtain shut. Our noses kissed, Eskimo-style. I felt my breasts sandwich against his chest. His eyes and hands warmed my face. All this would have started a Swedish sauna brewing in my underpants— if I'd had any on. He took my bottom lip in his teeth and licked its underside with that old confidence.

"See, that wasn't so hard," I said.

chapter 49

CLAIRE

I thought Tony would have to shut us down for the night when the ambulance came for Parker, but in true show-must-go-on spirit, Parker had lifted her head off the stretcher and announced imminent death to any who would dare cut short the evening. So Andreas and I launched into our final set with as much energy as we could muster, and the crowd responded in kind.

Brian and Ethan were in the front row. My boys. There was a time when the idea of singing in front of them would have felt as comfortable as a hair shirt, but now I was simply grateful and gratified to see their feet tapping in time with the music. After accompanying Parker to hospital, Anya returned, which I took as a sign that things were going to be all right. But why did she keep checking her watch like that? I winked at her and directed the next song toward her, this girl who could be my daughter-in-law, but she didn't smile, just tugged on Ethan's sleeve and tried to shout something in his ear, which apparently he couldn't hear, because he grinned and mimed noise and pulled her under his arm.

At around nine P.M., I told the crowd we were taking a break and Tony put on that Abba CD that always drove the crowd wild. I grabbed a beer and went outside on the terrace to get some fresh air.

"You're great tonight, Mum," said Ethan. He put his arm around me and I kissed his rough cheek.

"Thanks. It's been such a dream, all this. And it makes a big difference, you and Bri being here." My hand waved, as if to pull down the net of stars spread out over the water, then fell to the railing.

"Mum?"

"Hmm?"

"Do you think I'm doing the right thing?" My son's eyes were large and expectant in the moonlight, with the same gentle ripples of concern and awareness that had been there since he was a toddler. I still couldn't fathom how he'd gotten so *grown* so fast. When did that happen?

"About moving to America?" I said eventually.

"About moving to America, and moving in with Anya and leaving the partnership with Dad, and abandoning my house. . . . I guess that's it." He laughed.

"I'd say that's plenty." I plucked a loose string from my gypsy scarf and reached up to touch his face. "I wish I could promise you it's the right thing, Ethan, but I can't. The truth is, you won't know till you try. Even then you won't know! But I do know you won't have to live with the regret of not knowing if it could have worked out for you." I paused as the music kicked up inside. "You're a good man, and Anya's a lovely girl. Life is unpredictable. Grab it and run with it. That's all I know. Oh, God, I'm terrible at advice, aren't I?"

"No, you're wonderful, Mum. I'm going to miss you so much."

"Maybe I'll visit when Muse Records flies me over. I'll insist on a pied-à-terre apartment in San Francisco as part of my contract," I said lightly.

Ethan hugged me to his side. "Don't laugh, Mum. A smart woman once told me, 'Life's unpredictable, so grab it and run with it.' "

"Can I interrupt the lovefest for a minute?" Brian stood on my other side.

"We're just planning your brother's journey to conquer America," I said.

"The only thing he needs to conquer is his atrocious taste in women, and it looks like he's done that with Anya," Brian said.

Ethan reached around and grabbed Brian by the neck. "Yeah, well, don't get me started on your taste in men, little brother. I mean, the Italian? Bloody nightmare."

"At least he doesn't stalk me when I go on holiday."

"Probably because he can't remember your name."

"Ouch."

Ethan hesitated. "Yeah, sorry."

I laughed. "Boys, I'm glad you're here, because there's something I want to talk to you about."

"You're getting a haircut that costs more than five dollars?" said Brian hopefully.

"Shut up, idiot, let her talk."

"It's about me and your father," I said. Then, while the three of us discussed the end of Claire and Gary Dillon and what I would do when I returned to Australia, the last passenger ferry of the night chugged its way out of the harbor after disgorging its passengers, lights flickering in a Morse-like code I had yet to understand.

Andreas loomed over me. His shirt flapped open, revealing a triangle of glistening brown chest. For a moment, my mind wandered to the cooking class I'd taken with Brian. Something about the color and texture of that roux sauce . . .

Then a droplet of sweat poised for a moment in the hollow of his throat and fell onto my face, mixing with my own sheen of perspiration. That snapped me out of it; there's nothing like a classic soft-porn moment to shatter the tension. I smiled at

Andreas and turned back to the audience, which was screaming its approval at our impromptu dip as it surged in and out in a circular tide, performing the intricate steps of the *kalamatianos*. I whipped away from Andreas like the coquette I was playing and sang the refrain of the traditional Greek song Andreas had translated into English for me:

> *What is this thing called love, what is it?*
> *What is it that secretly drives our hearts,*
> *With so much nostalgia?*
> *What is this thing called love, what is it, what is it?*
> *It's a smile, a tear, sun and rain and*
> *The end of the start of our lives.*
> *Never, never has a wise man found the answer*
> *And the explanation to give us yet.*
> *What is this thing called love, what is it, what is it?*
> *That makes us to sing the song . . .*
>
> *I love you*
> *I love you*
> *I love you*

I closed my eyes and let the feel of the music wash over me. Like a drug, I'd grown addicted to it over the past months and knew I wouldn't give it up for anything or anyone, this time. I didn't need fame and fortune, but I did need the satisfaction of performing, of delivering the small slice of pleasure I could to an appreciative audience—and, yes, relishing the attention that went with it.

I opened my eyes and the first thing I saw was my husband leaning against the wall, drinking a beer.

The Greek-language refrain I'd memorized phonetically promptly departed my stunned brain, no doubt seeking succor somewhere it was better appreciated, like Páros or Rhodes. Andreas absorbed my flub a second before everyone else would and quickly jumped into the gap with an improvised acoustic guitar solo and strut that had the women shrieking their approval. I eased away from the circle's center with an idiot's grin on my face, miming approval of my accompanist's turn at the wheel. Shit. All the little gestures that had worked their way into my routine and had seemed sexy before now made me feel like an over-the-hill game-show hostess. Suddenly, the persona I'd spent three months refining—Claire Dillon, songstress, temptress, Pauline Collins wannabe—seemed as tired and spent as a deflated party balloon. Good Lord, what was Gary doing here, and what would he think, me onstage with my tits hanging out for all to see, a gypsy's cut of silk streaming down my shoulders and a Greek boy crooning into my ear?

I cut my eyes toward the wall where Gary was nursing his beer. I was trying—badly—to keep up the pretense of performing, as if a grin and a flourish with my skirt every sixty seconds qualified. Gary'd lost weight, pounds of it, looked like. His strong shoulders and great height seemed too heavy to be borne by his now-sinewy body, curving downward in the posture of an old man. His dirty-blond hair needed a cut, and the fine hazel eyes had a look in them I hadn't seen in years.

I felt Andreas beside me.

"Claire?" he whispered under the music.

"Hmm?"

"You will sing now?" He sounded worried.

In response, I picked up the microphone and started up again. Relieved, Andreas sat on the stool beside me and we settled into a groove, insofar as that was possible with my past slapping me in the face.

Then several things happened.

I glanced at Gary again. Reading only the pain of loss on his weathered face, my gaze swept down his familiar figure. Settled on his foot. Which was, I absorbed, *tapping*. Tapping! In time to the music. His fingers curled around the beer bottle, swinging it against his leg in the *kalamatianos*'s unusual 7/8 count. Next, the most extraordinary thing happened: The stage, the taverna, Corfu, the entire universe, even, was reduced to that modest movement.

I felt as if my very heartbeat had thudded into compliance with Gary's Blunnie boot, in a rhythm as vital, as life-affirming and un-practiced, as the orbit of the earth itself—and as unfathomable to the naked eye. As I met his eyes, a smile burgeoned at the edges of his mouth, wanting to sweep over his whole face. Without thinking, I felt an answering glow suffuse mine. Suddenly, it was 1976 again, and I was onstage singing my heart out to the tall, shy blond in the back row, and he was staring at me in that way that told me he wanted to protect me as much as he wanted to make love to me. The first one—the *only* one—who'd wanted to do both.

Out of the corner of my eye, I spied Ethan and Brian become aware of Gary on the other side of the room. Apprehension flooded my belly, but I sang on. As if in pantomime, Ethan mouthed *Dad?* and then my sons' father was pushing through the crowd, heedless of who he jostled, trying to get to his boys.

Gary's own hand closed briefly on Ethan's neck, then my hus-band turned to the son he hadn't seen in seven years. Gary's arm reached tentatively out and encircled Brian's shoulders, and I could see our son's back convulse under his father's hands before their foreheads came together and their fingers united in glad, trembling release. At the sight, tears flooded from my eyes, slip-ping off my nose and spattering the old stone at my feet. Andreas's warm, questioning hand at my neck only turned the spigot up and produced a fresh wave of gushing.

I wondered if Brian had conjured this moment too.

chapter 50

∿∿∿∿∿∿∿∿∿∿∿∿

KELAH

I was destroying a platter of dolmas and watching Tony do a uniquely obscene bump and grind with a Greek Cypriot supermodel twice his height when they came for me.

It was hardly surprising. After Parker keeled over into the moussaka and Claire's husband showed up looking like he wanted to punch Andreas in the conker, I figured it was only a matter of time before whatever malicious planets had lined up tonight had their fun with me too.

Nico pulled me aside. "Kelah, there is telephone for you in the kitchen."

"For me?" The only person I could think of who would call me here was . . . well, actually, there was no person.

"It is Joan. She is not nice woman," Nico said sadly.

Oh.

"No, she is not a nice woman," I muttered as I jogged into the kitchen's hole-in-the-wall office, which doubled as a changing room and, we suspected, a minute love nest.

"Joan?" I said into the receiver.

"Who do you think it is, Princess fucking Diana?" she growled. "Took long enough to find you on that godforsaken island of yours. Why they let those Greeks into the EU when their phone operators can't even speak the Queen's English, I have no idea." Hack, hack. "We've got a bit of a problem, love. We are deep in the proverbial merde, as our American friends like to say."

I didn't bother to inform her that *merde* was actually French, since she had probably studied it for eons in whatever posh prep school she and her parents and her parents' parents had attended.

"What?" I said, instead. Apprehension had hijacked my voice and mutated it into a piggy squeal. Oh, God, I'd mucked it up. I knew it! I racked my brain for possible cock-ups. Dire punctuation (I'd never figured out the difference between a colon and a semi-)? Plagiarism? Insufficient shagging?

Joan continued, "Apparently, there's somebody who doesn't think we've done enough to preserve the anonymity of those wayward innocents mentioned in that little column of yours. A Swedish gentlemen by the name of . . . where the hell is it? . . . here it is, Mr. Sven Olaffson. It seems that Mr. Olaffson has filed a civil suit against *Flounce* and a Ms. Kelah Morris and Ms. Morris's editors and, who knows, probably your fucking dentist as well. Let's see, what's it say . . . defamation of character, libel, loss of future earnings—*that's* rich, what's the bloody-minded man do for a living, run the bloody Vatican?—and about ten other quite intimidating-sounding things whose meaning escapes me. Anyway, suffice to say they're suing our bloody arses off," she said cheerfully.

"Are you pulling the column?" I felt dizzy.

"Pull the column? Whatever gave you that idea? On the contrary—this is the best thing that's happened to *Flounce* since Nigella started shagging that advertising person and gave us the exclusive. All the talk programs want to interview you. The dailies want a nibble too. Publicity's arranged for you to meet with Jewel Goldstone on Tuesday morning, and you'll be interviewed by Estella Sykes for the *Daily Mirror* in the afternoon. You're hot, my dear. Scalding, in fact." Her words dissolved into a chorus of tubercular coughs. Just when I thought she was going to chuck up a lung or two, she choked, "Fitch wants to extend your contract and give you a bonus. He's afraid you'll leave us for greener pastures. You wouldn't leave us, now, would you, little Kelah?"

All that came out of me was a disbelieving little grunt. Fitch, *Flounce*'s infamous editor in chief, existed in splendid mono-appellation, like Madonna and Cher. Also, like Cher, he was said to have had a nose job and slept with Gregg Allman. But, mainly, Fitch is infamous for having once presided over a magazine launch party at which a transsexual performance artist was violated onstage by a bottle of Beaujolais. Needless to say, journalistic credibility is not the man's reputational mainstay.

"Anyway, they want you here bright and early on Tuesday morning. Wear a suit, preferably something deep blue or another jewel color. No black and no white. Doesn't photograph well. What's your hair look like?" she asked suspiciously. Then, "Never mind. Dubois will deal with it. Oh, if you get a spot, don't worry yourself, we'll have Genevieve give you a bit of cortisone."

I imagined myself sweating fearfully under the camera lights, the demonic Dubois and Genevieve sticking me with needles and searing my flesh with flatirons, twin Dr. Mengeles reincarnated as Frog stylists.

We talked for a couple more minutes. Rather, Sloaney Joan spewed vulgarities and I tried to absorb this latest development. As usual, she hung up before we could actually resolve any logistics. I put the phone back in the cradle and wandered back to the dance floor in a daze.

A suit. Bollocks. Oxfam, here I come.

There's only so much a girl can stand before she goes stark raving mad. I mean, bloody hell, I'd slathered my face in makeup. I'd worn decent knickers. My skirt was short enough to moonlight as a serviette. I'd done everything but post a sign on my bum advertising my availability. What was it going to take to get Bozzie to see me as a fucking shaggable babe instead of terminally indecisive, insufficiently depilated friend material?

I wallflowered myself between the bar and the food table, furtively picking at stray bits of lamb and trying to understand the sea change I'd undergone vis-à-vis Boz. Three months ago, in what I now saw as my outrageous self-absorption and conceit, I'd wedged him into a high-walled space somewhere between friend and champion. Mine. A minion who wouldn't hesitate to tell a date to sod off if I rang him whinging about my breakdown of the week, who bailed my deadbeat brother out of jail and told me straight up when I was dressed so crap I wouldn't get a date in a prison block.

As near as I could tell, the sea change had something to do with the shift in focus that occurred when I found some sort of satisfaction and validation in my work. Before, I had the contextually bankrupt point of view of the obsessive. Since everything was about me, and my work—whatever *that* was—and, more importantly, about my deficiencies and my work's deficiencies, the fact that Boz found something to fancy in me didn't say much for him. In fact, it kind of disqualified him as a love interest, because who in his right mind would want to be with such a fuckup, right?

Understanding it didn't make me feel any better. I didn't want to be one of those people who only want what they can't have, who are only attracted to those who reject them. Fee called it the attraction–repulsion factor. Scrummy, she'd sigh, raking her round blue eyes over the new Canadian bloke who was killing himself to get her attention or the well-built artist who'd asked her out every week since she graduated Oxford. Then she'd turn around and say, But now I know they're interested, it sort of ruins it, doesn't it?

I felt a single finger on my neck and shivered.

"Who rang you?" Boz had crept up next to me. His glasses had slipped down his nose and his cheeks were pink with drink.

"Joan."

"Monstrous woman." He picked a piece of lint off my skirt, tantalizingly close to my crotch.

"She rang to tell me the magazine and I are being sued by some Swedish guy who didn't like his initial in the column."

"Really? They must be really chuffed."

"How'd you know that?"

He shrugged. "Isn't all publicity good?"

I stared at him admiringly. "Bozzie, why is it that lately you're always right and I'm always wrong?"

"I've been waiting for you to notice."

"Well, they want me on the telly." I preened a little bit.

"They want you on the telly?" he parroted.

"Don't act so surprised."

"I'm not. It's just . . . and you said yes?"

"Bloody right I said yes."

"Hmm."

"What does 'hmm' mean?" I said.

"Nothing."

"Everything means something."

"Okay, it means, I'm certainly not hearing any more complaints about sneaking Kelah's work onto the pages of *Flounce,* and she's going to be hacked off when they try to get her to wear a suit and comb her hair."

"Oh." This was getting downright creepy.

Andreas started playing a Greek folk dance and everyone screamed.

"Come on," Boz said. "Enough about television appearances and horrid Joan. Let's dance."

It was probably for the best.

Yes, definitely the most circumspect route.

Anything else would be unthinkable.

How many times have I said it myself? You don't fool around with friendship. Blokes will come and go, but a true-blue friend is a rarity in this world. It's something to preserve and protect, not muck up because you're on extended holiday and ouzo gives everything—including skinny guys with glasses and unfinished theses you've known forever—a lovely shimmery air of slightly bent mystery. With a little booze, turquoise seas, and the right light, even a gimlet-eyed swami bilking his followers for their last pound can start looking like the keeper of the secret of everlasting spiritual bliss. On holiday, it was like everything was tipped a couple of degrees south of its proper angle and looked delightfully, temptingly skewed, so one didn't know what to believe, even about the most familiar things.

But I was pretty sure about this one.

Everyone's entitled to a bout of madness once in a while. That's what makes life interesting. Otherwise we'd just go about our business awash in sanity and confident purpose, meeting deadlines, cheerfully dining with ex-lovers without a trace of bitterness, and snapping off our snagless stockings at the end of each perfect, productive, magnificently evolved day.

Bollocks.

I rolled over, taking the mound of blankets and sheets with me. It was warm and I didn't really need a mound, but it seemed right somehow. When you're mourning something—and one should never underestimate the power of a hobbled dream, no matter how foolish, recent, or short-lived—there are certain steps that must be followed, certain rituals observed. Sulking under a mound of covers is right up there with ringing exes at two A.M. and consuming a dozen Cadbury milks.

It would be easier when we got home on Monday. London would have a chilling effect on my addled mind. Plus, with the schedule Sloaney Joan had planned for me, I wouldn't have time to brush my teeth, let alone indulge in thoughts of Bozzie's myopic, thick-lashed gaze or his delicious rendering of the Monty Python classic "Every Sperm Is Sacred."

The digital travel clock flipped to 3:35.

I gave up and tiptoed to the window. The air had that smell that seeps out of the damp shrubbery and chilled asphalt in the

thin window between the witching hour and dawn: cool, stag-
nant, leafy, and slightly metallic. Outside in the little courtyard,
everything was completely still, from the clothesline sheeted with
neat squares of trousers, shirts, and towels to the bird feeder that
hung on a muscular branch of the loquat tree.

I stood for a while, until I felt the sharp edges of myself blend
into the heavy night air. My breathing slowed until my chest rose
and fell as leisurely as Tony's eyelids when a beautiful woman
walked into the taverna. A dense, unreasoning calm settled over
me. With it, a grain of an idea: What if I didn't have to *wait* for
something to happen? What if I took matters into my own hands?
What if I wasn't mad at all, just infuriatingly, self-defeatingly passive?

What if my friend vs. lover theory was crap?

Later, I would swear I didn't mean to do it. That it was dark
and I didn't know which room I entered. That I was still a little
drunk from the party. That I was, for a moment, mad.

Bozzie's room lay next to mine, a dusty twin box with tile floors
and a virginal bed. His door was ajar. Before I could talk myself
out of it, I slipped through the crack and moved toward the bed.
His familiar smell filled my nose. I felt my throat narrow with apprehension. Then I bucked myself up and reminded myself that
once we got back to London, all bets were off. I reminded myself
of my brilliant idea for the next iteration of my column. It was
now or never.

Then I stumbled over a minefield of what seemed like ten
pairs of shoes, rammed my knee on the bed frame, and yelped,
which kind of took the seductive part out of my seduction.

"Auggh," I moaned.

"*Bugger off!*" Boz yelled. He rose from the bed like a malodor-
ous phoenix, jabbing at me in the dark, and succeeded in smash-
ing me quite forcefully in the nose with a flailing elbow.

"Auggh," I moaned again.

"Kay?"

"Yeth."

"Oh, God. I'm sorry. I thought you were Alistair Brumley."

Alistair Brumley was Boz's nemesis throughout primary school. The fact that he still populated Boz's nightmares twelve years later spoke volumes about what a little schoolyard bullying will do to a scrawny boy's psyche.

"I think you gave me a bloody noth," I lisped.

"Let me turn the light on." He shuffled toward the door, tripped over the same pile of trainers I'd landed in, and cursed. Light drenched us, and I felt my pupils shrink in pain and possibly a little embarrassment. He came back and inspected me.

"It's not pouring, but it's a bit grotty-looking. Why don't you sit down and I'll get you a cloth and some ice."

I sat. This is what happens when girls like me attempt to swim in uncharted waters. I silently thanked God I hadn't got it into my head to don a body or some otherwise sexy garment that would have required me to quietly drown myself off the coast of Corfu.

Boz came back and handed me a dripping bag. I tilted my head back and held it against my nose. We sat that way for a few minutes. Eventually, I put the bag down and tentatively touched my face. It felt tender but not terribly damaged.

"It's not bleeding anymore," Boz said.

I looked down at my legs and realized what I was wearing was almost as bad as lingerie—a skimpy T-shirt and knickers that had once been white but had somehow turned a shameful shade of gray. Boz's own legs poked out from his uncharacteristically fashionable Calvin Klein skivvies like lightly furred maypoles.

"Boz, I have a confession to make," I said slowly.

He waited, saying nothing.

"I came in here to tell you I fancied you." Not exactly true, but who wants to hear about predawn commando sex missions from a girl with a crusty nose and stained underwear?

His stillness made me babble.

"I'd planned a whole line, you see. I don't recall it exactly, but it was something about surrendering and emotional risk and how if we really fancy each other, why waste a chance at love."

He frowned. "Sounds a bit, dunno, cheesy. I mean, surrender?"

"Quite."

Boz tilted his shaggy head, the way he always did before he proposed something outrageous. "What's this about love?" he said finally.

My cheeks burned. "Well, I meant, more like, fancying . . . you know . . . if you just want a shag, that's okay with me. . . . I mean, at one point I was fairly sure you felt the same way, like earlier in the summer . . . and if that's what—"

"I don't just want a shag."

I stood up. "I'll just go back to bed and we'll forget this ever happened."

He grabbed my arm. "Wait."

I covered my face with my hands. "I'm so embarrassed," I muttered between my fingers.

He pried each one of them off my face the way my friends and I used to play he-loves-me, he-loves-me-not with flower petals, one at a time. Then he gently pulled me onto the bed beside him.

"I do fancy you, Kay. I always have," he said.

"What?"

"I said, I fancy you and have been trying to make myself stop because it seemed like you just wanted to be friends. That's why I tried it with Inez. Stupid, really."

"Oh." There was no rebuttal, since everything he said was true.

"And now I find you sneaking into my bed in the middle of the night." He sounded pleased.

"Can't we just do it and get it over with?" I pleaded.

He stroked my cheek. "Your skin's so soft."

"If you change your mind after, I'll understand—"

"I love the way your hair springs out from your temples. Right here"—he twined a corkscrew around his finger—"it's almost blond. See?"

"Bozzie, maybe this isn't such a good idea—"

Boz leaned over and kissed me hard and quite skillfully on the mouth. I felt like my chest had been lit with electric resuscitation paddles and I was going to have a heart attack: *English Columnist,*

25, *Dies of Freak Cardiac Arrest Due to Unexpected Protestation of Love; Sex with Friends Proven Dangerous to Health in Landmark Study.*

"You need to stop talking," he said. His eyes glowed.

"But—"

"Shh!"

We kissed again, tasting this time. Our hands had taken heed of the new policy and ran over each other's body like prisoners pushing through a barbed-wire fence. I had the sensation of being closer—physically—to Boz than I'd been to any other human being. As if I'd kissed and made love to my other boyfriends through a gauzy curtain or a pane of glass. Our kisses got slower and deeper, until we were lying down on the bed. Boz leaned back and grinned at me. I wasn't sure whose chest was scrawnier, his or mine.

"What?" I said.

"I owe Fee ten quid."

We laughed so hard the little bed shook.

chapter 51

ANYA

"Why didn't you just tell me?" Ethan had said.

"I was about to, but then Neil showed up, and we went to the hospital, and by the time we got back and I saw your dad wasn't there, I thought he'd missed the ferry or something. I didn't know he'd stopped in town to rent a car."

Ethan's emotions were bouncing around from one extreme to the other, the psychological equivalent of heavy baggage on a bungee cord. When Gary showed up, and Brian froze, and Claire started crying uncontrollably, all the pent-up resentment and anguish of trying to please everyone and hold the Dillon family together had exploded in him and he'd simply stood, paralyzed and mute. Then I saw something hopelike light up his sherry eyes and I squeezed his hand and he squeezed it back—I thought, gratefully—before leaving to be alone with his family.

"One big happy family," someone said behind me.

I turned around. Evil Rachel had on a sharky smile, a cigarette, and a leather dress she wore as casually as flannel pajamas. Ugh.

"Definitely happier than before," I murmured.

The sleek, geometric cap of hair swished back. "I suppose congratulations are in order."

"For what?"

"Well, for Ethan. Looks like you nabbed him after all."

"I wasn't trying to *nab* anyone." I was annoyed. How could Ethan have gone out with this woman?

"Sweetheart, we're all trying to nab someone or something. I have to hand it to you. The whole innocent Catholic Spanish girl shtick? It totally worked. Ethan's a fixer, a saver. I was always too strong for him. What he really wants is someone fragile, someone who he can save from her own helplessness on a daily basis. A little geisha." She took a long pull off the cigarette between thin ruby lips. "I hear he's going to San Francisco with you."

I didn't bother to respond or rebut her characterization of me. I was so angry I was afraid I'd be tempted to do something crazy—like scream deliciously profane insults and ram my fingers into the glittering blue marbles of her eyes. I comforted myself with thoughts of what we'd have done to a nasty *cusca* like her in the schoolyard growing up. Well, what Carilu and her friends would have done. I was never much of a fighter, but before my little sister took the first hank of her opponent's hair in her hands and yanked, she used to slowly remove eight of her nine chunky gold rings and place them in her friend Diana's curled-up palm, leaving one threatening knob smack in the middle of her knuckles. For intimidation, she'd said, and it had always worked.

"Can I give you a piece of advice?" she said.

I folded my arms over my chest. Evil Rachel took that as a yes.

"You may want to—how should I say this?—stay up-to-date on the, um, art of love. Ethan may act like a lamb out of bed, but I think we both know he's a tiger between the sheets."

"*Gracias.* I'll keep that in mind," I said sarcastically. I'd had enough. I turned on my heel and started to walk away. I didn't want to stoop to her level, you know? Actually, I did want to. That's what scared me.

"Yeah, he was a real tiger. You'd think he hadn't been laid in eons," Evil Rachel purred.

I stopped.

"I mean, doing it on a lounge chair wasn't my first choice. All that sand! But it did add a certain something to the whole thing. I guess the idea of screwing in the dark three meters from the pub kind of turns me on."

I turned.

"Ethan likes it rough, you know. From behind, bondage, in public, you name it. Our first year together, I think we personally discovered at least ten new positions!" She laughed her wind-chime giggle. "And that was just with me on top!"

"Rachel"—her name tasted like curdled milk on my tongue— "Ethan told me about how you . . . got together. If you're trying to shock me, well, don't bother."

"Is that what he told you? That we 'got together'? Oh, how sweet. How American."

I stared her down.

"I'm sorry to have to break this to you, but Ethan and I got a lit-tle more carried away than that. As in 'just like old times' carried away."

I felt the familiar sense of inadequacy and fear of loss cool my blood, and I started to tremble. I closed my eyes for a split second, willing my body to not betray me. With every ounce of emotional intelligence I possessed, I knew I had not misjudged Ethan. I knew I no longer had it in me to be with someone who would skewer my heart that way. I knew he had not betrayed me.

Then, with a dexterity I hadn't known I had, I plucked the burning cigarette from Evil Rachel's fingers and ground it into the leather bodice of her dress, right between the ridiculous, astrally oriented boob things.

"Go to hell, you lying, anorexic, Pamela Anderson wannabe, white-bread, *gringa*, fake chichi, hard-up, pathetic little *puta*! Oh, and Rach? I'm not Spanish, I'm *Mexicana*." I worked the *equis* like my very life depended on it. "We have a saying in my culture. *Dios no le diá, alas a los alacranes*: God did not give wings to scorpions. *No*. They seem a little scary at first, but look how small they are, how bitter and ugly. They just have to crawl around in everybody else's *mierda,* waiting for the chance to sting someone. *Pobrecita* . . . don't it just suck to be a bottom-feeder? Don't it just?"

With that, I spun on my sharp little cone of a heel and did a passable Wonder Woman exit, my coat flying out behind me in a sheet of sky blue. Now, where the hell was my invisible jet?

Life is like a suitcase. You can leave it open, snap it closed, or crack it slightly, maintaining a modicum of privacy while you shuttle essentials in and out. If you do your homework, you'll find there's a range of quality, from the formidable contours of the Samsonite 800 series to the tender exterior of the dime-store duffel, easily pierced and not particularly well suited to the rigors of international travel. Some suitcases make it easy for you, rolling along on slick little rubber wheels, whereas others seem incapable of standing upright, tending to fall down or list sideways at the worst possible moments. Baggage comes in a variety of colors, patterns, and materials, reinforcing its owner's personality: bold leopard, electric blue, deceptively fragile flowers, and, of course, safe, blissfully anonymous, basic black.

Leaving tomorrow. A concept that had seemed as unlikely as quantum physics earlier in the summer was now as incontrovertible as a brick wall. Packing was something you did when you were running to or from something. Every pair of shorts or blouse or tatty bathing suit I tucked into my black American Tourister was imprinted with a summer memory: kissing Ethan for the first time at the ruins, confessing the reason for my involuntary holiday to Parker, my first choppy attempt at swimming, countless dinners at Tony's, stunning only for their simplicity, emotional sustenance, and basic goodness.

I'd finally found what I'd been looking for, and now it was about to end. It seemed cruel and unfair, somehow, giving someone a taste of such a thing and then whisking it away.

I had to tell Ethan about the Curse before we left for home. I'm a firm believer in foundations, and to leave Greece without telling him the truth once and for all was to carry our relationship into the real world on a bed of lies. We'll talk tomorrow, he'd said, when I asked if I could meet him later, after the party. And who wouldn't want to be with his family, when they'd just found one another again after all this time? So I'd kissed him and slipped away, buoyed and also intimidated by the picture of completeness the Dillon family made, Claire, Gary, Ethan, and Brian.

Where the heck did a *chola* from the Mission with a fat love curse on her head fit into *that* picture?

"Rachel's gone back to Oz," said Ethan.

"Oh, yeah?" I said innocently.

"Yeah, she pinned a note to my door saying, in effect, have a nice life. I guess she finally got the hint."

"Great."

I didn't tell him about the cigarette-in-the-bustier episode. I mean, there are lies and there are *lies*. It was one of those things that might seem a little psycho if you weren't there, you know?

"How're your mom and dad and Brian doing?" I said.

Ethan smiled hugely. "Really good. I think there's a lot of trust to be earned back, but things are going really well. Brian's even going to take over for me with Dad's business when I come to California. And Mum's going to keep singing. Dad's okay with it. I mean, Mum and Dad have been through a lot, and mistakes were definitely made on both sides, but, Anya, watching them together last night, I thought, I'd be lucky to have half as much love and . . . devotion, I guess you'd call it, in my own marriage, as my parents have. They've been through hard times, but I really think they'll be even stronger once they get through it. My mum looked happier than she's been in ages, really relaxed, and Dad looked ten years younger. Now that everything's on the table, all the secrets and lies, I think everybody feels such relief. I know I do."

I stopped wrapping the beach glass I'd collected. The time was now.

"Ethan?" I said.

"Yeah?"

"Come here."

He sat down in front of me on the bed and wrapped his arms around my waist.

"I'm going to tell you a story. Don't say anything until I'm done, okay?" I closed my eyes, felt the contours of his familiar face under my fingertips. "I'm going to tell you a story," I said again.

Angelo Contreras had pale green eyes, the color of ripe kiwifruit, under thick brows slashed like black arrows. His smile was crooked, his expression somnolent or watchful, depending on the situation. He was medium height, with square brown shoulders and a slender, watch-sprung body, which he kept slim by running five miles several times a week, playing *fútbol,* and doing sit-ups under the lemon tree in the yard my family shared with his. Angelo had a single tattoo of a cross on the knuckles of his right hand. It was drawn poorly in inky green and bled into the fissures of skin between his index and middle fingers. He said he kept it there because it reminded him of what might have been if God hadn't given him a second chance.

Angelo Contreras ran with the *El Norte* gang until he was sixteen. Then he underwent a transformation. Slowly, he disengaged himself from the sour bosom of his *vatos,* got his GED, and started reading books. Dozens of books. Gabriel García Márquez. Isabel Allende. Sandra Cisneros. Che Guevara and Cesar Chavez biographies. Books exploded from his cracked leather book bag and hung dog-eared from his fingertips. He brought them home from the library and the Modern Times bookstore, stinking from the moist fingers of his predecessors. Sometimes he ran into his former friends. Once, he came home with bruised eyes, a punctured eardrum, and a cracked fibula, but he remained stoic through his pain, his chipped front tooth giving him the rakish charm of a Don Quixote.

Angelo Contreras's transformation didn't happen overnight or without pain, but it did happen, and when he was eighteen,

Angelo entered seminary to become a priest. The neighborhood *abuelas* were proud of Angelo—imagine, one of our very own performing Mass someday—and peppered him with the food of love: homemade tamales, empanadas, softly wrinkled hands against his cheeks. After all, they said, he was studying all the time, it's the least they could do to give him a little pleasure.

I was fifteen the year Angelo entered seminary. Before the transformation, Angelo had little to say to me, a plump schoolgirl with averted eyes and oversize breasts straining at her white shirt, whose forehead gleamed by noon and tended to have a sprinkling of pimples hidden beneath a stiff wing of gelled bangs. I'd hurry home from St. Paul's Catholic School for Girls clutching my books to my chest, anxious to get inside before Angelo and his friends gathered on his doorstep. Angelo just smoked cigarettes and drank Negra Modelo beer out of bottles, but his friends yelled and whistled at me and Carilu like they owned us. *Hey, mamasitas,* they'd call out, *nice chi-chis! Hola, mama, ven aquí.* And I'd feel nauseous rage seep into my cheeks while Carilu gave them the finger and swished her long streaked hair around like a cat's tail. *Assholes!* she'd yell, prompting more laughter and catcalls. *Chinga tus madres!*

When Angelo changed, I avoided him even more rigorously, sure that the ugliness of my presence would sully his newfound purity. I didn't want the pitiful charity of his kindness. Something observant and still feral in those green eyes made me feel too exposed, as if he could see my insecurity and frustration beneath the carefully cultivated layers of innocent studiousness. It was not unusual for me to go so far as to turn my head away on the rare occasions he spoke to me, pretending a sudden interest in the clasp of my purse or a stalk of Mexican sage.

One day I was at the public library, writing an essay on Thomas Hardy's *Far from the Madding Crowd.*

"*Hola,* Anya," Angelo said. He had his usual teetering stack of books under his arm.

"Hello."

"What are you working on?"

I showed him the book.

"I read that last year. It's good, but I liked *The Return of the Native* better."

"The part where the shepherd pokes the sheep's bellies open so they won't explode . . . that was horrible," I said suddenly.

"Yes." The green eyes watched me carefully. "Do you like to read, or do you just do it for school?" he asked me.

"I like it."

"Maybe you'd like to read some of my books when I'm finished with them?"

"I guess."

"Why don't you come over and look them over sometime? My *mama* would be happy if I got rid of some of them. She says they're taking over the whole house." He smiled, revealing the chipped tooth.

"Okay."

That's how I started going over to the Contrerases' house in the afternoon after school. Nobody thought anything of it. It was obvious to everyone that Angelo had turned himself around, joined the priesthood, and, besides, my parents were too busy with their political activism to keep an eye on every little move I took. Anya is a good girl, they always said. See how she reads when other kids are watching TV?

The first time Angelo kissed me was at my *'uelo*'s wake. As far as kisses go, I see now that it was chaste in manner if not in intent, as truncated and feathery as a baptismal benediction. After that kiss in my mother's pantry, I thought of little else, the boy-priest next door's high-cheekboned visage superimposed on math tests, his name on my lips while I did the dishes, the house next door glowing with a kind of radioactive sickness as I lay in my bed listening to Carilu's light snore. In allowing Angelo to kiss me, I'd not only threatened my own innocence, I'd compromised his. Priest or student, it didn't matter—I was to Angelo what the poison apple was to Eve, and I was nearly paralyzed with guilt and fear. And desire. Of course, desire.

We avoided each other for two weeks.

One spring day, my doorbell rang.

"Anya?" he called. "It's Angelo."

I peered through the peephole.

"Anya?"

I opened the door. He still wore regular clothes back then. That day he had on jeans and a short-sleeved shirt. His eyes held something furtive and appealing I hadn't seen in them before. Fear?

"Anya, I have to apologize to you."

"You have nothing to apologize for." The words made my mouth ache.

He frowned. "Of course I do. I haven't taken my vows yet, but it was impure and wrong, what I did. I take full responsibility for it." He stared at a point behind my head. "I'm just a man, and you're a beautiful girl. They never told me it would be so hard. It's different for the older priests, the ones who've never had a woman before. *Dios*, I shouldn't be saying this stuff to you! God forgive me."

"I'm not beautiful," I said.

Angelo stepped in and shut the door behind us. I could feel his heart beating as if it was in my own chest, pumping blood. He grasped my arm in his hand. It hurt. I clenched my teeth at the pleasure of it.

"I'm just an ugly *puta*," I whispered.

"No, no."

"I hate myself."

Then we were kissing, tearing at each other's clothes, Angelo's hands pinching the flesh around my waist, my knee rising to wrap around his hip. We stumbled down the hallway toward the bedroom I shared with Carilu and fell onto my bed under the window, the view blocked by the enormous lemon tree.

Angelo's eyes had grown shuttered and remote, his breath hard and short. I licked the tattoo between his knuckles. It tasted like salt, like nothing. He groaned. He leaned back and looked at me without speaking.

"They're gone till eight P.M.," I said.

My skirt and blouse were still bunched around me like an inner tube when his penis pierced me. I screamed, and he clapped a moist hand that smelled like me over my mouth. I bit him and he slapped my face, lightly. He was crying when he came. His semen burned my thigh, itched all the way up to my womb. It smelled of powdered bleach.

The next day he left for Guatemala.

Six weeks later I knelt over the school toilet with knees wet from urine and dirty water and vomited my despair into the porcelain. After school, I took three buses across town and went to a drugstore in Sea Cliff, where the only Latinas were a few maids and nannies, nobody I knew. I peed onto the white stick in the bathroom of a Burger King. It was positive.

It took me three days to decide what to do. I was sick with indecision, with self-recrimination, with desire and hate. I could still close my eyes and feel Angelo inside me, summon the odor of his armpits, hear the peculiar animal cadence of my cries. I fantasized Angelo leaving the priesthood and marrying me under the lemon tree in our shared yard. I fantasized dying, my body impaled like Frida Kahlo's under a cable car. Another part of me wanted to do the unimaginable, to curse myself so I could keep the memories fetid and hot in my mind. In the end, I telephoned him in Guatemala at the parish where he was on a mission. His voice on the phone could have been anybody's. I told him I was pregnant.

"I'll wire the money tomorrow," he said, and gently hung up.

I refused to see what happened as a seduction. It didn't have the necessary orchestration. It was more like an impromptu dance, the partners willing but inept, drawing courage from the hot rush of blood to the hips rather than memorized steps explicated by a henna-haired instructor in a teal skirt and low-heeled pumps.

In the end, I did the thing that would best keep my secret inside me, and accepted my punishment and my memories. I learned to live with the Curse that caused my lovers to glance up from their coffee at just the moment their future soul mate raised her eyes from her newspaper across the café. The Curse that nudged my promises to myself off their pedestals and into the murky waters of neediness and self-deception. The Curse that made my *amigas'* eyes slide away from mine on the way home from Easter Mass.

I accepted the punishment of losing myself yet another time to a figment, a weightless, man-shaped idea.

"I can't have children," I whispered. "The abortion . . ."

"The doctor told you this?" Ethan said this calmly, but his face was chalky.

I shook my head. "I just know. My periods . . . they've always been . . . problematic. Endometriosis, I think." My voice rose. "I killed my baby, Ethan, and God's never going to forgive me for that. I took Angelo's money—I mean, Father Contreras's—and they cut my baby right out of me, vacuumed it away like a piece of bad meat—"

"Anya! Don't ever say that! God forgives you. Of course God forgives you! The real question is, why can't you forgive yourself?"

I ignored him. "So you see, I've been lying to you. It can't work, you and me. You want kids, and I can't give them to you. I can't even have a proper relationship. It's like a curse. I'm so sorry, Ethan, so sorry . . ." I dissolved in sobs. This was where it ended. This was where it always ended.

Ethan gripped my chin in his hands. The color had come back to his cheeks, and his eyes warmed my face. He rubbed my tears so they wouldn't stain me. I hiccuped while he gently rubbed my back with his other hand. I could hear my breath slowing to match his.

"Will you marry me?" he said.

epilogue

SIX MONThS LATER

Corfu

PARKER

Names aren't as inviolate as people think. For instance, my real name is Rosie, but for twenty-four years every single person I met or knew called me Parker. My parents, Leo and Sue Glass of the Berkeley Coalition for Progressive Social Change Glasses, made a few valiant attempts to call me by the name they'd given me back in the 1970s, but the icy silence they encountered in my eight-year-old self precluded a long battle over the fertile turf of my identity. Did I turn out differently because I lived nearly a quarter century of my life as Parker instead of Rosie? Did ideas I never would have entertained as Rosie Meadow Glass adhere to the walls of my mind and propagate themselves into an alternate universe populated by entirely different beings, thoughts, values? Did I love the same people I would have loved as Rosie, or the opposites of those people?

I don't know the answer to these questions. I mean, I could guess, but what good would it do? They're all variations of the same thing: What is real? I stopped thinking I knew what was real the day Neil left me and junketed to Uruguay. It took me nearly four months longer to realize I didn't care—what was real, that is. They were pretty bad months, and pretty good ones too.

Six months ago, when I signed the papers that transferred one hundred percent ownership of Tony's Taverna to me, I found my hand scrawling out *Rosie Meadow Glass* in the loopy, relaxed penmanship of a seasoned adventuress. Like a second language lost to time and distance, I tested the feel of the rusty syllables on my tongue and found them palatable. So now, even though we're closed for the winter, and all-weather shutters form a cedar barrier around Corfu's future most-popular taverna, the glorious woodcut sign above the hallowed blue doors reads *Rosie's Taverna: Est. 1935 and 2004.*

I feel pretty confident about our prospects. Aphrodite agreed to come back as head chef, as long as Tony, whom she still hasn't officially forgiven, was ten thousand miles away spring-testing casting couches in L.A. As part of our deal, she's getting a fat raise and I've secured a promise that my less-than-telegenic chef will visit Kelah's amazing French stylists when she and Nico visit London on their honeymoon in the spring. I have plans for Aphrodite and Rosie's, you see, and they don't include serving great food in obscurity or an unknown chef with a latent mustache. In fact, what with Claire's hit CD singing the praises of summering in Corfu and Tony's/Rosie's in particular, I'm probably going to have to beat off tourists with a stick. Not to mention the excellent phone meeting I had with Candace Grant-Morris's editor colleague, who thinks there's definitely a place for a glossy Greek travel/cookbook that reads more like *Lady Chatterley's Lover* than *Joy of Cooking* and doesn't run away from a little lard when necessary.

Even if things don't work out, I'm not terribly worried about the future. After she freaked out, Molly generously agreed to give me a year to change my mind about my share of Glass, Ng & Associates. Of course, Christopher Peña was disappointed that we wouldn't, after all, be working together, but with his last movie going straight to video and all, he's probably relieved to scale back the job a bit. Plus, for the first time ever, one of Molly's hapless foreign interns has managed, through night classes and a ruthless determination of which Stalin would have approved, to graduate to full-fledged associate. I think Molly was secretly pleased when she handed Jack and Jill off to the steely embrace of Farangis the Tajik, whom she had repackaged for public consumption as the latest hot design import from Prague. I just hope Mol can handle Christopher Peña, but then, there's little my former partner can't do with aplomb, up to and including standing in for me under power of attorney in the sale of my and Neil's condo, my half of which provided plenty of seed capital for Rosie's.

Sure, sometimes I wonder what would have happened if I'd gone home. Maybe I would have distinguished myself in the interior-design world, gone on to fame and fortune and the pages of *Dwell* magazine. Maybe I would have settled down into comfy domesticity with Josh Lido and produced two perfect snaggle-toothed offspring. Maybe Sharon Stone would have called and we'd be giggling together at a Hollywood premiere or shielding our eyes from the glare of the paparazzi at the Versace show at this very moment. Maybe.

But I didn't.

Corfu's a weird place to be in winter. At first, my decision to stay was greeted with disbelief and skepticism. It was one thing to earn acceptance as a long-term guest, another altogether to eke out a place among the off-season stalwarts. Many of the Greeks themselves traveled back to the mainland during the rainy months; it was almost inconceivable that Blakas and I would move into Tony's shabby quarters tacked onto the back of the taverna, would crisscross the island on foot for hours at a time, seeing few but the old people who were too tired to migrate to Athens or Thessaloníki just for Chinese food and a multi-plex. But after a few months and serious discussions with my biggest supporters—Nia Alexiou, Nick and Patricia Halkiopolous, Aphrodite and Nico, Mrs. Gianniotis—I'd slowly won over my detractors and the nonbelievers, and offers of help and more than a few more lascivious propositions (which I'd gently refused) had been forthcoming.

There's so much to do before next summer, the months are flying by. When I happen to look up at the calendar and count the weeks remaining until Leo and Sue, Carda and Tarra, Claire and Gary, Ethan and Anya, Brian and a man to be named later, and Kelah and Boz and even Fee are due to arrive for the *second* grand reopening of Rosie's next summer, I can hardly believe it.

At first, Kelah was unsure about making the reunion. Her first book, the anthology of her now-famous *Flounce* columns, has sold astronomically well, and her publisher was rushing her second book to press. It was fiction and told the story of a half English, half West Indian young woman who'd never thought she could be brilliant enough to please her parents. Kelah's mom, Candace, had acquired it with pleasure and the full support of her publishing house's editorial board. Since everyone knows that the book's semiautobiographical, Candace's assistant editor, Nicola, is editing. Kelah reports that she and Nicola are getting along swimmingly, especially since Nicola's boyfriend, Alistair Brumley—Boz's old enemy, now *completely* reformed, I've been assured—and Boz share such a strong interest in Latin American magical-realist literature.

The timing was perfect for Claire, though. I'd called her the other day, and she was already looking forward to what would be a needed vacation. At forty-six, she'd obviously thought her child-rearing days were over. But Gary's boys could apparently still swim and her eggs proved decidedly hard-boiled. They'd conceived the night Gary arrived in Pelekastritsa, in the very lawn chair where the sounds of a honeymooning young couple had, she'd told me, instilled such yearning in her she'd written a song about it. The baby, a girl, was due in June. After a cursory consultation with a beaming Gary, Claire had elected to call her Andrea Antonia Rose Dillon. Luckily, Claire had had an easy pregnancy, with little of the morning sickness she'd had with Ethan and Brian. Of course, she'd spent her first trimester in the States, courtesy of Muse Records, recording a CD under the watchful eye of Taylor Black, who did indeed have two ladies named Charlene/Sharleen in his life, both of whom were blond, stacked, and completely adept at manipulating Taylor Black. I'd laughed out loud when I'd gotten her first postcard a month ago, post-marked Nashville, Tennessee:

Dear Rosie Parker or whatever your name is these days,
    Got to Nashville in one piece and without chucking up, which was some feat, let me tell you. Highlights thus far include:

🔲 *Champagne on first-class flight, which I couldn't drink but Gary assured me was fabulous.*

🔲 *Driver sent by Muse Records to pick us up. Not Samoan unfortunately, but almost as good: hulking bloke straight from Papua New Guinea, happy to see neighbors from Down Under!*

🔲 *Excellent hotel accommodations with enormous neon electric guitar on roof.*

🔲 *Lots of lovely, horny pregnancy/reconciliation sex.*

🔲 *Excellent prenatal massage therapist (Gary abstained).*

    See you in July with the beautiful Andrea Antonia Rose in tow, darling.

                                        Love, Claire

I suppose the person I miss the most is Anya. I mean, we didn't exactly start the summer on the best footing, but I truly grew to love her like a sister. She was there for me when nobody else was, kicking me out of bed when I couldn't seem to summon the energy to do anything but strategize ways to drive a penknife into Neil's heart, flushing my drug arsenal down the toilet when I got so depressed I forgot to change my underwear for a week, and distracting me from my Josh Lido obsession with funny stories about her sprawling Mexican family and often disastrous swimming lessons.

I am going to do everything I can to see that her July wedding to Ethan Dillon at Rosie's is everything she's dreamed of all these years. I have big plans, let me tell you. Hundreds of candles. Pristine silky damask interiors the color of Devonshire cream. Classy cocktails. An exquisite cake. A buffet featuring Greek lamb so tender it would make Wolfgang Puck weep. Importing Anya's favorite mariachi band from San Francisco is still on the table, and a proposed water entrance by the bridesmaids in ivory wet suits, led by Johnny the erstwhile swim instructor, has not been summarily rejected. With a little luck and a lot of work, the Dillon–Soberanes nuptials will be the wedding of the season. *Town & Country* and *InStyle* have both been notified. The editor of *Martha Stewart Weddings* even called to see if she could get an exclusive, which, alas, was given to *Flounce,* which seemed only fair, since it was Joan Vance who slipped the wedding mention into the press release that went out when Kelah's book hit *The New York Times* best-seller list.

I was so relieved when Anya e-mailed to tell me the results of her fertility tests. According to her doctor, there's absolutely no reason why Ethan can't knock her up tomorrow if she wants. No reason at all. They've decided to wait until after the wedding, but I can tell they're going to be great parents. Ethan's turned out to have a gift for languages—Anya reports that his Spanish is already so good her aunties can no longer talk about him in front of his face—and he really likes San Francisco. After the wedding, though, they're going to spend some time in Australia and see if they might live there for a while. Claire will need help with the baby, of course, and Anya would probably enjoy spending time with her mother-in-law, and friend, particularly if she finds herself pregnant as well.

I bet you're wondering whatever happened to old Josh Lido in all this. If I'm still playing Nun Rosie, running around organizing everyone else's lives while my own ovaries shrivel up like rotten mangoes. If the only man regularly nestled between my sheets—and my legs—is on the hirsute side and prone to eating lawn furniture when he loses his rawhide bone.

I guess the answer is, yes and no.

The first time for Josh and me, in the hospital, really answered a lot of questions. Questions like: Is it possible to come three times when you've just had a catheter removed (yes), do adjustable hospital beds facilitate woman-superior intercourse (yes), and are short guys short just in vertical stature or everywhere (no). Suffice to say, sex with Josh is the best I've ever had, and by far the most relaxed. Like the time Blakas jumped on the bed with a used maxi pad in his mouth and stared at Josh's butt moving up and down on me, and I laughed so hard I bruised Josh and he had to put a bag of frozen peas on his unit. Or the time the condom broke and Josh pretended he was "Josh Lido, Custodial Engineer," and performed a thorough vacuuming with his—well, you get the idea.

(That last one has become a recurring fantasy game of ours, to my everlasting pleasure.)

Of course, we'd talked about him staying on with me, through the winter. But I think we both knew it wasn't the time. I love Josh Lido, I really do, and apparently he loves me, and I know someday we'll do something permanent about that—or as permanent, as *real,* as our illusions can make it—but for now I'm content with our weekly phone calls, our daily e-mails, and our occasional rendezvous in Paris, Rome, or, once, Malta (cheap flights on Aeroflot). Josh is coming next summer for three months, at which time Blakas and I will have to find ourselves a bigger villa, so the three of us can be comfortable. We're already talking about a quick trip to some of the other islands, where Josh can scout the local schools for English-language programs. He's spent the year getting his ESL certification, so he can teach English to non-native English speakers, and says it's the best thing he's ever done. He won't be practicing law again. Josh's parents, whom I met on the Malta trip a couple of months ago, turned out to be the type of benevolent and extremely affluent people I'd always wished Jack and Jill could be. Barrett and Jane Lido have endowed a trust in Raphael Lido's name to fund ESL schools around the world. Josh says he wants to pick up where Rafe left off, teaching English, not to rich kids whose multilingual skills are honed by arguing about bedtime with multicultural cadres of nannies, but rather to poor kids who wouldn't otherwise get a chance to claw their way up to something better.

In the meantime, Blakas and I are holding down the fort here in Pelekastritsa, Corfu, Ionian Islands, Greece. The streets are mostly empty, the bars closed, the formerly crimson bougainvillea snaking the shuttered doorways as naked as an olive branch. People are few, and those who remain walk against the wind with their heads tucked down, scarves wrapped around their heads. It's cold, and I go several days at a time without human contact. Still, I feel part of things in a way I never did before.

I never did get back into those size-six Earl jeans, but then, there's something to be said for eating dessert on a regular basis. Josh still calls me Park, too, and you know what? Mostly, that's okay by me.

ABOUT THE AUTHOR

KIM GREEN is the author of *Is That a Moose in Your Pocket?* She lives in San Francisco with her husband, Gabe, and their daughter, Lucca. Her past life includes several Greek holidays.